THE
FOURTH PERSPECTIVE

Other books by Robert Greer

The Devil's Hatband

The Devil's Red Nickel

The Devil's Backbone

Limited Time

Isolation and Other Stories

Heat Shock

Resurrecting Langston Blue

THE FOURTH PERSPECTIVE

A CJ Floyd Mystery

ROBERT GREER

Frog, Ltd.
Berkeley, California

Published by Frog, Ltd.
Frog, Ltd. books are distributed
by North Atlantic Books
P.O. Box 12327
Berkeley, California 94712

Cover and text design by Brad Greene
Printed in the United States of America

North Atlantic Books' publications are available through most bookstores. For further information, call 800-337-2665 or visit our website at www.northatlanticbooks.com.

Substantial discounts on bulk quantities are available to corporations, professional associations, and other organizations. For details and discount information, contact our special sales department.

Library of Congress Cataloging-in-Publication Data
Greer, Robert O.
The fourth perspective / by Robert Greer.
      p. cm.
Summary: "C.J. Floyd, the streetwise, Denver-based bail bondsman and Vietnam vet, gets embroiled in an investigation that reaches back to the building of the transcontinental railroad, leads him to a famous photograph, and has him tangled with eccentric power brokers and collectors who are after a slice of priceless American history"—Provided by publisher.
   ISBN-13: 978-1-58394-162-1
   ISBN-10: 1-58394-162-2
  1. Floyd, C. J. (Fictitious character)—Fiction. 2. African American men—Fiction. 3. Bail bond agents—Fiction. 4. Antiquarian booksellers—Fiction. 5. Denver (Colo.)—Fiction. I. Title.
   PS3557.R3997F68 2006
   813'.54—dc22

                                                      2006013248
                                                          CIP

1 2 3 4 5 6 7 8 9 SHERIDAN 10 09 08 07 06

Dedication

For Phyllis, ever-present in my heart.

Money and things never belong to anyone.
They just come and go and come again.

—Will Smith

Author's Note

The characters, events, and places that are depicted in *The Fourth Perspective* are spawned from the author's imagination. Certain Denver and Western locales are used fictitiously, and any resemblance between the novel's fictional inhabitants and actual persons living or dead is purely coincidental.

Acknowledgments

The sometimes hazy solitude required to write a novel is always brightened by the light of people other than the author who help bring that novel to life. I am fortunate to have a bevy of such lights.

To Kathleen Woodley, my dedicated secretary of nineteen years who struggled with the worst cold imaginable to somehow deliver the final typescript version of *The Fourth Perspective* to its recalcitrant, longhand writing, computer-illiterate author on time, my heartfelt thanks. To Connie Blanchard, who dropped everything to also chip in, I offer a round of thanks as well.

To Connie Oehring, who did her usual masterful copyediting, repairing my spliced sentences, inappropriate use of commas and semicolons, and sentence run-ons, thank you so much.

A bolus of research time was required with this effort. When I needed help about the specifics of a rare Oklahoma license plate, I turned to Jim Gummoe, whose knowledge in that arena far outstrips mine. I traveled twice to Santa Fe to learn all I could about masterpieces of nineteenth- and twentieth-century photography from John Boland and Christopher Marquez, of the Andrew Smith Gallery. Thank you both for offering your valuable insights and for giving *The Fourth Perspective* an authoritative historical hook. To John McDowell and Lyndia Carter, I thank you for sharing your "Golden Spike" historical knowledge.

Information about the antiquarian book trade and rare and not-so-rare books and photographs was generously provided to me by Bob Topp and Jim Gladney, and instruction in the art of bow hunting came from John Mullen.

Finally, to the publishing team behind me, especially my publicist, Caitlin Hamilton-Summie, and the entire editorial and publishing group at North Atlantic Books, as always, thank you for helping to bring my imagination to life.

THE
FOURTH
PERSPECTIVE

CHAPTER 1

They mockingly called her "Goat Head," or "Pretty Babe," or, dismissively, "the Guatemalan." She was in truth from Nicaragua, and it would have been the height of flattery to describe her even in the most generous terms as pretty. She was noticeably disfigured, her appearance the result of the childhood onset of a developmental bone disease known as cherubism, a disorder that had robbed her of potential beauty, turned her squat and pumpkin-faced, and so altered and recontoured the bones in her face and jaws that her eyes were perpetually cast skyward as if forever searching for heaven.

Most of the obstacles she had encountered during her thirty-nine years—her cherubism, the childhood taunts, the loss of her parents, her struggle to raise a fatherless child, and growing up in the midst of revolution and civil unrest—had only made her stronger, more determined, more focused on rising above her assigned lot of a Central American peasant born to faceless migrant fruit-pickers, an anomalous, disfigured burden in the eyes of the world. Schooled by circuit riding American nuns, she'd largely beaten the odds, learning to speak impeccable English by the age of seven and becoming accomplished at math and music by the age of ten. Ever charming and deferential in spite of her handicaps, she was on the road to avoiding a life of poverty and toil by her eighteenth birthday. But at nineteen, after a year of college, she fell in love with a guerrilla freedom fighter, had a child, and found herself consumed by obstacles once again.

When her husband of thirteen years was killed, a casualty of persistent revolution, she reluctantly left her child with relatives and traveled by train to the United States by way of Mexico, hidden inside the hopper of a rotary gondola car used for transporting coal. Still grieving and despondent, she rode for two days on a back corner of the coal car's small iron sill between the gondola and the wheels of the train, knees folded, her feet against her buttocks, the lower half of her body dangling outside two feet above the rails as her muscles screamed in agony. Hanging on with her arms, she endured the train's thundering starts and stops and dehumanizing jars as it made its way from Mexicali to Los Angeles, toward what she expected—no, demanded—to be a better life.

What she found in the City of Angels was a culture she was ill prepared for. The city's streets teemed with tens of thousands of lost immigrant souls just like her. It was a land of desperate indentured hostages there to serve those who would use and abuse them. However, she found work and a place to live that was light years better than where she'd come from. Within two days of her arrival, Theresa Mesa Salas Del Mora was employed in the housekeeping service of a Century City hotel with a penchant for hiring and just as quickly firing a ready stream of illegal immigrants.

The job paid minimum wage, and the hours were graveyard and grueling, but Theresa stuck with her plan, enduring eight long months of physically demanding, often demeaning work, with only two days off. Always looking to better herself, she left that job for a better one, then discarded that job for another at a boutique hotel in the Wilshire district, followed by jobs at

European-style hotels in Beverly Hills and Bel Air. Eventually, laden with references that trumpeted her reputation as a tireless worker, her honesty, and most of all her loyalty and humility, she left Los Angeles and ventured east to the Rockies to serve as manager of housekeeping at a posh Park City, Utah, ski resort. From there she moved on to Colorado to take charge of a similar crew at a trendy Aspen getaway.

It had taken her six years to make her way to Aspen. She'd endured those difficult, long, and lonely years without the essence of her life, her now nineteen-year-old son. Finally, with a nest egg to fall back on, the woman whose coworkers in the City of Angels had once mockingly called her "Goat Head," "the Guatemalan," or "Pretty Babe," uttering the names as if calling to a pet, took her biggest chance yet. She moved to Denver after being recruited in blatant big-business fashion by Howard Stafford, a man whose wealth was said to be difficult to measure even by those in the know, to oversee a service staff of eight who ran Stafford's lush fifteen-acre compound. The compound comprised a twenty-thousand-square-foot main house and outbuildings that included her own residence; her salary would have made any MBA envious. Before accepting the position, she'd been told by envious acquaintances who knew the old-moneyed Denver landscape that she would be working for an eccentric—a man who always sounded as if he had a high frontal cold; whose closets, TV cabinets, and kitchen pantry sported combination locks—an antisocial recluse who wore a newscaster's ever-present painted-on smile and owned scores of identical silk shirts, alligator shoes, lizard-skin cowboy boots, and black gabardine trousers. Ignoring the possible downside and the advice of friends, she grabbed for her American dream. A month after signing on with Stafford, feeling secure and stable at last, she decided that it was time for her son, Luis, now two months shy of his twentieth birthday, to join her in America.

Luis Alejandro Del Mora arrived in Denver on a Mexicana Airlines flight, with all his papers in order and a newly minted student visa, on a crystal-clear, picture-perfect early-November afternoon, eight weeks to the day after his mother began working for Howard Stafford. Dressed in sandals and a peasant's poncho, sporting a revolutionary-style Nicaraguan mountain highlands guerrilla's straw hat, and carrying a backpack filled with two thirty-two-ounce bladders of wine, Luis walked arm in arm with his mother down a Denver International Airport concourse bustling with Americans. During Theresa's six-year absence, Luis had been taught to despise all such people by the cousins of cousins and the friends of friends with whom he had lived. Luis had arrived on American soil not as a child seeking maternal reunion and comfort, as his mother envisioned, but as a young man soured by years of separation, embittered by a lost child's disappointment, and angry at having had to live in the underbelly of a Nicaraguan caste system underpinned by American capitalism. He was suspicious, agitated, insular, and independent.

"You're in America now," Theresa said, beaming as she stopped to wrap her arms around her only child. "You're safe."

Luis forced a half smile and squeezed his mother tightly as he watched the people around him scurry disjointedly in every direction, aware that the place that had given his mother such hope and purpose could never do the same for him.

Within weeks of his arrival, Luis Del Mora was doing what he had learned to do best—what in six years of living with the cousins of cousins in Nicaragua he had been taught to do—steal.

In Nicaragua he had stolen cars and stereos, fruit and furniture, and carted away truckloads of computers and TVs. In America he would do the same. However, he wouldn't steal the trivial tokens that Americans, fat with opulence, toyed with briefly and then discarded. His sights were set much higher, and thanks to his mother's perseverance and position, he planned to extend his thievery to include the rare and priceless.

And so it began. On days when he was supposed to be attending Denver's Metro State College, he instead honed his skills as a thief—selling, fencing, and bartering stolen goods. Things went well enough that two months after his arrival, with his mother able to see only warmth, charm, and goodness in her son, Luis informed Theresa that he had secured a part-time job as a translator's aide at a Denver language school. With his nonexistent college courses and fabricated job that kept him far from the watchful eye of his mother, Luis began to lay the groundwork to steal from Howard Stafford—from a house filled with books and art objects that stretched back to the fourteenth century. Ultimately, Luis knew he would be able to cherry-pick gems that included rare books, ephemera, pottery, textiles, and art; he hoped that a reclusive pack-rat hoarder such as Stafford, steeped in his own eccentricities, might never even miss these things.

Luis started with a series of trial runs, stealing unimportant history books, railroad timetables, and what he took to be insignificant things that Stafford was unlikely to miss in a thirty-thousand-volume library before setting his sights on the real prizes in the Stafford kingdom. Starting small, he told himself, would give him the inspiration he needed to complete the gambit. With his run of the grounds and Theresa's run of the house, it was easy to learn from the cooperative staff, and from a mother wearing blinders, what things in the hacienda were the most precious. His most significant moment came one day as he walked through the main house with his mother. They passed the door of the library, and Theresa told him that the room, with its massive oak doors and fourteen-foot-high cross-beamed ceilings, was forbidden territory.

"The library is off limits," she said as they walked by. "Even to me." She grabbed Luis by the hand and pulled him with her toward the kitchen. That experience moved Luis to read up on Stafford—study the man who was his mother's employer—infiltrate his thinking in order to find out what treasures he might have locked behind the massive oak library doors. It took some digging to ferret out the reclusive rich man's passions, but Luis spent days combing through books, newspapers, and the Internet. In the end, he learned that what mattered most to the fifty-eight-year-old reclusive native Coloradan was to amass the world's ultimate private collection of rare Western maps, vintage Western photographs, and books. With that knowledge in hand, five months after landing in America Luis Del Mora decided that the time for trial runs had passed, and the time for the serious business of stealing had arrived.

CHAPTER 2

The neon sign above the door to CJ Floyd's recently opened twelve-hundred-square-foot South Broadway Antique Row store screamed in glowing red letters: *Ike's Spot: Vintage Western Collectibles*. CJ had chosen the name to honor his deceased uncle, Ike Floyd, the man who had raised him, taught him right from wrong, loved and nurtured him while fighting his own lifelong battle with alcoholism. Ike had snatched CJ by the arm and thumped his "narrow ass" whenever his nephew had strayed from the straight and narrow.

Mavis Sundee, the lifelong drop of feminine sweetness in CJ's hard-edged life, and fiancée of eight months, had suggested the name. When he'd asked her why, Mavis had emphasized the point with a palm slap: "For the same reason Mae's Louisiana Kitchen isn't called Mavis's Place after me, or Willis Sundee's after my father." Aware that Mae's, the landmark seventy-year-old Denver soul food restaurant and one of the three businesses that Mavis ran for her aging father, had been named for Mavis's mother, a civil rights pioneer who had been born and bred in New Orleans, CJ had smiled and agreed.

Eight months earlier, after a brush with death in a remote New Mexico wilderness, CJ had stepped away from life as a bail bondsman and bounty hunter, the only job he'd known since coming home from two naval tours of Vietnam. After the New Mexico ordeal, he was determined to open a vintage Western collectibles store on Denver's famed Antique Row. He had worked the streets and sewer-rat haunts of Denver for more than thirty years, but that case had nearly claimed Mavis's life, so after dispatching it and leaving his bail-bonding business in the capable hands of his Las Vegas–showgirl–sized partner, Flora Jean Benson, CJ was happy now to call himself a former bail bondsman.

Flora Jean, a U.S. Marines intelligence sergeant during the Persian Gulf War, now operated Floyd & Benson's Bail Bonds out of the first floor of the stately old Victorian building on Bail Bondsman's Row that Ike had left CJ. CJ, who still lived upstairs in a converted four-room apartment, had sold Flora Jean the business and a partial interest in the building during a Christmas Eve title-document ritual. A month later, with a three-year lease and every dime he'd managed to scrape together, he'd invested in Ike's. CJ was now an antiques dealer.

Business had been slow for the entire month of March, and CJ was having second thoughts about his career move, but Lenny McCabe, an aging hippie antiques dealer, and CJ's landlord, who operated the shop on the other side of the duplex CJ leased and was one of the few dealers who'd welcomed CJ onto the street with open arms, chalked up the lull in business to springtime in the Rockies. In pep talks to CJ, he'd claimed that people don't like to part with their money during the time of slush and mud.

CJ wasn't certain he could believe a man who braved Denver's fluctuating springtime elements in a Hawaiian shirt and shorts, wore his hair in a ponytail down to his belt loops, and trudged around in flip-flops in the snow. But he had to trust someone's experience, and since Lenny, a ten-year resident of the Row, had gleefully leased him space and helped him move into it, CJ was willing to have some faith in him.

CJ had started amassing his collection of antiques, folk art, and Western memorabilia during his lonely preteen years, when his uncle's drinking and erratic hours had forced CJ to find something stable to immerse himself in. Although sports had served as a partial fix, the world of antiques and collectibles had been his permanent elixir.

His apartment was cluttered with coffee cans full of cat's-eye marbles, and jumbos and steelies too. In the basement of the building he had stacks of mint-condition records—78s, 45s, and vintage LPs stored in tomato crates gathering dust. In his four-decade quest to collect, he had amassed hundreds of tobacco tins and inkwells from all over the world, along with maps in every size, color, and shape, maps whose pages folded and zipped and accordioned into place as they documented every place CJ had ever been and many more.

CJ's collection of antique license plates said more about him than any other items in his collection. He had started that collection during his teenage years, when Ike's drinking had reached its peak and street rods and low riders had taken the place of family in his life. The prides of his license-plate collection were his 1916 Alaska plate and a 1915 Denver municipal tag. Both had been fabricated using the long-abandoned process of overlaying porcelain onto iron. Although the collection was impressive, it remained incomplete, and Mavis, one of the few people who had ever seen the entire collection, suspected that, like CJ, it very likely would never be whole.

It was approaching twilight as CJ and Lenny McCabe stood near the back of Ike's Spot behind a glass display case that housed the bulk of CJ's lifelong collection of antique tobacco tins, shooting the breeze and trying to guess the temperature as snow fell outside. Lenny was the first to see the customer walk in.

"You got business, CJ," Lenny said, tugging his ponytail and giving CJ a go-for-broke grin.

CJ nodded, realizing as the man approached and McCabe's grin softened into a stare that the nervous, gaunt man, whom CJ pegged to be nineteen, tops, was only the fourth customer of the day. He had melting snowflakes clinging to a cowlick of jet-black hair that draped down over a bulbous forehead that dwarfed the rest of his face. He wore a lightweight winter coat and a backpack. He breezed past all the displays without so much as a glance, eyed Lenny dismissively, and turned to CJ.

Before either CJ or Lenny could speak, the hostile-looking teenager said, "Your ad in the yellow pages says you deal in Western collectibles. I have a couple I want to sell. High-grade stuff, guaranteed. Now, who's Ike?" He grinned slyly at McCabe and then CJ.

The words sounded rehearsed. It wasn't every day that a brash, pumpkin-headed teen, sporting a hint of a goatee and barking demands in a thick Spanish accent—or anyone else for that matter—marched into any store on Antique Row and offered to guarantee what they were selling. Lenny, looking surprised and agitated, shot CJ a look that said, *Watch yourself, rookie; whatever the kid's peddlin' is probably stolen or fake.*

"Whattaya selling?" CJ asked finally.

The young man slipped out of his backpack, slammed it down on the display case, and unzipped it. Rummaging around in the backpack as if prolonging the search for effect, he extracted his wares. "Books. And don't try to take me. I know what they're worth." He placed two books gingerly on the countertop.

CJ suspected that the round-faced man, whose eyes angled skyward, accentuating their whites, was older than he'd first thought. He couldn't tell if the man was bluffing, but he knew for sure that his fourth customer of the day had attitude to burn and that the Spanish accent he was anchored to screamed, *Not from around here!* CJ eyed the two books casually, feigning lack of interest, and glanced toward the store's front window. It had stopped snowing, and someone outside, clad in a parka, hands cupped above their eyes, had stopped to admire the inkwell and tobacco tin displayed in the window. The person quickly disappeared as CJ turned his attention back to the books.

The larger of the two books, nine and a half by six and a half inches and bound in buckskin, intrigued him, primarily because there was no title on the front cover. Two initials, an M lying on its side and an adjacent D, were stamped into the buckskin where a title should have been. The name "Harvey T. Sethman" was embossed in gold near the bottom. CJ nudged the book aside and tried not to salivate as he moved his attention to the second, smaller book. He had recognized it the instant the customer had set it down on the counter. Although license plates were his passion and inkwells and tobacco tins among his well-researched specialties, he had no trouble recognizing a cattle-brand book when he saw one, and the 1883 Wyoming brand book sitting in front of him was as pristine an example of a rare and collectible cattle-trade gem as he'd ever seen. He had a rough idea of its worth, and he'd have known its value to the penny if his friend Billy DeLong, onetime foreman of Snake River Valley Ranch in Baggs, Wyoming, had been there. CJ picked the brand book up and gently turned the pages, eyeing column after column, page after page of cattle brands, owners, names, and addresses as the nervous seller and an impatient, obviously perturbed McCabe looked on.

"Where did you get them?" CJ asked finally as the gears in his head shifted from antiques dealer to hungry-bail-bondsman wary.

"They belonged to my uncle. He's dead."

"Was he a rancher?" asked CJ, nudging the brand book aside, flipping open the other book's cover, and reading the author's front note: "This book is number seventy-eight of a special limited edition of three hundred copies of *Medicine in the Making of Montana*, hand-bound in buckskin and identified with the registered brand of the Montana Medical Association. This edition was commissioned by the Association for the benefit of its members and friends."

"You from Montana?" CJ asked, now aware of the significance of the initials branded into the buckskin. "Lazy MD," he said to Lenny, handing him the open book so that McCabe could read the front note.

"Makes sense. But I would've chosen Rockin' MD myself." McCabe's attempt at levity seemed forced. Eyeing the seller suspiciously, he put the book down.

Ignoring McCabe, the man looked at CJ and said, "No. Venezuela—my uncle ran a cattle ranch down there."

Uncertain whether the man was lying, CJ asked, "You got any proof?"

"Have you got proof that you own what's in this store?" the young man said without flinching.

CJ eyed the man pensively. "You got a name?"

The boy swept the books back toward his backpack without answering.

"Possession's nine-tenths of the law," McCabe interjected.

"And stealing's a crime," CJ countered.

"I didn't steal them," the man said adamantly. He had zipped up his backpack and turned to leave when CJ, wanting to take back the words as soon as he'd uttered them, asked, "How much do you want for them?"

"Eighteen hundred."

Pegging the brand book's value at $2,500 to $3,000, CJ said, "I'll give you fifteen."

"Seventeen."

CJ looked quizzically at McCabe, then watched as the seller flashed McCabe a bold, cocky smile—a smile that said, *Stay the hell out of this deal, friend.*

Taking the hint, McCabe said, "You're on your own, CJ."

"You'll have to take a check," CJ said haltingly to the nervous man, as if he were looking for a way to squelch the deal.

"Cash only," the man retorted.

"I don't deal in cash with these kinds of transactions. Your books could be knockoffs."

The man laughed. "I'll take my books and leave, señor." His cheeks reddened and he took a step toward the front door before McCabe said eagerly to CJ, "I'll spot you the seventeen hundred. Write me a check."

"Too risky," CJ countered.

McCabe shook his head. "Balls, man. Balls. In this business you gotta have 'em." McCabe eyed the seller for a reaction but got none.

CJ stroked his chin and considered the scores of life-threatening situations he'd found himself stuck in during two tours of Vietnam and thirty years as a bounty hunter and bail bondsman. *No risk, no reward,* he thought. Concerned that he might be losing the edge that had always defined him, he reached for the inside pocket of his black leather gambler's vest, a wardrobe trademark, extracted his checkbook, hurriedly wrote out a check for $1,700, and handed it to McCabe.

"I'll have the cash for you in a couple of minutes," said McCabe, folding the check in half, slipping it into his shirt pocket, and heading for the front door.

The customer watched McCabe walk away, his eyes locked on every footfall until McCabe disappeared. He and CJ looked at one another in silence for a moment; then, eyes glued to the floor, the young man walked across the room to examine CJ's porcelain-license-plate display.

An arc of bewildered relief had spread across the man's face when they'd finally closed the deal. It was a look CJ knew well— the same bewildered look he'd given Ike when his uncle had came home broke, disoriented, and quivering after two nights of drinking and gambling. A look of detached disappointment that leaned heavily on the fact that the bearer carried a burden much heavier than should ever be expected of him. CJ wondered what burden the boyish-looking man was carrying—and, more importantly, for whom.

Ponytail swinging, Lenny returned with a wad of rubber-banded hundred-dollar bills. He walked the length of the store past the bookshelf and back to CJ. The book seller returned to the display case and watched, smiling, as Lenny counted out seventeen bills.

"We good to go?" he asked, placing the books he'd again slipped from his backpack on top of the display case.

"Yeah." Struck by how out of place the uniquely American phrase sounded in the man's thick Spanish accent, CJ handed over the stack of hundreds.

Without recounting them, the man shoved the bills into his pocket. "My pleasure." Turning to leave, he took one of CJ's business cards from a card holder on the countertop, eyed McCabe dismissively, and retreated.

"Want a receipt?" CJ called after him.

The man didn't answer. Within seconds he was at the front door, greeted as he exited by a new shower of heavy, wet snowflakes.

CJ watched the man move past the front window before sliding the two books toward him. Looking at Lenny in full-choke puzzlement he asked, "Whattaya think? Stolen?"

Lenny shrugged. "You never know in this business."

"Thought I left those days behind when I got out of the bail-bonding business."

"Could be you didn't." There was a hint of playfulness in McCabe's tone as he slipped CJ's check back out of his pocket, snapped it, and said, "But I'm sure as hell good to go."

CJ nodded, opened the brand book, and began flipping through its pages. "Two for the money," he said, reaching page thirty. "Thanks for fronting me the seventeen hundred."

McCabe smiled. "Had to in order to protect my interests. I need a tenant who's making money."

"No shit," said CJ, surprised by the seriousness in McCabe's tone. "I should make a nice little piece of change on the cattle-brand book." CJ eased the book aside, eyed its partner, the Montana medicine book, and shrugged. "This one, though, like they say, you never know."

The windshield of the Volkswagen his mother had leased for him was covered with snow by the time Luis Del Mora had made the eleven-block trek from Ike's Spot back to where he'd parked the car in an alley. He had intentionally parked almost a mile away from the store, fearful that nearby on-street parking would have made him too visible, vulnerable to being seen by someone who might recognize him or the car. He had angled the lime-green Beetle into a narrow space between two garages, well out of the way of the alley traffic.

He cleared the windshield with a swipe of his jacket sleeve, looked skyward at the approaching darkness, patted the two wads of bills in his pocket, CJ's $1,700 and the tightly packaged four-inch-thick $10,000 roll beneath it, and turned back to unlock the door.

The book sale had been easy—much easier than he'd expected. And to think that selling the two books had been an afterthought, an add-on to his earlier sale. He broke into a self-congratulatory grin, thinking that the black man at Ike's Spot showed that African Americans seemed just as eager for money as their green-back-grubbing white counterparts. His sales had been brisk for the past month, and he had no reason to expect they wouldn't keep rising. He swung open the door, slipped inside the Beetle, and cranked the engine. He'd just started to back out into the alley when a wash of light filled the Volkswagen. He looked back to see a vehicle blocking his way. He waited briefly for it to move. When it didn't, he swung his door open, stepped out of the car, and said, "Hey!"

Luis Del Mora never uttered another word. Two close-range, silenced shots from a .22 Magnum pistol jutting from the vehicle's window made certain of that. One bullet ripped apart his wind-pipe, ultimately lodging deep in his cervical spine. The other shattered the delicate cherubic bone of his forehead before gyrating end over end through his brain. There would be no more words, no more book sales, and no more four-inch-thick wads of money for Luis Alejandro Del Mora.

CHAPTER 3

Celeste Deepstream had been cultivating Alexie Borg for months, hoping to get the once high-profile Russian hockey player to kill for her, and now she was close. As close as Alexie was, as he enjoyed the final titillating seconds of making love to her, to reaching a climax. "Oh, my God, oh, my God, oh, yes, yes, yes!" he screamed.

"Alexie, you're squeezing me too tightly. I can't breathe." Celeste's words came out in a gasp as all 250 pounds of the gyrating Soviet transplant collapsed onto her and Alexie spent himself.

His face a contorted mask of erotic pleasure, Alexie released his bear hug.

"Get off me!" Celeste screamed.

Floating on a sea of pleasure, Alexie rolled from on top of the onetime Miss Acoma Indian Nation and former world-class swimmer and flopped spread-eagled onto the bed. "You're something," he said, exhaling. "A woman to make a man forfeit his dreams."

For Celeste, the feeling wasn't mutual. In all their months of lovemaking, Alexie had brought her to climax only once. He was burly, rough, and unschooled in the ways that made woman release their juices. But he was necessary—a cog that counted. He was a brutal oaf at best, but he would be her conduit to eliminating CJ Floyd, the man who had stolen her life, so in the long run it was Alexie Borg who would service *her* needs.

Relaxing onto a pillow and propping himself up, Alexie ran a rough, callused hand along Celeste's inner thigh until he reached the sweet softness that had given him so much pleasure. "This you Indians should mass-produce." He capped the remark with a snort and a less-than-gentle squeeze.

Celeste responded with a string-along smile.

Alexie frowned, recognizing the smile for what it was. "What? Alexie's not good enough for you?"

"You're plenty," Celeste said, her words programmed and robotic.

Alexie inched himself farther up in the bed and, running his eyes up and down Celeste's exquisite body, scrutinizing every inch of her as if there were parts he believed he owned, said, "You remember, of course, the wreck you were when I found you? Are you now so far removed from that wretched state that you no longer feel the need to service me?"

Celeste answered with silence, vividly remembering the state she'd been in when Alexie had found her. She had been depressed and recovering from wounds she'd suffered in a shoot-out with CJ Floyd in the New Mexico Sangre de Cristo mountains. She had been forty pounds overweight, a fugitive, and barely in touch with reality as she'd moved back and forth between Taos, New Mexico, and the surrounding mountains. Alexie had dropped out of the sky to save her from herself and temper her long-festering grudge against Floyd—but only temporarily.

She had been a University of New Mexico world-class swimmer and a recently selected Rhodes Scholar poised to study anthropology at the University of London when a collision between her drug-addicted twin brother, Bobby, and Floyd had derailed her plans. Her dreams had been swamped because of Floyd, and because of Floyd, Bobby was dead.

Thirty-two years earlier she and Bobby had been born six minutes apart on a kitchen table in a crumbling two-room Acoma Indian reservation adobe. All her life Celeste had been stronger, smarter, and wiser than Bobby, miles ahead of her brother in all the things that mattered, ascending as he spiraled downward. It was as if the couplet of DNA she had sprung from had harbored all of life's richest components, while Bobby's had been stripped bare. Until the day he died, Bobby's one claim to fame had been that he was the oldest.

She had turned down the Rhodes Scholarship to spend time detoxifying Bobby, who had been strung out on Ritalin, Percocet, alcohol, and model-airplane glue, and in time Bobby had won that war with drugs. But her painstaking intervention had transformed her from caring sister into Bobby's permanent crutch, and the bond between them, though no less tenacious, had degenerated into an unhealthy codependency fueled by Bobby's instability and her deep sense of guilt.

And then had come Floyd, an unrelenting bounty-hunting bear of a black man hired to track down her now dried-out, bond-skipping brother, who'd turned his talents to the work of a small-time fence. Floyd had tracked Bobby across two states before hog-tying him in chains, dumping him in the back of a pickup, and hauling him from Santa Fe to Denver to face charges of transporting stolen weapons and illegal fireworks across state lines.

While awaiting trial Bobby had tried to kill himself in the Denver County Jail. Guilt-ridden and enraged, Celeste had unmercifully beaten the seventy-five-year-old skinflint bail bondsman who had hired Floyd to track down Bobby, blaming that man for her brother's plight. When the old man had died from his injuries, Celeste had received a plea-bargained manslaughter conviction that had earned her a twelve-year prison sentence. She'd never again seen Bobby alive.

With five years of model-prisoner check marks next to her name, chits that included saving a prison guard's life, teaching college-credit courses to inmates, and founding a Native American prisoners' prerelease job opportunities program, she'd masterminded an early release, dumping buckets of remorse around the room at two critical parole hearings and playing the role of a long-suffering sister forced all her life to shoulder responsibility for her bad-seed twin. She was paroled after serving just under half of her original sentence.

She had tried to kill the brown-skinned, square-jawed, wiry-haired bail bondsman Floyd half-a-dozen times, but she'd always failed. This time she was determined not to. This time she had Alexie, a Russian bear who had briefly moved with her from Taos to the sparsely populated White Sands Missile Range country outside Alamogordo, New Mexico, far from the law and any hint of limelight. A man who had been forced to America by the fall of communism to seek the good life he had enjoyed as a pampered Soviet athlete. Now, as a member of an elite arm of the Russian mafia, he fenced stolen airplane parts, illegal weapons, and medical contraband and smuggled rare art objects and priceless tapestries.

No pain, no gain, Celeste thought, responding finally to Alexie's question by reaching down and cupping his penis. "I'm not too far removed from anything," she said, skating an index finger back and forth across his testicles. "I just had a temporary lockdown because of Floyd."

"You lock down far too often over the bail bondsman, and always it seems to occur in the midst of our lovemaking. I have told you, I, Alexie Borg, will handle this."

Celeste sat up in bed. "I've told you before, Alexie, Floyd's no longer a bail bondsman. Problem is," she hesitated momentarily and frowned, "he's just as shrewd and probably just as fearless."

Alexie smiled. It was the secure smile of someone with inside dope. "But he's American. He has weaknesses."

"Not the Sundee woman, if that's what you're thinking. I've tried that route already, remember?"

"Close," Alexie said with a chuckle.

"What, then?"

Running his finger in a circle around one of Celeste's firm, ample breasts, he said, "His possessions. The precious inventory he houses in that store he calls Ike's Spot."

"Floyd's the one I want eliminated," Celeste protested, grabbing Alexie's finger. "Not a store full of junk."

Alexie slipped his finger out of her grasp and licked it sensuously. "In Russia we have a saying: 'Some pigs must die at the trough.'"

"Meaning?"

"Meaning, I will soon have an international present for your Stetson-wearing African American cowboy. One that will be delivered to Ike's Spot, the trough that he eats from. A message that will be delivered directly from the Middle East."

"How soon?"

"Tomorrow. Perhaps the day after." Alexie slipped an arm beneath Celeste, forcefully rolled her on top of him, and ground his body into hers, quickly bringing himself to a new state of hardness. Within seconds he had slipped inside her.

Preparing herself for Alexie's spastic, cumbersome onslaught, Celeste kept thinking, *No pain, no gain*, recalling words that had once been part of an athletic training mantra that had driven her to Olympic-caliber level. It was a mantra she repeated to herself in silence as, ignoring Alexie's grunts and plunges, she envisioned the death of CJ Floyd.

Rare collectible finds always kept CJ preoccupied, to the point of often interfering with his sleep. Unearthing, researching, authenticating, and cataloging a rare porcelain license could consume him for days. So it wasn't unusual to find him at one a.m. trying to put a collector's face on the two books he'd bought. He was seated at the eighteenth-century French partner's desk that Mavis had given him the day he'd opened Ike's Spot. As CJ had watched Morgan Williams and Dittier Atkins, two down-on-their-luck former rodeo stars who had done odd jobs and a little surveillance for him when he was a bail bondsman, struggle into Ike's Spot carrying the 350-pound desk, he'd asked Mavis why such an expensive one. She'd said, "So you can do the authentication research you've always done on your kitchen table in style."

He had pretty much wrapped up dealing with the 1883 Wyoming cattle-brand book, having called his friend, the former ranch foreman, Billy DeLong, in Baggs, Wyoming, for the long and short of it. The now teetotaling, wiry, rough-cut sixty-five-year-old, who'd lost his left eye to diabetes and Old Crow, had said, "A 123-year-old book full of cow tattoos, now, that's sayin' somethin'." CJ knew he had a real find when Billy, a man prone to understatement, had told him the book was probably worth about five grand. CJ had screamed, "No shit!"

Aware that the brand book wasn't the kind of item he could put out in the store for looky-Lous and kids with Popsicle hands to paw over, he had priced the book, given it an inventory num-

— 24 —

ber, slipped it into a small safe in the doorless, unpainted cubby that served as his office, and moved on to the Montana medicine book.

CJ assigned *Medicine in the Making of Montana,* by Paul C. Phillips, published in 1962 by the Montana Medical Association and the Montana State University Press, inventory number 301 and the shorthand log-in name *The Lazy MD.*

The book opened with a preface on the history of the medical practices of Montana Indians in the 1830s and moved on in the first chapter to document a list of the medical supplies carried by the members of the Louis and Clark expedition, but what caused CJ to puzzle as he flipped page by page through the 564-page volume was not what was contained within the book's bound buckskin boards but what was missing. The front and back panels and the book's first and last pages opened into two identical buff-colored, center-creased maps of Montana. The map in the front of the book that showed the territories of a host of Montana Indian tribes looked original and pristine. The end map, however, had been damaged, and pieces of yellowed cellophane tape and fragments of what appeared to be either string or fishing line clung to the tape as it crisscrossed the map in a perfectly centered X. The string or line appeared to CJ to have at one time secured something to the back board. A barely visible note printed in lowercase letters near the upper right-hand corner of the map read, *page 298, Covington.*

Intrigued, CJ flipped to page 298 and began reading. The page began with a discussion of the election of a recording secretary to the Helena, Montana–based medical association before going on two paragraphs later to describe in dry, succinct terms the life of Jacob L. Covington:

Dr. Jacob L. Covington left little record of his early life, but from accounts of his younger brothers and other family members, he was born in Bucks County, Pennsylvania, in 1838. He graduated from the University of Pennsylvania Medical School in 1860 and practiced in Pennsylvania until 1866, when he moved to Helena. The reason he gave for the move was that he was attracted by the climate. In 1868 he moved to Laramie, Wyoming, to become a doctor for the Union Pacific Railroad. He worked for the Union Pacific from 1868 until 1870 but returned to Helena the next year and established his living quarters and office in the St. Louis Hotel. Covington, an avid photographer, worked and lived at the hotel until it burned down in 1880. The doctor narrowly escaped death by sliding down a pillar to the street, but his 470-volume library and his surgical instruments were destroyed, along with most of his photographs.

CJ reread the paragraph, deciding after the second reading and a perusal of the biographies of a dozen other doctors that there was nothing unusual enough about Covington's background, education, medical practice, or life's tragedies to distinguish him from the hundreds of others described in the book, many of whom had had hobbies that had ranged form ornithology to fly fishing, and most of whom had been educated back East. There was one thing that was strikingly different about the Covington biography, however: the entire bio had been underlined perfectly, and almost imperceptibly, in pencil. CJ flipped to the book's endboard and tried to match the underlining with the notation that had been penciled on the map of Montana, but he couldn't. He reread the biography a final time. Assured that he hadn't missed anything, he shrugged, closed the book, and nudged it aside, convinced that the Wyoming cattle-brand book had been the real find of the day.

He checked his watch and decided that one-forty would have to be the witching hour for the day. He thought about whether he should put the book he now thought of as *The Lazy MD* in the safe with the brand book. Deciding it wouldn't hurt, he walked over to the safe, knelt, and ran the combination. As he held the door open, he had the feeling that he'd missed something important in the book. He had noted that except for one minor page tear, some smudges, and three or four barely perceptible page crimps, the book appeared almost as pristine as the day it had been printed. He slipped it into the safe, wondering as he closed the door why he was so drawn to a drily written book on the history of medicine in the nation's third-largest state when he probably should have been more concerned about whether the book or its companion had been stolen, and whether the cops and the rightful owner would descend on him, confiscate his finds, and charge him with trafficking in stolen merchandise.

He rose and dimmed the store's lights, ready to head for Bail Bondsman's Row and home. Donning his Stetson and slipping on his jacket, he stepped outside to be greeted by a warm chinook breeze. The temperature had risen twenty degrees since the young man with the books had walked into Ike's Spot on a rush of frigid air. *Springtime in the Rockies,* CJ thought, heading for the sagging poor excuse for a garage where Lenny McCabe allowed him to park his 1957 drop-top Chevrolet Bel Air each morning. He slipped into the Bel Air, considered the day's events and the rapid double-digit rise in temperature, and shook his head, think-ing, *Rocky Mountain weather—you never know what to expect.*

CHAPTER 4

What greeted CJ the next morning as he raised the 1940s-vintage brown parchment shade on the glass-faced front door of Ike's, instead of a warm, comforting wind or a dusting of snowflakes, was the freckled face of a sunken-cheeked white man with a head of wiry red hair and a pencil-thin, equally red mustache staring back at him.

The man smiled, mouthed, "Open?" and stood back waiting for CJ to open the door.

"You're at it early," said CJ, taking in the man's lengthy torso and stilt-like legs.

The man, an inch taller than CJ, stepped across the threshold and into the store. "Started at seven. Always prefer to get a fast early break." The man, whom CJ judged to be no more than thirty, jammed a hand into his right pants pocket, extracted a business card, eyed the card as if it might not be what he'd reached for, and, handing the card to CJ, asked, "This one of yours?"

The way he said the word *yours*, as if he expected CJ to bolt for the back door, grovel, or start to hem and haw, told CJ everything he needed to know about the man. Vintage collectibles dealer or not, CJ still had the nose for sniffing out a cop. "Yeah. Got a problem, Officer?"

"You're quick on your feet, Mr. Floyd," the man said, surprised at how quickly he'd been made. He reached into the pocket of his loose-fitting seersucker jacket, pulled out a wallet that con-tained a business card and a badge, flashed the badge, and handed CJ the business card. "Sergeant Fritz Commons—as in, it hap-pens all the time. Seventh Precinct, Homicide." He smiled and slipped the wallet back into his pocket.

Poker-faced, CJ said, "And why do I have the early-morning pleasure?"

"That's easy, Mr. Floyd. Your business card plopped me right here on your doorstep. One of my forensic guys teased it out of the pants pocket of a man we found lying jack-face up, dead as a doornail, in an alley late last night, eleven blocks from here. He had a couple of nice-sized bullet holes in him. One dead cen-ter in his throat, one in his forehead." Commons flashed CJ the self-assured nod of someone who liked to get every fact straight, follow every rule just right. "Customer of yours?"

"Maybe."

"I need a lot more certainty than that, Mr. Floyd."

"Describe your dead man for me," said CJ, accustomed to play-ing cat-and-mouse with cops.

"Five-six, dark-complected, big round face—the hint of a goatee."

"Could be he was in yesterday," said CJ.

"About what time?"

"Late afternoon."

"Buy anything?"

"No."

"Sell you anything?" asked Commons.

"A couple of books."

"Got proof of the transaction?"

CJ's answer was diversionary and quick. "An eyewitness."

Commons smiled at the tactic and shook his head. "I'm talking receipt, as in the paper kind most businesses use."

"I paid in cash."

"And your eyewitness saw the man too?"

"Sure did. It was his cash."

"I see. Are the books you bought handy?"

"They're in my safe."

"Hmmm. That valuable?"

"One is for sure," said CJ, gauging Commons's reaction, uncertain how much the sergeant might already know about the books.

"Let's take a look," Commons said, glancing around the room and scanning the merchandise as he tried to determine whether he was dealing with a legitimate antiques dealer or a fence. "Nice merchandise," he said, his assessment apparently still incomplete.

CJ turned and headed for his unfinished office. He knelt in front of the safe, opened the door, reached inside, and handed Commons the two books. He watched the calculating red-headed detective examine the cattle-brand book first, knowing full well what Commons was thinking: *Why not pay the man for the books and get your investment right back by killing him?* Deciding to take the wind out of the pesky cop's sails, CJ said, "I didn't kill the man, Sergeant."

"Didn't say you did." Commons set the brand book aside and flipped through the Montana medicine book.

"But it's on your list of possibilities," countered CJ.

Commons laid the second book down on top of the first one. "You seem to know a lot about cops, Mr. Floyd. Ever been one?"

CJ smiled. "Nope. A long way from it."

Commons drank in CJ's smile, and his eyes narrowed to a suddenly less-than-friendly stare. "I've got a murder on my hands,

Floyd, and you were quite probably the victim's last contact. You've got what was assuredly his property locked in your safe and no documentation to prove that he willingly sold the merchandise to you. Bottom line here, friend, is you've got a problem."

"And I've got a witness to attest to the sale, remember?"

"Time to produce your witness, Floyd."

"Easy enough. He's right next door," said CJ, hoping that for once Lenny McCabe had opened his store on time.

"Then let's walk over and have a talk with him, and on the way maybe you'll tell me how it is you're so quick to spot a cop."

"Learned it in a previous life."

"Doing what?" Commons asked, following CJ toward the front door.

CJ paused, causing Commons to nearly stumble into him. "A thirty-year tour as a bail bondsman," he said, swinging open the door to McCabe's Matchless Gems and sighing in relief as he watched Lenny McCabe stride toward them.

Fifteen minutes later, after grudgingly accepting the fact that McCabe had indeed given CJ $1,700 to buy the dead man's books, Commons was gone. He'd departed only after McCabe had produced CJ's uncashed check with a note on the memo line that read, "Montana medicine book and Wyoming BB 1883"—and then only after he'd quizzed both men about the transaction three different ways from Sunday.

CJ had tried to squeeze more details out of Commons about how the book peddler with the thick Spanish accent had died, but the cagey homicide cop wouldn't step beyond his earlier revelation that the man had been shot.

Commons had left with strong words of advice for CJ: "Lock up the books, photocopy that check, and stay friends with your next-door neighbor. And by the way," he'd added, offering a departing salvo from McCabe's doorway, "when it comes to a murder case, leads are, as I'm sure you're well aware, a lot like muscle cramps. You have to massage them over and over to get out the knot. Count on it, I'll be back for another visit."

The unmarked police cruiser with blackwall tires, no hubcaps, and a volleyball-sized dent in the right rear quarter panel looked so out of place sitting in the cobblestone driveway in front of Howard Stafford's sprawling French country home that the two undocumented Latino gardeners who were trimming hedges along the driveway's western edge whispered in near unison to each other in Spanish, as Sergeant Commons exited the vehicle, "*Policía.*"

The noonday skies had turned overcast, promising a calm, dreary afternoon, but that calm had been shattered moments earlier by Theresa Del Mora's wails, her mournful sobs, and her pleas in Spanish for help.

Theresa had been supervising the placement of a 350-pound, centuries-old Grecian urn that with its twin would flank the tiled entry to Howard Stafford's home when Fritz Commons had pulled up. The entryway was normally gated, but two workmen had been installing a new entry keypad to the right of the gate, and the gate had been open, affording Commons the chance to circumvent a security clearance and breeze past them on a beeline to Stafford's house. On his way he'd sped past a mass of greenery, freshly planted spring flowers, fountains, rows of hedges, and a grouping of ornate cast-iron benches that looked as if they belonged on a Hollywood movie set.

He hadn't expected the mother of his murder victim to greet him as he'd walked up the front steps to the Stafford mansion, but Theresa Del Mora had, and when he'd announced who he was, relaying the unsettling news about Luis to her as she took a seat, she'd let out a wail and immediately begun to sob.

"You'll have to calm down, ma'am, if you want me to try to help," Commons said, uncertain how to cope with Theresa's hysteria. He turned to one of the hedge trimmers for help when a puzzled-looking, cowboy-booted, bush-hat-wearing Howard Stafford bounded up the steps toward him.

"What's going on?" shouted Stafford. "And who the hell are you?"

Commons slipped his badge wallet out of a coat pocket, flashed it at Stafford, who'd barely slowed his charge, and said, "Sergeant Fritz Commons, Denver Police."

Stafford, a tall, gaunt man with keen features, stopped inches from Commons. "What's happened?"

Theresa glanced up, sobbing. "Luis is dead." Her words were slurred and barely intelligible.

Stafford eyed Theresa and let out a sigh. "Oh, God!" He took Theresa's right hand in his and squeezed it reassuringly. "I'm sorry." Theresa choked back more sobs as Stafford, speaking to her in Spanish, helped her to her feet and walked her through the front door of the house into a bright marble-floored foyer. Accompanying her to a wooden bench that hugged one wall, he sat with her on the bench and nodded for the trailing Commons to take a seat on a nearby hassock.

They sat in silence as Theresa continued sobbing. When a woman wearing an apron and dressed in black, form-fitting slacks appeared from a barely visible nearby doorway, Stafford said, "Some water, please, for Theresa."

The woman scurried away and quickly returned with a serving tray, a carafe of ice water, and three chilled glasses. Stafford took the tray and waved her off dismissively.

"Try this," he said to Theresa, pouring her a glass full of water. "You too," he said to Commons, his manner as ingratiating as it had been rude to the woman who'd brought the water.

"Now," he said, sounding breathless and looking at Commons, "perhaps I can hear the rest of the story."

By the time Theresa Del Mora had calmed down enough to listen to Commons describe what had happened to Luis, including most of the circumstances surrounding his death, a half hour had passed and an empty carafe sat on top of an antique carpenter's chest across the foyer from them.

"And that was it?" asked Stafford, responding to the suddenly silent Commons. "No car tracks in the snow, no footprints, no other significant clues?"

"Only one," said Commons, deciding it was time to drop his bombshell about the books. "Luis had just sold an antiques dealer on South Broadway a couple of books. The seventeen hundred in cash the dealer had paid him was still in Luis's pocket."

"Then Luis wasn't robbed," said Stafford, eyeing a morbidly silent Theresa, elbows on her thighs, head bent, eyes on the floor.

Commons chose his words carefully. "Things don't seem to point that way at the moment."

"Seventeen hundred dollars. That's a pretty hefty sum for two books," said Stafford.

"They were rare ones. What collectors call antiquarian."

The muscles in Stafford's face were suddenly taut. He looked at Theresa, who still hadn't moved, and asked haltingly, "What were the titles?"

"Don't remember exactly," said Commons, bending the truth in order to see where Stafford would take him. "But one was a Wyoming book of cattle brands from the 1880s. The other was a historical account of Montana medicine."

Stafford shook his head and eyed Theresa disappointedly.

"Problem?" asked Commons.

"Maybe."

"Mind clueing me?"

"I'm a collector of many things, Sergeant, including books. The books you mentioned sound like two I have in my collection. But they're not so rare that I'd think people would steal or kill for them," said Stafford, trying not to sound accusatory.

"Can you check and see if your two books are missing?"

Instead of answering, Stafford rose from his seat and took three strides toward the doorway that the woman who'd brought them water had appeared from. He pushed aside a well-concealed sliding door, barked a command in Spanish, and walked back to join Commons. Moments later the woman reappeared.

"Take Theresa to her quarters," Stafford said authoritatively.

The woman dutifully helped Theresa from her seat. Wrapping an arm and a brightly colored shawl around her, she angled Theresa toward the front door.

"I'll check on her later," Stafford called out as he and Commons watched the two women disappear through the front door. Turning to Commons, he said, "I didn't want Theresa to hear or see any more of this. Let's take a walk to my library."

Commons followed the wealthy oil and gas baron, whose Western lineage stretched back to before Colorado's 1876 statehood, down a long, Spanish-tiled hallway that led into the house. They walked past a dozen priceless oil paintings, most of which depicted the trials of pioneering settlers or Indian conflict, before turning down a second limestone-floored hallway accented with strategically placed Persian and Indian tapestries. They breezed past a couple of thousand-year-old Mayan vases before reaching the hallway's end and the massive hand-carved double doors of Howard Stafford's library.

Stafford extracted a set of keys from his pocket, disarmed an alarm keypad on the outer wall, unlocked the doors, swung them open, and said, "Step into my world, Sergeant Commons."

As he entered the windowless forty-by-forty-foot library, Commons resisted the urge to say, *Wow*. The massive room, paneled in lightly stained cherry wood, had a captivating bookwormish, lost-to-the-world warmth. Exquisite hand-carved columns supported floor-to-ceiling bookshelves that encased the room. They were accented with lights, and some held rare nineteenth-century Pueblo Indian pottery, baskets, spurs, bridle bits, intricately beaded leather scabbards, and even a few seemingly out-of-place antique children's toys. Books in every size, shape, and color overflowed from the rest of the bookshelves.

Three coffin-sized, marble-topped, glass-fronted display cases chock-full of Western artifacts—from tomahawks to tepee hides, Indian moccasins to muskets—occupied the center of the room. A fourth case with locking wooden doors ran perpendicular to the other wall.

"What do you think?" asked Stafford, slipping his keys into

his pocket as he angled his way past the display cases and walked toward the far western corner of the room.

"Impressive."

"It's meant to be. It's my pride and joy. There're things in here the Library of Congress, the Smithsonian, and the National Archives would salivate over."

"Hope it's wired."

Stafford laughed. "To the teeth and then some. You'd need a couple of grenades and a Ph.D. in electrical engineering to get in here."

"Or a set of keys and an alarm code," Commons said casually.

Without responding, Stafford stopped, looked up toward a top shelf that was stacked support column to support column with books, and said, "Need a ladder." He stepped several paces to his left, retrieved a ladder that tracked around the room, and pulled it back to where he'd been standing. He mounted the first three steps until he could reach the shelf he'd eyed earlier. Slowly he ran a finger along the spines of several of the shelved books. Stopping abruptly in the middle of his run, he pulled half-a-dozen books off the shelf and cradled them in his right arm before slipping them back into place, leaving a three-inch-wide gap on the shelf. The look on his face was charged with amazement.

"They're gone. Both of them," he called down to Commons. "That's a damn shame."

"Anything else missing?"

"Not from this shelf. But I'll have to check everything. It'll take some time. Damn! And I thought Luis was different from the rest, like his mother. Guess I was wrong." Stafford eased his way down to the ladder's bottom step.

"Did the books have any distinguishing marks? Anything to prove your ownership?" asked Commons.

"No," said Stafford, flashing Commons an incredulous look. "Name plates only serve to deface books and detract from their value. But I can describe the books to a T, and of course my insurance records contain photos."

"I'll need both," said Commons, watching Stafford step down to the floor. "A few more questions."

Dusting off his hands, Stafford said, "Shoot."

"You wouldn't have had any serious differences with Luis Del Mora, would you?"

"I shouldn't grace that with an answer, Sergeant, but no."

"What about his mother? Any problem with her?"

"Are you blind, Sergeant? I have the deepest respect for Theresa. Six years ago she came to America penniless, a stowaway in the bottom of a coal car. Today she earns sixty-five thousand dollars a year."

"I see," Commons said with a quick nod. "Did her son have any enemies?"

"You'll have to ask his mother." Stafford's tone was indignant.

"I'll do that."

"Good." Stafford pivoted and headed for the door with Commons at his heels. "And while you're at it, you can work on recovering my books."

Commons didn't answer, knowing that Stafford's books would be logged in as evidence in a murder investigation just as soon as he'd paid CJ Floyd a second visit. The books wouldn't be returned, even to someone as powerful and influential as Stafford, until that murder investigation was finished. But at the moment, Commons saw no need to mention that.

CHAPTER 5

Platter-sized puddles, remnants of the previous day's intermittent snow showers, sat in a shaded spot just beyond the entry to Mae's Louisiana Kitchen. Minutes earlier the noonday temperature had peaked at fifty-five, and the early-April sun, not yet high enough in the sky to bring the Denver afternoon much greater highs, had moved on.

CJ was wrapping up lunch with Mavis and his best friend of more than forty years, Roosevelt Weeks. Weeks, known on the streets of Denver's historically black Five Points community simply as Rosie, was polishing off the last of his sweet-potato pie. Five Points, though still anchored by Mae's, Rosie's 1950s-style gas station and garage with its three banks of stately white-globed gas pumps, and the now defunct Rossonian Club, once the heart of the American jazz scene in the West, was moving closer to urban gentrification day by day.

Matching CJ bite for bite in an apparent contest to see who could finish Mae's sweet-potato pie, the restaurant's signature dessert, the fastest, Rosie glanced up at Mavis.

"You're worse than a couple of kids," Mavis said, shaking her head as she watched CJ and Rosie repeat the lunch-ending ritual they'd been practicing for decades.

Accepting defeat, CJ paused, took a sip of coffee, and eyed

Mavis. "Thin lunch crowd today," he said, scanning the half-empty restaurant.

"And it'll likely get thinner," Mavis said with a sigh. "At least until the yuppie land speculators finally settle in for good and figure out that fried chicken, red beans and rice, and sweet-potato pie are fare to die for."

"By then there won't be a black face in the neighborhood," said Rosie. "You see the prices they got on them condos they're buildin' up there on 28th? Hell, they're asking rich folks' prices." Rosie put down his fork, smiled at CJ's unfinished pie, and said, "Done."

"And they're selling," Mavis chimed in.

"What about the Five Points Businessmen's Association?" asked CJ, eyeing Mavis, the association's first female president, quizzically. "Aren't you pushing back?"

Mavis laughed. "Like the French did when Hitler took Paris. Lucius Allen sold that piece of land of his just up the street to a bank. He tried to keep it quiet, but Daddy found out. When Lucius came in for lunch yesterday, Daddy let him have it full-bore. I don't think Lucius'll want to see any more Willis Sundee for a while."

CJ shook his head and thought about what Five Points meant to him. In truth, "the Points," as it was called by locals, was no more than an intersection formed by the confluence of 27th Street, Welton and Washington Streets, and 26th Avenue, but it had been the cultural core of his life. He'd gone to school in Five Points. It was there that he'd made most of his lifelong friends and fallen for Mavis. And it was the place he'd come home to after his two soul-testing tours in Vietnam. "You'll have to keep pushing back," he said to Mavis. "You've got a business to protect."

"I'll survive." Mavis's response was matter-of-fact. "The question is, what about you?" She smiled and clasped CJ's right hand in hers. The engagement ring CJ had given her months earlier sparkled. "Give me the rundown on how it's going at Ike's."

"Yeah, man," said Rosie. "I wanta know whether it's more lucrative to push antique license plates and spurs or write bail bonds."

"Neither. Everybody knows the real money's in peddling fan belts and overpriced tune-ups," CJ shot back with a smile. "But I'm doing okay, and I caught a real good buy yesterday. Coughed up seventeen hundred for a couple of books. I was nervous as hell when I did it, but I called Billy DeLong up in Wyoming for verification on the value of one of them, and he told me the book was worth at least five grand."

Rosie whistled, pushed back from the table, and patted his midsection. All 260 pounds of the massive, no-neck man shook. "Now, that's what I'd call a smart investment. Two times your money and then some—I'd say you're kickin'."

"Now all you need is a buyer," said Mavis, toning down Rosie's exuberance.

"One will come," said CJ. "But there is one minor problem."

"With the books? They aren't fake, are they?"

"No. With the man I bought the books from. A few hours after he sold me the books, the cops found him shot to death in an alley."

"Uh-oh," said Rosie, eyes widening.

Mavis's response was silence. She'd ridden every possible high and low with CJ during his thirty-plus years as a bail bondsman and reluctant bounty hunter. She'd seen him beaten and shot. She'd spent days, nights, and occasionally weeks worried about whether he would come home safely after dueling and dealing with what her father aptly called society's pond scum. She'd watched him helpless, hapless, and sometimes even hopeful as he dogged robbers and fences, con artists, wife-beaters, and shills across much of the Rocky Mountain West, praying that one day he'd get his fill of the excitement of the chase and stop. But he hadn't until nine months earlier, when Celeste Deepstream had tried to kill them both in the remote New Mexico wilderness. That ordeal had exacted a toll, and when CJ had brought a physically and psychologically damaged Mavis home to recuperate, he'd promised her that his days as a bail bondsman and bounty hunter were over. CJ's story about the books and a murder sent Mavis spiraling back in time, and now, as she sat limp in her chair with a look of anguish frozen on her face, she couldn't help but think, *I knew it was too good to last.*

Squeezing her hand, smiling defensively, and playfully twisting the ring on her finger, CJ said, "Things are fine." The smile was quickly replaced by a chiseled frown when he glanced briefly toward the front of the restaurant to see Fritz Commons standing at the hostess station. Commons smiled at the hostess, sidestepped her, locked in on CJ, and walked briskly down the restaurant's center aisle. He smiled and respectfully nodded to Mavis, but the look he gave CJ and Rosie was more probing and official.

"Your friend Lenny told me I might be able to find you here," he said to CJ. "Seems McCabe's always on the money."

CJ shook his head, glancing at Rosie and then hesitantly at Mavis. "Lenny's got his finger on the pulse of it all. Our guest here is Sergeant Fritz Commons. What can I help you with, Sergeant?"

CJ's response, which Mavis had heard him serve up to policemen for years, had her stomach churning.

"We can talk in private if you'd like."

"No need. I'm among friends." CJ flashed Mavis a look that said, *I know, but everything will be okay.*

"Fine," Commons said with a shrug. "Turns out those books you bought yesterday were stolen."

"From whom?"

"That's confidential at the moment."

"What's your proof?"

"The owner can describe them to a T, and he's got insurance records and photos to back him up."

"And I've got proof that I bought them—legit," CJ shot back.

"Nobody's claiming you knew they were stolen, Floyd, but what they are now is evidence in a murder investigation. You'll have to turn them over."

"I don't bring my merchandise with me to lunch."

"Didn't figure you did. But the day's young, and if I remember right, the shade on the door of your place says, 'Open 10 to 5.'"

"I'll be back in the shop in an hour."

Commons smiled through splayed, badly yellowed teeth. "Take your time. We've got until five. I'll be there before you drop that shade." He nodded at Mavis, pivoted, and walked back up the aisle without another word.

The dryness in CJ's throat intensified as he watched Commons retreat. It was a nervous, anticipatory dryness—the kind he'd experienced whenever the 125-foot navy patrol boat he'd been a machine gunner on during the war in Vietnam had left for a mission. His nervousness, however, had nothing to do with the sweaty uneasiness that haunts a soldier during war. What had him on edge and drumming his fingers on the tabletop was that by purchasing two books he shouldn't have bought, he'd allowed himself to drift out of the safe harbor that he had spent nearly a year constructing and back into waters that were mined. Even worse, he had let Mavis down.

He glanced over at Mavis, searching for words to smooth things over, words that would let her know he'd had a simple lapse in judgment and that he wasn't headed back for troubled waters, but the words wouldn't come.

CHAPTER 6

Two hours later Sergeant Commons stood across the counter from CJ with the two stolen books in his hand. CJ had had the good sense to photocopy the page relating to Dr. Jacob L. Covington, the front and rear free endpapers, the pastedowns with the Montana maps, and the first three chapters and index of the Montana medicine book. He'd also photocopied all eighty-six pages of the 1883 Wyoming brand book.

Commons, who'd arrived at Ike's Spot ten minutes on the good side of CJ's duplicating efforts, handed CJ a property receipt initialed F.C. "On the off chance the books aren't stolen," he said, with a grin. "Better hold on to it."

CJ jammed the receipt into the frayed pocket of his riverboat gambler's vest, disgusted at himself for taking a flyer on the books and knowing that he'd set fire to his rent money for the month. He shook his head, looked up at Commons, and asked, "Got autopsy results on your victim yet?"

"That's no concern of yours, Floyd." As Commons pivoted to leave, CJ's porcelain-license-plate display caught his attention. He walked over to the display and picked up a coal-black 1914 Pennsylvania plate with embossed white numerals. "What would this plate set me back?" he asked, turning back to CJ.

"Right at five hundred."

"Steep. Antique license plates your specialty?"

"Yes."

Commons flashed CJ a sly, one-upping smile. "Take my advice. Stick with your strength and stay away from books." He put the license plate down and headed for the door.

"Wouldn't think of it," CJ called after him, suspecting that the gangly red-headed cop was probably right.

Business was snail's-pace slow for the rest of the day, and CJ's only sale of the afternoon came on the heels of Commons's visit: $35 worth of vintage Rocky Mountain National Park postcards that he sold to an elderly couple visiting from Louisiana.

A half hour before closing, he parked himself at his desk, eyed the wall behind him, and let out a sigh. He'd been an antiques dealer for two slow, disheartening months, and all he had to show for it were a couple of Lenny McCabe–authored rent statements he hadn't paid, less than a thousand dollars in total sales, a police property tag for two stolen books, and a record-breaking one day loss of $1,700.

Slipping his feet up onto the edge of his desk and deciding to make a call he knew would infuriate Mavis, he dialed the number to Denver Health and Hospitals, asked for extension 48, and waited for an answer. The mellow baritone voice on the other end of the line answered, "Vernon Lowe, Morgue."

Vernon, a five-foot-seven, bug-eyed, flashy-dressing slip of a black man and Denver Health's chief morgue attendant, had been in charge of prepping and eviscerating the dead for almost twenty-eight years. He'd been CJ's friend for thirty, and Ike's for even longer.

"What's up on the downside, V?" said CJ, offering Vernon the same signature greeting he'd been giving him for nearly three decades.

Vernon's response was automatic: "Nobody shakin' in this place but me. What's up with you, CJ?"

"Just tryin' to make a poor man's living, V."

"Ain't that the truth? I was just about to shut things down. Callin' pretty late in the day, aren't you, CJ?"

"I was hoping you could pin down a few details for me on someone who's no longer with us."

Vernon, who'd been feeding CJ "unofficial" autopsy information for years, said, "Figured as much."

"Need to know if you've done a post on a Spanish kid—nineteen or so—twenty-one tops—with a big melon head, dark skin, a hint of a goatee, and wide-set eyes that showed pretty much nothing but the whites? I'm pretty certain he took a bullet to the head and maybe one to the throat."

Vernon shook his head. "Thought you were outta the kinda business that would cause you to wanta know things like that, CJ."

"I am. But the kid and I had a connection."

Vernon looked around the room as if to make certain no one was eavesdropping. "Autopsied him this morning. Hold on and let me get his chart." He set the receiver down on a gurney, walked over to a bank of World War II–vintage metal filing cabinets, and extracted a chart. When he picked the receiver back up, CJ had pencil and notepad in hand. "Here's the poop," Vernon said cautiously. "Name was Luis Del Mora. Twenty. Nicaraguan. Rode into the good old U.S. of A. on a student visa. Took a .22 Mag to the brain and another one to the larynx."

"Sounds like he met up with a sharpshooter."

"Had to. You don't hit these kind of vitals without knowing how to bang. Especially since the coroner makes the time of death somewhere around dusk. You'd have to be one hell of a shot to be able to hit them two spots right on the money with your daylight droppin' outta the sky. But if you could, you'd doggone sure hit pay dirt, 'cause you know as well as me, a bullet from a .22 Mag tumbles right through your brain. Whoever popped the kid had to be a pro, or close."

"Anything else I should know?"

"As a matter of fact, yeah. Sort of strange, even for the knife-and-gun-club operation we run down here. A cop showed up at the post."

"Let me guess. Tall, red-headed, yellow teeth, skinny?"

"That's him. Rare to get a cop down here eyeballin' a post. Usually all they want are the autopsy results."

"Was he pretty closed-mouthed?"

"Pretty much. Just watched for the most part. But he seemed real interested in the entry and exit wounds in the kid's skull. I'm bettin' he pegged it as a professional job too. He did drop one little surprise though, right after Dr. Woodley finished examinin' the kid's brain. I was sewin' the skullcap back on when your cop said the kid had seventeen hundred bucks on him when they found him that wasn't even touched. Made the remark out of the blue, like he was lookin' to get some kinda response outta either me or the doc, like we could've been suspects. Real strange cop if you ask me."

"Damn! He still had the cash."

"Hell, CJ, you're makin' noise like the money was yours."

"It was."

"You're bullshittin'."

"I wish. Your dead man sold me a couple of stolen books. That was my seventeen hundred."

"Well, it ain't no more. The city and county ain't reimbursin', and neither's the kid."

"I know," CJ said with a sigh.

"One last thing. May not mean anything, though."

"Shoot."

"The kid was packin' a real high-rent address on his driver's license—top of the line. One of them rich white folks' addresses in Cherry Hills."

"Mighty top-drawer for a twenty-year-old immigrant on a student visa," said CJ.

"Maybe he had upper-crust kin."

"Could be." CJ stroked his chin thoughtfully. "These days you never know. Anything else?"

"That's it."

"You're the man, V."

"All the women tell me that," Vernon said with a smile that was deadly serious.

"You get anything else, clue me in," CJ said.

"Will do, and remember, you never heard nothin' from me."

"I've been hard of hearing for years—you know that," said CJ, offering Vernon his standard sign-off.

"Later." Vernon smiled and cradled the phone.

Denver's five-thirty p.m. rush-hour traffic had kicked into high gear on South Broadway. Once a quaint two-lane road that made its way from downtown to the suburb of Littleton, Broadway had never been meant to accommodate the urban jailbreak of traffic it was now forced to handle, and CJ had the feeling as he stood at the front door of Ike's, ready to drop the door shade on business for the day, that the Denver city fathers would be happy to see the street turned into an interstate if they thought it might add money to their coffers.

With his attention focused on a conga line of traffic, CJ didn't notice a small raven-haired woman approaching the store until she was framed in the front door's beveled glass. "I'm closed," he mouthed, waving her off.

"Please," the sad-eyed, defeated-looking woman called out unmistakably through the glass. Acquiescing, CJ swung the door open, suspecting that the gloomy-faced woman wanted either work or directions. Without a mask of beveled glass between them, he recognized the expression on the woman's face: it was the unmistakable look of grief. The same grief-stricken look he'd worn for months after Ike had died. "What can I help you with?" he asked, his tone suddenly a whisper.

"Are you Mr. Floyd?"

"Yes."

The woman, dressed in a black, Spanish-territorial, ankle-length cotton skirt, a loose-fitting turquoise blouse, and Western boots, extracted a wallet-sized leather coin purse from a slit at the side of her skirt, unzipped the purse, and pulled out a yellow sheet of paper. As she unfolded the paper, CJ realized that it had been torn from the yellow pages. Circled in Magic Marker, his boxed ad for Ike's Spot occupied the lower right-hand corner. Holding the ad open for CJ to see, the woman said, "I found this page from the phone book in my son's room beneath a stack of auto-racing magazines. I am Theresa Del Mora, and I have been told that you were probably the last person to see my son,

Luis, alive." Theresa's eyes glazed over and her lower lip began to quiver, but there was a sternness in her face that hadn't been there during the first hysterical hours after she'd learned that her son had been murdered.

The only words CJ could muster as he watched the dour-looking, round-faced woman try to control her emotions were, "I'm sorry."

"Thank you, Mr. Floyd. Unfortunately, at one time or another sorrow reaches the pulse of us all. It was simply my time." There was a tone of inevitability in Theresa Del Mora's voice, and her words, spoken with a barely noticeable Spanish accent, sounded practiced and pondered. She watched as CJ wrestled for a response. "I can see that you are searching for words of comfort, Mr. Floyd, and that is good. It tells me you have been in my shoes before. Like circumstances always breed compassion."

CJ responded with a nod.

"Then you understand how important it is for me to find out who killed my son. May I come in?"

"Please." CJ ushered Theresa in, led her the length of the store to his unfinished back office, and nodded for her to take a seat in one of the chairs that faced his desk. "Can I offer you a glass of water?" he asked, sitting and adjusting himself in his chair as he pondered why the chubby-cheeked woman sitting in front of him with her eyes cast skyward was there.

Declining the water, Theresa shook her head.

"I'm not sure how I can help you."

"You can help by first assuring me that you had nothing to do with my son's death."

"All I did was buy a couple of books from him."

"The books were stolen."

"I was unaware of that when I bought them."

"I understand, and the detective who is working to find Luis's killer agrees. Nonetheless, you used bad judgment when you purchased those books, Mr. Floyd."

Unprepared for the grief-stricken woman's directness, CJ said, "I didn't kill your son, Mrs. Del Mora, and you still haven't told me how I can help."

Having made her point, Theresa asked, "Did Luis seem at all nervous or agitated when he sold you the books?"

"Not particularly. In fact, he negotiated the sale like he'd done it lots of times before."

"He was accustomed to bartering in our native Nicaragua."

"It showed. How long had he been here in Denver?"

"Five months. He was a student at Metro State. He wanted to be a history teacher." Theresa's eyes glazed over, and she swallowed hard. "His dreams will never be met."

CJ paused momentarily before asking the next question. "Where did he get the books?" he said, careful not to use the word *steal*.

"From my employer, Howard Stafford."

"Is he a rare-book collector?"

"Books and much more."

CJ nodded, trying to place the name. "Do you know why your son chose the books he sold to me?"

Teary-eyed and suddenly aware that CJ had taken over the questioning, Theresa said, "I don't know."

"What does Stafford have to say about what happened?"

Embarrassed, Theresa said, "We haven't discussed it. But I spoke for a long while with that detective. He's been to see me twice. Once with the news of Luis's death, when I was largely incoherent, and a second time when he filled the air with questions."

"Is his last name Commons?"

"Yes."

"What kinds of questions did he ask?"

"Did Luis have any enemies—and what about friends? Had he been in trouble with the law either in Nicaragua or here? Did he have a girlfriend? Had he been acting strange lately? Was Luis doing drugs? Did he and Howard Stafford get along? What was Luis studying at Metro State?"

"And your answers were?"

"Luis was a loner, Mr. Floyd, and he had neither enemies nor a close group of friends. He behaved no differently from the day he arrived in this country until his death as far as I could tell. He certainly didn't do drugs. And as for Mr. Stafford, Luis was like most other people for him. No more than background noise. For him Luis probably never existed."

"Stafford's that far out?"

"He's different." Theresa Del Mora's eyes narrowed to an insightful squint.

"Different enough to kill someone to get his books back?"

"Unlikely. He can certainly purchase more."

"Then with me scratched off his list of suspects and Stafford pretty much a scratch too, I'd say Sergeant Commons has his work cut out for him," said CJ, hoping that Theresa Del Mora's response would tell him exactly where he and Howard Stafford stood on Sergeant Commons's list of murder suspects.

"I don't think either of you has been removed, Mr. Floyd. And that's partially why I'm here. I'm hoping to find a route that will take me to the truth about my son's death. You Americans call it justice. Too often in Nicaragua there is no such thing. You've heard of the Sandinista revolution, I am sure, Mr. Floyd?"

"Yes," said CJ, familiar with the 1979 Nicaraguan revolt that had kept the largest nation in Central America in turmoil for the next eleven years.

"There can be no justice, Mr. Floyd, when there is no law. And during my lifetime the law and all its apostles, whether here or in Nicaragua, have largely been unavailable to me. One can never trust lawyers or the law."

"And cops? How do you stand on trusting them?" CJ asked.

"The *policía* never, including your very polite Sergeant Commons!"

Looking confused, CJ asked, "Mind telling me where I fit in?"

"Your question deserves another, Mr. Floyd. Did you know that the seventeen hundred dollars you paid Luis for those two books was still in his pocket when they found him? Rolled tightly into a wad and secured with a rubber band?"

Sidestepping the question, CJ asked, "Who told you that?"

"Sergeant Commons. I think he told me to see how I'd react. I didn't. He also told me that you were once a bail bondsman and a bounty hunter."

"Once," said CJ, wondering where the small, moon-faced woman was headed.

"Do you still have friends in that business?"

"Yes, but you'd probably do better with a private detective."

"No, Mr. Floyd. I'm looking for a person who is much less official. Someone less closely linked to your American system of justice and your need to, above all else, maintain order. I suspect you probably qualify, Mr. Floyd."

"Why trust my judgment?"

Theresa responded as if she'd pondered the question at length. "Because you didn't rob my son, as I'm certain Sergeant Commons first expected. And because, like my employer, Howard Stafford, you collect treasures, and that means that somewhere along the line someone has treasured you. And finally because the trail to the murder of my son began and ends with you."

Theresa Del Mora's riddle-like response had an unnerving ring that reminded CJ of all the times he'd unsuccessfully tried to set justice right.

"This isn't Nicaragua," he warned. "The law works differently here, and the system, flawed as it may be, frowns on vigilantes. I'm afraid what I did in that area is in the past, which means I can't help you."

"But you must, however, know the kind of person I need," Theresa said disappointedly. "Can you please provide me with the name of someone who can help?"

"I know one person," CJ said after a thoughtful pause. "She's a former marine. She's no-nonsense, smart, and expensive."

"The name, Mr. Floyd. Please."

CJ opened the top drawer of his desk, extracted the business card of his former partner, Flora Jean Benson, and handed it to Theresa, who examined the card carefully. "How late is she open?"

"Till six-thirty, but being a bondsman means you're always on the job. Call the cell-phone number on that card. She'll respond."

"I'll call her on the way home," said Theresa. She abruptly turned to leave. "Thanks for Ms. Benson's name."

"You're welcome," said CJ, watching Theresa Del Mora scurry from the store.

Moments later CJ stood and walked the length of the store. As he again locked up for the day, he glanced out onto the sidewalk to look for the moon-faced Nicaraguan woman, but Theresa Del Mora had already vanished.

CHAPTER 7

The link between one person and another, the how and why of a relationship, the thing that crystallizes a friendship can be difficult to pinpoint, but the connection between Nasar Moradi-Nik and Alexie Borg was easily defined. Their passion for athletics and Russia's 1970s military intervention in Afghanistan would serve to link them forever. Both men had lost fathers in that conflict, and when, on the eve of the 1996 Olympic Summer Games, years after the Soviets had turned tail and run from Afghanistan, the two countries had an opportunity at the urging of the IOC to parade Alexie and Nasar in front of TV cameras and showcase their made-for-the-media camaraderie, the die was cast.

Alexie's post-Olympic fame was short-lived, Moradi-Nik's even briefer, but they'd stayed connected over the years, and as each man's homeland drifted in and out of political and economic chaos, they managed to survive in a world beyond athletics by honing skills far removed from those of an Olympian.

Moradi-Nik, quixotic, always fearful, with a personality verging on schizophrenia, had cemented his post-Olympic reputation in the underbelly of the world, operating as a high-priced torcher of buildings and an occasional bomber. An agnostic with no interest in or respect or tolerance for religion, Moradi-Nik was the antithesis of the American-conjured terrorizing demonic Middle Eastern zealot. He was, on the contrary, an ordinary-looking, dark-haired, fair-skinned, clean-shaven, Western-looking man of medium build who started fires and detonated bombs for a living—bombs and conflagrations that he liked to think were worthy of America—explosions and fires designed to take out one's business opponents and competitors, clear space for a new highrise, or rid one of an overly leveraged building. Nasar Moradi-Nik was, after all, as he was quick to point out to potential clients, an American businessman, a capitalist, available for the asking—at a price—to cleanse any ailing capitalist's entrepreneurial soul.

Although Moradi-Nik had built a solid reputation for efficient, untraceable work, Alexie disliked using him on jobs, especially small jobs, for two simple reasons. He was a nervous ninny who twitched and shook and looked over his shoulder incessantly, which made the gruff, ice-water-in-his-veins Russian uncomfortable. Moreover, Moradi-Nik had a tendency to pay far too little attention to detail when he considered a job and the paycheck beneath him.

In the face of these shortcomings, Alexie, on Celeste Deepstream's orders, found himself hunched up next to Moradi-Nik behind a Dumpster in an alley twenty yards from the back door to Ike's Spot, watching his shaking and quivering Afghan friend begin the initial phases of a plan to blow Ike's Spot to kingdom come.

CJ had left the antiques store two hours earlier, and his half of the Lenny McCabe–owned duplex had remained quiet until just before twilight, when Morgan Williams and Dittier Atkins, the two homeless former rodeo cowboys who most nights called the screened-in back porch of Ike's Spot home, had arrived to hunker down for the evening.

Alexie and Moradi-Nik had watched the two street bums settle in, and for the last twenty minutes they'd been trying to decide what to do. "Floyd must know they're there," Alexie whispered, peering around the edge of the Dumpster and watching Morgan and Dittier move around on the porch. "The short one with the shaved head had a key."

"Quiet," said Moradi-Nik, every muscle in his body quivering. Borg frowned, telling himself that he just might be risking too much for a mere piece of Acoma Indian pussy.

They watched Morgan and Dittier walk around in the porch's subdued light for another five minutes until Moradi-Nik, with Alexie reluctantly in tow, moved to take a closer look at his target from behind the garage that CJ used to house his Bel Air. The garage's wall intersected a fence that rimmed a tiny patch of backyard grass between it and the porch. Peering around the corner of the garage, Alexie estimated that the two street bums, who'd arrived at Ike's Spot pushing shopping carts filled to the brim with aluminum cans, were less than fifteen feet away. "Why are we wasting our time?" he whispered. "Let's come back when they're not here."

"Shut up," Moradi-Nik warned, wondering why the porch lights kept cycling on and off. "I need to know if they're going to stay or leave. There's a difference between blowing up an empty building and blowing up one with potential eyewitnesses. I don't care one bit about those two street bums being here when I take the place out, but when things settle I want the building and everyone inside it to be one hundred percent dead." Moradi-Nik's voice rose as he talked gleefully about death and destruction, and for the first time all evening he stopped shaking. "Come on, let's move back to the alley. I've seen what I came to see. This will be easy pickings." He duck-walked his way back toward the alley with Alexie nervously in tow.

Morgan Williams, a muscular cigar stump of a black man with a shaved head and skin as smooth as a carnival Nubian's, was busy fiddling with the disagreeable light switch that controlled the back porch's two ceiling lights. "Hell, I told CJ to get this thing fixed. It's a fire hazard," he complained to Dittier Atkins, his deaf-mute onetime rodeo partner.

Reading Morgan's lips, the former rodeo clown nodded in agreement, and his face, a leathery, sun-damaged dry wash of wrinkles, lit up when Morgan hammered the light-switch cover plate with his fist and the lights brightened instantly.

"There!" said Morgan. "Think that'll do it." He glanced across the room at Dittier and signed, "Did you bring your bedroll from your shopping cart?"

Dittier nodded.

"Then we're set for the night." Morgan took a seat, slipped a crumpled *Western Bits and Spur* magazine out of his own bedroll, and flipped the magazine open. "Saw a pair of Canyon City spurs advertised in here that I need to tell CJ about. Price seemed mighty appealin'," he signed to Dittier.

"They might be fakes," Dittier quickly signed back.

"Yeah, I was thinking that, but . . ."

Suddenly keen-eyed, Dittier stood and glanced toward the alley. Motioning for Morgan to stay put, he raised a finger to his lips and walked toward the back door.

"You feelin' somethin'?" Morgan signed rapidly, aware that although the sounds of the world had been lost to Dittier for-ever, Dittier still had the eyes of an eagle and could damn near feel the vibrations caused by a pebble hitting sand.

"Something's out there," Dittier signed, opening the door and moving into the doorway, unaware that Alexie Borg and Moradi-Nik were making their way toward a nearby Dumpster and safety.

"Could be a stray animal," said Morgan.

Dittier shook his head and emphatically mouthed, *No.*

"What, then?" Morgan asked, now standing directly behind Dittier.

"People!" mouthed Dittier. "People!" he reiterated, signing.

Morgan's eyes narrowed as he scanned the darkened alley, aware that Dittier was rarely wrong when it came to such matters, "I'll take a look. Let me get a flashlight." He walked back to his bedroll, extracted a battered World War II–vintage army-issue flashlight, and followed Dittier outside. Always protective of the man who'd saved him from being stomped by one-ton bulls more times than he could remember, Morgan stamped his right foot and yelled, "Hold up, Dittier." The shout sent Alexie and Moradi-Nik scrambling for new cover into a shed across the alley.

Reacting to the stamp, Dittier held up until Morgan joined him. Morgan swung the flashlight in a wide arch along the fence line. "Don't see anything." He moved to the far end of the garage, looping the flashlight to and fro. "Nothin' out here." Shaking his head, he turned to look back for Dittier to find him kneeling next to where the backyard picket fence intersected Lenny McCabe's sagging excuse for a garage. Agitated, Dittier motioned for Morgan to shine his light toward the ground.

Morgan homed in his light on a spot that Dittier was patting. Fresh-looking footprints remained in the loose dirt and gravel.

"Somebody was out here," Dittier signed up into the light.

"Yeah."

"What do you think they were up to?" Dittier signed.

"Don't know," said Morgan, glancing up and down the dark empty alley and rolling his tongue back and forth along his lower lip, the way he used to do before mounting an angry bull. "Don't know," he repeated, motioning for Dittier to follow him back to the porch. "But we sure as hell better tell CJ."

"I don't care what it costs," Howard Stafford shouted from the middle of his library. "I just want it fixed," he added just as loudly to the two men standing directly in front of him.

The shorter of the two, a muscular white man with crooked teeth and pockmarked skin, shook his head and said authoritatively, "I told you not to install divided-light glass in those display-case doors in the first place," as the other man, tall, stately, and black with close-cropped salt-and-pepper hair, nodded in agreement.

"It's a library for Christ's sake. Not Fort Knox. I thought all your space-age security gadgetry was supposed to do the trick," said Stafford, dressing down the acne-scarred Arthur Vannick.

"Well, it didn't because your burglar had a key," Vannick said defensively.

"We're not certain about that," countered the other man.

Vannick shot the black man a look of contempt. "Stick to what you know, Counts."

Theodore Counts bit his tongue reluctantly. He and Vannick, a flamboyant, self-professed onetime Secret Service agent turned security specialist, had butted heads over the entire five months that Counts, a onetime Denver Public Schools chief librarian, had served as lead consultant on the down-to-the-studs remodeling of Howard Stafford's library a year and a half earlier.

Vannick had pushed for a friend of his own who was a high-profile architect to design and manage the construction, to which Stafford had agreed, but he'd given Counts the nod as a consultant because a *Denver Post* article had touted Counts as a bibliophile's messiah when it came to library design, and Counts had been the fuse and gunpowder behind a 1980s refurbishing and revitalization of Denver's high school libraries.

Stafford, a risk taker, had chosen Counts over Vannick's protests, and Counts, in concert with the project's architects, had modified the design of the University of Southern California's prestigious Doheny Memorial Library to render by project's end, at least as far as Stafford was concerned, an absolute masterpiece.

"I did stick with what I knew," Counts said defensively. "Take a look around. All of Howard's books are here but two. You're the one who screwed up. Security was the problem."

"Would you two stop? You're here now for one reason only: to get together and correct any visible shelving and display-design flaws and install a security system that works." Stafford scanned the library thoughtfully. "Maybe what I really need is a bunch of safes."

"That defeats your purpose," said Counts. "You've always said you want your books to be out so you can enjoy them."

"Maybe it's time I modify my thinking, Ted."

"I'd say so," Vannick snapped.

"The bottom line is this," Stafford said. "You've got two weeks to come back to me with a library and security reconfiguration that allows me to enjoy my books visually. Do you read me?"

Both men nodded.

"Good. Now that we're all on the same page, maybe we can finally get around to those drinks." Stafford pushed a call button that was set into a nearby countertop.

"I'm afraid I'll have to pass," said Counts.

"Nonsense. The drinks are on their way."

"Not like the old days, huh, Counts?" said Vannick, aware that a problem with alcohol had been one of the things that had nudged Counts out of the Denver Public Schools system and into early retirement.

"Better than being a con," Counts shot back.

"Can it or I'll use someone else," said Stafford, aware that, far more than the satisfaction of being right, what both men craved was money. "I took the liberty of ordering for you," Stafford added as a young woman walked into the room carrying a tray of drinks that had been prepared by Theresa only moments earlier. The woman placed the tray on a nearby table and left immediately.

"Scotch on the rocks." Stafford smiled and handed a tumbler to Vannick. "And a Tom Collins for you," he said, handing a second drink to Counts.

Unwilling to offend Stafford, Counts accepted the drink.

"To fixing a problem," said Stafford, hoisting his glass in a toast.

"To the fix," Vannick chimed in. Watching Counts barely bring his glass to his lips and smiling, Vannick decided he would do some additional checking on the man who'd been such a nemesis. It was the prudent thing to do, he told himself, especially since he knew Counts had already spoken to a police sergeant named Fritz Commons about him.

Counts and Vannick had disappeared into the crisp April evening when Howard Stafford wrapped up his evaluation of their meeting. Entering a neatly printed note into a leather-bound journal, he enumerated five reasons for putting Counts and Vannick at the top of his very personal list of robbery suspects.

CHAPTER 8

Pen in hand, Flora Jean Benson sat in CJ's former office, hunched over a legal pad, taking notes and listening to Theresa Del Mora's story. Mahogany-skinned with deep-set dark-brown eyes and unabashedly African American, Flora Jean had the build and carriage of a Las Vegas showgirl, and she still spoke, after living for nearly twenty years in Denver, with a Midwestern East St. Louis heart-of-the-hood twang. Even seated, she seemed to dwarf the much shorter, light-complected, cherubic-looking Theresa.

Noticeably nervous, Theresa had arrived at eight a.m. sharp. After introducing herself, she'd asked Flora Jean why the sign over the door still read, "Floyd & Benson's Bail Bonds," since CJ claimed to be retired. Flora Jean had chuckled and said, "Floyd's a brand name in the bail-bondin' business here in Denver—still brings me in a good seventy percent of my clients. You don't change thoroughbreds in the middle of the derby, sugar; it's bad business."

Theresa had liked Flora Jean's no-nonsense demeanor right off, and as she watched Flora Jean flip the page on her legal pad, she had the sense that she'd struck investigative gold.

Flora Jean paused from her note taking and looked up at Theresa. "Now, tell me a little more about why you think your son might've been plannin' to lift more than the two books he stole from Howard Stafford's library."

"It was the way he acted—moping, secretive, more and more distant the longer he was here. That and the fact that a week before Luis was killed, I found five one-hundred-dollar bills taped to the bottom of one of his dresser drawers. Do you need to see them?"

"Nope," said Flora Jean, amazed at Theresa's near flawless English. Jotting down a note about the money, she asked, "How long you been here in the States, sugar?"

"Six years."

"You sound like you been here all your life."

Theresa forced a smile. "I guess I should thank your American-made circuit-riding Catholic nuns."

Flora Jean nodded. "And Luis, how long had he been here?"

"Five months," said Theresa, blinking back tears.

"Plenty of time to get the lay of the land at Stafford's."

"Yes."

"What did he do besides hang out at the Stafford compound?"

"He was studying history and political science at Metro State. He had classes two days a week."

"Good school," said Flora Jean, who, at the insistence of the other rock of strength in her life besides CJ, retired marine two-star general Alden Grace, had enrolled in night classes in criminology at Metro State. With life experience credits that included a tour in the Persian Gulf War, where she and the general had fallen in love, and two semesters of course work behind her, Flora Jean was halfway toward earning a criminology degree. "Question is, did he go to class?" Flora Jean tapped the business end of her pen on the legal pad and eyed Theresa quizzically.

"I'm sure he did. I found grade slips and a note from one of his professors in his room." Failing to mention that she'd also found a jewelry box full of her son's most personal possessions in the back of a closet, she bent down and began rummaging through a canvas shopping bag at her feet. She sat up and handed Flora Jean several Metropolitan State Collage grade slips and an eight-by-eleven-inch black binder.

Flora Jean examined the grade slips and nodded approvingly. "He seemed to be doing pretty good. As and Bs." She set the grade slips aside and flipped the binder open. "The Role of the Transcontinental Railroad in the Opening of the West" was typed halfway down the title page. An "A," circled in red, sat like a bull's-eye just below the obvious term paper's title. A note below that read, "Keep up the good work and I'll teach you more." The comment, which struck Flora Jean as somehow strangely out of place, was one that Flora Jean decided she'd best remember if she took on the case.

Flora Jean flipped through the term paper's twenty-four pages of text, scrutinizing them carefully, including the final two pages of references. At the end of the references a boxed note read, "Submitted in partial fulfillment of requirements for History of the American West, MSCH 201, Course Director Professor Oliver Lyman, Ph.D."

"Looks like your son had a nose for history," said Flora Jean, setting down the binder.

"He did, and in Nicaragua as well." Theresa sighed. "Luis was mesmerized by history's untold stories. But he was too unseasoned to understand that the stories of the past are usually told by those who are the winners—never the losers. In too many ways he was so much like his father." Theresa's voice trailed off to a whisper.

"And his father was?"

"A loser, not as a man but as a revolutionary, like his brother and the sons of his brother, Luis's cousins."

"And you think Luis saw himself as a revolutionary?"

"Not once he was here. But I'm afraid he brought that kind of mind-set with him from Nicaragua."

"I see. Did he have friends, enemies, heroes, mentors?"

"No."

"Any axes to grind?"

Theresa shook her head.

"What about places he hung out? Did he have a favorite restaurant or chat room? Any special coffee house or bars?"

"None that I know of." Theresa turned teary-eyed. "I should have been more of a mother."

"I'm bettin' you did all you could, sugar." Flora Jean reached over and patted Theresa's hand. "Your son was twenty years old. Don't know much about Nicaragua, but that's pretty much a grown man here."

Theresa frowned, recalling her own youthful years spent in the midst of revolution, where the sight of nine-year-olds carrying machine guns was commonplace. "Age is relative," she said insightfully.

"Ain't that the truth?" Flora Jean smiled and thought about the sixteen-year age difference between Alden Grace and her. "You sure you don't wanta rely on the cops?" she asked, eyeing Theresa thoughtfully.

Theresa's eyes narrowed, and suddenly she was pale. "Men in uniform calling themselves policemen killed my husband and set his car on fire, with him in it, in our village square. Revolution and death are harsh teachers, Ms. Benson. You would have no reason to really understand. No! Never do I wish to interact with your so-called cops."

Flora Jean resisted the urge to respond to the sad-faced woman sitting across the desk from her. A woman who had no way of knowing that as a marine intelligence sergeant during the Persian Gulf War, Flora Jean had seen death, destruction, and dehumanization that surely rivaled the worst that the Nicaraguan civil war could have offered. Or that as the unwanted child of a St. Louis prostitute, she had been shuttled between her mother's friends, abusive relatives, and juvenile hall more times than she cared to count. She understood very well what it was like to be a marginalized human being, and what mattered was that, like Theresa, she had survived.

Realizing that now wasn't the time for either poor-mouthing or one-upmanship, she flashed Theresa a smile. "I'll take the job. I'll start with a visit to your son's history professor over at Metro State." She picked up the term-paper binder and flipped to the back. "Oliver Lyman," she said, reading the name aloud. "What else do I have to start with? After that I'll move on to Howard Stafford, if that's okay."

"Do what you have to, but do your best."

"I charge two hundred fifty dollars a day, plus expenses. My associates get one fifty."

"Associates?"

"I use a couple of former rodeo cowboys to help me with loose ends, and occasionally I have to touch base with an attorney to make sure I'm inside the bounds of the law. I might even need a little insight from the man who sent you here, CJ Floyd."

"I thought he was retired."

"And so did Nellie," said Flora Jean, grinning knowingly. "She thought she was eatin' ice cream, but she was eatin' jelly. Trust me, sugar, the man ain't retired. He's just restin' up for the next lap."

Theresa nodded, understanding. "We have a similar saying in

Nicaragua: *It's the road you know best that takes you home safely; be wary of the one that has just been discovered.* When will you start?" she asked, slipping a checkbook stuffed with bills out of the bag at her feet.

"Right this second." Flora Jean flipped through the overstuffed Rolodex on her desk, slipped out a card, picked up the phone, and punched in the number on the card. After a brief pause, she said to the person who'd answered, "Department of History, please." Waiting to be connected, she cupped the receiver against her shoulder and reiterated to Theresa, "Right this second, sugar."

Metro State College, just south of downtown Denver, rose from the ashes of Denver's skid row and an adjacent, mostly Hispanic, solidly Catholic neighborhood during urban-renewal efforts of the late 1960s and '70s. In the four decades since the nascent educational institution had begun writing its history, the college had grown from an enrollment in the hundreds to a sprawling urban campus now called Auraria that also included the University of Colorado at Denver, the Community College of Denver, and a student body of thirty-three thousand.

The campus, a darling of urban-based, vote-hungry politicians, had gobbled up a swath of scenic acreage along the banks of Cherry Creek and the South Platte River and was now held in check only by Invesco Field at Mile High Stadium, home of the Denver Broncos, and I-25, the lifeblood of its commuter students.

Finding a parking space on the Auraria Campus was impossible, so Flora Jean walked the mile from her Delaware Street office on Bail Bondsman's Row and down the Speer Boulevard bike path that curved its way along Cherry Creek to intersect the

Auraria Campus. Before leaving the office, she assured a sad-eyed Theresa Del Mora that she would find her son's killer. She'd then ushered Theresa off with an assignment to do mop-up duty on Luis's contacts and police his room one last time. "And this time, search the place like you're a cop," Flora Jean had emphasized after Theresa had told her that a homicide detective named Commons had spent nearly an hour searching Luis's room. "I'll do the same, soon as I get a chance," Flora Jean had added.

Puffy banks of low-hanging clouds, a cinch to produce afternoon showers, draped the Front Range of the Rockies as Flora Jean crossed the light-rail commuter tracks that marked the eastern edge of the campus. It was a quarter past ten, and the short-notice meeting she'd set up with a very accommodating Oliver Lyman an hour earlier on the pretense of being a nontraditional minority student interested in pursuing a master's degree in Western history was scheduled for ten-thirty.

She slipped her student ID out of her pocket, clipped it to the pocket of her form-fitting leather jacket, and headed diagonally across campus toward the King Center, home to the Department of History, telling herself as two pimple-faced eighteen-year-olds ogled her breasts that it was a good thing for them and their reckless eyeballing, that she'd returned to college at the mature age of thirty-seven.

The King Center was a late-twentieth-century example of functionally adequate, aesthetically unappetizing university construction. Oliver Lyman's fifth-floor office anchored the southwest corner of a hallway that emitted the lingering smell of stale fast food and youthful hormones. Lyman's office hours, typed neatly on a sheet of paper posted to the right of his office door, read, "Monday, Wednesday, Friday—10 a.m. to 12 noon."

Flora Jean found herself wondering what the Western history professor did with the rest of his time as she knocked on the door, expecting for some reason to be greeted by someone looking stereotypically professorial—tweeds, pipe, an elbow-patched sport coat—or perhaps a man sporting a swoop of long hair, retro frameless glasses, and Birkenstocks. Instead, Oliver Lyman, a rotund man of fifty with close-cropped graying hair, a black handlebar mustache, and teeth a size too large for his mouth, greeted her with a "Howdy" that rose from the depths of his midsection.

"Back at you," Flora Jean said to the much shorter professor, who wore ropers boots and blue jeans. "I'm Flora Jean Benson."

She moved into the room as Lyman, his gaze locked on her chest, reached out to shake hands. "Oliver Lyman," he said, gripping Flora Jean's hand firmly. "Come on in."

Flora Jean followed Lyman into a sunny fourteen-foot-square room with a single window that faced the Rockies. A mid-1950s-vintage junior high school–style library table covered with books and papers occupied the middle of the room. Barrister-style bookcases overflowing with books covered two of the room's walls. A diploma from the University of Washington granting Oliver T. Lyman all the rights and privileges of the degree Doctor of Philosophy in history hung, along with a photograph of Mt. Kilimanjaro, on the south-facing wall.

Lyman scooted around the back side of the library table, took a seat, and motioned for Flora Jean to have a seat on the other side. "So you want to do graduate-level Western history? Good choice. As you can see, I'm rather fond of the West myself." Lyman smiled as Flora Jean took in every square inch of his Western garb. "There's not a book in this room without at least a nugget of Western history between the covers," Lyman boasted. "How far along the way are you toward your undergraduate degree?"

"I'm just over half done," said Flora Jean, relieved that Lyman hadn't asked her about her major.

Lyman nodded approvingly. "And what makes you think you want to pursue a master's degree?"

Flora Jean moved quickly to get what she'd come after. "A friend of mine, Luis Del Mora, recommended it. And I have a real interest in the West." She watched for Lyman's reaction, hoping she hadn't telegraphed the fact that she was lying. "He's in one of your classes."

Lyman paused and stroked his chin. "Luis. Yes, he's quite a good student. He's in my History 201 class." The response was matter-of-fact.

"Yeah, he showed me a term paper he wrote—on railroads in the West."

"An excellent paper," Lyman said proudly. "And an easy one to recall because it was so well done. Luis received an A. And I'm not that generous with As, Ms. Benson. My upper-level courses are designed to be a true test of one's abilities. You should know that up front."

"No problem. Are there tests as well as term-paper assignments in that 201 course?"

"Yes. Two of them."

"Who chooses the term-paper topics?"

"I assign them," said Lyman, puzzled by the question.

Uncertain whether she was dealing with a thoughtful, unflappable killer or simply a college professor who was a cowboy wannabe, Flora Jean decided to press the term-paper issue. "Then I guess I can't do a makeover on Luis's paper," she said, sitting up straight in her chair, watching Lyman's eyes follow the curve of her breasts.

"Certainly not."

"No matter. Like I said, I like Western history. Might as well give your course a fling."

"Are you a history major now?" asked Lyman, deciding to do a little probing of his own.

"Nope. I'm studyin' criminology."

"Ummm," said Lyman, his expression unchanged. "That would make your move to Western history a pretty good stretch. But there were certainly plenty of criminals in the Old West," he added with a smile.

"And in the new one too," Flora Jean countered.

"Could be a topic for a term paper," said Lyman, eyeing his watch and standing to indicate that the session was over. "I look forward to seeing you in my class, Ms. Benson."

"Lookin' forward to takin' it. I'll try to get it on my fall semester schedule."

"Sign up early. The course fills up fast," said Lyman, heading toward the door.

"You're that good?"

"I've been told so." There wasn't a hint of modesty in Lyman's tone.

"I'll tell Luis that I talked to you," said Flora Jean, hoping to elicit some kind of reaction.

"Do that, and remember, no duplication of term papers in my courses. I keep very good records."

"No worry," said Flora Jean, moving through the doorway. "I've got plenty of topics of my own."

Lyman responded with a smile, turned, and gently closed the door.

Flora Jean made her way back across campus, uncertain whether her approach to Lyman had been the right one. There was no real reason to suspect he'd killed Luis Del Mora, but she'd had to begin her investigation somewhere. Sooner or later Lyman would stumble across the fact that Luis was dead, and it was a certainty that she'd never get as cordial an audience with the professor a second time. He hadn't seemed one bit nervous during their talk, and the only solid connection between him and Luis remained a strange note on a term paper about post–Civil War railroads. Nonetheless, she had the feeling that, calm demeanor aside, Oliver Lyman and Luis Del Mora had had a connection that extended beyond that of student and teacher. And she had one other thing—something she hadn't sprung on Lyman. Something that could wait until lunch at the Satire Lounge, where she was due to meet CJ and their friend and attorney, Julie Madrid. At lunch they would all have a chance to mull over the fact that one of the books Luis Del Mora had stolen, which CJ had briefed her on that morning after Theresa had left during a three-way phone conversation with Julie, had appeared as a reference in his term paper. It had been CJ who'd suggested that she hold back the truth about Del Mora during her meeting with Lyman in order to gauge the man's reaction—see if he might be lying. She had played the game CJ's way, and Lyman had turned up smelling pretty rosy, but she couldn't help but wonder what kind of aroma would have filled the air if she'd mentioned that Luis Del Mora had been murdered.

CHAPTER 9

Denver's Colfax Avenue, billed as the longest street in the United States, starts in Aurora, a sprawling eastern suburb, and ends twenty-seven miles later in the Rocky Mountain foothills to the west. During its 120-year existence, the street has boasted every imaginable tenant, from silver miners to defrocked politicians, from $10-a-pop sexual fantasy motels to Kitty's House of Porn. In recent years the two-mile stretch between the Colorado state capitol downtown and National Jewish Hospital to the east had undergone a gentrification facelift so that once again, for Colfax Avenue, change was in the wind.

The Satire Lounge stood at the corner of Colfax and Race Street, anchoring a blue-collar, racially mixed neighborhood of small businesses and apartment dwellers—and the Satire, with its brain-numbing margaritas and burritos, chock-full of juicy sweet beef pickled in spices, unlike Colfax, wasn't about to change.

A twenty-mile-per-hour wind gust laced with rain and riding the leading edge of a cold front had blown CJ, Flora Jean, and Julie Madrid through the Satire Lounge's front door fifteen minutes earlier. Now, as they sat in one of the eatery's shiny, well-worn Naugahyde booths feasting on tortilla chips and bitter-hot salsa, sloppy wet burritos, and long-neck drafts, CJ finally slipped the papers that Julie had given him earlier off his lap. Fumbling with the top sheet, leaving it fingerprinted with grease, he reread the summary that Julie's law clerk had given her on Jacob Covington. "So Covington was more than just a sawbones," he said, eyeing Julie and reaching for a couple of chips.

Julie nodded. "According to my law clerk's quick-and-dirty Internet search." A decade earlier Julie had been CJ's secretary. Petite, Puerto Rican, and *West Side Story* sexy, she had left CJ's employ six years earlier to fight her way through law school at night. That exit had made way for Flora Jean.

Grabbing a couple more chips, CJ said, "Sounds like Dr. Covington could've been a professional photographer." He set the papers down on the table and wiped a layer of salt from his fingers.

"Maybe so, but there was still more money in settin' bones and deliverin' babies than in takin' pictures, even back then," said Flora Jean. "His shutterbuggin' was just a hobby."

"And a real serious one, according to these papers," said CJ, reading from a Covington bio: "'A respected Union Pacific Railroad doctor, Covington is also credited with taking hundreds of photos of the progression of the transcontinental railroad as it made its way west, including scores of photographs of toiling Union Pacific workers, photographs of the harsh surrounding landscape, and photographs of the Grand Tetons and Yellowstone Park. His portfolio documented a changing West.' Wonder if it was enough of a hobby to end up getting somebody killed one hundred thirty–some years later."

"Reasonable thought. Anything else catch your fancy?" asked Julie, wiping CJ's greasy fingerprints from the page as he handed it back to her.

"Not much, just a note your law clerk made confirming that

after Covington lost most of his photographs in that fire, the one the Montana medicine book talks about, he pretty much disappeared."

Julie shook her head and turned to Flora Jean. "Then, as we say in the trade, somebody's gonna have to do some more digging. I'd go talk to that great-great-niece of Covington's that my law clerk outed in his Internet search if I were you." Julie picked up a second sheet of paper that CJ had been reading and said, "I'll try not to get grease all over it," as she ran a finger down the page, stopping near the bottom. "The niece's name's Amanda Hunter, and she runs a seven-thousand-acre cattle ranch north of Cheyenne." Realizing by the look on his face that her law clerk's facility at data-gathering had shocked the computer-phobic CJ, Julie added, "The Internet works in mysterious ways, Mr. Floyd." Wagging her finger, she flashed CJ a wink.

"I agree with Julie," said Flora Jean. "We need to find ourselves a better source on Covington than some junior-league reference to a book on Montana medicine in a dead college kid's term paper. I say we go talk to Covington's niece."

CJ nodded thoughtfully. "What about that Metro State history professor you talked to? Think he was stonewalling?"

"Don't know," said Flora Jean. "I didn't ask him about Covington. I was just tryin' to get a feel for what he knew about the Del Mora kid. He seemed pretty genuine to me."

"Think he could've killed Del Mora?"

Flora Jean shrugged and took a sip of beer. "Who knows? Question is, why would he have?"

"I'd say your answer's probably inside the pages of that term paper Del Mora wrote," Julie interjected. "People lied, killed, stole, borrowed, cheated, and begged in order to build the transcontinental railroad. Could be your murder's linked to laying those tracks of steel."

"And the Wyoming cattle-brand book? What about it?" Flora Jean asked, finishing her beer. "Seems to me, with this Wyoming cattle-ranchin' niece of Covington's poppin' up outta nowhere, that brand book could still be the real murder connection."

"That's CJ's territory," said Julie. "I don't know beans about cattle-brand books." She eyed CJ quizzically.

CJ shrugged. "You got me. All I know is that the brand book's worth three times what I paid for it, according to Billy DeLong. I can show the photocopy I made of it to Billy. He may have a better take on how it could be connected to a murder."

"Then we need to talk to both Billy and that niece of Covington's," said Flora Jean. "Hell, they both live in Wyoming, and I'm bettin' a dime to a dollar that if her uncle was as well known as that bio of his claims, the niece'll know a whole lot more about him than the Internet can tell us. You up for a trip to visit Billy in Wyoming?" she added, looking at CJ.

CJ shook his head. "I'm out of the bail-bonding, bounty-hunting, and murder-investigation business, remember?"

"But Billy ain't," Flora Jean countered.

CJ shook his head. "Billy's the kind of person you need backing you up in a firefight, not the one directing it. You know that, Flora Jean."

Continuing her urging, Flora Jean said, "Then go along with him to see Covington's niece. No bounty huntin' or chasin' down bond skippers involved. Nothin' even close."

"It's investigating a murder, Flora Jean!"

This time it was Flora Jean who shook her head. "Damn, CJ. You're out there in that antiques store every day hustlin' collectibles, tryin' to make a dime, and every time I see you these days, you look more and more like somethin' dying on the vine." Surprised by her own directness, Flora Jean looked to Julie for support.

Julie took a sip of beer and remained silent, aware that CJ had promised Mavis days before their engagement that he would leave the bail-bonding business and its associated risk behind forever. She couldn't fathom why Flora Jean was so intent on encouraging CJ to break that promise.

"I'll give it some thought," said CJ, feeling guilty the second the words left his mouth. He looked at Julie for guidance, but she judiciously took another sip of beer, unprepared to take sides in what had the potential to become a war among friends.

Caught between a strange desire to get back into a game he'd sworn off forever and keeping his word to Mavis, CJ said to Flora Jean, "What's your take on Theresa Del Mora?" hoping to steer the conversation in another direction.

"The woman's hurtin', no question. She wanted to meet with me last night, but I couldn't. She was sittin' on my doorstep at eight this mornin'. Practically begged me to take the case. She paid me for two weeks' work up front, in cash. Could've been money from the five hundred-dollar bills I told you she found taped to the bottom of one of her son's dresser drawers. Anyway, I took it."

"Think she's hiding anything?" CJ asked, making a mental note of Theresa Del Mora's windfall.

"If she is, I didn't pick up on it. I think her angle's more along the lines of revenge."

"Whatever her angle is, she sounds pretty flush," said Julie.

"Why not?" said Flora Jean. "She works for a man who's supposedly worth close to a hundred million."

"Could be she's also working for her son's killer," Julie countered.

"I considered that. But then I asked myself, why would you, if you're worth a hundred million, murder somebody over a couple of books? Couldn't come up with a good answer."

Julie scooped a dollop of guacamole onto a chip and took a bite. Then, waving Luis Del Mora's term paper in the air, she said, "You wouldn't unless something in a term paper written by some college kid rocked your world. Railroads. I've said it before. Leland Stanford, Mark Hopkins, Edward Harriman, Jay Gould. They were the Bill Gateses of their day. Anybody hearing my tune?"

"I hear you, Julie. But what's Howard Stafford's connection to a bunch of long-dead railroad tycoons other than the fact that like them, he's got beaucoup bucks?" Flora Jean asked.

"Don't ask me," said Julie. "But right now my barrister's antennae are gyrating out of control. Seems to me that Stafford's been awfully quiet up to now for someone who's been robbed."

"I'm with you there, and from what Theresa Del Mora says, he sure ain't been screamin' to the cops. The only people he's hammered, accordin' to her, and I talked to her just before comin' here, is the guy who designed the library his books were stolen from and some security-systems ace he hired to wire the place. She claims word around the Stafford compound is the two of them better have the place redesigned and as solid as Fort Knox real quick or there'll be hell to pay."

"Have you got their names?" asked CJ.

"Not with me, but I've got 'em back at the office."

Looking unimpressed by the new revelation, Julie said, "Rich people like Stafford usually want more than their share when it comes to a pound of flesh. I'm surprised Stafford hasn't gone after Theresa Del Mora. After all, it was her son who stole his books."

"Could be he and the lady from Nicaragua have somethin' goin'," said Flora Jean. "Who knows?"

"I'd get the full skinny on both of them if I were you," said Julie. "Stafford sounds way too placid for a kingfish who's been robbed. And for all we know, Theresa Del Mora could've been in on the heist with her son."

"So what's the agenda from here?" asked CJ, who'd been inexplicably quiet.

"I'm gonna find out more about our history professor, Dr. Lyman, draw a bead on the guy who designed Stafford's library, and hunt down Stafford's security man," Flora Jean said forcefully.

"And I'll dig up what I can on Stafford," said Julie. "Should be easy. When you're worth a hundred million, gossip abounds."

Suddenly both women's eyes were locked on CJ. "I'm just an antiques dealer, here for the beer and chips," CJ said defensively.

"Well, Mr. Antiques Dealer, do you think I can talk you into going to see Jacob Covington's niece?" asked Flora Jean. "Hell, you and Billy could do a little fishin' up on the Laramie or the North Platte, snag yourselves some fat little spring runoff trout, and then run by and have a talk with the lady at her ranch."

"We could," said CJ, feeling both enticed and squeezed. Peddling antiques was fun—and he enjoyed it—but there just wasn't enough day-to-day excitement. The excitement for him when it came to antiques and collectibles, he now realized, had always been not selling but rather chasing down a find. The Del Mora case had him suddenly feeling whole and necessary again.

"Think it over," said Flora Jean, recognizing that the gears in CJ's head were churning. "There has to be some way you can drive up to Wyoming for a little information-gatherin' and a fishin' trip without going back on your word to Mavis."

CJ didn't answer. He was too busy trying to figure out how to broach the subject with Mavis.

An hour later, having left CJ to ponder her offer and giving Julie the green light to initiate a Stafford probe, Flora Jean sat at her office desk, phone in hand, trying to schedule a meeting with Arthur Vannick. She'd easily been able to schedule a meeting with the retired librarian, Theodore Counts, by telling him that she was interested in transcontinental railroad lore from the perspective of a school librarian with regional expertise, but getting an audience with Vannick was proving difficult. She'd been transferred to his appointment secretary, who'd placed her on hold, where for the past five minutes she'd been forced to listen repeatedly to a twenty-second promotion for Vannick's security-systems business. Frustrated, she held for another minute and listened to Vannick's promo one last time before shaking her head in disgust and slamming down the phone. Adjusting the half-dozen African bracelets that encircled her lower right arm, she was about to go get a cup of coffee to soothe her frustration when the phone rang.

"Floyd & Benson's Bail Bonds," Flora Jean answered robotically.

"It's Julie."

"What's up, sugar? You got gas from all the guac and chips?" Julie's tone was all business. "Nope. This is more serious."

Looking perplexed, Flora Jean said, "Sing your song, sugar."

"Okay, but answer me straight. Why all the pushing and shoving to get CJ back into the game that just about finished him?"

Flora Jean took a long, deep breath. She'd sensed Julie's discomfort near the end of their lunch. "'Cause the man's dyin'. Inside and out. You can see it in his eyes!"

"Maybe so. But you're about to make him go back on one hell of a promise with that trip to Wyoming. Come on, Flora Jean, there has to be another reason you're pushing so hard."

"I'm not forcin' him to do nothin', Julie. Just suggestin'. I've got my reasons."

"Mind sharing them with me?"

Flora Jean gnawed at her lower lip, uncertain how to respond. She didn't want to break a confidence, but there was no way she could continue to lie to Julie.

"Flora Jean? Come on." The insistent tone of a criminal defense attorney was evident in Julie's tone.

"I'm thinkin'," said Flora Jean. She rose from her seat and, phone in hand, headed across the room to get her cup of coffee. On her way she glanced back toward her desk—the same desk CJ had worked at for years. She eyed the back wall and the rows of photographs of the hundreds of bond skippers he had apprehended over the years and thought about how CJ had plucked her from a dead-end pool of secretarial temps, taught her the bail-bonding business, supplied her with cases she could handle on her own, and, in the end, pretty much dropped a business that made money—albeit not a lot of money—into her lap. Unable to stonewall any longer, she said, "CJ's got money woes, Julie, and he ain't about to tell nobody about 'em, not even us."

"He's always had money problems."

"Not like this. I got it straight from the horse's mouth. That guy he rents Ike's Spot from, the guy in the other half of that duplex, Lenny McCabe, says CJ's upside down in his rent. Claims

CJ ain't paid him a dime in two months. Told me CJ gambled the last seventeen hundred dollars he had on earth on them books that were stolen. CJ dropped way too much into them lease-hold improvements when he fixed up the damn place. Fancy lit-up display counters, floor-to-ceilin' shelves, havin' McCabe prop up that lean-to of a garage behind the place for the Bel Air. I think CJ thought he had more money to play around with from sellin' me the business than he actually did."

"But he's got money coming in. You pay him rent on your office space in the Victorian. I drew up the papers. And I know what he's paying to lease Ike's Spot. It should be close to a wash."

"I know all that, sugar. But like I said, the money I'm payin' him every month don't begin to cover the cost of all them improvements he made in the space he's leasin' and the rent to boot. Bottom line is, the man ain't makin' no sales."

"Why hasn't he said something?"

"Come on, sugar, you know CJ. He ain't never goin' to say nothin', ever. That's why I was pushin' so hard for him to go take that trip to Wyoming. Take himself a couple of days off and on top of it earn a little pay."

"But he'd lose that much in sales being out of the store."

There was a lengthy pause before Flora Jean finally responded: "Mavis might mind the place."

"You told Mavis about CJ's money problems?"

"The whole nine yards. I had to do somethin'."

"I sure hope CJ never finds out."

"You and me both," Flora Jean said softly.

Julie let out a sigh. "Oh, what a tangled web we weave when first . . ."

"What?"

"Nothing," said Julie. "Let me think about calling Mavis."

"What are you gonna tell her?"

"I'll ask her to give CJ some operating room. To let him have enough space to do a little of what he's best at—investigating. A trip to Wyoming to talk to that niece of Covington's isn't a bounty-hunting or bail-bonding job. All he's doing is gathering facts. It should be safe enough."

"What if Mavis ain't okay with that?"

"She'll be okay with it."

"You sure?"

"As sure as I am that CJ Floyd's the main reason I have a law degree."

"Then go for it. 'Cause I ain't sure I've got the strength to face the man if he ever finds out I told Mavis he was up against it financially."

"Come on, Flora Jean. You're an ex-marine," Julie said, anticipating Flora Jean's standard once-a-marine-always-a-marine response.

"And CJ manned a .50-caliber machine gun on the back of a gunboat during a war that was one hell of a lot worse than mine. Go on. Talk to Mavis and help me dig myself outta this hole I got myself in."

"Just remember exactly who the *me* in this is if things start to go south on us," said Julie, pondering how to broach the subject with Mavis.

Flora Jean nodded without answering as Julie carefully cradled the phone.

CHAPTER 10

CJ's mind was made up: he was going to take a trip to Wyoming. With one foot up on his desk, he continued blowing smoke rings skyward, reminding himself that now all he had to do was explain his decision to Mavis.

It had been easier than he'd thought to locate Amanda Hunter, Jacob Covington's twice-removed niece. When you are looking for a woman in her midforties who's been a Cheyenne Frontier Days rodeo queen, and who owns and operates a seven-thousand-acre cattle ranch, fingers start to point you in the right direction pretty quickly. The Wyoming State Livestock Board and the State Stock Growers Association not only provided CJ with the phone number to Hunter's Triangle Bar Ranch, they practically gave him directions on how to get there. Wyoming, open space and friendly and populated by just over five-hundred-thousand residents, still had what in the past thirty years Colorado had forever lost.

CJ called Billy DeLong from Ike's Spot just before three o'clock, laid out the Luis Del Mora story for him, and asked the wiry cowboy with one glass eye if he was up for a road trip.

After some arm-twisting, Billy agreed to meet CJ that evening in Cheyenne, where they would coordinate a visit to the Triangle Bar Ranch the next morning, a visit that CJ admitted hesitantly he hadn't quite set up. Telling Billy he'd call him back if things didn't pan out, CJ hung up to call Amanda Hunter.

CJ's phone conversation with Amanda Hunter was disjointed and a hard sell. It took five minutes for the person who answered the phone to locate Hunter, and several more minutes of introduction and explanation before Hunter, a woman with a sexy, gravelly voice, consented to listen to what CJ had to say. After ten more minutes of conversation, Hunter finally agreed to meet CJ the next morning at the ranch. "Seven a.m. sharp," she said. "I'll be repairing one of our windmills." She gave CJ directions to the ranch's Laramie Mountains foothills entrance, fired off directions to where she'd be, "smack in the middle of our Casement pasture," and then, surprising CJ with her candor, added, "I've been concerned for years that one of these days it would come down to this." When CJ pushed her for an explanation, she said matter-of-factly, "Down to somebody getting killed over my Uncle Jake's hobby. We'll talk about it tomorrow," she said, abruptly ending the conversation.

Should be an interesting visit, CJ thought, stubbing out the cheroot he'd smoked down to a nub and swinging a boot onto the edge of his desktop. He ran through a checklist of the things he needed to do before heading for Wyoming, a list that included calling Billy back to tell him things were a go and that he'd hook up with him in Cheyenne that evening, asking Lenny McCabe to cover Ike's Spot for him the next day, checking in with Flora Jean and Julie to let them know what was up and see how they'd fared with their own assignments, and finally and most importantly calling Mavis.

A half hour later, he'd made every phone call but one. He finished stowing his fishing gear in the back of his aging Jeep, the

Bel Air's road-trip surrogate that Rosie Weeks kept running for him, sighed, and slipped his cell phone off his belt. He punched in the number to Mae's Louisiana Kitchen to let Mavis know he'd be by her house a little past five. He wasn't sure how he would explain that he'd gotten himself entangled in the web of a murder investigation, but as the phone rang, echoing loudly in his ear, he knew he'd better come up with one hell of a story.

Mavis Sundee lived in a beautifully restored turn-of-the-century Queen Anne in Denver's Curtis Park neighborhood, where housing prices were rising daily and longtime Curtis Park residents, like their Five Points neighbors, were getting the kind of money they'd once only dreamed of for homes only blocks from downtown and running for cover.

CJ had a thousand-dollar smile on his face as he mounted the front steps to the Queen Anne, a smile bolstered by the fact that just before he'd headed out to see Mavis, a customer had walked into Ike's Spot, nosed through a stack of 1940s *Life* magazines sealed in Ziploc bags, and bought a dozen magazines along with a $300 Plow Boy tobacco canister, circa 1944. Five hundred dollars wealthier than he'd been a half hour earlier and feeling flush, CJ rang Mavis's doorbell with his smile locked on high beam.

Mavis answered the door seconds later. She was dressed in loose-fitting chinos and a blaze-orange blouse. Her close-cropped, curly jet-black hair framed an oval cocoa-brown face devoid of wrinkles. Sometimes when they were making love, CJ would teasingly ask her how she'd managed, at forty-six, to retain her youthful good looks. Her answer was always the same: "Good genes, baby, good genes." She locked a hand in CJ's, guided him over the threshold, and kissed him softly on the lips. "You're looking awfully happy. Didn't realize my kisses were that powerful."

"I am, and they are," said CJ, running a hand across Mavis's derriere.

"Come on, CJ. You're barely in the house." She removed his hand, slapped it, and, recupping it in hers, led CJ through the first-floor living room, down a hallway plastered with family photos, and into the sun room off the kitchen. "Park it," she said with a wink.

CJ took a seat at a ceramic-topped table, sensing as he did that Mavis, always even-keeled, seemed more bubbly than usual.

"Beer, wine, coffee?" she asked, slipping behind a half wall that separated the sunroom from the kitchen and stepping over to a below-the-counter refrigerator.

"You."

"What's with this one-track sex-video mind of yours, CJ Floyd?"

CJ grinned. "Just wound up over a sale." He hoped the good news would pave the way for the less palatable news to follow.

"Great. What sold?"

"A whole stack of vintage magazines and a hefty-priced tobacco canister."

"Reason enough to celebrate. You pick the libation," Mavis said, swinging open the refrigerator door.

The look on CJ's face was suddenly serious. "Coke."

"Are you sure?"

"Yeah."

Mavis slipped two Cokes out of the refrigerator, walked back over to the table, and pulled up a chair. "You're traveling light," she said, popping the tabs on the sodas and handing one to CJ.

"I got a problem, Mae," he said, calling Mavis by her middle name, a coded distress signal they'd shared for more than four decades and one that always served as a prelude to any discussion of serious matters.

Mavis's eyes widened and her voice dropped an octave, "Have you got a number?"

CJ, who during his bail-bonding and bounty-hunting days had ranked bond-skip cases on a scale of one to ten, realized where Mavis was headed with the question. Cases garnering a ten represented worst-case scenarios—life-threatening treks that could cost CJ a portion of, or sometimes all, the bond assurance money he'd put up, saddle him with sleepless nights, and quite possibly put him in a face-off with a family member of the bond skipper, the skipper himself, a lover, the bond skipper's victim, or a cop. "A one, maybe a two at best," he said hesitantly.

Remaining silent, Mavis twisted her engagement ring around on her finger. There was no hint in her expression that she'd already talked to Julie.

"Flora Jean asked me to help her with a case. All I have to do is gather a little information for her up in Wyoming," he said, hoping Mavis wouldn't press him for details.

"Information about what?" The words came out rapid-fire, as if they were one.

"Info about those books I bought that were stolen."

"Then it's about a murder." Mavis strained to maintain her composure.

CJ shook his head in protest. "No, I'm just going to talk to a woman who's a relative of someone who's mentioned in one of the books. She runs a ranch an hour or so northwest of Cheyenne. Billy's going with me. He's driving over from Baggs to meet me in Cheyenne this evening."

Eyes narrowed, Mavis asked, "How did Flora Jean get involved?"

"I gave her name to the mother of that kid who was killed. Since I was the last one to see her son alive, the kid's mother came by Ike's the other day to find out if there was any way I could help her find out who killed her son. I put her in touch with Flora Jean."

"You're heading down a road you promised to never travel again." Mavis's words traveled across the table with force.

CJ reached out, clasped Mavis's right hand, and began toying with her engagement ring. "It is an overnight trip, Mavis. I'll ask the woman a few questions first thing tomorrow morning and be done by nine. After that Billy and I will spend a few hours fishing, and I'll be home in time for the six o'clock news."

Mavis's response was silence.

CJ released her hand, sat back in his chair, and forced back a sigh. His next words came out slowly as, hanging his head, CJ came as close to admitting defeat as he'd ever come in his life. "I'm up against it financially, Mavis. I need the money Flora Jean's gonna pay me."

Mavis swallowed hard, feeling partially responsible for CJ's plight. She was the one who'd demanded that he make a choice between the kind of disjointed, precarious life he'd been living and her. Suddenly she remembered something Flora Jean had told her one night almost nine months earlier during the agonizing time that Flora Jean and CJ had alternated staying with her after Celeste Deepstream had beaten and kidnapped her and imprisoned her in an iron lung on the top of a mountain in a remote cabin in the New Mexico mountains. It was the same thing Julie Madrid had called to remind her of in a slightly different way just thirty minutes earlier. But it was Flora Jean's words that kept cycling through her head: *You're comin' off a bad time right now, sugar, but it won't stay that way forever. You got me here to ease the hurt, and you got your man. And although you may not think so right now, you gonna pretty much need him the way he's always been. Trust me, CJ ain't the kind that can spend the rest of his life peddlin' antiques.*

Recognizing that CJ was in pain—hurting down deep from trying to please her—suffering as a result of forcing himself to try to change who he was, she slipped her hand into his. "Who'll cover the store?" she asked softly, a clear hint of acquiescence in her tone.

"Lenny," CJ said, surprised by Mavis's response. "He knows my inventory, my reserve prices, and he's my landlord to boot. He can handle things for one day. And Dittier and Morgan will be out back for security," CJ added, euphoric that for some inexplicable reason Mavis had bought in to his plans. Realizing from the sudden frown on Mavis's face that he shouldn't have mentioned the issue of security, he mouthed an inaudible *Damn.*

"Security?" said Mavis, looking confused.

"Yeah, but it's nothing. Dittier and Morgan thought they heard somebody rummaging around in the alley behind the store the other night. They probably heard a raccoon or some wino looking for a spot to bed down," said CJ, knowing that Dittier had found two fresh sets of human footprints in the alley.

Mavis eased back in her chair and eyed the love of her life thoughtfully. "CJ, are you happy?"

CJ looked puzzled.

"Are you happy being an antiques dealer, I mean?"

"Sure."

"You don't think that I pushed you somewhere you didn't want to go, do you?"

"Mavis, come on."

Mavis took a deep breath, hesitant to ask the next question. "What triggered the money problems, CJ?"

Surprised by the question, CJ shrugged, trying his best to look and sound calm. "My eyes were just too big for my stomach, I guess. I overdid the tenant finish, and I haven't had the sales to keep up."

"What can I do to help?"

"You're doing it. Hanging in there with me."

"And you're only going to Wyoming to gather information?" she asked, her tone almost pleading.

"And to do a little fishing."

"Please let it stop there, CJ."

"I will."

"How do you plan to get out of your money jam without taking on more jobs for Flora Jean?"

"Simple. Sell more merchandise. Lenny says that once the weather breaks, things'll pick up."

"I hope he's right."

"He should be. He's been hawking antiques and just about anything that's collectible for years."

Mavis nodded, unconvinced. "When do you plan to leave to meet Billy?"

"In about an hour."

"Can I have a bit of that time?"

"All of it," said CJ, leaning over and kissing Mavis softly on the lips.

"Tell Billy hi for me," she said, returning the kiss and letting it linger before scooting her chair next to CJ's and snuggling into the crook of his arm.

"I will. If I don't start something here that keeps me stuck in Denver."

"I'll work on that." Mavis eased her way over onto CJ's lap. Wriggling herself against his incipient erection, she relaxed comfortably into his grasp.

"Mavis Sundee!" CJ feigned shock.

Mavis smiled. "You started it when you walked in the door, and it's your job to finish it," she said, feeling CJ harden beneath her as he gently cupped her breasts and his mouth met hers.

Billy DeLong, a five-foot-nine-inch, 150-pound coiled spring of a man, sat hunched over a frosted mug of apple juice at one end of the stale-smelling bar in the Holiday Inn at the Cheyenne I-80 exit just southwest of the city center. He was nursing the juice as if it were his last and reminiscing with the bartender, who'd been serving Billy and CJ for the past half hour.

The bartender, a onetime wrangler boss of a twenty-five-thousand-acre ranch outside Saratoga, Wyoming—a ranch whose northern border kissed the southern edge of an adjacent fifty-thousand-acre ranch Billy had been foreman of at the time—mopped up a bar spill and nodded. The now robotic nod had started in response to something Billy had said, but the bartender's eyes were locked on CJ, whose handwoven turquoise-and-gold Chimayo vest seemed to have the man hypnotized. "Hell, Billy, I ain't thought about that in years," the bartender said finally. "The way them two megamillionaires was going at it over who had the responsibility for maintaining some piss-assed quarter of a mile of fence when we had seventy-five thousand goddamned acres to worry about was flat-out stupid. When you told Old Man Holcomb that you'd stick a fence post up his ass the next time you had to send your people out after two hundred head of strays 'cause of some fence break he refused to fix, that damn sure closed the door on the issue."

"Holcomb was a toad. Had his brains up his ass." Billy took a slow sip of apple juice. "Never treated his people right neither, and that always rubbed me."

Nodding in agreement, the bartender said to CJ, "Billy's always been one for straight talk."

"I know."

Responding to his two friends' assessment, Billy said, "Well, then, here's a little inside dope for you, CJ. Go light with the pressure on the Hunter woman tomorrow mornin'. We ain't gonna be dealin' with one of your bond skippers. Play it loose and we'll learn a lot more."

"I know the lay of the land, Billy."

"I know you do. Just makin' certain." Billy slipped a stick of Doublemint gum out of his pocket and popped it into his mouth to freshen his ever-present wad. "Here's one final scoop," he said. "It's got nothin' to do with the Hunter woman and a lot to do with you. Know what you said to me when you first got here about someone nosin' around in the alley behind Ike's Spot?"

"Yes."

"Well, you best look into why somebody's so interested in your rear entry. Ain't nobody with good intentions ever lookin' for the back entrance to nothin'." Billy finished the last of his apple juice and nudged the empty mug across the bar to the bartender. "Done for the evenin'."

"Same," said CJ. The bartender hooked the handles of the two empty mugs with a pinkie and headed for the sink.

"Wonder who's casing my place?" asked CJ, knowing that Billy, who'd obviously been considering the issue for over an hour, would methodically zero in on one answer.

"Could be the same person who took out Luis Del Mora," Billy said, stroking his chin.

CJ shook his head. "Don't think so. I don't even have the books Del Mora stole anymore."

"A burglar, then," said Billy, working his way down a well-thought-out list.

"Could be. But why try and finesse your way past built-in security like Morgan and Dittier when there are easier pickings to be had?"

"Enemies from your bail-bonding days, then?" asked Billy, headed for closure.

"Possibly. But why?"

Billy wanted to say, *You know why.* Instead he said, "To even things up, maybe settle a score."

CJ shook his head. "Most of my enemies have turned halfway straight, or they're over the hill or in jail."

"Don't con yourself, CJ. It's bad for your health. You know what I'm drivin' at."

CJ looked Billy straight in the eye. "There's no way, Billy. She disappeared nine months ago down the mouth of a dried-up creek bed in the Taos Mountains."

"Yeah, man, I know. I was there." Billy sat up straight, grinned at CJ, and said, "Let me tell you a story. When I was in the service, I had an old sergeant who'd served in the Korean War. He had a name for people like Celeste Deepstream. Called 'em walkin' ghosts. Said that sometimes after he thought he'd killed a man, the man would come back at him, risin' straight up from death, aimin' to even the score right on the spot." Billy nodded and smacked his gum wad. "A walkin' ghost, yeah, that's pretty much what I'd call her."

CJ eyed his old friend pensively, thinking, *No way.* Celeste Deepstream wouldn't come after him again. She'd failed too many times, and if she wasn't crippled or paralyzed from the blast from his 30.06 that had sent her scurrying into the Taos Mountains, she was still a fugitive on the run. He'd checked. She was most-wanted material in at least three Western states, a dangerous felon in violation of her patrol. *It couldn't be Celeste,* he told himself. *There is no way she'd come back after me again.* CJ patted his vest pocket for his cheroots. The carton he pulled out was empty. He eyed the box, shook his head, and tossed the box onto the bar. "Let's go," he said to Billy as he turned to head for the door. "A walkin' ghost," CJ said, moving toward the exit. "Must be a hell of an image to try and get a fix on."

"Sure is," said Billy. "And if I was you, I'd start my triangu-latin' right now."

CHAPTER 11

The terrorist bombs that killed 191 people on four commuter trains in Madrid in the spring of 2004 consisted of 220 pounds of explosives in ten backpacks. Timothy McVeigh packed a rental truck with 4,800 pounds of ammonium nitrate fertilizer, oil, and commercial explosives in his quest to blow up the Alfred P. Murrah Federal Building in Oklahoma City in the spring of 1995, killing 168 people. The multiple terrorists' bombs that destroyed three London Underground train cars and a double-decker bus during the summer of 2005, killing more than fifty, weighed less than ten pounds each.

Nasar Moradi-Nik, his project much less ambitious, used just under twenty pounds of black-market plastic explosives from the Czech Republic to construct the unsophisticated bomb he planned to use to blow up Ike's Spot. The device, set to go off with a command from a doctored TV channel changer, was one of the smallest he had ever cobbled together and far more bang for the buck than he thought necessary to take out a simple two-by-four-framed duplex. But Alexie Borg, who was footing the bill for his services, had insisted on a device that would be certain to level the building, including the store next door, and kill any unlucky occupants. "I don't want any comebacks," Alexie had insisted when he'd dropped by Moradi-Nik's garage and bomb-making shop just before midnight to inspect his accomplice's handiwork.

"Send the bail bondsman's worthless trinkets flying to the sky," he'd told his bomber encouragingly, handing a perspiring and twitching Moradi-Nik an envelope that contained half of the $5,000 he'd demanded for the job.

Now, as Moradi-Nik lay prone in the alley just south of the garage behind Ike's Spot, sweating profusely in the three a.m. chill, he began to shake. He'd watched the building for an hour, looking for activity on the back porch. After concluding that no one was inside the building, he'd decided to place the bomb behind the failing latticework that covered the crawl space beneath the duplex's back porch. He'd detonate the bomb from a spot fifty yards down the alley.

As a rule he didn't take jobs where he received only half of his money up front, but he had known Alexie since their youthful days as Olympians, and he'd done jobs for the big Russian's handlers and had always been paid, so he'd made an exception. Besides, he preferred assignments where the risk of blowing yourself up or being caught were minimal. Twitching and sweating like an overworked beast of burden, he crawled through an opening in the picket fence that rimmed the backyard with his bomb in his backpack and his TV remote tucked safely in his shirt pocket. Moradi-Nik was ready to begin the final leg of his assignment.

Since midnight Morgan and Dittier had been out scavenging, rummaging through the Dumpsters and trash cans in search of aluminum cans. As they pushed their shopping carts down the alley that led back home, both men were all smiles. In three hours they had loaded their carts six times, pushed each load to a convenient self-serve twenty-four-hour can crusher less than a mile from home, and garnered $18 each, enough for Morgan to get the expensive run-over Luchesse boots he'd once rodeoed in a new set of heels and to afford Dittier a new chambray shirt.

Lagging behind Dittier, Morgan stopped to glance up toward a white-hot-looking full moon. "Damn near as bright as day out here," he muttered, surprised that with all the moonlight they hadn't once been spotted or run off by some overeager security guard or paranoid homeowner. Thirty yards from Ike's Spot, Morgan stopped to check his watch. The glow-in-the-dark dial of the sixty-year-old Bulova he'd found five years earlier at the bottom of a trash bag read 3:20. As he moved to catch up with Dittier, Dittier stopped and abruptly spun his shopping cart on one of its rear wheels to face him. It was a sign the streetwise former rodeo clown and Morgan used to signal to one another that there might be trouble ahead.

Morgan tiptoed his way up to Dittier. "Whattaya see?" he said slowly, watching Dittier read his lips.

"Somebody's outside the back of the store," Dittier signed, taking a knee. "I can feel the movement."

Morgan brought an index finger to his lips and said, "Quiet," as he slipped the lariat he'd used during his rodeo days from the strip of rawhide securing it to the handle of his shopping cart. He tapped the cart's handle, a signal for Dittier to stay put. Leaning against the cart for support, he removed his boots and moved cautiously up the alley.

A streetlight on the opposite side of the alley flickered on and off as Morgan closed in on the duplex. He spotted the outline of a lone figure near a hole in the backyard fence that he and Dittier used to roll their shopping carts through. In the same instant a quivering, perspiring Moradi-Nik spotted him.

"Hey, what the hell are you doin'?" Morgan shouted as Moradi-Nik bolted, racing for the narrow strip of space that separated the duplex from the neighboring building to the south and exiting onto Broadway as he headed for the safety of his pickup.

Morgan, who'd begun his rodeo career as a steer roper, had no trouble looping the business end of his lariat around Moradi-Nik's left foot. He gave the lariat a yank, and as Moradi-Nik, sweating, twitching, and screaming profanities, reached out to break his fall, his TV remote slipped out of his shirt pocket. The remote took a single skip along the ground face up before Moradi-Nik's elbow came crashing down on it, triggering the bomb and a freight train–like explosion that rocked the building's foundation. The back porch of Ike's Spot disintegrated instantly, sending roof tile, drywall, aluminum siding, wood splinters, and chunks of cinder block and mortar flying in every direction as Morgan and Dittier hit the ground spread-eagled.

Trapped between ground zero and the building next door, Moradi-Nik stood no chance. The rocket-propelled scythe of galvanized downspout metal that slammed into his neck severed his carotid artery and stopped his twitching for good.

CJ and Billy DeLong reached Wheatland, a small Wyoming prairie town seventy-five miles north of Cheyenne, at sunrise. They'd left Cheyenne in darkness, their fishing gear snuggled tightly against the back door of the Jeep, grabbed coffee and what turned out to be four stale donuts at a 7-11, and headed north for the Laramie Mountains and the Triangle Bar Ranch.

"This exit's a bugger," Billy said, smacking on a fresh four-stick wad of Doublemint as CJ slowed the Jeep to take the second

Wheatland exit. "Gets one or two real bad semi rollovers every few months."

The Jeep fishtailed momentarily the instant CJ tapped his brakes.

"Told you."

CJ nodded, his eyes locked on the mountains to the west. The narrow rising sweep of the chip-sealed secondary road he'd turned onto now afforded him an unobstructed view of the snow-capped 10,272-foot Laramie Peak to the northwest. As the entire panorama of the Laramie Mountains unfolded before them, Billy said, "Prettier than a picture."

"And then some. How much farther do you figure, Billy?"

"Ten, twelve miles at the most."

CJ checked his watch. "Looks like we've got ourselves a little time to spare." He slowed the Jeep to take in the view.

"High, wide, and handsome," said Billy as the two men drank in the landscape where the myth of the American cowboy was born.

The Denver bomb-squad lieutenant had been floating on a cushion of beer-induced sleep when he'd gotten word that there had been an apparent bombing on South Broadway. He'd climbed out of bed, rinsed the stale taste of weak poker-party beer and Tostitos out of his mouth, and called his onetime police academy classmate, Fritz Commons, who several hours earlier had scored the smallest pot of the night, to tell him well in advance of foot-dragging police procedural protocol that he had a homicide on his plate.

As the sun tightened its grip on the day, Commons sat on a trash can taking Morgan and Dittier's statement in the alley behind what was left of Ike's Spot as Rosie Weeks looked on. Morgan had considered calling Mavis with the news that Ike's Spot had been bombed, but he'd called Rosie instead. Neither of them could understand why Rosie's half-dozen frantic calls to CJ's cell phone had gone unanswered.

The rear third of the duplex that CJ and Lenny McCabe shared was scattered up and down the alley. Two cinder blocks from the foundation still mortared together and the twisted metal framework of Morgan's army cot rested inches from Dittier and Morgan's feet. A gaggle of neighbors stood in a yard across the alley, some still dressed in pajamas and bathrobes, drinking in the carnage.

Missing, however, from the cordoned-off war zone–like area was much of the infrastructure of Ike's Spot itself. Lenny McCabe's half of the duplex had suffered all the serious damage, probably largely because, according to what the bomb-squad lieutenant had told Commons, Ike's Spot's back porch had been filled with Morgan and Dittier's stash of salvaged wicker furniture and bedding, bedrolls, cots, mattresses, and a storehouse of clothing. The porch had served as a buffer zone with sheets and blankets draping the windows along with two blast-stopping refrigerators that Morgan and Dittier used to store their beer, bologna, fresh fruit, and bread. Both appliances now sat in the middle of the backyard, their doors blown off, kissing one another, head to toe. CJ's office had suffered minor damage, his partner's desk being the biggest loss, but his safe and the rest of the store's contents remained pretty much intact.

Lenny McCabe's back porch, with no more than a lounge chair and a wrought-iron table to absorb the blast, had served as a conduit to his store, leaving most of it a shambles and turning his nineteenth-century glassware collection and his storehouse of Rocky Mountain National Park ephemera into a crazy quilt of glass and pulp.

McCabe sat across the yard talking to the bomb-squad lieutenant. Dressed in shorts and sandals, his ponytail drooping, McCabe looked utterly exhausted. When a rangy, beak-nosed bomb-squad technician jogged up and interrupted the conversation, McCabe looked relieved. "Macy found a fragment of plastic he thinks you should have a look at, Lieutenant," the technician said excitedly.

The veteran bomb-squad officer, suspicious of building owners who had just seen their building snuffed out by an explosion or fire, said, "Okay," to the technician and turned back to McCabe. "Gonna pass you off to the homicide officer in charge, Sergeant Commons. He tells me he's visited your little establishment before. Should be a great homecoming." The lieutenant glanced down at the field tarp that covered the remains of Moradi-Nik and shook his head. As he walked away, eyes bloodshot, his breath stale with beer and with the eager-beaver technician trailing him, he smiled at an approaching Fritz Commons. "Hell of a way to start the morning, Fritzie."

"At least you woke up to a pocket full of silver," Commons said, turning an empty pants pocket inside out as he walked past. Commons slipped a small spiral-bound writing tablet out of the inside pocket of his leather jacket as he approached McCabe. "Sure seems to be a lot of action down here on Antique Row, and an overabundance of dead people, McCabe. And for some reason, you always seem to be in the mix."

McCabe glanced down at Moradi-Nik's covered remains without responding.

"Where's your buddy Floyd?" asked Commons, attempting to see if he'd get the same response he'd gotten from Morgan and Dittier.

"He had to go to Wyoming."

"Business or pleasure?"

"A little bit of both, I think."

"And how's your business?"

"It's been good until now," McCabe said despondently.

"And Floyd's?"

"You'll have to ask him."

Commons smiled. "The two of you wouldn't have had any reason to, say, ummm, blow up your building?"

"Are you crazy, Sergeant?"

"Nope, just looking where I always look when I'm talking to the owner of a building that's just been blown up and I have the remains of a dead man sprinkled at my feet." Commons shot McCabe an incisive stare. "So your answer to my question is?"

"No!"

"Did you take a look at the dead man?"

"What was left of him," McCabe said, frowning.

"Know him?"

"No."

Commons nodded toward where Morgan, Dittier, and Rosie remained huddled. "Do you know those two street bums I was talking to or that guy with them who looks like he should be an NFL nose tackle?"

"Yes. And they're not bums. The one with the shaved head has his bust down in Colorado Springs in the Pro Rodeo Hall of Fame. Name's Morgan Williams."

"And the deaf one?"

"Dittier Atkins. He's a six-time pro-rodeo clown of the year. The big guy's name is Rosie Weeks. He's Floyd's best friend."

"I see. And you, McCabe? What's your claim to fame?"

"Don't have one."

"It sure doesn't seem as if you do. And you know what? That makes me want to dig a little deeper into this bombing. I did a little checking on you and your buddy Floyd. Turns out Floyd has a pretty impressive service record. Two tours of Vietnam, a Navy Cross, a genuine war hero. And would you believe he's still alive after working for more than thirty years as a bounty hunter and bail bondsman? But you know all of that, don't you, McCabe?" Commons flipped his writing tablet open. "Now, here's what I found out about you. You've sold cars and used kitchen appliances. You've peddled aluminum siding, brokered secondhand furniture, hawked comic books, sold lawn-aerating equipment, and even peddled scrap metal. Seems you even dabbled in selling health food and real estate for a while. A pretty hit-and-miss career, don't you think, McCabe?"

McCabe bristled. "And I've had a very successful business down here on South Broadway for the past ten years."

"So you hit a lucky streak."

"Call it what you want, Sergeant."

"You got any enemies, McCabe?"

"We all do, Sergeant. Friends and enemies; it's what makes the world go around."

"And Floyd, he got any—enemies, that is?"

"Don't know."

"What about the two rodeo cowboys?"

"Didn't you ask them?" McCabe answered smugly.

Commons frowned. "I'll let you in on something, McCabe.

My friend over there from the bomb squad's gonna look at you long and hard. He'll take a gander at the lease agreement you have with Floyd, and he'll scrutinize any insurance policies you and Floyd might have. And after that he'll nose into your debts and check out how many girlfriends you've got and look into how regularly you and Floyd pay your bills. Maybe even add up your tabs down at the liquor store."

McCabe cut Commons off. "Maybe he should find out if our mothers are still virgins! Come off it, Sergeant. I didn't bomb the place, and neither did CJ."

Ignoring McCabe's outburst, Commons smiled and continued. "That's what my bomb-squad friend will do. My job will be to find out as much as I can about our friend over there under the tarp. Look into whether he blew himself up by mistake or somebody, a building owner perhaps, set him up. I sure hope for your and Floyd's sake that everything I dig up turns out to be miles and miles away from any connection between the three of you."

CHAPTER 12

The Laramie Mountains provided enough cell-phone signal interference to ensure that Rosie Weeks's calls to CJ remained unanswered. Oblivious to the problems that awaited him in Denver,
and with Billy drinking in the grandeur, CJ drove beneath the
massive log cross-timbers of the Triangle Bar's eighteen-foot-high
entry arch and onto the ranch property a few minutes before seven.

They bumped along a winding gravel road for the next mile
before the road dipped to cut a two-car-wide swath between three
hundred acres of irrigated pasture and a section of grazing land.
The pasture was still brown and dormant, the grazing section
dotted with cattle. Barbed-wire fences, their strands glistening
in the sun, hugged both sides of the road, and the entire Laramie
Mountains range seemed to arise directly on Triangle Bar property as the early-morning sunlight poked seductively from behind
the edges of low-hanging clouds.

"Pretty," said Billy as CJ, following Amanda Hunter's directions, nosed the Jeep across a century-old split-timber bridge
spanning the Laramie River. "Bet the fishin' down there's world
class," Billy added, eyeing the swift-running waters. When CJ
didn't respond, Billy leaned forward in his seat and, chomping
on his gum, said, "What's troublin' you?"

"Nothing. Just wondering whether I should've kept on doing
what I was good at."

"Meanin'?"

"Meaning, maybe I should've stuck with the bail bonding and what I know."

"Bullshit! You know more about Western collectibles than most folks do who went to school for it. Quit your moanin' and mopin', man, we've got business at hand," Billy said, spotting a windmill and a nearby pickup about a third of a mile down the road. "And don't let no guilt feelin's about goin' back on your word to Mavis get you to second-guessin' why we're here. We're here on business, plain and simple. We get that done, we toss a line in the Laramie, and we head back home."

CJ nodded, remaining silent until he'd pulled up next to a battered red pickup. The Triangle Bar brand was stenciled in black on the driver's-side door. "Guess I better bring my dupes with me," CJ said, slipping the photocopied pages of the Montana medicine book and the Wyoming brand book from under the front seat. He tucked the copies under his left arm and got out of the Jeep; he and Billy strode toward a woman kneeling a few feet from the stock-watering tank at the foot of a windmill.

They were within fifteen feet of Amanda Hunter before she looked up. Bent over two rusty windmill blades that looked as if someone had tried to saw them in half along the long axis, Hunter was dressed in faded jeans, a wrinkled chambray shirt with a badly frayed collar, and run-over ropers boots. A baseball cap sporting the Triangle Bar brand sat in the dirt a few feet from one knee. She reached for the cap, positioned it carefully on her head, and stood.

"I'm hoping you're Amanda Hunter," CJ said cordially.

"I am," she said, looking CJ directly in the eye. She was chunky and attractive in an outdoor, athletic way. Her face was prematurely wrinkled from years of working in the sun, and her eyes sparkled with a neighborly warmth. Somehow she reminded CJ of some of his Uncle Ike's people from the Cotton Belt south. "And I'm guessing you're CJ Floyd." She said the name as if they'd been friends for years and took a generous step forward to shake CJ's hand.

CJ pumped her hand twice and nodded at Billy. "The man wearing the Stetson with the Montana block is my friend Billy DeLong."

"Are you out of Baggs?" Amanda Hunter's face lit up as Billy nodded and tipped his hat.

"Sure am," said Billy, looking puzzled.

"Well, I'll be. *The* Billy DeLong. Never figured I'd ever have the chance to meet you." She looked at CJ. "Guess you know you have one of twentieth-century Wyoming's most famous cattlemen for a friend?"

"Sure do," said CJ, uncertain where Amanda Hunter was headed.

"*Legendary*'s a more proper word." Amanda eyed Billy wonderingly. "Word has it that you once drove seven hundred head of cattle through a snow break in the Never Summer Range during a blizzard, and never lost a calf—and that you're the only man on the face of the planet who ever has put Andy Holcomb in his place."

Billy smiled self-consciously. "Give a story some age and a little yeast and it'll start to rise on you."

"Age, yeast, whatever. It's a pleasure to meet you." Grinning like a charmed schoolgirl, Amanda reached out and shook Billy's hand. Realizing she must have looked a little giddy, she shot a quick glance toward the two windmill blades at her feet. "Thought

I might be able to fix my windmill problem here on the spot." She hefted one of the blades and shook her head. "Turns out I was wrong. Lightning latched on to both these puppies. They'll need some welding, maybe more. Mind following me back to my shop? It's right at my house, and we can have coffee or something close to it while we tell one another our stories. Besides, there're some things I should probably show you back at the house."

"Fine by me," said CJ.

"Good. Just follow my truck." Amanda picked up one of the windmill blades as Billy hoisted the other. "Thanks," she said, smiling at Billy and shaking her head in disbelief. "Billy DeLong. Uh, uh, uh. My foreman had to go to Casper for tractor parts. Left at daybreak and won't be back till late this evening. Shame. Clovis would've paid money to meet you."

Billy smiled as he and CJ followed Amanda to the pickup. They dropped the damaged blades into a truck bed filled with tires and spare parts. Moments later the two vehicles were headed south on a road that CJ hadn't noticed on their way in. As they bumped along the rutted road, both trucks jiggling, CJ said, "Didn't know I was traveling with a superstar."

"Me either," said Billy with a shrug. "But who knows? Could just be the thing we need to grease the skids that'll help us find that Del Mora kid's killer."

Billy and CJ had been given the Cook's tour of Amanda Hunter's hundred-year-old National Historic Registry–listed home, and the two early-nineteenth-century grandfather clocks on either side of the entry to the house's big-game trophy room where they now sat were chiming half past eight when Amanda finally got to the heart of the story about her uncle. Both CJ and Billy, who was well into his third cup of coffee, were well primed.

Taking a sip of coffee as she tried to digest CJ's strange tale of stolen books and murder, Amanda said, "And you say the young man who was killed wrote a term paper that was sprinkled with a heavy dose of my Uncle Jake?"

"He referenced your uncle in four different places," said CJ, now so familiar with Luis Del Mora's term paper that he felt as if he'd written it. "Twice when he talks about Union Pacific doctors working out of a hospital in Cheyenne, once when he discusses how your uncle lost his photographs in a Helena, Montana, fire, and finally when he makes a reference to Jake dying at the age of seventy-two in 1910." CJ handed the term paper to Amanda. "I tabbed the references, have a look. And by the way, that term paper's one of the only documents I've seen with any information on him. A lawyer friend of mine had one of her people search the Internet for information on your uncle, looking for references about him in the years after he lost his photos in that fire in Helena. Nothing," CJ said with a shrug.

"And there's good reason," said Amanda. "He pretty much turned into a recluse after that fire. Medicine was his vocation, but photography was what really made him tick, at least according to my grandfather, who'd just turned fourteen when Uncle Jake died. Grandpa always claimed that Jake was as smart as Einstein, as artistic as Picasso, as fearless as Jack Johnson, and as stubborn as ten teams of Death Valley mules. His watercolors were good enough to have been entered in the 1889 Paris Exposition. He engineered the entire irrigation system on this ranch, all seven thousand acres of it, for his brother. He photographed most of the Laramie range, the Tetons, a good measure of Yellowstone, and the Platte River basin, and he surveyed a good part of the Bighorn River and the eastern half of the Snake. He was never married. He didn't drink, and according to my granddad he continued to take photographs until the week he died."

"Sounds like one unique fellow," said Billy.

"They broke the mold." Amanda nodded proudly.

"There's no disputing that your uncle was a very special man," said CJ. "The question is, how does his life tie in to the murder of a kid from Nicaragua ninety-six years after his death?"

"Simple. His photography. Like I told you on the phone yesterday evening, I'm not surprised that things have come down to someone getting killed."

"Why not?"

Amanda rose and adjusted the plantation shutters that encased the room's massive bay window, reducing the glare of sunlight that filled the room. "For several reasons. Six months back I had a break-in here at the ranch, and a strange call soon afterward. It's pretty unusual to lose anything to thieves around here except for the occasional hay bale, or of course a stray cow. But I'm sure that whoever broke into my old machine shed was after what was left of my Uncle Jake's photos."

"Did they find what they were after?" Billy asked.

"No, because what they were after is locked up in a safe here in the house. But the whole episode unnerved me, and believe me, Mr. DeLong, I don't unnerve easily. At my foreman's insistence, I had a security system installed in the house and the shed and even the tractor barn down the road."

"What was your grandfather's take on the break-in?" asked CJ.

The expression on Amanda's face saddened. "He died six months before it happened. But I can tell you what he would've said." Amanda paused to let her words gather steam. "*Mandy, baby, you should've shot the bastards. And I would've if I'd caught them.*"

Billy and CJ smiled. It was evident that Amanda Hunter's lineage included not only thinkers and artists but someone who could be as plainspoken as the people of Five Points.

"I can show you what I think the thief or thieves were after if you'd like."

"Sure would," said CJ.

Amanda rose, looked directly at Billy as if CJ weren't there, and said, "Come with me."

They followed Amanda from the trophy room down a hallway lined with photos of blue-ribbon-winning quarter horses and steers and through a large kitchen with expensive-looking custom-crafted cherry cabinets and a massive six-burner stove. When CJ spotted a photo of President Franklin Delano Roosevelt seated in a wheelchair shaking hands with a willowy-looking, deeply tanned man in a narrow-brimmed Stetson, he asked, "Isn't that FDR?"

Amanda glanced back at the photograph. "And my granddad. He was an original New Deal Democrat," she said, proudly, smiling at Billy.

Movers and shakers, CJ thought, taking in Amanda's smile and wondering whether she would have been nearly as accommodating if Billy hadn't been along.

Amanda turned a corner near the rear of the house, ducked into a low-ceilinged alcove, and said, "Watch your step." She flipped a light switch on the wall and started down a narrow, poorly lit stairway. "From here on out, the house is pretty much the way it was a hundred and five years ago. Watch your head."

They descended twelve broad-planked steps, heads tucked,

into a musty-smelling adobe-walled cellar with a floor constructed of uneven handmade mortarless bricks. "The ceilings down here are only six and a half feet. It's a little claustrophobic at first, but you get used to it," said Amanda, flipping on another light switch and striding across the forty-by-forty-foot room. "Over here," she said, stopping next to a squat olive-green safe with gold-leaf lettering on the door that read, "San Francisco Safe Company." A barrel-faced steamer trunk stood a few feet away.

Amanda eyed the safe and shook her head. "I don't know how my grandfather ever got this thing down here. He never said. My father always claimed that they must've set it in place with a crane before they put on the first floor. It's been sitting here in pretty much the same spot all my life."

CJ surveyed what he now realized was only a partial basement. Other than the steamer trunk, the safe, a dozen or so antique canning jars that lined a row of shelves attached to the wall to their left, and a couple of floor-to-ceiling half-empty bookcases that hugged the opposite wall, the large, dimly lit space was pretty much empty.

"I'll have the safe open for you in a sec," said Amanda, spinning the ship's lock–style combination. "Don't peek," she said, winking at Billy, who stepped back, looking embarrassed. "There." She swung the door open. "Let's have a look," she said, removing a 1950s-style wooden pop-bottle crate, placing it on the floor, then quickly retrieving a second.

CJ stepped forward to find himself looking down on what appeared to be rows of metal picture frames packed domino-style, back to back inside the two crates. There were at least a couple of dozen of the frames to a row. He estimated that each box probably held at least sixty.

"Here's what they were after," said Amanda. "My Uncle Jake's daguerreotypes." She teased two of the framed photo plates out of place, handing one to CJ and the other to Billy.

"Well, I'll be," said Billy, recognizing the art form. Peeking into the safe, he asked, "How many more boxes of these you got in there?"

"A half-dozen. Close to three hundred and fifty photos all told."

Billy, who had a lifelong interest in silversmithing, spur and bit making, and saddlery and a minor interest in photography, whistled loudly. "Quite a stash!"

CJ held the baseball-card-sized photograph he was holding up to the subdued light and moved it in and out of focus. He'd seen metal-plated daguerreotypes before, but he'd never seen three hundred fifty of them in one place, and he clearly lacked Billy's and Amanda's familiarity. "Mind clueing me in on what makes these little puppies so desirable?"

"They aren't by themselves," said Amanda. "A single photo's probably worth three, four hundred dollars. But according to my grandfather, my Uncle Jake produced close to a thousand of them. What you're holding is a daguerreotype 'whole' plate. It has a fifty-four-inch viewing surface that's cobbled together in a frame with a mat. In essence, it's a one-of-a-kind photograph on a copper-plated surface that has been silver coated."

"Heck of a process," said Billy, admiring the daguerreotype of the Grand Tetons that he was holding.

"My grandfather said Uncle Jake always referred to the daguer-reotype process as a mixture of mechanical tinkering and chemical magic. He brought the technique out West with him after learning it during his medical school days back East. The process had been first successfully demonstrated in France in the late 1830s by the French painter Louis Daguerre. According to my grandfather, the process both mystified and mesmerized my uncle, who before his medical studies had been a graduate chemist. I'm told that when he wasn't practicing medicine, Jake was using the magic of the daguerreotype process to take pictures of the land and the landscape he loved."

CJ stroked his chin thoughtfully. "But that Montana medicine book claims he lost all of his photographs in a hotel fire in Helena." He slipped the folded photocopies he'd taken of the book's important pages and endboards out of his shirt pocket.

Amanda smiled. "Nope. What he lost in that fire were his albumen prints, and a few of his daguerreotypes. Like I said, Jake was a very stubborn man. The newfangled albumen-print process never caught on with him, so he stuck with what he knew. But the daguerreotype's popularity only lasted in the U.S. for about twenty years, roughly 1840 to 1860, when the process was replaced by albumen-print photography. Uncle Jake, however, continued using the daguerreotype process as his staple well into the early 1870s."

"What process did he use after that?" asked Billy.

"None." Amanda's eyes glazed over. "He spent most of the time in the late 1870s and early 1880s, after the Helena hotel fire, practicing medicine. That's why your lawyer's Internet search turned up nothing. In 1881 he was nearly killed in a buckboard accident here on the ranch. For the rest of his life, all twenty-nine years of it, most of it spent right here, he was a severely brain-damaged invalid. When my granddad said Jake practiced photography, his passion, till the very end, what he meant was that he practiced it in his head."

"Sad for such a brilliant man," said Billy.

Amanda nodded without responding.

CJ gave Amanda a moment to compose herself before asking, "What do you think all of these photos are worth?"

"My friend Loretta Sheets, a former University of Wyoming museum curator, claims that what you see here's probably worth about a hundred thousand. If his life's work had been photography alone and not a mixture of photography and medicine, she claims you could pretty much double that."

CJ made a mental note of the woman's name, shook his head, and eyed Billy knowingly. "Money, money, money."

"Ain't it always?" said Billy.

Turning his attention back to Amanda, CJ said, "Think I have a handle—at least a partial one—on why Luis Del Mora was murdered." He unfolded the photocopy of the back endboard of the Montana medicine book he'd been holding, and centered the daguerreotype photo on top of it. "Have a look," he said, motioning for Amanda and Billy to look closer. "The sheet beneath the daguerreotype is a photocopy of the endboard from the Montana medicine book that Luis Del Mora stole. Notice anything strange about it?"

"Not really," said Billy. "Except for them four faint black lines on your photocopy. The ones shootin' out at forty-five degree angles from the corners of the daguerreotype."

"Uh-huh," said CJ. "Those lines represent photocopies of pieces of string or fishing line or something pretty close that were taped to the endboards of the book. Now, one of you remove the daguerreotype."

Amanda reached over and lifted the daguerreotype photo plate. There was a faint gray outline on the photocopy that coincided exactly with where the daguerreotype had rested. "Damn," said Amanda, running a finger gingerly over the photocopy's surface. "Pretty close to a perfect match. Do you think somebody secured one of my uncle's photos to the back of that book?"

"More than likely," said CJ.

"But why?"

"Money, money, money."

Amanda shook her head. "What single photograph could Jake have possibly taken that would be worth killing someone over?"

"I don't know," said CJ. "But there was a daguerreotype photograph strung to the back of that Montana medicine book. I'm certain of it." He paused and thought about a couple of the rare finds he'd stumbled across during his forty-plus years as a collector. A 1915 porcelain Denver municipal license plate worth $1,200 that he'd bought at a yard sale for $11. A 1920s-era Navajo wedding basket that had cost him fifty cents at a flea market outside Phoenix that turned out to be worth $750. "And I'd be willing to bet it's probably worth a lot more than the hundred thousand that museum curator quoted you for everything you've got here."

"What kinda photo could be worth that?" asked Billy.

CJ shrugged. "Don't know. But I've got a feeling that Luis Del Mora's term paper is a blueprint for where we ought to be looking."

CHAPTER 13

Celeste Deepstream stood tapping her foot and fuming in the living room of Alexie Borg's Lower Downtown Denver condominium, $750,000 worth of high-rise real estate a stone's throw from Coors Field. "No more excuses, Alexie. You screwed up."

"No, Moradi-Nik screwed up. And he paid for it," said Alexie, his tone unsympathetic. He'd learned while cruising South Broadway earlier that morning for his usual postmission confirmation to make certain that things had gone as planned that Moradi-Nik had bungled his assignment and blown himself up. When he'd seen a half-dozen police cars and a coroner's wagon lined up in front of the target, he'd known he had trouble. The job had called for Moradi-Nik to make certain that no one was killed in the bombing. Murder always brought far too much scrutiny. When he'd stopped to ask a bystander what had happened, the woman, her hair adorned in curlers and sporting a frayed terrycloth robe, had said, "Somebody blew themselves up."

Alexie didn't wait for details. He left the scene in a rush and, monitoring the police-band radio airwaves for the next hour, confirmed that Denver police had a South Broadway bombing and perhaps even a homicide on their hands.

Aware that Alexie, who never took the blame for anything, wasn't about to take the blame for Moradi-Nik's death, Celeste said, this time in a hushed tone, "Your screwup, Alexie," and casually walked over to the condo's floor-to-ceiling dining room window to drink in the view of the Rockies.

She had once dreamed of living on Colorado's Jurassic-rich Western Slope and working as an archaeologist until CJ Floyd had dashed her dreams and taken away Bobby. The only thing she dreamed of now was seeing Floyd dead, and she knew that the same inner drive that had delivered her from reservation poverty, molded her into an Olympic-caliber swimmer, and made her a Rhodes Scholar would assure her of eventual success. She knew it. Just as she knew that she'd had it with Alexie, his incompetent friends, and his insatiable need for sex.

She turned to see him walking toward her, his pants front bulging, his eyes glazed with desire. "We can settle our little difference of opinion with a refresher sprint," he said, using the phrase that Russian coaches had used to describe the final endurance challenge they required of Olympic-caliber athletes when capping a grueling workout. He wrapped an arm around Celeste's waist.

"Sorry," she said, spinning away. "I've got work to do."

Offended, Alexie said, "I'll get a replacement for Nasar."

"You had your chance, Alexie. And you muffed it." Celeste sidestepped the big Russian's attempt to grab her arm.

"I can fix it," Alexie said in a near whine as he trailed Celeste toward the door.

Like you can fix your ill manners, your premature ejaculations, your incompetence, and your oafish ways? "No, thanks. I'll handle the problem myself." She swung the front door open and stepped out into the corridor. "I'll call you if there's a need," she said, walking away, leaving the still aroused Alexie staring at her backside, angry and befuddled.

CJ was in the midst of releasing a twenty-inch rainbow, his fourth twenty-incher of the morning, when Billy, standing in swifter, waist-deep water thirty feet away, screamed, "Son of a bitch!"

CJ looked up to see a football-shaped two-and-a-half-foot trout knife out of the water until, at Billy's chest level, the huge rainbow plunged headfirst into the safety of the cold rushing waters of the Laramie River.

The fish knifed out of the water three more times. Each jump was nearly equal to the first as Billy tried to gain control. His line screamed as the fish submerged and made a new run. "Tied into a lunker!" Billy hollered to CJ. "I'll work him toward the shore." In the five minutes it took Billy to land the rainbow, the fish never again showed itself, and neither man saw its real girth until Billy, as wily and cagey a fly fisherman as he was a cowman, his arms tired from playing the fish, netted the big rainbow a few yards from shore. "Monster," he said, looking up at CJ, who stood just a few feet away. Billy snapped a surgical hemostat off a metal loop on a pocket of his fishing vest, clasped the number-16 Adams fly that had been the fish's undoing with it, and removed the hook from the corner of the fish's mouth. Shaking his head, he said, "Must be my lucky day; sucker was barely hooked." He moved the spent fish back and forth in the current, forcing water into its gills. "One more good jump and he'd'a slipped me for sure."

"But he didn't." CJ watched the rainbow swim in place for several seconds before darting away to blend in with the rocky river bottom.

"Hell of a fish." Billy grinned. "Ain't hooked one that big in a long time."

"Premium water," said CJ. Stepping out of the river and onto the grassy bank, he watched the Laramie ripple by.

"You got that right. I'd wager ain't nobody but Amanda Hunter and her hired help fished this stretch in the past twenty years." Billy rested his fishing net against a nearby rock and unbuttoned the bottom button of his vest. "What did you think of her?"

"Tough lady."

"And real class," Billy added.

CJ hesitated before offering a second response, suspecting that Billy had come as close as he believed Billy could ever come to being smitten. "Think she told us the truth?" he asked finally.

"Yep." The short, clipped answer was clearly meant to end any debate.

"What about that story of hers about some librarian calling her and asking about her uncle's photos months before the break-in? Awfully coincidental. And she didn't bring it up until we were about to leave."

"It probably slipped her mind," Billy said defensively. "Remember, she was dealin' with some hurtful family history. Besides, in case you missed it, the lady's already rich, and she's got her uncle's whole daguerreotype collection sittin' right under her nose. Why would she want one more?"

"Money, money, money."

"Horseshit! If you want to look at somebody closer, try that librarian lead she gave us. Didn't you say on the way that Flora Jean was sniffing up the shorts of some library type back in Denver?"

"Yeah. A guy named Counts."

"Then that's the trail I'd ride," said Billy. "Let's stick to what we agreed on earlier. I'll try the Sheets woman over in Cheyenne at that museum Amanda told us she runs, and you follow up with Flora Jean on the library guy. Trust me, Amanda's clean on this, CJ. And on top of everything else, she never heard of that guy whose books were stolen, Stafford."

"That's a little bothersome, don't you think, Billy? Money runs with money. That's always been my experience."

"But ranchin' money ain't Howard Stafford's kinda money. He and Amanda ain't cut from nowhere near the same cloth."

"No argument from me," CJ said, suspecting he'd ruffled Billy's feathers enough. "Think we should head back south while our fishing luck holds?"

Pleased that CJ was off Amanda Hunter's case, Billy grinned. "Fair enough. That way when we get back home and spin our fishin' tales, there'll be no need for lies."

CJ winked, leaned against a boulder, and started taking off his waders. *Amanda Hunter is an unusual breed*, he thought, watching Billy break down his fly rod—but then, so was Billy DeLong, and CJ trusted Billy's judgment with his life.

Billy was behind the wheel of the Jeep, fighting a thirty-five-mile-per-hour crosswind just south of Wheatland, when three chimes from CJ's cell phone signaled that he had voice mail. "Four calls," said CJ, looking surprised as he eyed the message screen. "Must've been out of signal range."

"Mavis?" asked Billy, his eyes glued to the road.

"Probably." CJ called up the first message from Rosie Weeks. There was an urgency in Rosie's voice. "CJ, call me back as soon as you get this. Got a problem at your store." Rosie's next two identical messages, "Call me back, CJ. It's important," had CJ gnawing nervously at his lower lip. Rosie's final message, "When you get this, head straight home. Somebody's bombed Ike's," drew a "Shit!" as CJ's eyes widened and every muscle in his face went taut. He glanced at Billy, looking bewildered. "Step on it, Billy. Got a serious problem back home."

"Mavis?" asked Billy, drinking in the look of anxiety on CJ's face. The Jeep's speedometer nosed past ninety.

"No. The messages were from Rosie. Somebody bombed Ike's."

Billy gripped the steering wheel with both hands. "You're shittin'!"

CJ stared straight ahead without responding, his eyes fixed on the stark Wyoming landscape. His left eye suddenly began to twitch, the way it had since Vietnam whenever stress overwhelmed him. Running his tongue slowly and thoughtfully around the inside of his lower lip, he punched Rosie Weeks's number into his cell phone as a cold, detached look spread across his face. It was the same look he'd worn every day for close to two years after coming home from Vietnam.

The grease monkey who answered the phone had Rosie on the line within seconds. "Where you been, CJ?" asked Rosie, wiping a glob of grease off his forearm with a shop rag.

"Wyoming. What happened?"

"Somebody tried to take you out."

"Are Morgan and Dittier okay?"

"Yeah. They're fine. They're the ones who spotted the bomber. And the dumbass SOB blew hisself up. By the time I got to Ike's after Morgan called me, cops were all over the place."

CJ shook his head. Floating on a sea of disbelief, he stared out the window and watched the Wyoming scenery rush past. "How bad's the damage?" he asked finally.

"Yours ain't that bad. Mostly your back porch. But that guy next door to you, McCabe, he's outta business for sure."

When a waggle of static interrupted the conversation, CJ yelled, "Rosie? You there? You there?"

"Calm down, man. Like I said, your store's okay."

"Have you said anything to Mavis?"

"No."

"Don't."

"Won't matter. The bombing was the lead story on the noonday news. She's bound to find out."

CJ sighed and slumped in his seat.

"Want me to head back to Denver with you?" asked Billy, eyeing his despondent friend.

"No. You go on ahead and check on that museum lady, Loretta Sheets."

"Who the heck are you talking to, CJ?" asked Rosie.

"Billy DeLong. He's with me."

"Good," said Rosie, sounding relieved.

CJ checked his watch. "We're thirty miles north of Cheyenne. I should be back in Denver by six."

"No rush," said Rosie. "Morgan and Dittier have pretty much secured everything at Ike's. Even stuffed a few of your most valuable things in a shopping cart and hauled 'em off before the cops showed up. I've got the stuff here at the garage."

"Thanks for looking out for me, Rosie."

"No problem."

"Any leads on the bomber?"

"No. But they'll ID him soon enough."

"Anything else I need to know?" asked CJ.

"Only that that red-headed cop who showed up at lunchtime the other day showed up and grilled the hell outta me and Morgan."

"Commons? Wonder why he was there."

"I think he was checkin' out a homicide angle for your bomber."

"And probably looking for a tie-in to another murder," said CJ.

"Why's that?" asked Rosie.

"I'll tell you when I get home," said CJ. "See you about six."

"Gotcha," said Rosie, hanging up, leaving CJ looking as frustrated as he was confused.

CJ didn't utter another word, nor did Billy, until Billy eased off the accelerator on the outskirts of Cheyenne.

"How bad's the damage?" asked Billy.

"Survivable."

"Any line on the bomber?"

"Nope. He blew himself up."

The two friends eyed one another, looking as if they'd both found the answer to some long-held secret. "Somebody out there doesn't like me, Billy," CJ finally said wryly.

Billy nodded. "And I'm guessin' her name's Celeste."

"Wouldn't bet against you," said CJ, watching a sea of tract homes rise out of the rolling grasslands. Shaking his head and stroking his chin, CJ added, "Wouldn't bet one dime" as he contemplated how to deal with an acute new problem.

CHAPTER 14

Agitated and sweating, Oliver Lyman paced the floor of his Metro State College office, both ears ringing as he whispered into the mouthpiece of his cell phone: "I told you we should've taken more precautions. I'm worried my next visitor won't be some snoop pretending to be a student; it'll be some cop."

"You're paranoid, Ollie. Calm down and stop wetting your pants. I'll handle damage control."

Lyman swiped his brow with a forearm. "I never should've told you about Luis Del Mora."

"But you did. What you shouldn't have done was let Del Mora write a term paper that mentioned Jacob Covington. That was stupid."

"Bullshit!" Lyman plopped into a chair and started removing one of his boots. "There's no way anyone can make a connection between Covington, some obscure college term paper, and that photograph in a thousand years."

"What about your Amazon pretending to be a student?"

"She's bluffing. What I can't figure out is how in the heck she ever got wind of that term paper in the first place."

"Maybe she had help."

"Could be," said Lyman.

"Trust me. She was fishing—hoping for a bite. If she surfaces again, feed her the same damn line."

"Okay. But I don't mind telling you, she's got me out of sync."

"Then you better get refocused if you ever want to get paid."

"Don't get heavy-handed with me, you arrogant shit," Lyman said with a frown. "I expect to be paid, and soon."

"You will, but like I said from the start, things could get rough."

"I know, but there's gold at the end of this rainbow. I'll roll with the waves."

"Good. Just sit tight, keep your mouth shut, and if the Benson woman pays you a return visit, let me know."

"Oh, you'll hear all right. Now, how soon can I expect my money?" Lyman demanded.

"Within the week, ten days at most. As soon as my negotiations are done."

"Fifty thousand like we agreed?" Lyman asked.

"Like we agreed. Gotta go. We've talked too long."

"Just reminding you of our deal."

"I'm reminded."

The line went dead before Lyman could respond. Shaking his head, he slipped off his other boot and eyed his desktop, where the cardboard backing from a spent legal pad sat. He looked down at his right boot and back up at the backing several times before reaching for the cardboard. He picked up the boot and placed it on the cardboard, grabbed a pen, and traced the sole and heel of the boot on the cardboard. Hunched over and squinting, he retraced the outline several more times until he was certain the cut-out, and the insurance policy he was about to make, would fit the boot perfectly.

Flora Jean ate a late lunch at Mae's and stayed until close to three o'clock talking to a visibly shaken Mavis about the bombing of Ike's. Uncertain whether the bombing was a sign that Celeste Deepstream had reared her vengeful head or whether it was tied to the Luis Del Mora killing, both women agreed that CJ was once again swimming with sharks in the same troubled waters that always seemed to lap at him.

Flora Jean left Mae's for the three-block walk to the Five Points Blair-Caldwell African American Research Library and a meeting with Theodore Counts, more concerned for CJ's safety than she'd been in years.

On the walk from Mae's to the library, she ran into Roosevelt Weeks coming out of the Points' only bank. Stashing a deposit slip and a wad of twenties in his pocket, Rosie stopped to tell her he'd talked to CJ earlier and that by now CJ should be pretty close to home. When she asked Rosie how CJ had taken the news of the bombing, Rosie offered, "Not good, not real bad either. It was sorta like deep down he'd been expectin' a streak of bad to come along." Flora Jean left the encounter feeling perplexed.

She entered the library's spacious foyer determined to size Counts up better than she'd sized up Oliver Lyman. She still couldn't decide what Lyman's connection to the Luis Del Mora killing was, but she'd thought about the wannabe cowboy's possible involvement long enough to have convinced herself that no matter how clean Lyman had come off during their Metro State chat, he was linked to Del Mora's murder.

A helpful librarian politely directed Flora Jean to Theodore Counts's second-floor office. Smiling as she waved Flora Jean toward a bank of elevators, she said, "Room 201," and then, sounding as if she actually meant it, "Have a nice day."

Flora Jean had initially thought of running the same kind of bait-and-switch routine she'd used on Lyman, but she decided to modify that approach because the Lyman visit had yielded so little information. She'd done a little more homework on Counts, and her research told her that what Counts liked more than anything was a good dose of ego stroking. Deciding to accommodate him, she pushed open the door to Room 201 and found herself in a small outer office. A petite, boyish-looking woman manning a desk that filled most of the room looked up at her quizzically. Smiling at the woman, Flora Jean said, "I'm here to see Mr. Counts. Flora Jean Benson."

The woman shoved aside the magazine she'd been reading, glanced at the open day planner to her left, picked up the phone, punched in what seemed to Flora Jean to be an inordinate amount of numbers, and said into the mouthpiece, "Your three o'clock's here." Looking up at Flora Jean, she said, "Mr. Counts will be with you in a moment," before robotically cradling the phone.

As Flora Jean scanned the tiny room for somewhere to sit, Theodore Counts appeared in the doorway to his office. He walked across the room and greeted Flora Jean with a handshake and a smile that reeked of self-importance.

"Come on in, Ms. Benson," he said, directing Flora Jean around the secretary's desk and into an office that was just a hair's breadth larger than the secretary's.

The cramped, windowless room was all pomp and circumstance—a monument to Theodore Counts's achievements. Plaques, citations, and awards touting various milestones in his career adorned every wall. A degree in library science from Morgan State College hung at eye level directly behind an antique rolltop desk. A garish blood-red, high-backed Louis XIV chair sat behind the desk. "Impressive digs," said Flora Jean, initiating the conversation with a bit of low-flying flattery.

Counts smiled. "Comfortable enough for a public servant and school-system retiree. Have a seat."

Flora Jean eased down into an uncomfortable side chair. "Looks like you've accomplished a lot," she said, nodding at the wall testimonials.

"I've had a fulfilling career." Counts was all business as he looked Flora Jean up and down. "Now, refresh my memory about why you needed to talk to me so urgently." His words had an unmistakable ring of superiority.

Suppressing the urge to say, *Oh, shucks, captain, I's here to find out if your pompous ass is connected to a murder,* Flora Jean instead said, "I'm lookin' into how you helped build the Denver Public Schools library system into a national model. Its part of the research I'm doin' for my master's degree over at Metro."

Counts flashed a self-congratulatory smile. "Hard work, Ms. Benson. And the unselfish support of the good people around me," he added obligatorily.

"How long did you work for the DPS?" asked Flora Jean, extracting a notepad from her tote bag.

"Thirty-six years. And all of them amazingly productive ones."

Sure, Flora Jean thought. "Durin' that time how many libraries were you responsible for remodeling?"

Counts stroked his chin as if searching for an answer he'd long ago memorized. "Not just remodeled, Ms. Benson—reconstructed. Twenty-two in all. I touched every library in the system in one way or another during my career. Got them everything from new lighting and carpet to state-of-the-art computer systems and space-age purchasing and inventory-control programs."

Flora Jean piled on the fluff. "Sounds like you were as much a systems designer as a librarian."

"I was. Still am. Most of what you see in this building is my doing."

Flora Jean choked back another thoughtful *Sure*. "Did people ever tap your expertise outside the DPS system?"

"Of course."

"Can you give me a few examples?" Flora Jean tapped her pen's point on the notepad for effect.

"The University of Colorado, a half-dozen county libraries surrounding Denver, libraries on the Eastern Plains, places as far away as Durango." Counts was all bluster.

"What about the private sector?"

Counts sat up in his chair, shoulders raised haughtily. "Does the name Coors ring a bell?"

Flora Jean nodded, thinking, *Gotcha!* "How about Howard Stafford? Ever work for him?"

Counts cocked an eyebrow and relaxed back in his seat. "I have."

"Recently?"

"Are you headed somewhere with this, Ms. Benson?" Counts asked, a tinge of suspicion in his response.

"Sure am. A young man named Luis Del Mora was killed a few days ago. Bought a couple of bullets to the head and neck region. Turns out he lifted a couple of books from Howard Stafford's library, and it probably cost him his life. Any chance you might've known him?"

Caught off guard, Counts muttered, "No."

"How about Stafford—good person to work for?" Flora Jean asked, uncertain whether Counts was lying and certain that as soon as he recovered from her broadside she'd be asked to leave.

"He was always good to me."

"Candid," said Flora Jean, surprised that Counts wasn't showing her the exit.

"I tend to be." Counts grinned slyly.

If there's something in it for you, Flora Jean thought. "Did you know Theresa Del Mora?"

"Peripherally."

"Anything special about her and Stafford's relationship?"

"Not that I ever saw." Counts eyed Flora Jean sternly. Tempering his anger, he asked, "Who are you really, Ms. Benson? And what's your angle?"

"Everybody don't have an angle, Mr. Counts. But to answer your question, Theresa Del Mora hired me to find out who killed her son."

"You're a PI?"

Flora Jean shook her head. "Nope. Do bail bondin' for a livin'."

"I see. Well, here's a take for you, bond lady. The work I did for Howard Stafford involved making certain that his library was state-of-the-art. But I bet you already knew that, didn't you?"

Flora Jean remained silent.

Counts smiled and continued. "Here's what you didn't know. I was simply one consultant on the Stafford project. Since you're looking into a murder you think was triggered by a theft, I suggest you talk to Stafford's security-systems man, Arthur Vannick."

"An enemy of yours, I take it?"

"Just talk to him, Ms. Benson." Counts continued smiling. "I hear he's connected, mob style, if you know what I mean."

"Think he'd say the same sweet things about you?" asked Flora Jean, trying to decide if Counts was attempting to deflect suspicion by sending her on a wild-goose chase.

Counts dug in his heels. "I never knew how the library was ultimately secured, and the Del Mora woman had the run of the place. Talk to them."

"Maybe a thief wouldn't need to get to Stafford's books by breachin' security. What about . . ."

"I think you should probably go, Ms. Benson." Counts rose and moved around his desk.

"One last question. Any other folks around the Stafford estate with a motive for murder?"

"Go." Counts reached for Flora Jean's arm.

"Don't do somethin' you'll be sorry for later, sugar." Flora Jean jerked her arm out of reach, prepared to splinter every bone in Counts's hand if he moved it any closer.

Regaining his composure, Counts walked to the door, swung it open, and said, "Don't come back, Ms. Benson."

Flora Jean smiled. "The sign in the lobby says *public* library."

"I can make things extremely difficult for you."

Flora Jean looked Counts up and down, and the look was sergeant-major marine corps steely. "Works both ways, sugar," she said, moving to leave.

Counts stood in the doorway of his outer office and watched Flora Jean walk toward the elevator at the end of the corridor. He slammed the door and raced back into his office for the phone the instant she stepped inside.

By the time Flora Jean reached the first-floor reference librarian's desk, Theodore Counts was near the end of his brief phone conversation. "Bottom line is, we've got ourselves a heavy-duty problem," he said, out of breath.

"We've simply run up against unintended consequences," came the reply. "We'll deal with it."

"How?"

"There'll be a way."

Counts sighed as he listened to the dial tone.

❦

During the eight long years she'd unsuccessfully tried to kill CJ Floyd, Celeste Deepstream had used everything from a set of homemade propane firebombs to a high-powered rifle. Now she had a new plan. She only needed the perfect spot to carry it out. *Nowhere to run, nowhere to hide, Mr. Floyd,* she thought as she walked to retrieve the instrument that would drain the life from Floyd. She looked back down the thirty-yard path she'd worn in the soft pine-needle-covered dirt over the past two days. Chastising herself for again acquiescing to Alexie, she stared back at the tree she'd started from and finally skyward. As she eyed the crystal-blue Colorado sky, it came to her. The perfect place. The perfect spot. It had been there all the time. Old and ugly, dilapidated and dark, public yet private, easily accessible and easy to leave from. She couldn't believe she'd never thought of the spot before. She stooped, picked up her killing tool, and thought, *A little more practice, just a little more practice,* as she rose and turned to walk back to the tree she'd started from.

❦

CJ walked around Ike's Spot slowly, zigzagging his way through a maze of toppled antiques, glassless display cases, bookcases on their sides, and scattered treasures. Sergeant Fritz Commons was glued to CJ's side.

"I'm only letting you have a look around the place to see if you can spot anything that might help me with my investigation," said Commons. "An access point, a door that shouldn't be open, a missing antique, something that looks strangely out of place."

CJ nodded. Numb with disbelief, he knew that Commons had also probably let him enter the crime scene so he could size up whether CJ had ordered the bombing himself.

"That tale your two rodeo cowboy friends came up with is a real doozy, Floyd. Roping the damn bomber in the act. Pretty hard to swallow."

"Never known either one of them to be liars," CJ said defensively.

"Didn't say they were. Just said their story's a tad unbelievable. I let them walk, didn't I?"

CJ scanned the room without responding. The store's contents were scattered around the room like superfluous junk, but most had barely been damaged. He still had a store and most of his inventory. There was no electricity, half the rear wall was missing, and there was no heat or water, but he still had a business. There'd be mop-up required, and there was no telling when the structural engineering bureaucrats who controlled such things would give him the okay to reoccupy the space—months, he suspected—but at least he wasn't in Lenny McCabe's shoes. And even if he had no income, a shaky future, and still owed McCabe two months' back rent, he wasn't a casualty.

One of his prized tobacco cylinders rested on the floor inches from his feet. When he reached down to retrieve the $700 antique, Commons wagged a finger. "Uh-uh. I told you no touching."

Ignoring the directive, CJ took a handkerchief out of his jeans pocket, picked up the cylinder with the handkerchief wrapped around his hand, and placed the antique on a nearby countertop.

Deciding not to press the issue, since he expected it would be a minor skirmish in a very long battle, Commons smiled and tagged the cylinder with a yellow sticky note on which he'd scribbled, *Floor near the back door.* Nudging the cylinder a bit to the left, he said, "You've got enemies, Floyd. I've checked. Could be they want you either out of the antique business or dead."

Recognizing the probing methods of a homicide cop who was trying to splice together the loose connections between a murder and a bombing, CJ nodded and said, "Yeah."

"I'm betting it's that Indian lady who holds you responsible for the death of her brother."

"Could be."

"Can the con, Floyd. I checked the records. Her name's Celeste Deepstream. She did five years for manslaughter. She's tried to kill you at least twice, according to what I dug up, and probably a few more times you've never told anybody about. She kidnapped your girlfriend nine months back; her parole officer hasn't seen her in over a year, and my guess is that if you and your buddy McCabe next door aren't looking to scam your insurance companies out of a few bucks, or if whoever killed the Del Mora kid isn't looking to throw a world-class scare into your ass, the Deepstream woman is out to finally settle her score."

"That's a lot of ifs, Sergeant."

Commons shrugged. "Play it your way, Floyd. If she pops your ass, she does. If I were you, though, I'd rent a set of eyes for the back of my head. You see what you ended up with here."

"My problem, Sergeant. I'll deal with it."

"You do that," said Commons, double-checking to make certain the sticky note was still stuck to the tobacco cylinder. "Ever heard of a guy named Moradi-Nik?" he asked, patting the top of the cylinder.

"No."

Commons nodded thoughtfully. "Well, he was your bomber. A pro. Would've totaled the place if it hadn't been for your two rodeo buddies living out back."

"Looks to me like he wasn't on top of his game."

Commons shook his head, exasperated. "You're a tough nut, Floyd. Hope it doesn't end up getting you killed." He turned abruptly, announced, "Tour's over," and headed for the garage-door-sized window of daylight streaking through the back wall. CJ followed, stepping gingerly as if sleepwalking his way through a dream.

Moments later they stood outside, where a twenty-foot-square perimeter of crime-scene tape surrounded them. Commons eyed his watch. "McCabe's due to meet me here in a few minutes. When I talked to him earlier, he wasn't making much sense."

CJ eyed what was left of Lenny McCabe's half of the duplex. "Would you have been?"

Commons ignored the question. "This place is off limits until further notice, Floyd. You just had your last tour." He looked around to see a late model Ford pickup headed up the alley toward them. The bright-red truck, with door logos that read, "McCabe's Matchless Gems," pulled parallel to the property's garage and stopped. Ashen-faced, Lenny McCabe stepped out and walked toward CJ and Commons, eyes to the sky as if he were either pleading or praying. "Bad day at Black Rock?" he asked, stopping a few steps from CJ.

"Worse," CJ countered.

"Who'd we piss off?" McCabe asked.

Before CJ could respond, Commons said, "My money's on a very determined and vengeful lady," stopping McCabe in his tracks.

CHAPTER 15

Rosie's garage was a long-established Five Points gathering place and more. The garage's massive back storage room, referred to as "the den" by locals, offered Five Points denizens the opportunity to gamble, play the numbers, buy liquor on Sundays—still against Colorado law—or, if they had a mind to, just hang out all day and shoot the breeze. Rosie didn't mind customers loitering, since that usually meant money in his pocket, but if he caught them cursing in front of a woman, or if one of their poker games turned sour and ended in a fight, he sent everyone packing. Local politicians knew full well what went on in Rosie's back room, but few ever made mention of it, and law enforcement largely ignored it.

Rosie stood inventorying the den's liquor cabinet, making certain he had enough whiskey and beer for the weekend, when CJ walked in, Lenny McCabe in his wake. Both men had the look of haggard ghosts as they closed in on the liquor cabinet.

Rosie didn't know much about McCabe—he'd met him only once, the day CJ had celebrated signing the lease on Ike's Spot—but as he moved around the bar to greet the two men, the foggy-eyed, trance-like look in CJ's eyes told his lifelong friend that CJ was in deep trouble.

"How you doing, CJ?" Rosie said, draping an arm over CJ's shoulders.

"Not that great, Red," said CJ, calling Rosie by the nickname that only CJ, Rosie's wife, Etta Lee, and Mavis were privileged to use. "The store's a wreck, and like you said on the phone, I've got a hell of a reclamation project on my hands. Lenny's place is worse."

McCabe's head bobbed up and down, punctuating the point.

"Sorry to hear that," said Rosie, patting McCabe on the shoulder. Turning back to CJ, he added, "How can I help?"

CJ's words came reluctantly. "Thanks. I haven't really had time to think things through, but there are a couple things you could do." CJ eyed the floor, embarrassed.

"Shoot," said Rosie, surprised by CJ's reticence.

"Let Morgan and Dittier stay here for a night or so until I can fix up a place for them in my garage. I've got Mavis working on it."

"Easy enough. How'd Mavis take the news?"

"Not good. But it's not like she hasn't been through rough times with me before. I've only talked to her once since I got back from Wyoming, but I'm headed to see her as soon as I leave here."

"What else do you need?" Rosie asked.

CJ eyed McCabe. "Lenny here's in bad shape. He's pretty much lost everything. I owe him a couple of months' back rent. I was hoping you might be able to help me out."

"I'll do what I can," said Rosie, recalling that the last time CJ had asked him for money was when they'd been in the tenth grade and CJ had left his book-deposit money at home. "That it?"

"Yeah." CJ's response was barely a whisper. He looked at McCabe, who tried his best to mount a smile.

"What about all them antiques of yours that are still in the store? Think they're safe?" Rosie asked.

"Hope so. The cops have the place roped off, and they won't let me bring in anyone to board up the hole in the back wall until the city engineer says the building's okay structurally." CJ glanced at McCabe. "They won't let Lenny set foot in his place."

"Then we gotta make an end run around their asses," Rosie said, smiling. "And the nighttime's the right time, if you know what I mean. We'll use one of my trucks to load up your stuff. I'll get Dittier and Morgan to help out."

"Don't get caught. That cop Commons has his teeth sunk way down deep into this," warned McCabe.

Recognizing that McCabe might not understand the way black folks, especially black folks who stood to lose everything they had, viewed the law, Rosie said, "Don't matter. He's white, and he's slow." He flashed McCabe a no-harm-intended look, glanced back at CJ, and said, "I'll handle it. You best head on over and see Mavis. Let's head back up front and I'll get to work on that money for you."

CJ and McCabe followed the six-foot-four-inch, 260-pound, self-made Five Points businessman toward the den's front door. There was a bit less hesitation in CJ's gait than when he'd entered, but McCabe's downtrodden shuffle was still painfully obvious.

Six years in the U.S. Marine Corps and a tour of duty in the Persian Gulf War had taught Flora Jean to always expect the unexpected. Now, as she waited for Arthur Vannick to exit the 24 Hour Fitness club he belonged to, she couldn't help but wonder whether Vannick, who claimed to be a former member of the

Secret Service and whose security business website touted the fact that he'd been a human shield for presidents, had during his years in that business developed the kind of sixth sense that would alert him to the fact that he was being followed.

When she'd heard from a subdued, road-weary CJ via cell phone a few hours earlier that Ike's had been bombed but his and Billy's Wyoming trip had been fruitful, she'd considered canceling her Vannick stakeout to meet with CJ and console him, but CJ had insisted that she go ahead with her plans.

A light southwesterly breeze kicked up as Flora Jean, outfitted in a tight-fitting Windbreaker, sweatpants, and sneakers, eyed the fitness center's entrance waiting for her mark to appear. She hoped the photo of a smiling Vannick she'd downloaded off his website was a good match. She didn't want to confront the wrong person.

Most of the people entering and exiting the fitness center appeared to be in their twenties or thirties, and the majority, decked out in designer sweats and sneakers, gym bags looped over their shoulders, looked as if they were headed not for a workout but for a date. Flora Jean shook her head, mumbled, "White folks on the make," chuckled at the fact that sweating and grunting one's way to fitness had been moved way up on the social scale, and went back to scanning the patrons for Arthur Vannick.

Two twenty-somethings who looked like actors in a beer commercial, caps on backward, $150 running shoes paving their way, gawked at her as they ambled toward the front door of the building. The no-excuses-sir marine corps stare she gave the two men caused them to pick up their pace.

Vannick swept out the front door so quickly that Flora Jean almost missed him, and she would have if he'd been wearing a hat or cap. He was three shades paler than his website's airbrushed, suntanned photo, and his pockmarked skin stood out. He was also fifteen pounds heavier than depicted in the photo.

Vannick moved toward the elevator of the fitness center's three-story parking structure as if he were on a mission, so rapidly that Flora Jean could barely keep pace with him.

Rethinking the background information that Julie Madrid had e-mailed to her earlier, information that didn't fully mesh with the propaganda on Vannick's company website, Flora Jean picked up her pace and closed the gap between them.

As Vannick stepped into the elevator alone, she raced for a nearby stairwell. Taking the steps three at a time, she barely beat the elevator to the second floor. When Vannick didn't exit, she bounded up a second flight of stairs. She was standing on the third-floor landing, barely winded, waiting for the elevator doors to open before Vannick even heard the third-floor arrival ding.

The brightly lit third level, a concrete floor walled in by cinder block, was empty except for a car and two expensive-looking pickups as Vannick headed across it. Surprised that anyone calling himself a former Secret Service agent would let a six-foot-one-inch woman wearing a scratchy-sounding Windbreaker close in on him so quickly, Flora Jean overtook her mark.

"Mr. Vannick," she called out, watching Vannick react with a start. "Finally! I've been tryin' to catch up with you all day."

Still walking and squinting over his shoulder at Flora Jean as if she were an apparition, Vannick tightened his grip on the strap of his gym bag. "Pardon me?"

"Been tryin' to get a chance to speak with you all day. I'm Flora Jean Benson, and I'm lookin' into the Luis Del Mora murder. We need to talk."

"Can't help you." Vannick's upper lip curled indignantly.

"I've been told you can."

"By whom?" Vannick angled across the floor toward the lone car.

"Theodore Counts," said Flora Jean, matching Vannick stride for stride.

Vannick stopped and turned to face Flora Jean. "And how does that asshole claim I can help you?"

"He says the security system you designed for Howard Stafford's library may have been faulty."

"That's about what I'd expect out of a full-time piece of shit like Counts. And while he was trying to link me to a murder, did he happen to tell you why, after thirty years of working for the Denver Public Schools system, he took an early-retirement powder?"

"No."

"Didn't figure he would've. Well, here's why: He left because he was embezzling money. No proof, of course; that's the way things operate in a bureaucracy. The dirt gets swept under the carpet so that all the Counts in the world end up with a hall pass to their golden years."

"You sound bitter, Mr. Vannick."

"I sure as hell am. I don't like my tax dollars being skimmed off by equal-opportunity cons like Counts. Now, instead of pestering me, go dog him before you end up being sorry."

Flora Jean bristled. "I'd lighten up on the threats, sugar. Might take you somewhere you don't wanta go."

Vannick flashed a half-cocked smile. "Sorry, sista, didn't mean to hurt your feelings."

Flora Jean took a half step forward. "Got any more innuendos you need to get off your chest, sonny?"

Vannick stood his ground. "Don't push your luck, lady. I'm from a different world than you."

"So I've heard. Had a lawyer friend of mine check you out. She says you claim to be connected. Well, friend, believe it or not, I know a few people from that side of the universe too. Think I'll run your name by 'em."

"Knock yourself out, but don't bother me again—ever."

"You tellin' or askin'?"

"You figure it out." Vannick shot Flora Jean one cold final stare before walking away.

"I'll try," Flora Jean called after him. "But remember, I might not get it right. After all, I'm just your basic sista."

Vannick turned and mouthed, *Fuck you, bitch.*

"Save it for your mother," said Flora Jean, watching Vannick slip into a late-model Porsche and gun the engine. He zoomed by her seconds later, cutting the intimidating pass as close as he dared. As he slowed to take the ramp down to the next level, she found herself wondering whether Vannick, as Julie Madrid had suggested during their afternoon phone conversation, was simply a con man running a bluff or an organized crime wiseguy, as he liked to intimate. It would be easy enough to determine. She didn't have the contacts to fully scope Vannick out, but CJ did. An old curmudgeon named Mario Satoni, a onetime genuine Mile High City wiseguy, though he was reluctant to admit it, had been one of CJ's Uncle Ike's longtime gambling buddies. Satoni would know if Arthur Vannick was lying about his purported underworld contacts. More importantly, Satoni still had the juice to make Vannick stop running his bluff.

Mavis had turned off all the lights in the house except for a hall-way nightlight and a bedroom reading lamp. She was seated naked on CJ's lap with a pair of University of Colorado running shorts at her feet. CJ, clad in a matching pair of shorts, rocked her gently back and forth, trying not to think about the bombing, his store, the overdue rent, his decision to get out of the bail-bonding business, or Celeste.

They had rehashed the day's events to the point that there wasn't anything left to discuss. Mavis had been the one to suggest they slip into the jogging shorts that a close friend and Vietnam comrade of CJ's had given them eight months earlier as a lighthearted gift the day they'd announced their engagement, saying, "Now you're really a pair." Whenever their relationship seemed to be teetering, Mavis would retrieve the gift to help calm the waters. "When do you think they'll let you back in the store?" she asked tentatively, one arm wrapped loosely around CJ's neck.

"I don't know." CJ raised his head until their lips met.

"Is all your stuff safe?"

"As safe as things that really don't matter can be."

"CJ, please. You've spent a lifetime collecting those things. Don't act as if they don't matter to you."

CJ shrugged. "And look what I've got to show for it. Debt up to my eyeballs, a bombed-out shell of a store, and nothing left of the bail-bonding business it took Ike a lifetime to build."

"It wasn't all Ike's doing. You put in your share of time, and the name over the door still reads, 'Floyd & Benson's.'"

"I sold the business to Flora Jean, Mavis." CJ stopped rocking the only woman he'd ever loved and looked her squarely in the eye. "I don't know which way to go, babe."

"Do what you do best, CJ," said Mavis, uttering words she'd thought she'd never say. She had no desire to see CJ step back into a world that had caused the two of them more pain and grief than she cared to remember, or to watch him immerse himself once again in a business that had nearly gotten her killed, but she knew CJ needed something to give him a sense of purpose and a lift out of the morass he was stuck in. "How badly does Flora Jean need you?"

"She can use the help."

"Then help her," said Mavis, hoping she sounded sincere.

CJ wrapped his arms around Mavis's waist and sat back in his chair. "Things could end up like they were before. I could end up chasing bottom feeders all day long."

"Things can't get much worse than they are, CJ."

"Guess not." He squeezed Mavis tightly.

"What about Celeste?"

"She's always been out there somewhere, Mavis. The bombing just proved it."

"Have you called the police?"

"Didn't have to. They came calling on their own."

"Who?"

"That red-headed sergeant, Commons, the one who tracked me down at Mae's the other day. He knows all about my problems with Ms. Deepstream."

The look on Mavis's face was suddenly as devoid of expression as CJ had ever seen.

"If she comes after us again, CJ . . ."

"She won't," CJ said, still taking in the look.

"She won't because I won't let her." Mavis wrapped her arm around CJ's neck. "I'll kill her first."

There'll be a time and a place, Celeste told herself as she watched Mavis Sundee's house go dark. She'd been following Floyd all day, and although she hadn't been able to get as close to him as she'd hoped, she could smell his scent and the scent of his bitch. She walked down the alley that separated Mavis's house from a cluster of recently renovated Victorians on the next street and headed for her pickup. Now that she knew how and where she would dispense with Floyd, she would zero in on his routine, catalog the way he lived, and chart his every move before she extracted his life from him.

CHAPTER 16

Billy DeLong's trout-filled cooler sat across from him on the seat of his pickup. After leading a morose CJ from the Holiday Inn back to I-25 the previous day and waving good-bye to him as their vehicles headed off in different directions southwest of City Center, Billy had spent the rest of the day landing fish after fish on the North Platte River.

Now as he headed for Loretta Sheets's Equal Rights Western Heritage Museum, refreshed from a gold-medal day of fishing and a good night's sleep, his fingers tapping out a rhythmic beat on top of his cooler, he was thinking more about the midsummer eating pleasure he'd enjoy every time he sat down to a meal of smoked Rocky Mountain trout, baked beans, coleslaw, and lemonade than about discussing century-old photographs in some drafty museum. Chewing on his wad of Doublemint, he turned onto downtown Cheyenne's Central Avenue and slowed his pickup, eyeing the declining address numbers until he pulled to a stop in front of 966, got out, dusted off his jeans, and headed for the museum.

The previous evening, when he'd asked his Holiday Inn bartender friend about Sheets's museum, the bartender had smiled and said, "If you go inside, be sure to tie down your wiener. The woman who runs the place ain't got nothin' but contempt in her heart for men. Be sure and read the little brass plaque to the right of the door before you set foot in the place. You'll see what I mean." He'd winked at Billy, refreshed his lemonade, and clammed up.

Following the barkeep's advice, Billy stopped to read the five lines of raised lettering on the plaque: "Wyoming, state of vast places and first government of the world to grant women equal rights. Please enter this museum with that historical information in mind." Billy walked through the museum's ten-foot-high double doors at ten-fifteen, his mind historically primed and open.

The vaulted, open room that greeted him was musty but well lit. Three gigantic Tiffany chandeliers hung from the ceiling, and claw-footed antique oak tables filled with books, ephemera, and artifacts encircled at least half of the fifty-by-fifty-foot room. Two glass-fronted cases containing plaques, photographs, tapestries, and a dozen or so old fur trappers hats sat at the room's center. The walls were adorned with photographs of women riding horseback, hunting, driving race cars, holding test tubes, and standing at lecterns.

A half-open door with an off-kilter overhead transom occupied the center of the back wall. A set of keys hung from the door lock. "Be with you in a minute," a woman's voice called authoritatively from the back of the room. It took Billy a moment to realize the greeting had come from a tiny, stoop-shouldered woman who was sitting almost out of sight just in front of a five-foot-high chest of drawers to the left of the door with the keys. When the woman, her head barely even with the top of the chest, moved to greet him, Billy saw that on her right foot she was wearing a shiny black orthopedic shoe with a three-inch-high built-up heel and sole. She looked to be in her mid- to late forties, and she walked with the barest hint of a limp.

"How can I help you?" she said, stopping a few paces away.

"I'm just having a look around," Billy said noncommittally. "Interesting place."

"I'd like to think so, and please do—look, that is. I'm Loretta Sheets. I curate the museum," she added proudly.

"Pleasure." Without announcing his own name, Billy reached out and shook the dark-haired bifocaled woman's hand, wondering why his bartender friend had described the seemingly pleasant woman in such demonic terms.

"How long has the museum been here?" Billy asked, releasing his grip on her exceptionally warm hand.

Eyeing Billy intently, as if trying her best to place him, she said, "Eleven years in this location. I was over on Lincolnway three years before that. Are you from around here?"

"Nope. Baggs."

Loretta Sheets's eyes lit up. "Butch Cassidy and the Great Train Robbery country. Believe it or not, as long as I've lived in this state, I've only been to Baggs once. But I'm aware that it's a place filled with lots of history." She cleared her throat as if preparing to begin a lecture. "Were you aware that when Butch Cassidy and the Sundance Kid pulled off the Belle Fourche robbery in the Black Hills in 1897, they had help from a woman? And she wasn't that pretty little schoolmarm that Hollywood depicted in that terrible movie. Her name was Lucinda Frewen, a cousin to the famous Frewen brothers of the Powder River Cattle Company."

"The ones with the 76 cattle brand?"

"Yes."

"Never knew that."

"There's a lot of people don't know about women," said Sheets, now eyeing Billy as if she knew him but couldn't place his name.

She stepped to her right, picked up a clear plastic folder filled with postcards and photographs of Little America, a Cheyenne-based I-80 gas station, truck stop, and motel that was arguably the largest gas station in the world, and handed it to Billy. "Little America, for instance. It was started by a woman."

"Didn't know that." Billy eyed the folder's contents, handed it back to Sheets, and waited for the punch line.

"Sure was. The brainchild of the wife of the original owner. He was just a gas jockey. She was the one with vision." Sheets grinned. "Vision enough to parlay what started out as just a little truck stop into a twenty-million-dollar business."

"No argument here," said Billy. Realizing that if he didn't quickly cut to the chase, he'd have Loretta Sheets lecturing him on the untouted deeds of women for the rest of the morning, Billy said in a downhill rush of words, "Got any daguerreotypes around? Amanda Hunter said I should drop in and have a look, and that while I was at it, I should get an expert's lowdown on the value of her Uncle Jake's collection."

"Oh, did she?" Sheets eyed Billy with a clear hint of recognition. "Got any proof as to who you are, Mr. DeLong?"

Startled that he'd been made, Billy said, "Just my driver's license."

Sheets smiled. "That's okay. I've got something that'll suffice. Why don't you follow me?"

Billy trailed the tiny woman to a card table stacked high with clear plastic Tupperware containers that were filled with pamphlets. Sheets picked up a container that was labeled in bold black letters, *1980–1985*, popped the top, eyed Billy, and said, "Wyoming Cattleman's Association newsletters. They go back more than twenty years. It's here somewhere," she said, flipping through the newsletters. "Yes, here it is." She slipped an insert out of one of the newsletters and handed it to Billy.

Billy broke into a smile as he thumbed through the pamphlet's familiar pages. "Price of cattle's gone way up since they printed this thing." He stopped at page twelve, where there was a full-page photograph of him standing next to his now deceased quarter horse, Smokey. A banner headline above the photograph read, "Wyoming Cattleman's Association's Cattleman of the Year— Billy DeLong."

"Knew I'd seen you somewhere before," said Sheets. "Just needed a little time for things inside my head to click. Heck of a story in there about you," she said, eyeing the pamphlet. "Some of it sounds a little—if I can say this without offending—well, Hollywood." Sheets smiled, primed to deliver her punch line. "But I'm told by the *woman* who edited that story, a woman who still edits the newsletter, by the way, that the Cattleman's Association bulletin deals only in fact."

Realizing now why a story about a man had found its way into the Equal Rights Western Heritage Museum, Billy said, "Appreciate the history lesson. So now that my credentials are in order, do you think I could get a rundown on those daguerreotypes and Covington?"

"Sure thing." Sheets glanced toward the museum's entrance, where a tubby man and a young girl stood. "Let me take care of them, and I'll be right back."

Billy thumbed through the pamphlet, recalling his often turbulent but rewarding days as a top-rung ranch foreman. He remained the only black man in the history of Wyoming to be named Cattleman of the Year and only the second man in the state's history to receive that honor not as a cattle owner and producer but as a foreman. He'd been at the top of his game back then—back when he could gauge the weight of a first-calf heifer or a rambunctious yearling within a couple of pounds while on horseback from a good thirty yards away. Back when he still had twenty-twenty vision and both of his eyes—back before insulin shots and wounds that hadn't healed quite right had become his penance for consuming too much Johnnie Walker Black for too many years. He eyed the pamphlet nostalgically one last time before setting it aside.

Loretta Sheets was back, two $20 bills clutched in her right hand, before Billy knew it. "The young girl collects old-time pulp novels with women protagonists. I find them and sell them to her."

"Looks like her daddy's hanging right in there with her," said Billy as he watched the girl and the man walk out of the museum hand in hand.

"The man with her is her grandfather," said Sheets. "Her father's in jail for beating her mother to death last month."

Billy simply shook his head.

"My sentiments exactly. Men. Sometimes I wonder if they're really human beings," Sheets said matter-of-factly. She slipped the $20 bills into a jeans pocket and dusted off her hands dismissively. "Now, back to those Covington daguerreotypes. How can I help?"

"Amanda says that you once put a value on the stash of her uncle's daguerreotypes she's got out at the Triangle Bar."

"Sure did. A year or so ago. Somewhere around a hundred thousand."

"Did you know somebody tried to break into her place about six months back? She thinks they were probably after the photos," said Billy.

"Sure did. But I think Amanda's wrong about what they were after, and I've told her that. Whoever tried to break in out there wasn't after bunches of photos, Mr. DeLong. They were more than likely after a single photo, and an impeccable, irreplaceable piece of American history, if in fact the photo exists."

"Go on," said Billy, deciding not to let Sheets in on the fact just yet that he was the Wyoming arm of a team that was investigating a murder.

"There's been speculation in academia and in the railroad collectibles community for years that Jacob Covington was present at the 1869 joining-of-the-rails ceremony at Utah's Promontory Summit, when the Golden Spike commemorating the completion of the transcontinental railroad was driven. And that he was not only there, but there with his camera. Guess you weren't expecting that," said Sheets, drinking in the surprised look on Billy's face. "Now, let me top things off with a cherry and put it all into historical perspective for you. The ceremony that day marked the completion of the last set of ties and spikes set by construction crews from the Union Pacific and the Central Pacific Railroads. The whole affair was disorganized at best, and the crowd that gathered pressed so close to the two train engines that were parked head to head on the final length of rails, the Union Pacific's Number 119 and the Central Pacific's *Jupiter,* that reporters could barely see or hear what was actually said."

"I see," said Billy. "In other words, there's lots of different versions of what actually happened that day besides what's in the history books."

"Exactly. But some things remain indisputable. The two train engines were lined up facing one another on the tracks, separated by the width of only one rail. And at twelve-forty-seven p.m., the actual last spike, an ordinary iron spike, not a golden one, was driven into a railroad tie. Now, that's where Jacob Covington and the other photographs of the event come in," said Sheets, watching the anticipatory look on Billy's face broaden.

"Three important photographs—photographs that are now world famous—arose out of the Golden Spike ceremony. One by Alfred Hart, a photographer hired by Leland Stanford, president of the Central Pacific Railroad, to make a record in still film of the construction of the entire transcontinental railroad process. A second by Colonel C. R. Savage, most notable for his documentation of Mormon involvement, or the absence of it, in the transcontinental railway process, and the third and most famous by Andrew Russell, primary photographer for the Union Pacific Railroad. The photographs all show essentially the same thing: the *Jupiter* and Number 119 sitting nose to nose with one another, pilots touching, as the two competing railroad crews form a wedge radiating out toward the camera from the two engines' point of contact. Men atop each engine, clinging to the smokestacks, can be seen hoisting bottles of champagne high in the air as down on the tracks the two chief project engineers, Samuel Montague of the Central Pacific and General Grenville Dodge of the Union Pacific, clasp hands across the very last tie at their feet."

Billy nodded, capturing the scene in his mind's eye. He paused as if memorizing a phone number, then said, "So if all three photographers shot pretty much the same picture, what's so special about Jacob Covington's photo? If it even exists?"

"That, Mr. DeLong, is the grand and glorious rub. If there is a Covington photograph, and if it still exists, it would undeniably be a daguerreotype. A daguerreotype of one of the most significant events in American history. A photograph done in a dying art form, not a wet plate, as were the photos of Hart, Savage, and Russell. And a photo shot by someone recognized today as having a significant body of very impressive but underappreciated work. In other words, the photograph would represent that needle-in-a-haystack kind of confluence of circumstances that historians and serious collectors are always looking for."

"What makes you think there really is a missin' Covington daguerreotype of the Golden Spike ceremony?"

"What else, Mr. DeLong? A woman. Like most of the photographers of that time, Jacob Covington didn't operate alone. He couldn't have. He required an assistant. Regardless of the process you were using at that time—wet print, the precursor of the modern photo we know today, with its all-important negative, or daguerreotyping—the process of producing an image was time consuming. Under the circumstances, producing a Golden Spike ceremony daguerreotype would have been exceptionally difficult. Daguerreotype cameras were awkward and cumbersome. Simply preparing the photo plate to accept an image could take twenty minutes or more. The exposures that were required were at least two to eight minutes, and the developing, fixing, and gilding of the daguerreotype itself was a five- to ten-minute chemically dependent process. Finally, the hand-coloring of the image and the all-important step of protecting and preserving the finished product demanded a final tedious five minutes." Loretta Sheets smiled. "In order to get it just right, one almost certainly had to rely on the skills of a helper, an assistant or a companion. And in Jacob Covington's case, that person was a woman."

"I get the drift," said Billy. "Who was she?"

"No one knows for sure, and I haven't been able to pin it down exactly in over twenty years of researching the subject, but the closest anyone has come to determining who Covington's assistant was, appeared in an early-1980s scholarly article out of the University of Montana. According to the paper's author, the assistant was a full-blooded Sioux Indian and a direct descendant of the famous Sioux Chief Red Cloud. The only written record of who she might have been comes from a post–Golden Spike ceremony letter of Covington's that was found in the floorboards of a hotel that burned to the ground in Helena, Montana, in the 1880s. In that letter Covington stated that a Sioux Indian woman named Sweet Owl, who, and I'm quoting pretty closely here, was skilled in the mixing of chemicals and gifted with a panoramic eye equal to that of a camera, assisted him with his photography until she disappeared after helping him at the Promontory Summit ceremony."

"And there's no mention of her anywhere else?"

"Not that I know of."

Billy pondered the new information and wondered why Amanda Hunter hadn't mentioned any of this to him. "Does Amanda know any of this?"

"I'm not sure."

"Hmmm. How'd you stumble onto it?"

"I didn't, Mr. DeLong." Loretta Sheets's tone became indignant. "Before I was a museum curator, I was a history professor over in Laramie at the University of Wyoming. I have a Ph.D. in American history, and my oft-cited dissertation, 'Women in Nineteenth-Century American Transportation,' is considered a seminal work."

"Sorry."

"No problem," said Sheets. "Look at how difficult it was for me to peg you as a famous cowman."

"Touché," said Billy with a wink. "But photography's a pretty good stretch from transportation, don't you think?"

"Not when you're dealing with the intricacies of a dissertation involving the entire history of American transportation. There's no way that photography couldn't be a part of that discussion."

"Where'd you do your studies?"

"The University of Colorado."

"Got your dissertation handy?" asked Billy.

"Yes. But only if you answer a question for me before I dig it up."

"Shoot."

"Explain to me why a break-in at the Triangle Bar Ranch would garner so much attention and send you here to the museum on what can only be described as some kind of investigation when, according to Amanda Hunter, the would-be robbers left empty-handed."

"Fair enough," said Billy. "If you'll tell me what that needle-in-a-haystack missin' daguerreotype, if it exists, might be worth."

"It would be invaluable."

"Put a number on it for me," Billy insisted.

"Let's see. An 1869 wet-plate photo done at the actual laying-of-the-rails ceremony by Russell, the priciest of the whole known triumvirate, would go for about two hundred thousand. And believe it or not, there're still some of them around. Bottom line, however, is that unlike a daguerreotype, the photo still wouldn't be one of a kind."

"What about a negative of the event? Wouldn't one of them be worth a pretty penny?"

Sheets shook her head. "No. In the world of photography, it's the original authenticated work from 1869 that has value, not the negative. Heck, they make prints of the Golden Spike ceremony today from readily available negatives that sell on the Internet for twelve ninety-five. The key to the photo's value is whether the print was actually done in 1869."

"Still need a bottom line on that price," said Billy.

Sheets paused. She looked skyward, deep in thought, and said, "A million—a million and a half. Even more if someone can validate the role that Sweet Owl played in the photo's production."

Billy let out a lengthy whistle. "Serious money."

"And then some. Let me get my dissertation for you," Sheets said proudly, walking away and limping much more noticeably than when Billy had first entered the museum.

Billy picked up a book, *African American Women in Twentieth-Century Medicine*, from a nearby table and began thumbing through it. Loretta Sheets returned, dissertation in hand, before he could finish reading the three-page introduction.

"Here you are," she said, handing Billy her bound 180-page dissertation. "Read it and weep. Now, since you still haven't told me what all the fuss is about, besides a phantom photograph and a minor break-in, mind setting the record straight?"

"Murder," said Billy, his eyes locked on hers.

Sheets took a half step backward. "What?"

"You wanted the facts," Billy said with a shrug. "A few days ago a kid named Luis Del Mora was murdered down in Denver." Billy studied Sheets's face carefully, trying to judge whether the look of shock on her face was genuine. "Del Mora was more than likely killed because he was carryin' around a book that had that high-dollar, needle-in-a-haystack daguerreotype you've been talkin' about strapped to the back cover."

"God! You're investigating a murder?"

"Nope, just helpin' out a friend." Billy opened Sheets's dissertation and scanned the title page briefly before flipping to the next. The second page contained a list of four names. Above each name there was a signature. Pointing to one of the signatures, Billy asked, "Who are these folks?"

"My committee members. Three internal and one from outside the university."

"Seems like overkill to me," said Billy, scrutinizing the bottom name and signature.

"Check and balance, Mr. DeLong. It's always good to have someone from outside the nest lend an unjaundiced eye to any evaluation."

"Did the external guy listed here give you a hard time?" asked Billy.

"No. Quite the contrary. He helped me immensely. Especially when it came to trying to dig out the truth about the Jacob Covington–Sweet Owl connection."

"I see." Billy hefted the dissertation. "How many pages you got in here about her?"

"Two, maybe three. No more than that."

"Can you photocopy 'em for me? And while you're at it, I'd appreciate a copy of that sheet with your dissertation committee members' names."

Looking surprised, Sheets said, "Fine. But why the interest in my committee members?"

Billy ran his finger along the boldly scripted signature of the lone external committee member: *Oliver Lyman, Ph.D.* "Says under Oliver Lyman's name that he's a professor at Metropolitan State College. Ain't that in Denver?"

"Yes."

"Is Lyman still there?"

"As far as I know," Sheets said hesitantly.

"Good, 'cause he's close enough to home base that he deserves at least a sniff."

Sheets laughed. It was a nervous, halfhearted, almost impetuous laugh. "Oliver Lyman a murderer? No way. The man's a leftover flower child from the 1960s. All peace and love, if you know what I mean."

"When it comes to murder, ain't no hall passes, Ms. Sheets. Not for flower children or even your highbrow professors." Billy handed Sheets the dissertation. "I'd sure appreciate it if you'd make me them copies."

Looking at Billy as if she were suddenly just a hair off her game, she said, "Sure thing," turned, and limped toward the front of the museum. Billy followed closely, pondering just how Loretta Sheets fitted into the broad scope of things.

CHAPTER 17

Billy's drive from Cheyenne, a drive that would take him south of Wyoming's famed Snowy Range Mountains and ultimately home to Baggs, started as a troubled one. During the first half hour, all he could think about was whether Amanda Hunter had told the truth about her uncle's photographs. It seemed strange to him that she wouldn't have known about a daguerreotype photograph worth a million dollars or more, and stranger still that during his and CJ's visit, Amanda had never gotten around to mentioning her uncle's Union Pacific Railroad connection. Covington had been a Union Pacific doctor, after all. It was spelled out in black and white in the Montana medicine book. CJ had said so himself. That connection alone could be the key to the missing one-of-a-kind daguerreotype, Billy told himself as he gassed up his ten-year-old dually in the foothills town of Woods Landing. There had to be an explanation for the oversight, Billy tried to convince himself.

He paid for his gas and called CJ from his cell phone, aware that something about Amanda Hunter had penetrated his rough-cut cowboy exterior.

"CJ, you there?" Billy said into the mouthpiece, his unmistakable gravelly baritone competing with a rumbling convoy of flatbed trucks loaded with hay for high-country cattle. "Got the lowdown on why the Del Mora kid probably bought it."

"Shout it out, Billy. The background noise is drowning you out."

"I said, I know why Del Mora bought it. He was probably packin' around a photograph worth at least a million inside that book he sold you. Loretta Sheets, that museum lady Amanda told us about, claims Jacob Covington took one of them daguerreotype photos of the transcontinental railroad Golden Spike ceremony back in 1869. Accordin' to her, the photo's been floatin' around out there somewhere for years."

"Gives you a motive for murder, doesn't it?" said CJ. "What's the museum lady's tie-in to all this?"

Billy lowered his voice as the last truck in the convoy rumbled past. "She used to be a college history professor. Did her Ph.D. dissertation on the history of women in the transportation industry. Her link to Covington is hooked up to the fact that our picture-takin' sawbones supposedly had an assistant, an Indian woman that Sheets stumbled across while she was doin' her research. And believe me, after talkin' with Sheets, you can take it as gospel that this woman existed 'cause Sheets never would've been interested in Covington's photos if there wasn't a woman linked to 'em somehow."

"Interesting. More interesting if you include the good Professor Lyman back here in Denver. All of a sudden we've got history professors coming out both ears. Anything else she let you in on?"

Hesitant to share his concerns about Amanda Hunter until he'd had more time to think things through, Billy said, "Got some more on Lyman that'll interest you." He was about to go into detail when a second bevy of semis rumbled by. "Gonna lose you to the noise," Billy shouted.

"Where are you?" CJ asked, yelling into the phone.

"Woods Landing."

"Call me back when the traffic dies down."

"Will do," said Billy. "Gotta run and buy a couple of packs of Doublemint anyway. Talk to you in a couple of minutes," he said, hanging up. He watched the line of trucks lumber by in the mid-day sun, concerned more than ever that Amanda Hunter probably knew more about the missing daguerreotype than she was telling.

Theresa Del Mora had tried all morning to grease the wheels so Flora Jean could talk to Howard Stafford, but without any luck. She'd finally called Flora Jean to admit that Stafford would probably be more accommodating and candid if he could talk to a man. "He's not a bad man," Theresa lamented. "Just set in his ways."

Puzzled over Theresa's wellspring of loyalty, Flora Jean countered, "You sure stick up for that man, sugar. The two of you got somethin' goin'?"

"He signs my check," Theresa said, noticeably offended. "And I sign yours. You're going to have to find out what you want to know about him on your own," she added curtly and hung up.

Twenty minutes later, still puzzled by the Theresa Del Mora–Howard Stafford connection, Flora Jean sat across from a buoyant-looking CJ in her office. CJ, his feet propped up on a chair, had just finished laying out the needle-in-a-haystack daguerreotype story Billy had told him. "Now we have something to go on."

Flora Jean shook her head. "Trust me, we ain't goin' nowhere with this Del Mora thing without knowin' more about Stafford, and he ain't talkin'."

CJ toyed with the stubbed-out remnant of a cheroot and smiled. "There's always more than one way to skin a cat, Flora Jean. For instance, Morgan and Dittier spent most of last night moving themselves and everything worth a nickel out of Ike's and into my garage. I decided that it was in my best interest to do an end-around Sergeant Commons, city engineers, and any other ruling party with not a thing in the world to lose if all my shit got stolen from under their noses."

"And your point is?"

"Just this. We do an end-around Stafford. Find out more about him than he knows about himself—from somebody else."

"Got any candidates?"

"One. Paul Grimes."

"You kiddin' me? That lowlife, muckrakin', yellow journalism snot?"

"He helped us with the Langston Blue case last year, didn't he?"

"And he also almost got your ass killed by some rogue CIA agent in the process, in case you forgot."

"I haven't forgotten. You got a better angle for us to pursue?"

"Not at the moment," said Flora Jean, looking as though she'd just been checkmated.

"Good. Because not even somebody as rich as Stafford likes losing something worth a million dollars, and if anybody has inside dope on Stafford, it'll be Grimes."

"Gotta admit this whole Del Mora killin' seems kinda rich-folk freaky to me. First off, why would anyone keep a photograph worth that much money sittin' around on a library shelf inside a book?"

"Could be it wasn't. Maybe the book or the photo were some-where else when they were stolen."

"Where?"

"Haven't figured that out. And maybe the photo was in the library and inside the book all along. I'm just saying we need to keep an open mind."

"Fine," Flora Jean said. "For the moment, I'll give Stafford the benefit of the doubt. But I ain't changin' my take on Oliver Lyman. Lyman's in this thing up to his nose hairs. His signature on the front page of Loretta Sheets's dissertation proves he knew about the photograph. Might be worth me payin' him another visit."

"Probably, but there's always the possibility that Sheets played Billy a little so we'd go tracking after Lyman instead of her."

"So which way do we head?" asked Flora Jean.

"I root out Stafford using Paul Grimes, you have your second dance with Lyman, and we regroup."

"That'll work. What about Counts and that security guy Van-nick? I've got a boatload on the two of them."

"Bad people?" CJ asked, checking his watch.

Flora Jean shrugged. "Vannick would like you to think he is. As for Counts, he ain't nothin' but a bag full of stale air."

"Think either one of them could've killed Del Mora?" asked CJ, picking up Flora Jean's phone, hoping to catch up with Paul Grimes before he headed out for his noonday jaunt to the Den-ver Press Club to drink his lunch.

Flora Jean smiled and watched CJ dial. "For a photograph worth a million bucks, sugar? Ain't no doubt about it in the world."

The Denver Press Club, a watering hole where hard-drinking newshounds could commiserate and vent their spleen, had undergone a much-needed recent interior facelift. Luckily the renovations hadn't cost the venerable old club its sense of history or the offbeat press-room charm that patrons loved.

Paul Grimes, a press club member for close to thirty years, spent three late afternoons a week, elbows anchored to the far end of the first-floor bar, tossing back gin and tonics and chasing them with handfuls of whole walnuts that he carried with him by the mason jar.

Grimes usually arrived at the club for thirty minutes of imbibing before a five-thirty meal. He'd agreed to meet CJ at four-thirty because it would mean an extra hundred dollars and an additional half hour at the bar. Ill-mannered, crass, New York City abrasive, and as good an investigative reporter as the *Rocky Mountain News* had ever seen, Grimes was standing near the club's leaded glass front windows, gin and tonic in hand, when CJ walked in.

"CJ, my man," Grimes called out, spotting CJ as he reached the top of the stairway that led into the club's front lounge, a room dominated by its bar and the smell of whiskey, leather chairs, and oak.

CJ removed his Stetson and set it on a nearby table. "Paul." He smiled and pumped Grimes's drink-free hand.

"What are you drinking?" Grimes asked as if CJ were missing an article of clothing.

"I'll do a beer. Negra Modelo if they've got it."

Grimes turned and called out to the bartender, "A Negra Modelo over here for my riverboat-machine-gunning friend." Turning back to CJ, he said, "Park it over there," motioning for CJ to take a seat in one of the room's high-backed leather chairs. "I'll get your beer." Grimes strolled to the bar, aware from the look on CJ's face that his machine-gunner remark had tweaked a deep-rooted nerve in CJ's psyche but unfazed by the reaction.

Hoping to get the information he needed from the quixotic reporter as quickly as possible, CJ asked as Grimes handed him a Negra Modelo in the bottle with a wedge of lime, "Did you bring that interview you mentioned on the phone?"

"Not so fast, my antique-dealing friend. First we need to settle up."

CJ pulled out his wallet and extracted a $100 bill.

Grimes smiled. "Hell, man, I don't mean that settlement. I'm talking about the real money the two of us are gonna make on the story I'm thinking of piecing together about that antiques store of yours getting blown to smithereens."

"What?"

"Don't look so torn and twisted, my man. Hell, you're sitting on a natural-born, made-for-TV gold mine of a story, my friend." Grimes raised both arms, held up two fingers of each hand, and jiggled them quotation-marks style. "Navy Cross–winning bail bondsman turned antiques dealer stalked by vengeful Rhodes Scholar Indian maiden. Hell, the story's got Hollywood stamped all over it. And it's tabloid fodder for sure."

"Are you out of your mind?"

Grimes looked offended. "You've gotta seize the moment, friend."

"What the hell do you know about *my* story, Grimes?"

Grimes mounted an ear-to-ear grin. "All there is to know, my man. All there is. Shit, I've been piecing *your* story together since late last year. Getting the facts, knitting together the whole nine yards, filling in holes that other people would've certainly missed. I got wind of the Deepstream woman wanting to settle a score with you from one of the boys down at Homicide right in the middle of when I was researching that Langston Blue thing for you last year. Been following up ever since. Shit, what we've got here, CJ, is pretty much a daytime soap-opera serial. And right on cue, just like magic, the whole thing gets programmed for sweeps week when our Indian maiden bombs the hell out of your store. Catch her or kill her and you can pretty much name your price."

Unable to check his temper, CJ grabbed Grimes by his jacket lapels and lifted the suddenly wide-eyed 145-pound man off the floor. "People have told me you're crazy," said CJ, nose to nose with Grimes. "And you just proved it. I don't know how you worked your way into this Deepstream thing, who the cop was that gave you inside dope, or why you ever thought I'd agree to you sifting around in my life, but it's time to stop the presses." CJ released his grip, and, landing askew, Grimes wobbled momentarily from side to side.

Trying his best to look unperturbed, Grimes gulped in a breath of air. Eyeing CJ and the suddenly nervous-looking bartender, Grimes said, "Didn't know I'd tickle such a raw nerve."

"You did. Try not to tickle it again."

"Read you," said Grimes, breathing heavily as he tried to reenergize the two most powerful tools in his investigative journalism arsenal: his gall and his composure.

"Glad you do," said CJ, realizing that his heart was racing. "Now, can we get back to the reason we're here?"

"Got that Stafford piece right here." Grimes slipped the yellowed, trifolded newspaper feature he'd done on Howard Stafford ten years earlier out of his shirt pocket. "Sized Stafford up right off when I did this piece. Not an ounce of bullshit in it. The man's all about money and collectibles." Grimes unfolded the paper and handed it to CJ.

CJ scanned the story's headline: "Serious and Selective: Howard Stafford Unvarnished." He asked, "How'd you get Stafford to agree to talk to you?"

Grimes flashed CJ the sly, penetrating smile of a manipulator. "Easy. I intimated to him that I'd give him the chance to set the record straight on all the bad press he'd gotten over the years, counter the stories about him being a half-off-his-rocker pervert of a recluse. Of course I didn't say it like that. I simply said that I'd give him the opportunity to talk about his interests, his triumphs, and his everyday decency. And that I'd give him space to talk about his number-one passion: collecting the rarest of the rare."

"And he bit, just like that? Strange. From what I've heard about the man, I'd've figured he'd never let a muckraker like you through the front gate."

Grimes jaw muscles flexed, and both eyes narrowed. "Don't sell me short, Floyd. I wasn't always what I am now. I was top-drawer material back when you were babysitting that machine gun of yours during Vietnam." Grimes grunted dismissively and continued proudly, "Read my article and see what I got. In case you don't, here's the bottom line. Stafford's family made their money brokering oil and gas leases in Kansas, Colorado, Utah, and Wyoming right after World War II. His father was a D-Day veteran and a son of a bitch. His grandfather was meaner still. His mother drank, and his two brothers, both of 'em dead by the time I interviewed him, whored. He collects rare artifacts, ephemera, tapestries, pottery, and books because, according to him—and this is a direct quote—they suit him, tell a story, and most of all, they don't talk back. He made a point of telling me three times during our interview that never once during a near lifelong trek through the antique and rare collectibles world has he ever been outbid at an auction."

"Sounds determined."

"As a fucking pit bull," Grimes said, nodding. "My guess is you'd have to kill him to get him off if he ever sank his teeth into you." Grimes shook his head. "Believe me, he's one hell of a dichotomous man. The SOB raises prize roses by the truckload. Showed me a strain of prizewinning Mr. Lincolns that go back a hundred and fifty years. He champions people he sees as downtrodden and powerless because, according to him, his old man whipped his young powerless ass a couple of times a day. And on top of all that, he claims to read four or five books on American history every week."

"Complex man."

"And a sad one. I came away from our interview feeling like I'd been peeking in the women's bathroom, and for me that's saying a hell of a lot."

"Did Stafford put any limits on what you could say in the story?"

"No. Just asked me to let him see the piece before I ran it. And I did. The only thing he changed was a reference I made to him being worth close to a hundred and fifty million. Blacked it out and inserted one seventy-five."

"Narcissistic bugger."

"Absolutely. And he's proud of it."

"Did your story do what he expected?"

"I'm not sure. He never complained about it, though."

"Ever talk to him again?"

"Just once. At a Rockies game, a couple of years after that sorry excuse for a baseball franchise landed here in Colorado. He was seated alone in the next-to-last row of one of the Coors Field upper decks. I guess he sticks to the cheap seats to preserve his anonymity in public. I remembered from the interview that he was a baseball nut. He recognized me and said hi. The Rockies were behind by a couple of runs. When I asked him if he thought they'd ever win a pennant, he smiled and said, 'Nope,' adding pointedly, like someone with inside knowledge, that top to bottom, the whole damn organization lacked guts."

"He was right on that point," said CJ, a hapless Rockies fan himself. CJ eyed Grimes's article one last time before folding it slowly. "Mine to keep?"

"Sure is."

"I'll make it my bedtime story."

"Good reading," said Grimes. "But you won't find any more gold nuggets in there than what I just handed you." He eyed CJ quizzically. "Why are you dogging Stafford anyway?"

When CJ didn't answer, Grimes said, "I mine swamp gas for a living, Floyd, or have you forgotten? You can tell me now or I'll find out later."

Aware that Grimes was telling the truth, CJ said, "The son of one of Stafford's employees turned up dead a few days back."

"And you think Stafford's involved?"

"Don't know. Right now, as you'd say, I'm just mining for nuggets."

Grimes thoughtfully fingered the cleft in his chin. "Why'd the kid buy it?"

"The best I can figure, he stole a photograph of Stafford's that was worth a lot of money, and somebody either wanted it or wanted it back."

"How much money?"

"A million at least."

"Chump change for Stafford," said Grimes, shaking his head. "Don't think he'd get involved in anything as squirrelly as a murder for that kind of money."

"Maybe he hired out the job."

"Nope," Grimes said with a grin. "Read my article. He's not the kind that uses middlemen. Got any other suspects?"

"Damn, Grimes. You sound like a cop."

"Just trying to offer you a free point of view."

CJ shrugged. "I've got a few maybes and a couple of Stafford contacts I want to take a hard look at. A onetime librarian named Counts and a security-systems specialist, Arthur Vannick."

Grimes's head arched back. "You're shittin' me!"

"No reason to do that."

"Then you've stumbled onto one hell of a gigantic nugget today, my friend. Counts I've never heard of. But Vannick, now, he's a whole different story. He's a self-promoting loudmouth with a boatload full of bullshit. He says he was in the Secret Service. He wasn't. Claims to be a Vietnam vet. He's not. Boasts that he has underworld connections. I doubt it. *And* he's got a record. Did four years in our state's delightful penal institution for men in Canon City. Should've gotten life."

CJ whistled. "And your connection to Vannick is?"

"I did a *Denver Post* exposé on him back when he was running a commodities scheme based out of Miami. He was milking wads of money out of a couple of leaders of half-baked *juntas* down

Central America way and squeezing shekels out of a dozen or so Miami businessmen and politicians dumb enough to listen to his song and dance."

CJ's eyes widened. "Did he do any business in Nicaragua?"

"Couldn't prove he did. Why? You got anybody from Central America on your suspects list?"

CJ slipped a pack of cheroots out of his vest pocket and tapped one out. "My, my, my. Nope. But the kid who was killed was from Nicaragua."

"Well, if he screwed with Vannick, he screwed with the wrong man," Grimes said knowingly.

"Why's that?"

"Those four years Vannick did in Canon City weren't because of his Ponzi deals and white-collar stuff. The time he did was for manslaughter."

"Who'd he kill?"

"A business partner. Accidentally, of course."

CJ lit his cheroot, glanced out one of the press club's windows toward a line of slow-moving traffic, and said, "How much time have you got, Grimes? I'd like to hear more about Mr. Vannick."

Grimes looked over toward the bar and smiled. "All evening if need be."

"Why so giving?"

"Just call it my early-April Christmas spirit," said Grimes, both eyes narrowing to a hateful squint. "After my story on Vannick ran, the son of a bitch threatened me, and believe it or not, warm and loving human that I am, until now I've never had a chance to return the favor."

CHAPTER 18

Celeste Deepstream had just finished inspecting her kill spot: a peeling unmaintained billboard that touted the gastronomic virtues of a long-defunct Denver restaurant. It rose thirty-five feet above a self-serve parking lot on the south side of 13th Avenue and sat a mere thirty yards from the Victorian building that housed Floyd & Benson's Bail Bonds and CJ Floyd's apartment. Fortunately for her, the antiquated advertising canvas lacked the stadium-style halogen lighting of its contemporary counterparts.

Now, as she sat in the half-full parking lot below looking up at the billboard, locked safely behind the tinted windows of the pickup that Alexie Borg had lent her after she'd crawled back to him and acquiescently given him the sexual ride of his life, she couldn't help but think that after so many failures and false starts, she was about to finally enjoy success.

The night time is the right time, she told herself, humming the refrain from the Ray Charles classic. Her execution would have to be letter-perfect, and she'd have to kill Floyd in that fleeting, perfect time between the end of day and the cusp of darkness, when there was still enough light for her to see her target but insufficient light for the random bystander or passing motorist to see her. She knew she could do it.

She still needed scores of additional practice runs down at

Alexie's second home in the Black Forest outside Colorado Springs. But she'd find perfection. She'd have to learn to scale the ladder that led to the billboard's catwalk a bit more quickly, and she now knew that she would have to crawl instead of duck-walk along the catwalk in order to take advantage of its protective twilight shadows. She knew she could do all that as well.

For now, in the light of day she would simply drink in the lay of the land and watch Floyd's Victorian for activity. During the twenty-five minutes she'd been there, Floyd hadn't made an appearance. But she knew he would. Sooner or later, everyone had to come back home.

Calculating distances and imagining trajectories in her head, she took in the surroundings for several more minutes before, disappointed at not seeing Floyd, she cranked the truck's engine, aware that thirty minutes on the premises made her a parking patron; any longer stay risked transforming her into a recognizable nuisance. As she drove out of the parking lot, she watched a petite woman carrying a leather briefcase mount the front steps of Floyd's building. The woman, dressed in a light tan trench-coat and fashionable business pumps, had the unmistakable look of a lawyer. She was probably there to meet Floyd's partner, the Benson woman, and massage some legal angle that would wrangle a client out of jail, Celeste reasoned.

But she was wrong. What the briefcase-toting green-eyed Puerto Rican woman was delivering to Flora Jean was background information on the building of the transcontinental railroad, along with a dossier filled with information about a fugitive onetime Olympian, and former Rhodes Scholar, who had been on the run from the law for more than two years. Celeste also had no way of knowing, as Flora Jean Benson and Julie Madrid hugged each other in the building's doorway, that the two women were as tenacious about protecting Floyd as she was determined to kill him.

Theodore Counts's half scowl mirrored Arthur Vannick's angular, tight-lipped glare. For the past half hour the two men had been staring one another down and nursing mugs of bitter black coffee in the dimly lit alcove of the Boar's Breath restaurant and bar, a seedy, out-of-the-way watering hole for ski bums and mountain men cloistered behind a string of spruce trees in the mountain town of Silverthorne, Colorado, sixty-nine miles west of Denver.

Neither man had enjoyed the trek to the mountains, but since they couldn't risk being seen arm in arm with one another in Denver, the Boar's Breath, a favorite weekend haunt of Vannick's during his college days twenty years earlier, though he hadn't set foot in it for close to two decades, had been chosen.

Counts set aside his coffee mug, scooped up a handful of pretzels from a wooden bowl in the center of their table, and pointed a finger accusingly at Vannick. "You're the one with shit stains in his drawers, my friend, and that Benson woman was savvy enough to sniff them out."

"Ease up on the finger pointing, Counts. She just happened to contact me more recently. The issue here isn't her timing— the issue is, we've got a problem that needs resolving."

"For once you're right. If that Benson bitch digs deep enough into your bag of dirty laundry, she's going to find out that we have a connection, and if she's got a brain that's half the size of her tits, she'll start piecing things together. I told you to be wary of that Del Mora kid from the start."

"Screw what you told me, Teddy," said Vannick, aware that the effeminate Counts preferred to be called Theodore or Ted—anything but Teddy. "I went with what I thought was the best game plan."

"And it didn't work."

"It scored us twenty-six grand, didn't it?"

Counts let out a snort. "When the upside was scoring a million. There you go again, trying to add sugar to a bitter taste. I knew I never should've hooked up with your prevaricating ass."

Vannick grinned. "But you did, didn't you, Teddy?" He reached out and pinched Counts's cheek. "Now, since you're so sad about that twenty-six grand, maybe you should just give back your half of it."

"Touch me again and I'll give you more than that."

"Can the tough stuff, Teddy. You haven't got the balls."

"Wanta try me?" Counts teased back the lapel of his sport coat. The butt of a .38 jutted from the inside pocket.

"Flash that thing again, you fucking halfwit, and I'll make you eat it."

"Sure, you will." Counts laughed and patted his coat pocket. "Don't try and con me, Arthur. I've seen your whole sorry act. What you need to be doing, Mr. Secret Service man, instead of selling me a bunch of wolf tickets you can't back up, is covering our rear. That Benson woman's one thing. Cops are a whole different matter."

"Don't tell me what to do when it comes to cops, Teddy. I've already had a visit from the red-headed bumbler in charge of the Del Mora case. Some junior-leaguer named Commons."

"What?"

"Don't blow a gasket, Teddy-boy. He's been talking to anybody who had anything to do with the remodeling of the Stafford library, right down to the guys who stained the oak. He'll get around to you soon enough."

"And you haven't said a word to me about it until now?"

"Shit, man. You've got a gun." Vannick forced back a snicker. "When he gets around to your lame ass, why not just shoot him?"

"Don't laugh, you idiot. There's a difference between a real cop and some overeager big-titted sista."

"Calm down, Teddy. Commons simply asked me what my role was in remodeling Stafford's new library. I told him security. Every question after that was gravy."

"Did he ask about me?"

"Of course. And I told him the truth. That you're a pompous wannabe self-important asshole. Doesn't matter what I said anyway. He'll never figure we're connected in a million years."

"Did he know about the daguerreotype?"

"Shit, no. He barely knew about the Montana medicine book. Hell, I ended up getting more information out of him than he got out of me. Found out that the last guy to have the book in his possession was a South Broadway antiques dealer named Floyd. A black guy. And believe it or not, the other day somebody blew up Floyd's store."

Counts stroked his chin thoughtfully. "What did your cop say Floyd's first name was?"

"Didn't have one. Seems to like using his initials. CT, or maybe it was TG, something like that," said Vannick.

"Damn!"

"You know him?"

"I know of him by way of my community connections. The last I heard, though, he was a bail bondsman."

"Guess he changed careers."

"Yeah, a big change. Most of what I know about him comes from the do-gooder father of the woman Floyd's sweet on, a guy named Willis Sundee. The old fucker." Counts sucked a stream of air between the gap in his front teeth. "I'll do some checking."

"You sound ticked, Teddy. What did the girlfriend's daddy do you out of?"

"My job and almost my pension," Counts said, his voice charged with anger. "Somehow I recall someone mentioning that Floyd and that Benson woman were connected." Counts shot a quizzical glance at Vannick.

"Don't look at me. Five Points is your territory, Teddy."

"Appears I haven't been doing a good enough job of mining it."

Vannick shook his head. "So what's new? You're that fucking out of touch? Shit, no wonder word on the street has it you're a damn Oreo."

"Screw you. I've got a wire, and I've got my reasons for keeping the folks on the Points at arm's length."

"And I bet it has a bunch to do with that downscaled pension you're always griping about. Folks down there got something on your ass you don't want to talk about, Teddy?"

"Mind your own business, Vannick."

"I am, and my business right now is finding out where that missing daguerreotype is. The one you claimed you had a laser lock on, in case you've forgotten."

"Who knows? It could be on its way to Europe or Central America by now."

"I don't think so. We're talking American history here, not the history of Europe or the week-long story of some banana republic. That photo's right here in the States; you can count on it."

"Yeah. And so's the Empire State Building. Bottom line is, after all my years of chasing the thing, I still don't have it."

"But we have that Floyd connection. Could be that whoever blew up his store has the photo."

"Maybe." Counts sounded unconvinced. "But my guess is that Floyd's prior life as a bail bondsman bought him a whole suitcase full of enemies."

"Wasn't you who blew up his place, was it?" asked Vannick with a wink.

"No. Besides, unlike some people, I don't profess to have under-world connections."

Vannick cocked an eye in defiance. "My people would've killed Floyd if they had any hint he had that photo, trust me."

"Yeah, yeah, yeah."

"Don't mock me, you fucking gun toter! I can have you killed in half the time it takes to inhale. Could be you killed the Del Mora kid and you already have the damn photo."

"Ditto, my friend."

The two men stared each other down until Counts finally said, "Best come up with a plan, Mr. Wiseguy."

"And if I don't?"

"Then a million bucks walks, and we come out of this clearing a paltry twenty-six thousand."

Vannick took a sip of his tepid coffee and nodded thought-fully. "Brings us back to Floyd."

"And our Stafford problem. Don't forget he gave us a time-line for coming up with a new library design and security plan."

"Screw Stafford. We need to have somebody take a long, hard look at your former bail bondsman," said Vannick.

"Got somebody in mind?"

"Sure do."

"Who?"

Vannick laughed, suddenly all bravado. "You blind, Teddy? I did Secret Service detail, remember? Who do you think can zero in on Floyd better than me?"

Counts didn't answer, wondering as he watched Vannick's eyes light up in anticipation whether the prevaricating security-systems salesman had ever been to DC, much less served as a Secret Service agent, and whether he actually had what it took to track a man like Floyd. Even more, he wondered if Vannick possessed that essence of darkness that he knew it took to kill someone.

Everything seemed out of scale and more ominous to Celeste now that it was dusk. The billboard's catwalk seemed that much higher, the empty parking lot looked larger and more intimidating, and the distances, especially the thirty yards between the billboard and Floyd's office, seemed somehow to have doubled. But none of that mattered. What mattered was the pain of losing her brother and the sorrow she'd lived with for the past eight years—and, of course, killing Floyd.

She climbed the ladder and slipped through the catwalk access as the quiet of the evening enveloped the day. The air was unusually moist, and the temperature, which had been falling since late afternoon, now hovered at forty degrees.

Dressed from head to toe in black, she was wearing leather gloves with the thumb, index, and middle fingers cut back to the knuckle. A four-foot-long boomerang-shaped hard plastic case sat on the catwalk next to her. She stretched out prone twenty feet above the asphalt, looked directly at the front door of Floyd's building, and watched a light-beige pickup pull away from the curb in front. A neon sign in Floyd's front yard flashed alternating red and yellow messages—"Bail Bonds Anytime—24 Hours a Day." Moments earlier a woman had rushed out of the building next door and jumped into the truck. Binoculars to her eyes, Celeste could see that the woman was crying. She wondered what the crime of the person the woman cared enough about to bring tears had been. Perhaps she was crying for her brother.

The truck moved toward Celeste, its headlights aimed directly at the billboard's I-beam supports before it turned onto 13th Avenue and faded into the twilight. The glare was unnerving and disconcerting enough to cause Celeste to momentarily rethink her plan. Maybe she needed to kill Floyd in the blackness of night, when she could be certain that no one would be around to witness it, or perhaps she should dispense with him at first light, killing him before the city awoke. She eyed the plastic case and brought it to her as if it were a long-lost lover. *No,* she told herself. *I've practiced too hard, spent too much time perfecting my timing, and logged too many hours honing an escape because of Moradi-Nik's stupidity to change things now.*

For now she would remain a flat board in darkness, a loose piece of scaffolding that no one could see, and she'd do what she'd come to do without altering her plan. Confident that she'd seen enough for one evening, she scooted along the catwalk and descended the ladder, wondering whether the woman who'd rushed from the building next to Floyd's was still crying and whether, like her, the woman would be seared inside and guilt-ridden forever because she hadn't done all she could for her loved one.

CJ smiled at Morgan and Dittier's inventiveness. After losing their home on the back porch of Ike's Spot, they'd set up new digs in the back of his garage without missing a beat. "You're back off the streets, for now at least. Bunk here as long as you like," said CJ, shaking his head in amazement at the garage's cluttered transformation. "It's not as stylish as what you had, but it's livable."

"It'll work, won't it, Dittier?" said Morgan.

Reading Morgan's lips, Dittier shot Morgan an affirmative thumbs-up grin.

"Dittier looks like he just ate the canary," said CJ, turning to leave.

"Nope," said Morgan, mussing what was left of the skinny rodeo clown's thinning hair. "He's just happy to have a place to call home. And so am I. Thanks," Morgan called out to a retreating CJ.

A late-evening, misty mountain chill filled the Queen City's air as Oliver Lyman, cell phone clutched in his right hand, headed for his car with a bucket of chicken tucked under his other arm. Three eager undergrads from his honors elective in American history were waiting for Lyman and the chicken back at the Metro State campus, and experience had taught him that the bucket's contents would be devoured in no time. Teaching had its drawbacks, but it also had perks. The money stank, but the youthful energy of a college campus clearly made up for it, and soon the money, or lack of it, wouldn't matter. Soon the only thing that would matter would be enjoying a way of life he'd worked for years to carve out for himself. He'd done his time in the academic trenches, twenty-five years, and in all that time he'd been patient, less than controversial, and compliant. And now, after all that time, after all the boring faculty dinners, the kissing up to petty administrators, and the traveling to meaningless conferences, he'd have his big score.

He reached his car, looked back toward the glow from the brightly lit KFC bucket in the mist, opened the door, and placed the bucket of chicken on the front seat. He flipped his cell phone open, punched in a phone number, and shut the car door before uncapping the bucket, extracting a chicken wing, and taking a bite. "I'm still waiting on my money," he said into the phone the instant he heard the familiar voice on the other end.

"Are you eating something?"

"Chicken."

"Didn't your mother tell you it's impolite to talk with food in your mouth?"

"I never had a mother. Just like I don't have my money. I'm getting tired of waiting."

"No need to wait much longer. Your ship came in today."

"You've said that before," Lyman protested.

"And I was wrong. Today I'm right."

"That would be a change."

"Don't press it, Professor. I could change my mind." The high-pitched response brimmed with irritation.

"You wouldn't chance it."

"Don't be so sure."

"Don't cross me." Lyman took another bite of chicken. "I delivered on my part of the deal."

"Not exactly."

"So there were some glitches. You got the photo."

"That I did."

"So cough up my money!"

"You'll get it tonight. Same place as before."

"Good. And then we're done," said Lyman.

"Done."

"Don't short-change me," warned Lyman. "I've documented everything, and I've got myself a hole card just in case."

"I'm not stupid, Professor."

"Didn't think so. How about meeting in fifteen minutes?"

"Works for me."

"How big a wad is forty thousand dollars?"

"Big enough to fill a tote bag."

"I like that," said Lyman. "Sounds so life-expanding."

"Save the philosophy session for class, and be there in fifteen minutes."

"I'll be there," said Lyman, taking a final bite of chicken and tossing the bone out the window. "And I intend to count every dollar before leaving."

"Your call."

"It's been my call from the beginning, or have you forgotten who hooked this up? I'll see you in a few minutes."

Lyman closed his cell phone, opened the car's glove compartment, slipped out a four-inch-long hunting knife, which he placed on the seat next to him, and wiggled the toes of his right foot, making certain his insurance policy was right where he'd put it two hours earlier. Moments later he was heading south on Speer Boulevard, cruising along at nearly double the thirty-miles-per-hour speed limit, oblivious to the meeting with his students—that, after all, could wait.

CHAPTER 19

Arthur Vannick browsed the Silverthorne Outlet Mall for close to half an hour after his meeting with Counts, ending his shopping trek with a fish sandwich and fries at an empty Burger King before topping off his gas tank and heading back for Denver. Scoring less than $30,000 on a million-dollar gambit was a bad return, and having to share half the money with a self-hating black man was even worse, he kept reminding himself all the way home to the Queen City.

Once home his thoughts turned to where things might have gone wrong in his quest to find the missing daguerreotype. All the thefts of books from the Stafford library had gone like clockwork, so he couldn't help but wonder if Counts wasn't lying to him, and whether he'd already found and disposed of the daguerreotype. Counts, after all, had been bold enough to flash a gun at him up in Silverthorne. Could be he'd had the balls to use the gun on Del Mora. He'd give it some thought while he went about finding out about the antiques dealer Counts had now mentioned twice, CJ Floyd.

"Bad choice," said Flora Jean, standing in the middle of her office and shaking her head at CJ. "Whattaya plan to do when Sergeant

Commons gets wind of the fact that you took all your stuff outta Ike's? Sure as hell, he ain't gonna like it."

"I'll tell him I was robbed," CJ said with a smile.

"Come off it, CJ. The man ain't stupid."

"Screw him. It's my stuff. It's not material to the Del Mora murder, and Commons has already sifted through it twice. Worst comes to worst, I'll plead ignorance."

Flora Jean grinned. "You been talkin' to Julie?"

"Who else? She said that if Commons presses the issue, the most any judge would do would be to give me a lecture about not interfering with an ongoing police investigation, slap me with a trespassing charge, and fine me a couple of hundred bucks."

"Speakin' of your own personal Clarence Darrow in a skirt, she dropped some books off for you yesterday just as I was gettin' ready to leave for the day. They're over on the table next to the coffee bar."

"Great," said CJ, walking over to the coffee alcove. "I called her after I talked to Paul Grimes. Asked her to dig up everything she could on Howard Stafford and to find me some books on the 1869 laying-of-the-rails ceremony."

"Well, she did. And I took a look through 'em, hopin' to give myself a history lesson worth a million bucks."

CJ hefted the books one by one, scanning the titles. *Building the Pacific Railway; Nothing Like It in the World; Iron Horses to Promontory;* and *Westward to Promontory.* "Wonder where she found these?"

"From a book store that specializes in railroad history over on South Broadway," she said. "And she said for me to tell you that you owe her fifty-five bucks."

CJ smiled, aware that when he offered to reimburse his former secretary, whom he'd extracted from a physically abusive marriage by jamming her then-husband's head down a toilet and threatening to fracture his skull or worse the next time he bothered her, Julie would refuse the money.

CJ opened the second-largest of the three books, *Iron Horses to Promontory*, thumbed through the table of contents, and flipped to page fifty-five. "Here's what all the fuss is about," he said, walking back to Flora Jean and pointing to Andrew Russell's famous laying-of-the-rails photograph.

"Who are all the men millin' around the tracks and hangin' off them two train engines?" Flora Jean asked, studying the photo.

"A mix of everyday workers and the two chief engineers of the project, the caption says."

"Not a woman among them or a black face either," protested Flora Jean.

"It was 1869, Flora Jean."

"So history turns out to be a bunch of scraggly-lookin' white boys puffin' and posturin' for the camera, lookin' for all the world like they just hit the Lotto. A million bucks for a photo of that. Shit, looks pretty much like a picture of one of them University of Colorado fraternity parties to me."

"It's not the people in the photo that make it valuable. What makes it valuable, according to what Billy DeLong's told me, is the fact that there were so few real-time photos actually taken of such a historic event." CJ set down the open book, picked up a smaller green book, *Building the Pacific Railway*, scanned the table of contents, and flipped to the C. R. Savage photo. "Pretty much the same," he said, comparing the two photographs. "And I'm betting the third photograph, the one by Hart, is probably identical. Looks like I'll have to do some reading. Did Julie have any insights?"

"Not really. The only thing she said as she was leavin' was, 'And they think we have robber barons now.'"

Looking pensive, CJ closed the books and set them aside. "So much for our history lesson. How about filling me in on what you came up with on Counts and Vannick?"

"No need to read up on those two. They're pretty much open books. Counts is a pompous Oreo. How he ended up with an office in a library in the middle of Five Points is beyond me."

"Contacts, I'd wager," said CJ.

"Or havin' dirt on somebody."

"Umm, maybe. Did it seem to you like Counts had what it would take to kill someone?"

"Couldn't tell. He was too busy blowin' smoke and oglin' my chest."

"Looks like we'll have to do a little more serious checking on Brother Counts," said CJ.

"Where you gonna look?"

"I've got sources."

"Willis?" Flora Jean said knowingly.

"Who else?" said CJ, aware that if anyone could come up with the goods on a bombastic wannabe-white windbag like Counts, it would be Mavis Sundee's seventy-nine-year-old civil rights-pioneering father, Willis. "What did you dig up on Vannick?"

"Not much other than the fact that he tried a little brush-back move on me with his car, and he claims to be connected."

"To what? A firehose?"

"Nope. Intimates that he's a wiseguy. Had me shakin' in my boots," Flora Jean said sarcastically.

"I'll do some checking on him too."

"I'd be a little more careful with Vannick, CJ. Wiseguy or not, he sure ain't no Counts. He's the kind that would kill you if he had to, or at least hire it out."

"I'll remember that when I talk to Mario Satoni. I'm waiting to hear back from him about who's out there doing freelance bombing these days."

"Good place to start," said Flora Jean. She'd never been told the whole story of CJ's Uncle Ike's link to Denver's community of wiseguys, but she knew that connection and CJ's and Mario's passion for collecting antiques and Western memorabilia had made them friends over the years. "Think Mario still has his finger on the pulse of things?"

"Not like he used to, but he'll be able to point me in the right direction on Vannick, and he'll have inside dope on who's the setup man to talk to if you're planning a store bombing."

"And if you find out anything, you're gonna let the cops handle it, right?"

"Damn, Flora Jean. You're starting to sound like Mavis."

"I'm tryin' to sound like somebody who don't want you gettin' your head blown off. You know as well as I do that Celeste Deepstream's more than likely the brains behind that bombing. Ain't you had enough of playin' cat-and-mouse with that nutcase?"

"She likes me."

Flora Jean flashed CJ a no-nonsense scowl. "Can it, CJ. You ain't jokin' with the boys down at Rosie's. She'll kill you if she gets the chance. Call the cops."

"No need. Commons knows the whole Celeste Deepstream story, even warned me to keep my head down, as if he really gives a shit. What's he gonna do, really?" CJ shrugged. "He's just a homicide cop who happened to stumble into my feud with a psychopath."

"Then call in somebody else."

"I did. I talked to Danny Kearnes about keeping an eye on Mavis."

"Danny's still wet behind the ears, CJ. He's only been on the force eight months."

"You got somebody better?"

"No." Eyeing CJ pensively, she asked, "You armed?"

CJ nodded.

"Guess your good sense is finally showin' through, sugar. So now that I know you ain't lookin' to end up a self-sacrifice, where do we head next with the Del Mora murder?"

CJ stroked his chin thoughtfully. "I think we've got the Denver scene pretty much handled for now, but there's still a Wyoming connection. I'm just not sure how that Sheets woman I told you about and that ranch lady Billy has a sweet tooth for, Amanda Hunter, fit in except for the fact that Sheets has a loose connection to your Metro State professor, Lyman."

"Lyman I can check on, but I thought you said Billy gave Amanda Hunter a clean bill of health."

"He did—I didn't. She seemed a little too blasé about that break-in at her place, and for my money she didn't seem concerned enough about somebody calling to ask about her uncle's daguerreotypes a few months back."

"Think she's hiding something?"

"I don't know, but I did find out something about her that she didn't tell either me or Billy when we were there. Julie dug it up when she did a Google search on her. Called and told me first thing this morning. Turns out the woman's a lot more than your basic cowgirl. She's got a master's degree in fine arts from the University of Arizona. Wanta take a stab at what her area of expertise happens to be?"

"Got me."

"She's a sculptor who minored in photography."

"Sounds like maybe she didn't tell you everything. But why would she steal from herself? You said she has a safe full of daguerreotypes."

"But not the all-important missing one. Maybe she needed to kill someone to get it back. I'll call Billy and tell him to put a little pressure on her. In the meantime, why don't you do a double-check on Lyman, and when you do, ask him about Sheets?"

"Will do." Flora Jean looked noticeably perturbed. "But before I hit the streets, I need to remind you of somethin', CJ Floyd."

"Shoot."

"I know this Del Mora thing has your juices flowin', sugar. It's stamped all over your face. And believe me, I need every drop of expertise I can get. But Theresa Del Mora hired me to find out who killed her son, and bottom line is, in the end I'm the one who's gotta deliver."

The room fell silent until CJ finally cleared his throat. "Sorry. Guess I just found myself back on my old beat and liking it. I know it's your show. It's just that right now I've got no antiques business, no bail-bonding business, and not a damn place to go."

"Wrong! What you've got, CJ Floyd, is me, and Mavis, and Julie, and Billy, and Rosie, and half-a-dozen other people who care about you that you ain't even stopped to count. You just gotta figure out how to prioritize things so they're workin' in your favor." Flora Jean dropped a comforting arm over CJ's shoulders. "So we do what you just laid out, only a little slower, 'cause Alden's up from Colorado Springs and we're barbecuing this afternoon."

Aware that Alden Grace, Flora Jean's long-standing love interest, could turn the normally "once a marine, always a marine"

Flora Jean into a pool of feminine softness, CJ grinned and said, "No room for guests?"

Flora Jean winked. "It ain't that kind of barbecue, sugar."

"Then get to Lyman when you can, and tell the general I said I still don't see a ring on your finger."

"Believe me, there'd be one there if he had his way. I'm the one who's skittish, you know that. We're salt and pepper, remember?"

"What did you just tell me?" CJ said pointedly, well aware that as the daughter of an East St. Louis, Illinois, prostitute, Flora Jean had watched her mother sell herself to men with drugs, money, or power until the day she'd died of tuberculosis. He understood Flora Jean's fear of relationships, especially one that involved her falling in love with a powerful white man.

"That you need to prioritize things so they work in your favor," Flora Jean said sheepishly.

"It works both ways, Ms. Benson."

"I'll think about it."

"Do that, and while you're at it, give Alden my best."

"Will do." Flora Jean walked over to her desk, opened a drawer, and took out an envelope. "Theresa Del Mora dropped off another check first thing this morning. Figured I better pay you before you got antsy." She handed the envelope to CJ. "I told her that sooner or later I'd have to talk to her boss. She seemed upset."

"You think she's afraid of him?" asked CJ.

"Yes."

"Then we'll have to figure out a way to undress the wealthy Mr. Stafford without involving her," said CJ.

Flora Jean let out a sigh and shook her head. "White men with power always scare me, CJ."

"There'll be a way to get to Stafford," CJ said reassuringly. "Like they say, even power has limits."

After twenty-five years in law enforcement, twenty-three years of it as a Denver homicide cop, Jumbo Jim Nicoletti had seen it all—scalded babies relegated to burn units and life support because their fourteen-year-old mothers couldn't stand their incessant crying, headless torsos, torsoless heads—so finding a dead man who was naked except for his socks, with road base dumped from a front-end loader covering most of him, wasn't out of the ordinary.

It had taken Nicoletti twenty minutes to fight his way through South Denver traffic and Colorado Boulevard standstills before working his way to the crime scene through a maze of I-25 T-REX highway-widening construction vehicles that included a crane moving a bridge girder. He had finally arrived at the site, smoking an illegal Cuban and wearing a twenty-year-old bullet-proof vest. The District Three sergeant who'd interrupted Nicoletti's lunch to request detective-level crime-scene support and a patrol officer who'd happened on the scene had cordoned off a fifteen-by-ten-foot area with crime-scene tape that looked as if it had been through a taffy pull.

"What the hell happened to your tape, Sarge?" asked Nicoletti, walking down a dirt embankment that T-REX construction crews would eventually engineer for drainage, groom, and line with stamped concrete noise-abatement walls.

"Got it knotted up in the dispenser." A greasy, tarpaper-black tape dispenser swung from the index finger of the sergeant's right hand.

Nicoletti eyed the dispenser and shook his head. "You need a new one."

"No way. I'm taking this one with me to the grave. I've had it fifteen years," he said, following Nicoletti beneath the tape.

"He's a John Doe as far as we can tell," said the sergeant as they approached the body. "No ID."

Nicoletti looked down at the nearly naked, partially dirt-covered lifeless form at his feet. The torso looked pretty normal except for a hole the size of a quarter, puckered and ragged at the edges, that sat like a bull's-eye in the center of the dead man's chest. "Somebody must've needed a set of clothes for the prom," said Nicoletti, staring at the man. "Whattaya say, Sarge? Maybe forty-five, fifty?"

"That would be my guess. Crime-scene boys are on their way; they'll peg it closer."

Nicoletti took a knee and examined the exit wound in the man's chest. "Bought it from behind," he said.

"Yeah," said the sergeant. "But he wasn't lying out like that originally. The guy standing over there by that front-end loader scooped him up and dumped him here."

Nicoletti glanced toward a man leaning on the front tire of a bright yellow front-end loader.

"Told him you'd want to talk to him," said the sergeant. "I didn't have enough tape to cordon off the path the loader took from where the operator scooped the body up, but I dropped some pebbles next to the tire tracks all the way back down that hill." He nodded toward a set of tire tracks. "Wanta take a look?"

Nicoletti nodded, wrestling with the idea that besides the fact that he was naked, something else seemed strange about the dead man. He followed the pudgy, balding sergeant down a second embankment that leveled off a few yards from I-25. Four lanes of cars zoomed past a double row of concrete barriers that separated traffic from where they stood.

"Lord," said Nicoletti. "Acid rock on wheels."

The sergeant nodded and shouted over the traffic noise, "The front-end-loader guy said the trench over there's for drainage." He pointed toward a long, six-foot-deep trench that ran to the southeast and past them a few yards away. The trench was flanked by a row of concrete conduits.

"Guess whoever popped our John Doe wanted the T-REX boys to be in charge of his burial," said Nicoletti.

"That was my take too." Noticing movement up above, the sergeant shaded his eyes and looked back up the embankment. "Looks like the crime-scene boys are here."

"Let's get back up top," said Nicoletti, glancing back at what would have been one very lengthy grave for their John Doe.

Winded from climbing back up the hill, his shoes covered in dust, Nicoletti stopped to take a final look at the victim. The man looked peaceful enough, even with the hole in his chest and dirt covering him from his hip joints to his knees. As Nicoletti knelt to take a final look at the victim, he realized what was so unusual about the body. It was the man's socks, and the fact that not only were they slightly different colors but the right sock had a noticeable bulge in it just above the ankle. Nicoletti slipped a latex glove out of his back pocket, pulled it on, and tugged at the top of the puffy right sock.

"Crime-scene boys wouldn't approve," said the sergeant.

"So let 'em sue me," said Nicoletti, removing the sock. He turned the sock inside out, extracting a small hunting knife and a moist piece of cardboard that had molded itself to the dead man's foot. "Looks like our John Doe here was carrying around a little protection."

"Protection he didn't get to use," said the sergeant.

"Yeah," said Nicoletti, eyeing the cardboard. "But he told us where to look for his killer." Adjusting the cardboard in the light, he read the two neatly printed lines that ran its full length: *Problem—Benson and Sergeant Commons. Solution—Loretta Sheets.* Beneath the printing was a drawing of what looked like either a ladder on its side or a railroad track.

"Anything important?" asked the sergeant.

"Maybe. That is, if there's not another Denver homicide detective named Commons."

"What?"

"Nothing," said Nicoletti, slipping the sock back onto the dead man's foot and adjusting the cardboard and hunting knife back in place. "Think I'll let the crime-scene boys do the honors on that foot," he added as he watched a man carrying a black crime-scene tackle box in one hand and a partially eaten Egg McMuffin in the other stride casually toward them.

CHAPTER 20

Things at Homer Smith's Tonsorial Parlor had just started to take their usual shape for the day when CJ stuck his head in the barbershop's doorway and yelled, "Hey, Petey-Boy, how about a shine?"

Petey-Boy Lumus, a forty-year-old, three-foot-eight-inch-tall dwarf who had overcome spina bifida, mocking, and childhood abandonment, looked up from the tooled, leather-bound, 1930s-style salesman's traveling case that held his shoe-shine paraphernalia and smiled. "Don't know if I got enough polish to handle them shit-stompers of yours, CJ."

"Then order some in," CJ shot back, tossing Petey-Boy the same follow-up line he'd been giving him for the past twenty years.

"It'll cost you double."

"What's money when you bathe in it?" CJ asked jokingly, taking a seat, pulling off his boots, and handing them to Petey-Boy. Petey lined up the boots next to a pair of spit-shined wingtips. Eyeing the wingtips, CJ said, "See Willis is here."

"In the back." Petey-Boy nodded toward a door across the room.

CJ walked stocking-footed across the shop's spotless black-and-white-tiled floor, then shot Petey-Boy a look that asked, *Okay?* as he approached the door and stopped.

Petey-Boy nodded as CJ pushed the door open and quickly disappeared into the room where Willis Sundee and another man stood talking. When they saw CJ, both men called out, "CJ," in unison.

"Willis, Homer, what's happenin'?"

"Same ol', same ol'," Homer Smith said, hefting a double-bagged Safeway grocery sack that contained the numbers money Homer had collected from barbershop customers, runners, Five Points housewives, teachers, drunks, construction workers, and even a few in-the-know suburbanites the previous day. Homer stapled the bag shut, wrote the previous day's date in bold numbers along the top edge of the bag with a Sharpie, and delicately etched the number 3 on both sides of the bag before setting it aside on a nearby table.

Homer looked at Willis and shook his head. "Pretty light. Ain't like the old days," he said. "Nine hundred ninety-eight dollars. Not even a grand. Nobody wants to gamble around here like in the old days, except over at the den. Shit, I remember when I could run ten grand a day through this place. And maybe even a little more if Ella Fitzgerald and Duke Ellington was playin' down the street at the Rossonian. Hell, I remember when Welton Street jumped all night and you could get a full-course gourmet meal served to you at three-thirty in the a.m."

"Those days are gone," Willis shot back. "Hell, you've got legalized gambling right up the road in Central City and Black Hawk. The state runs a lottery, and you've got a dozen New Mexico Indian reservations stealing your thunder all the way down I-25. Who's gonna risk placing an illegal bet or making a wild-haired guess on a couple of numbers that somebody pulls out of a hat when they've got all that other stuff available to them?

What matters, Homer, is that you're still in the game. So quit your bitchin'." Willis walked over to CJ, draped an arm sympathetically over his shoulders, and asked, "How you copin'? With the bombin' and all?"

"Best I can," CJ said to his future father-in-law.

"Heard about that," said Homer, turning up the room's lights. "Sorry, CJ."

"Thanks."

"Mavis thinks that Deepstream woman's involved," Willis said.

"More than likely," CJ admitted hesitantly.

"You gotta put an end to your feud with her, CJ," said Willis, every bit the worried father. "You and Mavis can't stand to go another round with that psychopath."

CJ almost said that he just wanted Celeste to go away and leave him alone. But he would have been lying. He wasn't looking for a truce. Deep down he wanted to pay Celeste back for kidnapping and brutally beating Mavis, for trying to fracture his skull with a tire iron two years earlier, and for once trying to asphyxiate him. Most of all, he wanted to settle up with her for insinuating herself into the back reaches of his mind and bubbling up to the surface at will.

"I'm handling it," he finally said. "Things'll be okay."

"Hope so," said Willis. "'Cause you got a wound that's festering, and that's never good."

"Let's say we forget about my Celeste Deepstream problems for the moment. I'm here on other business. Been working up a case for Flora Jean, and I need some help. What do the two of you know about a guy named Theodore Counts?"

"I know he's an asshole," Homer shot back.

"Willis?"

"I could say worse, but I won't."

"Guess you both know the man, then."

"Yeah, we know the skinny cream-colored wannabe-white SOB. And we know he's a lying thief." The veins in Homer's neck pulsated.

Willis nodded. "He's what we used to call a hit-and-run nigger when I was a boy down in Louisiana. Keeps his foot in the black community, glad-handing and kissing up so he can steal what little they've got. After he's milked folks raw, he parks his behind as close as he can to the straw boss's house. Surprised you've never run across him."

"Guess he hangs out in different circles from me."

"Fucker should be hangin' out in prison," said Homer. "SOB's a flat-out crook. Five, maybe six years ago he was runnin' a scam where he and some white boy were stealing rare books from libraries all over the state."

"They sold the books to collectors," Willis chimed in. "And when the bubble burst, it was pretty much hush-hush because of Counts's political connections. Next thing I hear, Counts has some bullshit position at our library right here in Five Points. From what I hear, all he does now is sit around and take up space."

CJ nodded as Petey-Boy swung open the door and waddled into the room. Eyeing Homer as if he were a truant, Petey-Boy said, "You got a customer waiting, Homer."

"Who?" Homer shot back, upset that his story had been interrupted.

"Charlie Renfroe. He said for me to come get you before you and Mr. Sundee talked away all his appointment time."

"Think Counts is capable of killing someone?" CJ asked as Homer headed for the door.

Homer laughed. "Shit, no. The man's a pussy."

"What about that book-stealing buddy of his?" asked CJ. "Got a name for me?"

"Nope. But I know that didn't nothin' happen to him either." Homer eyed Petey-Boy. "Tell Charlie I'm comin'," he said, watching Petey-Boy scoot from the room before turning back to CJ. "What's Counts done now?"

"I think he's back to his old book-stealing ways. But this time it looks like he's tapping the private sector."

"Boldness knows no boundaries," said Willis, trailing CJ to the exit. "You and Flora Jean gonna put the clamps on Counts?"

"We're trying," said CJ, heading across the barbershop to get his boots. CJ handed Petey-Boy a $5 bill, picked up his boots, planted himself on the top step of Petey-Boy's shoe-shine stand, and slipped both boots on. He was almost to the door when Homer, clippers in hand, called out, "We're lookin' for you to bat cleanup on Counts, CJ. Don't nobody like inhaling the stink on shit."

The ride from Five Points to Mario Satoni's mostly Italian neighborhood in North Denver normally took CJ fifteen minutes, but by the time he'd stopped for gas, inhaled two glazed donuts at LaMar's Donuts on 6th and Klamath, and checked in with Mavis, pleading with her during the conversation to bake his favorite dessert, a sweet-potato pie, nearly an hour had passed. As he entered Satoni's neighborhood, he realized that he was spending his whole morning sparring with feisty octogenarians.

Satoni, an eighty-one-year-old curmudgeon who ran a secondhand furniture store a few blocks from the house he'd lived in for fifty-five years, smoked foul-smelling cheap cigars that he imported from back East, wolfed down provolone cheese by the wedge, and ate Italian sausage half-smokes for dinner most days of the week. The thing that had sparked and ultimately cemented Satoni and CJ's lasting friendship, besides the fact that Satoni had known Ike, was the fact that Satoni had the largest collection of mint-condition license plates CJ had ever seen.

CJ had called ahead to make certain that Mario would be home, knowing the call was probably unnecessary since Satoni came home from his secondhand furniture store for lunch every day promptly at eleven a.m. to enjoy a peanut-butter-and-jelly sandwich on toasted Jewish rye, a bottle of Dad's Old Fashioned root beer, which he bought by the case from a store in Los Angeles, a dill pickle, and a salted lime.

After discarding a cloak of early-morning clouds, the day had turned bright, and Mario's mustard-colored bungalow, its basement chock-full of antiques and Western collectibles, seemed to glow in the noonday sun. CJ pulled the coral red Bel Air into Satoni's driveway, got out, stretched, eyed the crystal-blue sky, and realized that with all his problems, he'd still rather be right where he was than any other place.

He didn't see Mario approaching until the former Denver crime boss was nearly on top of him. Beltless, dressed in droopy khakis, an unironed dingy white shirt, and a chest-protector-wide tie, Satoni adjusted one of the dozens of sets of glasses that he kept around the house, brought CJ into focus, and on the heels of an ear-to-ear grin said, "Calvin, this could be your lucky day."

No one had ever called CJ by his given name, Calvin, except Ike—generally when Ike needed to press a point—but Mario, a man for whom protocol still mattered, had called CJ Calvin since the first time they'd met, reminding CJ whenever he asked to be called by the initials he preferred that Calvin, his God-given name, was the one he would be greeted with if and when he ever reached the pearly gates.

"How's that?" CJ asked, smiling and pumping Satoni's right hand. The old man, once nearly six feet tall, was now shriveled and stoop-shouldered.

Beaming like a child who'd just found the prize at the bottom of his Cracker Jack box, Satoni said, "Right after you called to say you were coming over, a guy walked into the furniture store and said, 'I hear you collect license plates,' then handed me the sweetest deal I've run across in decades. Come on in; I'll show you."

CJ followed Mario across his backyard and into the house, through the kitchen, and down a hallway whose walls were filled with photographs of mobsters and Colorado movers and shakers from another era before stepping into what Mario liked to call his theater—a windowless dark box of a room with a fifty-seven-inch flat-screen TV, two matching La-Z-Boy chairs, and a reenameled fifty-year-old Kelvinator refrigerator. "There it is, over there on the TV tray next to the fridge " said Mario. "Have a look."

CJ walked over to a TV tray that held an empty Coke can and a bowl of stale-looking popcorn. A porcelain license plate rested between them.

"Go ahead, pick it up," said Mario, watching CJ salivate.

CJ hefted a license plate that had been constructed by the long-abandoned process of overlaying porcelain onto iron and held it up to the light.

"Whattaya think? And for just five hundred bucks. Did I get a steal, or did I get a steal?"

CJ rotated the license plate, as near to mint as any porcelain plate he'd ever laid eyes on, in the light, knowing that it had to be the rarest of the rare since that was all Mario collected. "Can the suspense, Mario," he said finally. "Fill me in."

Mario grinned. "You ever seen a 1915 Oklahoma first-state?"

"A couple, at shows."

"Ever laid eyes on a prestate?"

"No."

"Well, you have now. You're holding a 1914 Chickasha Oklahoma premie. Easily worth four grand."

CJ ran three fingers along the smooth, green, porcelain surface, then back across the plate's raised white numerals, and smiled.

Uttering a phrase that he used only when he'd plucked a rare gem from a slush pile, Mario said, "Jesus wept. Now maybe I'll let you have a couple of those second-stringers that I keep downstairs, on the cheap."

"Wish I could take you up on that," said CJ disappointedly. "But I'm pretty much tapped out."

"Figured that, with the bombing and all, but the darkest hour's always before the dawn. Things'll work out. If they don't, come see me. There's a story about Ike and me I've never told you. A story that someday you're gonna need to hear."

CJ flashed Mario a look of surprise. It had only been in the past year that he had learned that Mario and Ike had been friends, and he couldn't imagine what the 1950s Italian crime boss and a black bail bondsman could have had in common besides their gambling jones, their love of jazz, and the fact that they rubbed shoulders with similar clientele.

"I will," said CJ, his tone dismissive. Stories about Ike usually saddened him.

Mario nodded and smiled knowingly. He'd spent a lifetime

sizing up loan sharks and weekend sinners, hit men, and whores, and he could still read the minds of crooked politicians and sniff out flag-waving crew cuts from the FBI in a crowd. Zeroing in on CJ's thoughts was minor league. "In a lot of ways you're just like him. In other ways you're not." Mario watched CJ run his hand across the license plate again, this time almost affectionately, and said, "So what's this business you said you needed me to help you with? And mind you, now, you know the rules. I'm in the furniture business, Calvin. Nothing else."

"I know," said CJ, cognizant of Mario's rules and aware that overstepping Mario's boundaries could end their friendship. There could be no talking about what Mario had done in the past, no mention of Mario's money-grubbing lawyer of a nephew who wanted the man carted off to a nursing home, and never, ever a word about Mario's late wife, Angie. "I need the lowdown on some folks."

"The ones you think might've blown up your store?"

"Nope."

Mario looked surprised. "You mean you ain't looking for the people who did the place?"

"I am. But that's a different matter."

Confused, Mario asked, "Then whattaya after?"

"A killer. Somebody who stole a photograph worth a million bucks."

"Ummm. Got any names for me to take a crack at?"

"Oliver Lyman," said CJ, starting at the top of his list. "He's a college-professor type."

"Never heard of him."

"How about Loretta Sheets? She's a museum curator up in Cheyenne."

Mario shook his head. "Never heard of her either."

"Theodore Counts?"

"Nope."

CJ paused, having saved the name he hoped would trigger recognition from Mario until last. "Arthur Vannick?"

Mario's eyes narrowed. "You know the rules, Calvin."

"I know the rules, Mario. Just hear me out."

"Okay, but you're pushing the envelope."

"Do you know him?"

"I know of him."

CJ hesitated, uncertain how to couch his next question. "Vannick claims he's got ties to the kind of people who count. Connected types, if you get my drift."

"I wouldn't know any of those kind of people," said Mario, his tone suddenly distant.

CJ smiled. "Never figured a legitimate furniture-store owner like you would. But I thought you might be able to steer me toward somebody who might. I'm looking for a killer, Mario. I don't know if Vannick's my man, but I know one thing for certain. The people he claims he's connected to don't take kindly to people who lie about their affiliations."

"I've heard that," said Mario. "Liars. They're the worst kind of people." He turned, walked over to a nearby table, retrieved a photograph, walked back, and handed the photograph to CJ. "Know who that is in the photograph with me?" he said, watching CJ eye a photograph that showed a much younger, fiftyish Mario standing next to a man who looked to be in his early twenties. Both men were dressed in expensive-looking summer-weight pinstripe suits.

"No," CJ said.

"My fucking nephew, Rollie."

CJ's face went slack, uncertain where Mario, who'd just broken his own iron-clad rule, was headed.

Mario took the picture back and replaced it on the table. "Like I said, liars, they're the worst kind of people. When Angie died, the SOB in that picture promised me that he'd always be there to look after me. He lied. I keep that picture around to remind me of that. All he's done for the past five years is to try and get me locked away in some shithole nursing home. Thinks he can get my money. Fucker!" Mario eyed CJ sternly. "He lies about his Sicilian roots because he's embarrassed by them. He lies about his education, says he went to Stanford Law when he went to LA State. And he lies to his wife. He's got a woman he keeps, a little Mexican girl, down in Colorado Springs. To sum it all up, he's a shitfaced snot without any sense of the past, and in my book, Calvin, that's the worst kinda somebody you can be."

The look on Mario's face had turned vengeful. "I'm bending a cardinal rule here, Calvin, and I want you to always remember that. I'm gonna hook you up with somebody who'll set you straight about your Mr. Vannick. Somebody who did a tour of duty in the military the same time as you during that little skirmish of ours over in Southeast Asia a while back. Somebody you already know."

Looking puzzled, CJ asked, "Who's that?"

Mario smiled. "Pinkie Niedemeyer."

CJ's jaw dropped as Mario added, "And don't worry about finding him; he'll find you." As far as Mario was concerned, the subject was closed, and CJ knew there'd be no more mention of Mario's backstabbing nephew or Pinkie Niedemeyer that day.

"Now, let's take a closer look at that Chickasha plate," said

Mario, picking up the license plate. "Four thousand bucks on five hundred. Now, that's how a man should use his money." He broke into a broad, toothy grin and handed the license plate lovingly to CJ.

A few minutes later, deep in thought, a cheroot tucked loosely in the corner of his mouth, CJ eased the Bel Air away from Satoni's. He'd figured all along that anyone who boasted about being a wiseguy almost assuredly wasn't one, but he'd never imagined that Mario, thirty-five years removed from the heyday of his underworld entanglements, would be so offended by Vannick's boast. He had Rollie Orsetti, Mario's nephew, to thank for that.

Breaking into a self-satisfied smile, he turned up the volume on the bluesy B. B. King lament he was listening to and cruised up 23rd Avenue past an empty, forlorn-looking Coors Field, the baseball park that was only weeks away from another certain Colorado Rockies losing season. His smile faded as he thought about the fact that he'd now have Pinkie Niedemeyer, arguably the Italian underworld's top Rocky Mountain "settlement agent," dogging his ass.

Pinkie no doubt would savor the opportunity, enjoying the fact that he'd picked the time, the place, and the circumstances under which the two would talk. CJ expected that the rail-thin, curly-headed hit man, who'd been dyeing his prematurely gray hair black almost from the day he'd returned home from Vietnam, would probably stretch out the detail, hoping to make CJ sweat a little.

As CJ turned right onto Broadway, nosing the Bel Air south for a meeting with Lenny McCabe, he wondered how he'd cope with being shadowed by Niedemeyer and quite possibly stalked at the same time by Celeste. *Funny the way things play out,* he thought, accelerating past a string of South Broadway fast-food eateries as B. B. reached the end of his rueful song.

The song's sorrowful words stuck in CJ's head all the way down Broadway, never ending until he pulled into Lenny McCabe's brother's used-car lot.

CHAPTER 21

Flora Jean and Alden Grace recognized that they both stood out, and neither of them liked it much. But they'd long ago learned to deal with the idiosyncrasies of a black-white love affair, coming to grips with the fact that a tall, buxom black woman walking hand in hand with a six-foot-four-inch, square-jawed, blue-eyed white man with a crew cut would certainly—during their lifetime and perhaps forever—draw stares in America.

Even though they'd fought a war together, participated in life-threatening clandestine intelligence games, engaged in tension-filled life-and-death pitty-pat with heads of state, and once made love in the midst of a raging oil fire in the Persian Gulf, Flora Jean had never been able to come to grips with the fact that she had fallen in love with a white man.

As Grace carried the bag of groceries they'd purchased for an early-evening barbecue at Flora Jean's across a crowded supermarket parking lot—a barbecue that Flora Jean had been promising him for more than a week—two black teenagers zoomed past them on skateboards. After eyeing Flora Jean, the smaller of the two boys glanced back briefly at Grace, flashed Grace the high sign, and yelled, "Big and fine, my man." Grace grinned as the boy skateboarded away.

Never comfortable with being a sex object, though it was something she'd endured all her life, Flora Jean simply shook her head.

"He's only calling it like he sees it," Grace said with a smile. "Didn't realize you had such a grip on the young."

"I don't." Flora Jean reached out and squeezed Grace's hand. "I work my magic on the old and infirm," she said to the athletic-looking former general, who was sixteen years older than she.

"I see," said Grace. "Well, my dear Sergeant, we'll see just how magical you are later on."

"That we will," said Flora Jean, pouting sensually and giving Grace a wink as they reached his pickup, a camper-topped silver extended-cab that had had its bed modified to handle the surveillance and intelligence endeavors that Grace still occasionally found himself involved in. Grace opened a rear door and placed the groceries on the backseat as Flora Jean skirted the front of the vehicle to get in on the other side. Grace had just shut the door when a voice at the rear of the truck called out, "Ms. Benson? I'd like to speak to you for a moment, if I may."

Flora Jean looked back to see Fritz Commons moving toward her. He was four paces away when Alden Grace stepped between them. Eye to eye with Commons, Grace said, "Can I help you?" His words were meant to bite.

"Alden!" Flora Jean's voice rose an octave as she grabbed the former general by the hand.

His right hand jammed into the left inside pocket of his jacket, Commons took a half step back.

"Do you know this guy, Flora Jean?"

"Yes." Flora Jean stepped between the two men, nudging Grace aside. "Sergeant Fritz Commons, I'd like you to meet General Alden Grace."

"General," said Commons.

"Sergeant."

"What can I help you with, Sergeant?" asked Flora Jean, watching Commons slip his hand out of his jacket pocket.

"I'm hoping you can help me with a problem that's cropped up," said Commons.

"Which is?"

"Another homicide. One that has a real solid link to you."

"I don't remember killin' anybody recently," Flora Jean said with a smile.

"Don't get flip, Ms. Benson. We can have an informal chat here in the parking lot or a more formal discussion downtown."

"Here's just fine."

"Appreciate the cooperation," Commons said sarcastically. "Do you know a man named Oliver Lyman?"

"Yes. He your murder victim?"

"Yes." Commons glanced at Grace. "Since none of this concerns you, General, why don't you have a seat in the truck?"

"If it concerns Flora Jean, it concerns me."

"The truck, General," Commons reiterated.

"Alden, it might be smart," said Flora Jean.

Well schooled in police procedure and realizing the risk Flora Jean took by talking off the record, Grace shook his head defiantly. "We're going downtown."

"But Alden . . ."

"Downtown, Flora Jean."

"You heard the man, Sergeant. I guess we're goin' downtown."

"Happy to accommodate," Commons said, uncertain what hold the authoritative-sounding general had on Flora Jean and wanting to know more. "You can both come." He nodded in the direction of an unmarked police car one row over.

"What about our barbecue?" Flora Jean said disappointedly to Grace as they headed for the cruiser.

"It can wait." Grace thought about the first POWs his intelligence teams had interrogated during the Persian Gulf War, recalling that the toughest nuts to crack were always those who volunteered to be questioned and aware that the POWs always seemed to come away from those interrogations learning something too. Helping Flora Jean into the cruiser, Grace whispered, "Remember, Flora Jean, first man up always tells the least."

Flora Jean winked and slipped into the backseat of the police cruiser as Grace followed.

"Got a refrigerator where we're headed?" Grace asked.

"Sure do," said Commons. "And a microwave and dinnerware too. Just about everything you need to set up housekeeping, but I don't think we'll be that long." Commons cranked the cruiser's engine. Glancing across the seat back, he flashed a smile. "But then, you never really know how long anything's gonna take these days, do you?"

"Twenty-three, twenty-four." CJ sounded winded as he counted out the last of the $2,400 Rosie Weeks had lent him onto the dust-covered, coffee-stained table and shoved the money toward the waiting hands of Lenny McCabe. "We're even."

"Yeah." McCabe divided the money into smaller stacks, sat forward in his seat, and, shoving the cash into his front pants pocket, despondently repeated, "Even. I've got a bombed-out building, no inventory, half an ounce of hope, and twenty-four hundred bucks. That should take me places."

"Better than me," CJ countered, glancing around the small

room they were seated in. A room that reeked of oil and rancid automotive-shop rags. A rathole of a room inside a double-wide trailer that listed to the right; a room in which Lenny McCabe's used-car-selling brother closed his car deals, ate most of his meals, fornicated, and commiserated.

The trailer, parked in the middle of the used-car lot, was less than a mile from Ike's Spot. Triple A Auto Sales had been Lenny's last stop on a downward spiral of dead-end jobs before he'd accidentally stumbled into the antiques business. Storeless now, and with little more than CJ's $2,400 to his name, Lenny was back where he'd started, inhaling the nauseating smell of soil, sweat, and his brother's semen.

McCabe patted his pockets, making certain the money was still there, and eyed CJ. "My insurance company's balking at picking up the tab for that bombing. What about yours?"

"Same thing. They're looking into whether the bombing was an act of terrorism. If they can nudge it into that bailiwick, they won't have to shell out a dime. But mostly they're stalling, just like yours. At least most of my inventory's intact. Sure sorry about your half of the building taking the brunt of it."

"Fuckin' bastards. They don't want a poor man to ever make a dime. But trust me, we'll ride this thing out." McCabe eyed CJ sympathetically. "At least I don't have some bitch with a wild hair up her ass looking to dust my ass."

"At least," said CJ, surprised that McCabe wasn't more upset over the fact that their predicament could be placed squarely on his doorstep. They had talked at length, and although they both assumed there could still be an off chance that the bombing was tied to the Del Mora murder, they'd pretty much settled on the conclusion that Celeste Deepstream had been the one pulling the bomber's strings. "I'm sorry about what happened," CJ reiterated.

"Shit happens. Hell, I've been on the bottom rung before." He looked around the room. "I used to eat, sleep, piss, party, and pick my toenails in this shithole. Ain't like I've never seen the sewer trap before. I'm just hoping that those insurance boys come through before we're both out of business too long. You lose your client base in the business we're in, and you're dead."

Surprised at McCabe's resiliency, CJ asked, "What if our insurance companies decide to kick us to the curb, invoke the terrorist-clause fine print? The bomber was an Arab, after all."

"They wouldn't dare. Shit, I don't have any terrorist links. Do you?"

"Are you crazy, Lenny?"

McCabe let out a hollow laugh. "See where despair takes you?" he said, looking relieved. "Now, if you don't mind me taking the liberty, let me offer up some advice. I know you spent half your life dealing with skaters and criminals, con men and cops. But I'd wager you never had to deal with them under our current circumstances."

Uncertain where McCabe was headed with his advice, CJ said, "No."

"So listen up. Right now we're at the mercy of insurance companies, city bureaucracy, whatever friends we got, and cops. And we're gonna have to, at least temporarily, play their game." McCabe paused and stroked his chin thoughtfully. "I see you moved most of your goods out of your space."

"Yeah."

McCabe shook his head. "Big mistake. Should've left the stuff. Now Sergeant Commons has a reason to ride your ass, ticket you, so to speak, for any kinda minor infraction, rub your nose in it because you violated one of his crime-scene rules."

"Screw Commons. Just about everything I owned in the world that was worth anything was inside a building with a hole the size of a car in the back wall waiting to be carted off by some enterprising thief."

"I know that. I just would've handled it differently. Greased a few palms, talked to one of Commons's superiors, got myself some bullshit semblance of a permission before I did what you did. Couldn't have hurt."

"I did what I had to, Lenny."

"So you did. But here's what I don't want you doing next. I don't want you screwing around with contractors or building inspectors or city engineers. And I don't want you eyeballing the rebuild, second-guessing the construction, or looking too hard at who's been hired to do the job. Okay?"

"You've lost me, Lenny," CJ said, frowning. "I've got insurance on my space and the contents. The way I handle my insurance settlement's up to me."

McCabe smiled. "CJ, my man, you're lost in the forest. Can't you see the opportunity here? What we need to do in the face of this whole unfortunate deal is make a little progress on our misfortune. Grab ourselves a nest egg as we pull ourselves back up out of the mire. What we need when all's said and done is to have enough money in our pockets to make up for our temporary out-of-business slump. And to do that we'll have to pool our resources, build ourselves enough of a kitty to be able to buy a few engineering and construction shortcuts—buy down the cost of rebuilding. See where I'm headed on this?"

CJ didn't answer, recognizing that what he'd earlier mistaken for McCabe's tough-edged resiliency was in fact the armor of an opportunist. CJ wasn't averse to greasing a few bureaucratic palms in order to move things ahead, and he certainly had no interest in dealing with a gaggle of contractors—McCabe could do that. But CJ wasn't willing to green-light the reconstruction of a building that might potentially collapse on his head just so he could pocket a little money, and he wasn't about to pool his insurance money with anyone. Eyeing McCabe sternly, he said, "Lenny, I think we might be headed in opposite directions."

"How's that?"

"I can handle redoing the lease-hold improvements in my half of the duplex on my own."

"I see," said McCabe. "Then tell me this. Can you handle an engineering mandate that calls for steel-beam reinforcement and masonry construction of a building that wasn't really much more than a bunch of two-by-fours to begin with? That's how they'll make me redo the place, I guarantee it." McCabe forced a sly smile. "And in the end, that'll end up tripling your rent."

"And you need my insurance money to make certain that you aren't faced with that kind of construction."

McCabe beamed. "Exactly."

"So in other words, I've gotta go along to get along."

"Your words, CJ."

"Looks like I've got a lot to think about," said CJ.

"Not really," said McCabe, looking up to see his brother Ritchie bounding through the trailer's front door.

"Got me a live one on that '98 Mazda sittin' out front," Ritchie boasted to Lenny, oblivious to CJ. "New paint, a cheap set of tires, a spruce-up on the interior—never ceases to amaze me what people'll buy." Taking note of CJ, he finally said to Lenny,

"Thought you were here by yourself," grabbed several sheets of paper off a desk in the corner, and rushed back out the door.

Unperturbed, Lenny said, "All you really gotta think about, CJ, is how soon both of us can get back in the money-making business."

CJ nodded, extracted a cheroot from a box in his vest pocket, and lit up, realizing as he watched smoke swirl toward the ceiling that there was no need to think about reopening Ike's Spot, at least in its current location, and there was no further need to ponder reconstruction and money-pooling and cutting corners and slicing up insurance-settlement pie. He'd move. Recalling one of Ike's favorite sayings, *Don't never give a kid who's cheatin' off your test the right answer 'cause the son of a bitch just might end up usin' that answer against you,* he took a long drag on the cheroot.

"You thinkin'?" asked Lenny, drinking in the look of concentration on CJ's face.

"Nope, just remembering," said CJ, smiling and blowing a series of smoke rings into the air.

Colorado's two-hundred-thousand-acre Black Forest is a heavily wooded and characteristically rural expanse that hugs the Palmer Divide just before the Rockies swoop down to meet the wide valley that becomes Colorado Springs. The acreage had been named by a German immigrant who'd thought the dark hue of the forest's dominating ponderosa pines resembled the famed Black Forest of his homeland. Once a pristine enclave of flora and fauna, the forest had gradually evolved since the late 1960s into a hodgepodge of five- to thirty-five-acre parcels of second-home dream escapism. In it, campers, log cabins, A-frame homes, and gas-guzzling RVs had become home to people looking for the bucolic life, including glassy-eyed retirees, loners, and a handful of survivalists.

Alexie Borg had purchased the twenty-acre parcel of land and the five-room log cabin that Celeste Deepstream had called home for the past six months four years earlier for $150,000. In that time he had doubled the value of his investment. But what mattered to him most about the isolated acreage was not the upslope of his money but the fact that six months earlier he'd first made love to a heavily intoxicated and thoroughly depressed Celeste Deepstream on the floor of the cabin after two months of rebuffed advances.

After their brief disagreement at his condominium in Denver, Celeste had come back home, where for the past two days she'd been fighting her own quiet demons, once again dependent on Alexie. Dependent on the house he provided, the money he gave her, and the secrecy he ensured and forced to accept his volatility, bad manners, and sexual whims. She suspected that Alexie had known all along that she'd come running back, had even savored the fact. She was, after all, a parole-violating fugitive and kidnapper with nowhere else to go.

She looked around the sparsely furnished cabin, frowning at the smell of the lacquered log walls that reeked of pine tar and creosote. It was a noxious smell that reminded her of her poverty-stricken childhood. A smell left behind by Bureau of Indian Affairs seasonal workers hired to seal the termite-infested logs that formed the cinder-block-walled crawl spaces beneath the poorly constructed cookie-cutter tract homes the government had marched across the open spaces of the Acoma reservation. She rose from the rocker she was seated in, grabbed her leather jacket, and said to Alexie who was making himself a vodka martini, "Let's go outside. The smell in here's making me sick. Besides, I need to practice."

Alexie shrugged and, drink in hand, followed her out the door. The mountain air was crisp, the temperature a half notch above freezing. Spreading her arms, Celeste inhaled the pristine air. "You can almost taste the freshness."

Borg, his mind cluttered with sexual fantasies, snorted perfunctorily before cupping Celeste's derriere in his left hand.

Celeste stepped out of his grasp, took another deep, intoxicating breath, and said, "Alexie, please. I should practice."

"But I need you right now."

"What did we agree to, Alexie?" Celeste turned and stared the big Russian down.

"That I wouldn't interfere with your plans to kill Floyd."

"You're interfering, Alexie."

"But . . ."

"Go back inside, Alexie. I'll only practice for a little while. Thirty minutes at the most. Besides, you'll enjoy it more if you have to wait for it." She tried not to choke on her words.

Borg drank in the outline of Celeste's body, imagining the firmness of her nipples in the chilled mountain air. "No longer than a half hour. I can't stand it."

Celeste walked away sensually without uttering another word, leaving Borg with an erection and sipping his drink. She quickly covered the twenty yards between the house and a tool shed that hugged the property line, leaving her footprints in a shaded skiff of snow. She stepped into the tool shed and flipped on a light switch, watching her breath stream out in front of her. She walked to a workbench in the center of the shed, picked up the instrument she'd handpicked to kill Floyd, and smiled. *Thirty minutes of practice,* she told herself, a solid twenty or thirty attempts, and an equal number of trips up and down the tree-stand ladder to check on her shots, and that would be it. It would tax her stamina, but in the end it was always practice that made perfect. It was practice that had turned her into an Olympic-caliber swimmer, patience that had helped her maintain the kind of self-control that had gotten her through five years in prison, and discipline that had enabled her to shed forty pounds of prison fat and recapture her figure and exotic good looks.

Practice, patience, and discipline, she silently repeated to herself again and again as, clutching the weapon she would use to kill Floyd, she walked away from the workbench, across the room, and back outside. She eyed the tree stand that Alexie had built for her six months earlier, when she'd demanded a private spot where she could retreat from her demons. The stand filled the lower branches of a forlorn-looking pine tree. *Thirty minutes of practice,* she told herself. Just thirty uninterrupted minutes to practice killing.

Her eyes were moist with anger, anger she wanted to draw on and linger, anger that would intensify when she had to go back inside to the Russian. Anger that had grown into a festering boil of hate that would explode the instant she dispensed with Floyd.

Haste makes waste, Theodore Counts kept reminding himself as, standing in his bedroom, he jammed clothes into a suitcase. Reacting in fear, his actions had been totally disjointed since he'd heard on a six o'clock news report that Oliver Lyman was dead. Suspecting that a police investigation would link him to Lyman, he'd decided to run.

He slipped a pair of penny loafers into the suitcase, layered the shoes with two cashmere sweaters, and scanned his bedroom for his running shoes. *I never should've started dealing in stolen books again,* he told himself, darting around the room, searching for the shoes—and he never should have told Vannick about the daguerreotype.

Now he was riding a wave with a dead man, a man he'd supplied with barely a dozen stolen books. He was certain Lyman had been the one who'd sicced Flora Jean Benson on him.

He tossed a Baggie filled with toiletries into his suitcase, uncertain how long he'd be gone. It really didn't matter. He needed breathing room. He'd spend the night at a friend's place southeast of Denver in the sleepy town of Kiowa, distancing himself from Lyman. As soon as he found his running shoes, he'd be gone.

CHAPTER 22

Russet, Amanda Hunter's six-year-old border collie, heard the noise first. The dog was at the front door spinning in circles and whining well before Amanda realized that she'd heard something too.

"Something out there, girl?" asked Amanda, surprised that a barely perceptible noise had triggered such an agitated response in the dog. Suddenly Russet stopped spinning and, with her nose inches from the door, let out a low-pitched, troubled growl. Amanda rose from her favorite chair, set aside the book she'd been reading, and, brow furrowed, walked over to the front window to peer into the blackness. Patting Russet on the head, she said, "Let's say we take a look."

Russet stopped growling, but her nose remained aimed squarely at the door as Amanda flipped the switch to a bank of outdoor floodlights and the front of the house was suddenly awash in light. She flipped a second switch, and a string of lights that her father had always called his runway lights flashed on along the thirty yards of the gravel driveway that led from the house to the nearby storage shed. She heard the unmistakable thud of the door to the storage shed bang into the outside of the shed when she reached for a third switch.

Most of the shed had been dug into a hillside so only its front timbers were visible. Amanda hefted the loaded shotgun she kept next to the front door, snapped it closed, grabbed four additional shells from a nearby table, flashed Russet a hand signal to stay, opened the front door, and stepped out onto the porch.

She could see from twenty yards away that the door to the shed was open. So much for her security system. A few steps from the open doorway, someone dressed from head to toe in black sprinted away from her down the driveway. The next instant Russet darted after the streaking figure.

"Russet!" Amanda screamed, racing down the front steps. Russet was within five feet of the intruder when the dark figure stopped, turned, and fired a .22 point-blank at the dog. Russet let out a yelp as two ear-shattering blasts from Amanda's over-and-under echoed in the mountain darkness.

"You son of a bitch!" she shouted, reloading the shotgun and firing off two additional rounds. Russet, undaunted by the coat-brushing sting from the .22, was about to bolt once again, but Amanda's sure hand on her collar stopped the dog short. The sound of a vehicle roaring to life in the distance coincided with the sound of the over-and-under snapping open again. Amanda reloaded, snapped the shotgun closed one-handed, scooped up the quivering forty-five-pound border collie, and, anger seeping from her pores, headed back toward the house.

Rosie's den was packed, jammed to its recently painted enamel-white cinder-block walls. It was a crisp, calm, quarter-mooned Saturday night, and cars lined both sides of Welton Street for almost three blocks on either side of the den.

As CJ negotiated his way through the boisterous gambling throng inside and toward a roulette table, Rosie Weeks called out to him, "Glad you could show up, Mr. Wonderful."

Only when CJ reached an island of calm just beyond the roulette table did he realize that Flora Jean was standing with Rosie. Flora Jean flashed a half-cocked smile. "Watch out, CJ; Rosie's ticked."

"Over what?"

"Over the fact that the Broncos traded one of their draft choices for some washed-up running back. When I told him the Broncos should have my problems and that the cops had found a dead men with my name written on a piece of cardboard inside his sock, he ignored me, claimin' that he could probably outrun that back."

"Yeah, I heard—about Lyman, I mean," said CJ. "Julie called me just after I had a business strategy meeting with Lenny McCabe this afternoon. Fed me the whole nine yards. Said Sergeant Commons wanted a piece of you."

"A big piece. Alden and Julie got him to back off, but not before I'd spent two hours in his dingy little office with him breathing green-chili breath in my face."

"Sounds like a pain."

Flora Jean shook her head. "Gotta admit, though, he's pretty damn smart. He's up to speed on the whole daguerreotype story. While I was sittin' there in his office, waitin' for Julie to toss around a little of her barrister's muscle, don't you know that damn Joe Friday contacted Loretta Sheets, talked to the Hunter woman at her ranch, and had a chat with Stafford!"

CJ look peeved. "You mean in two hours he dug up everything it took us days to uncover?"

"Sure did. Extracted it all from a note he said he found in Lyman's sock. Sheets told him about Amanda Hunter. He talked on the phone for a good ten minutes with Stafford, and my guess is that he's pretty much even with us when it comes to Counts and Vannick."

"Damn," said CJ as a woman who was painted into a red sequined cocktail dress screamed, "Full house! Show me the money! Show me the money!"

"Shit, Aquanetta Dunn just hit," Rosie lamented. "I'm gonna have to go get her some money. She'll want all her winnings in hundreds so she can slip the wad inside her bra and spend the rest of the night flashin'." Rosie moved toward the screaming woman, shaking his head as he watched her raise her arms and wiggle them skyward.

Flora Jean watched Aquanetta follow Rosie toward the den's portable cashier's cage. Looking back at CJ, she asked, "Did you see the six o'clock news?"

"Sure did, and you can bet whoever did in Lyman saw it too. One good thing, though—they don't know about that note in Lyman's sock, and thanks to Commons, we do."

"Think I'll check out Lyman's office and his house. See what I can dig up. As for the note in his sock, why do you think he did that?"

"More than likely because he needed an ace in the hole. Something the person who killed him wouldn't know about. He probably put the note there on real short notice."

"Why not just leave a written note back at his office?"

"Because it might not have been found, not to mention the fact that whoever killed him could've destroyed it."

Flora Jean shook her head. "Maybe. But writin' a note on a piece of cardboard and stickin' it inside your damn sock! I don't know, CJ."

"Doesn't matter, Flora Jean. It worked. And . . ." The chime from CJ's cell phone interrupted them. "Hold on a minute. It's probably Mavis." CJ flipped his cell phone open. "Floyd here."

"CJ, it's Billy. I'm headed for the Triangle Bar. Amanda Hunter just called. Said she had a break-in at the ranch. Somebody busted into her storage shed."

"She okay?" asked CJ, shouting over the background noise.

"She's fine. Her dog got grazed by a .22 before Amanda let whoever broke in have a double taste of buckshot from her over-and-under. The lady's tough."

"Where are you?"

"South of the Snowy Range Mountains, about two and a half hours away from the ranch if I step on it. Just bought myself a new pair of boots over in Laramie, and I was headed back home. I'm guessin' Amanda can use some peppin' up. Who knows, my visit just might shine some light on that murderer you're after too." Billy paused and pinched one ear shut. "What's all the noise in the background? You at an arcade?"

"I'm at the den."

Billy laughed. "Rosie's still sucker-punchin' all them dumbass Denver gamblers?"

"That he is."

"Flora Jean there with you by any chance?"

"Yeah. We just finished talking about one of our suspects buy-ing the farm. Oliver Lyman, that professor who was one of Loretta Sheets's dissertation advisers, well, somebody killed him earlier today."

"Guess I can strike Lyman off the list of people who might've broke in at Amanda's. Any idea who might've killed him?"

"No. But he left a note behind pointing a finger at Sheets. A piece of cardboard the cops found inside his sock."

"Ummm. Let me know if you need any more help with Sheets. She ain't but a hop, skip, and a jump away from the Triangle Bar."

"I will." CJ turned to Flora Jean. "You need to say anything to Billy? I've got him here on the phone."

Flora Jean shook her head.

"I'll keep you posted, Billy," said CJ, shouting into the phone. "Let me know what you come up with at Amanda's. And Billy, while you're there, why don't you ask her about her degrees. Found out she has one in photography."

"Okay. Talk to you later." Billy hung up. The photography news left him suddenly deflated.

CJ closed his cell phone, slipped it into his vest pocket, and turned to Flora Jean. "Somebody broke into Amanda Hunter's storage shed this evening. Billy's on his way there."

"Think it could've been the Del Mora kid's killer?"

"Maybe, or even Lyman's. Billy'll keep us posted." CJ turned and surveyed the room. "Too much noise in here for me," he said, looking at Flora Jean. "Think I'm gonna call it an evening." He checked his watch. "Got one final meeting to make before I call it quits."

"With who?"

"Pinkie Niedemeyer."

"The hit man!"

"Purported hit man, Flora Jean. There's a difference."

"Only if you're the damn press. I'd watch my back if I were you, CJ."

"Always do. You staying?"

"For a while. But I won't stay long. I need to have enough early-morning energy to worm my way into ol' Professor Lyman's office."

"Be careful, Flora Jean. Amanda Hunter already let whoever broke into her place tonight have a taste of buckshot. Wouldn't want you to get caught rooting around Lyman's office and getting more of the same, or worse."

"No worries," Flora Jean said, patting her buns. "I'm buckshot-proof."

"Hope so," said CJ, smiling and heading for the exit that he'd been working his way toward ever since he'd entered the den.

CJ was a half block from the Bel Air when Fritz Commons angled across Welton Street to intercept him.

"Knew you'd have to come back for your chariot, Floyd. Admire your taste in cars."

"You're a genius, Sergeant. Smart enough to realize, I hope, that it's Saturday night in Five Points and we need to get our asses out of the middle of Welton Street."

They stepped around the front of the Bel Air and up onto the sidewalk. "Win any money?" asked Commons, turning to face CJ, his breath reeking of green chili.

"I try not to gamble, Sergeant."

"Same here." Commons smiled. "Strange how an illegal joint like the den keeps chugging along after all these years. Guess Weeks has some kind of fairy godmother."

"Could be."

"Better hope you have one too. I talked to your friend Ms. Benson earlier today. Expect you already know that. I found her name on the most unusual insole I've ever seen, inside a dead man's sock, and that took me north to Cheyenne and a woman named Sheets, who had the strangest story about a missing million-dollar photograph. You wouldn't happen to know anything about that photo or its whereabouts, would you, Floyd?"

"I can't help you, Sergeant."

"I figured your answer would be something like that, so I told myself I needed a response that would let you see things from my perspective. Here it is: disappear into the woodwork, Floyd. You're still a suspect in a murder, and so is your friend Ms. Benson. You're out of your league in this one. We're not talking petty bond skippers here."

"Any more advice, Sergeant?"

Commons looked CJ up and down as he tried to put his finger on exactly how the recalcitrant former bail bondsman fitted into his murder case. "Yes. You're sucking up my investigative air, Floyd. If I find out you're breathing in information that's pertinent to a murder investigation and not exhaling it, you'll regret it."

"Appreciate the warning, Sergeant. Are we done?"

"For now," said Commons. "And Floyd, don't get too high-hatted. I've checked, and unlike your friend, Weeks, you don't have friends in high places, much less a fairy godmother. Drive defensively," he added with a smile.

CJ stepped off the curb and moved to get into the Bel Air.

It was just past midnight and pitch black at the Triangle Bar Ranch. Amanda Hunter and Billy DeLong stood in the middle of the poorly lit storage shed that had suffered the break-in, rehashing the night's events. The dirt-floored shed was filled with odds and ends that included spare tractor parts, salvaged furniture, and outdated equipment. A couple of boxes that had contained Amanda's grandfather's things, including his tally books, cattle-auction receipts, and brand books, were overturned on the floor in front of Billy. Most things in the shed looked undisturbed except for several boxes that had been rifled and an overturned riding mower that Amanda used to cut grass around the house. The mower's gas tank had leaked fuel onto the dirt floor in a perfect circle.

"Smells like the inside of a gas tank in here. Let's get this thing back on its feet," said Billy, turning the mower upright and dusting off his hands.

"The burglar probably broke in sometime around eight o'clock," said Amanda. "That's about the time I usually start reading or painting." Amanda eyed the shed's double-hung Douglas fir door. "What drew my attention and Russet's was the sound of that door over there banging into the outside of the shed. After a lifetime of living out here, I'd know that sound in my sleep."

Billy nodded and watched Russet, not one bit gun-shy after her encounter with a .22, sniff her way around the shed. "What do you think they were after?"

"My uncle's daguerreotypes, I suspect. Unfortunately, as you know, they picked the wrong place."

Billy nodded and looked around the shed. "Ain't too much in here outta place," he said, picking up a displaced saddle yoke he'd overlooked and examining it.

"That yoke was hooked to the wall over here," said Amanda, pointing to a jutting treble hook.

Billy walked over to where the yoke had been hanging, eyed the treble hook, and said, "Five foot high, wouldn't you think?"

"Closer to five and a half."

Billy eyed the hook, the wall, and finally the floor. "Think we've got somethin'." Billy fingered the edge of the treble hook. "There's a fragment of what looks like a piece of plastic caught here." He teased the object off the hook and handed it to Amanda. "What do you make of it?"

"Beats me," said Amanda, scrutinizing the one-and-a-half-inch-long mud-brown fragment, "but you're right; it's plastic."

"I think we should keep it. Got somethin' I can put it in?"

"I've got a Baggie in the house."

"Good enough." Billy slipped a handkerchief out of his back pocket and wrapped the plastic fragment in it. "Small bugger," he said, slipping the handkerchief back into his pocket. "What-taya think it broke off of?"

"Glasses frames maybe, or perhaps a comb."

"That would be my guess too." Billy looked around the room. "Did you find anything missing?"

"No. But I'm thinking our thief may have left behind something else."

"What?"

"Fingerprints, unless of course he was wearing gloves. Come take a look."

"Or she," Billy countered, following Amanda to a far corner of the shed.

Amanda stopped next to a box and picked up a postcard that she'd set on top of it before Billy's arrival. "This postcard didn't jump out of this box on its own," she said, handing a colorful postcard hawking the 1936 Cheyenne Frontier Days Rodeo to Billy. "The box isn't even overturned."

"Your thief would have had to have been pretty stupid to handle somethin' like this without gloves," said Billy, holding the card by the edges.

"Maybe he was."

"We'll bag it," said Billy. "Might lead us somewhere; who

knows? I've got a friend in Denver whose boyfriend used to be a top-level intelligence guy in the marines. He's helped me and CJ with prints before." Billy scanned the room one last time, drinking in every nook and cranny. "That about it?"

"I think so." Amanda checked her watch. "It's almost one o'clock. I can put you up for the night if you'd like."

"Thanks. But I better warn you, I've got some questions I'm gonna need answered about a missing daguerreotype that you didn't mention the last time I was here. One that I've been told is worth a million bucks, maybe more. More than likely that's what your burglar was looking for this evenin'."

"The Golden Spike photo, I'd bet," said Amanda, turning to leave the shed.

"Yeah."

"I figured you'd find out about it from Loretta Sheets."

"I did. So why didn't you tell CJ and me about it the first time we were here?"

Amanda's eyes welled with tears. "Because that so-called missing photograph pretty much killed my father. He spent his whole life looking for it, never knowing whether it really existed. His search almost cost us this ranch." Amanda turned off the shed's lights and closed the door as she and Billy stepped out into the driveway lights. "The first time you were here, I wasn't ready for you to pull the scab off that wound. To tell you the truth, I'm still not."

As they walked up the driveway toward the house, Russet took the lead, happy to be headed home. "Afraid the wound's open now," said Billy.

"I know," said Amanda, her tone resentful. "And believe me, it's stinging real bad."

CHAPTER 23

Pinkie Niedemeyer had lost all of his front teeth, top to bottom, eyetooth to eyetooth, and the pinkie finger of his left hand during a New Year's Eve firefight outside the village of Song Ve three days before he was scheduled to come home from a year-long tour of duty in Vietnam. He'd received a Purple Heart for doing his duty that day, and earned a nickname.

Now, thirty-six years later, Pinkie stood on the earthen shoulder of Denver's High Line Canal, a sixty-six-mile-long man-made waterway that wove its way through the city. He was rocking side to side, talking in a hushed tone to a very wary CJ.

It was one-thirty a.m. and peacefully quiet as the two men whose paths had crossed occasionally over the years, causing sparks each time, chatted.

"Things aren't always what they seem, CJ," said Niedemeyer, taking a step sideways. "Like you and me, for instance. Look at us. We're both the same age, fought the same war, and we've lived in Denver all of our lives. Only real difference is we got dipped in different skin-tone tanks at birth. But if you ask anybody, even people who think they're in the know, who's 'handled' more people over the years, I'd always end up getting the nod."

CJ, well aware of the meaning of the word *handled*, nodded and waited for Pinkie to continue.

"But that ain't reality, 'cause you and I both know those patrol-boat .50-calibers you babysat back when we were both *in country* took out more people during your year in 'Nam than I could possibly handle in a lifetime. So you see, CJ, things get twisted around in this crazy world, and facts sometimes end up turning into fiction." Pinkie, suddenly defensive, smiled and cleared his throat as if trying to rid himself of a bad taste. "Whattaya think, man? I started out to do what I do? Dreamed about it when I was a kid, like wanting to grow up to be a football player or Superman?" Pinkie shook his head in protest. "No way. Shit, when I was a kid, I wanted to be a butcher and own a little neighborhood store where I could sell steaks and specialty meats, like my Uncle Ernie. Betcha didn't know I'm part Jewish on my mother's side. Hell, I could've been a butcher, or maybe even a mohel."

CJ neither smiled nor answered. He simply eyed the haze-covered quarter moon, slipped a cheroot out of the pocket of his vest, and took a long drag before glancing back at Pinkie through a stream of rising smoke. "You're a hired killer, Pinkie, any way you spin it."

"You're hurting me, CJ," Pinkie countered. "Don't forget, I'm here on a payback. I could've chose not to come. But you're Mario's boy, so I'm here."

The look on CJ's face let Pinkie know he'd just turned the wrong phrase. Pinkie might as well have said, *You're Mario's nigger, and I know it.*

"I didn't mean it that way, CJ. You know me; I don't play them kinda games. You know what I mean. Mario respects you, talks about you like a son. Hell, ain't a black man in Denver who has a free pass to act out his ass any day of the week without consequences but you."

CJ blew a ring of smoke skyward. "You ever seen me act out my ass, Pinkie?"

"It's a figure of speech, man."

CJ tipped a bullet of ash from his cheroot, aware that if he and Niedemeyer didn't soon get to the real reason for their meeting, things would degenerate beyond repair. "Let's handle our business, Pinkie. That's why we're here."

"Fine. We're on the same page," said Pinkie, aware that as Mario Satoni's emissary he was to do as he'd been told.

CJ dropped his half-smoked cheroot onto the canal's equestrian path and stubbed it out with the heel of his boot. "I need a couple of pieces of info, Pinkie, bottom line. First off, I need the lowdown on a guy named Arthur Vannick, where he comes from, where he's been, and most of all whether or not he's connected. Got him pegged as a murder suspect."

Pinkie laughed. "Vannick? Ain't that nothin'. But it don't surprise me. He's from nowhere. He ain't goin' nowhere, and the only thing he's gonna be connected to if he keeps dropping tales around the region about being a member of a club he ain't never been asked to join is life support."

"Enough said. Here's my second question and it might be a little harder. Who's the top explosives jobber around the Queen City these days?"

Pinkie smiled. "Come on, CJ. You know I can't tell you that. But I know where you're headed. Heard about that antique store of yours catching a few pounds of jelly." Pinkie rubbed his chin thoughtfully. "My guess is, you bought yourself a problem with the Russians. They love plastic. It's readily available, it's cheap, and they've got connections to the kind of nutcases who like to use it. Mostly Arabs, like the stooge I'm told did in your place."

"Got a name for me?"

"Yeah. And a warning. The name's Alexie Borg." Pinkie slipped a piece of paper out of the left pocket of his Windbreaker. "Figured you might ask me a question or two about bombers, so I came prepared." He handed CJ the paper. "Everything you need to know is right there. Here's a heads-up. The Russki has a place in LoDo, high-end to the hilt. Takes up most of the fourth floor of his building. I sketched it out for you on the paper. But before you go screwing around with one of them Russian bears, here's some advice. They operate by a set of rules you ain't used to, CJ. As far as they're concerned, you really are flat-out just a nigger. Most of all, you fuck with them, you sure as hell won't have Mario Satoni running interference. They'll kill you, man, sure as shootin'." He paused and eyed CJ intently. "Why the hell they have it in for you anyway?"

"I'm not sure. But my guess is, if you're right and it was a Russian-sponsored bombing, someone who doesn't like me very much did the hiring. Know anything else significant about Borg?"

"Only that once upon a time he was an Olympic athlete."

The muscles in CJ's face went taut. "Son of a bitch!"

"Strike a chord?"

"Oh yeah."

"Think you know who hired out the job?"

"Yep. More than likely a sweet little Indian princess."

Niedemeyer looked perplexed. "A woman? My, my, my. World's gettin' meaner and meaner every day. Any more questions before I head off?"

"Nope."

"Okay. I'll leave you with this. Your Mr. Vannick's been spoutin' off for way too long about having certain connections. Until now he's been left alone because his mouthing off hasn't gotten him crossways with any ah, company rules. But havin' Mario ask me for a favor on your behalf just pushed Mr. Vannick across the line. I'm on orders to put things back in balance. And unfortunately for Vannick, those orders supersede any call Mario can make."

"How bad's the lesson gonna be?" CJ asked, aware that Arthur Vannick may have talked his way into a death warrant.

"Don't worry." Pinkie smiled. "It won't come down to much more than a serious talking-to. If he's uncooperative, he'll feel some pain; that's about it. First time around anyway."

"You could be dealing with a murderer, you know."

"I know," said Pinkie, laughing. "Mario filled me in on that case you're working and the kid from Nicaragua buying it. Trust me, Vannick's nothing more than a babe in the woods. If he killed anybody, it was probably on the humbug. I damn sure don't think he's used to dealing with the likes of me." The earnestness in Pinkie Niedemeyer's voice was chilling.

"I know you've gotta handle what you've gotta, Pinkie, but try not to overstep your orders. I don't want Denver's finest trying to link one of your assignments up to me."

Niedemeyer looked hurt. "You're not talking to one of them Russian bears, CJ. We still have rules."

"So I hear," said CJ, suppressing an urge to remind Pinkie that there was a difference between killing during wartime and murdering someone on the street, but the urge passed quickly. After half a lifetime of often sleepless nights, CJ had come to know that in the end, killing was simply killing.

CJ drove from his meeting with Pinkie Niedemeyer to the downtown Denver address that Niedemeyer had written on the piece of paper he was now clutching. He had lumbered slowly along the empty Denver streets, hoping that by drawing the trip out, he would somehow be able to gain the insight he needed to come up with a solution for his Celeste Deepstream problem. That strategy hadn't worked, and as he parked the Bel Air a half block north of Alexie Borg's building and gazed into the star-filled sky, he was not one bit closer to a solution.

Borg's penthouse took up half the top floor of a renovated four-story Blake Street building that had once been a warehouse. CJ placed Niedemeyer's sketch on the front seat and locked his gaze on the northeast corner of the fourth floor. All he could make out in the darkness was that the building was brick and that Borg's condo had a picture window that wrapped around the corner of the building, giving the transplanted Russian mobster a view of not just Blake Street but also Coors Field.

He rolled down a front window, inhaled crisp night air, and slumped down in his seat in order to take in the full view of Borg's condo. He tried to imagine what Borg and Celeste, if she was there, might be doing inside. Were they asleep, making love, planning a new assault? Were they even there? He wondered if maybe he hadn't jumped the gun, uniting them in a bombing scheme simply because they'd both been Olympians. Pinkie Niedemeyer could have been wrong about Borg being the brains and support behind the now dead Arab bomber, and there was always the off chance that the bombing was indeed tied to the Luis Del Mora murder. Nonetheless, he was still betting on Celeste. He had to. If he didn't, he had the feeling that given another chance, Celeste would succeed in killing him. He slipped the navy-issue field binoculars he'd carried through two tours of Vietnam out of the glove compartment and trained them on Borg's penthouse. The binoculars seemed only to magnify his dilemma, offering him no more than a close-up view of an old brick building and a lengthy expanse of window.

Momentarily frustrated, he placed the binoculars back in the glove compartment, slipped his cell phone off his belt, and punched in the number that rang in the back workshop area of his garage.

Four rings later a groggy Morgan Williams answered, "Yeah?"

"Morgan, it's CJ."

"Where are you, man?"

"On a stakeout in LoDo. One that I need you and Dittier to take over."

"Now?"

"No, in the morning."

"Shit, CJ. Couldn't it have waited?"

CJ thought for a moment, imagining the look of consternation plastered on the face of the sleepy, shaved-headed rodeo Hall of Famer. "No."

"You comin' home?"

"No. I'm headed for Mavis's."

"Then I'll talk to you in the mornin'," said Morgan, looking over at Dittier, who was stretched out on an old army cot a few feet away, dead to the world.

"First thing," said CJ.

"First thing," echoed Morgan, hanging up.

CJ cleared the line and called Mavis.

Sounding breathless, Mavis answered on the first ring.

"It's CJ. I'm on my way there."

"You okay?"

"Yes."

Mavis glanced at the alarm clock on her nightstand. "It's two-thirty, CJ; you're scaring me. You're slipping back into your old ways."

"I'm just clearing up a problem."

"You can talk to me about that later. Just get here, and soon."

"I'm on my way," CJ said, flipping the cell phone closed. He eyed Borg's penthouse one last time, started the Bel Air, and thought about the warmth of Mavis next to him, the smell of her, the softness of her skin. The next instant that thought was gone, replaced by the image of a 125-foot navy patrol boat navigating the murky night waters of the Mekong River and the cold, hard feel and oily smell of a .50-caliber machine gun.

The day broke cold and overcast, and as Flora Jean made her way up the stairs to Oliver Lyman's fifth-floor office, she had the sense that it would stay that way. It had been easy as she'd worked her way across the Auraria Campus to dodge the campus rent-a-cops; easier still to access the King Center as, dressed as a hairnetted cafeteria worker, she'd followed a wedge of five-thirty a.m. food-service and maintenance workers into the building.

What hadn't been easy was breaking into Lyman's office. She jimmied the door using an orthopedic surgeon's mallet and a bone chisel she'd gotten as a Christmas present from an Amerasian doctor friend of hers who'd signed the accompanying Christmas card, "Here's some tools of the trade—use them skillfully. Always your sista, Carmen."

Perspiring and hoping that the office didn't have an alarm,

she let out a sigh of relief when the door, its locking hardware now history, popped open in silence. Flashlight in hand, she quickly searched through Lyman's things, hoping Denver's finest hadn't gotten there first.

She moved to Lyman's desk and a stack of books, maps, and miniature Western photographs resting on top of it. She suspected that most of what was in the stack represented the treasures of a collector. The only thing she found that seemed out of place, piquing her interest as gloved, she sorted through the pile, was a miniature cigar box. She thought of CJ and his cheroots as she opened the box. Inside she found a cache of pawnbroker's receipts. She flipped through them hastily. The majority were made out in Lyman's name, but two of the receipts were filled out with the name Loretta Sheets. Flora Jean pocketed the receipts, thinking as she did that the connection between Sheets and Lyman had to be more than the professor-to-student link Billy DeLong had mentioned.

As she turned back to search through the pile on Lyman's desk a final time, she heard a noise in the hallway. Checking her watch, she realized that she had been in Lyman's office for more than half an hour. She turned off her flashlight, moved into a half squat, hoping that whoever was in the hallway wouldn't spot the jimmied door, and arranged the stash she planned to take with her into a pile.

She heard two distinctly male voices and the tramp of feet moving toward the office. The voices were suddenly directly outside the door. She pressed her back against the wall behind the door, deciding that if someone swung it open, she'd boomerang the door back into their head, hoping to daze them, and make a run for it. She found herself sweating as one man let out a rumbling belly laugh, and she dropped to a crouch. Prepared to spring, she heard a sharp slap of hands. One of the two men said, "Catch you later," and hurried footsteps took off in opposite directions.

She waited for the sound of footsteps to disappear. Slipping off her hairnet, she opened the door, grabbed her stash, and stepped out into the hallway. She looked left but headed right toward the stairwell. Moments later she was outside in the welcome chilly overcast grayness. As she moved toward one of the numerous bike paths that cut across campus, she heard a man let out a loud laugh, reminding her of her earlier scare as she looked up to see a couple of maintenance workers trimming a hedge. As she walked past the men, she smiled and, with her left hand deep in her pocket, fingered the pawnbroker's stubs she'd taken from Lyman's office. Picking up her pace, she walked briskly to the edge of campus until the laughing maintenance worker became just another man in the distance.

CHAPTER 24

O'Brien's, a plain-vanilla box of a cafe, sat at the junction of State Route 67 and US-85. The no-nonsense eatery twenty-five miles south of Denver featured retro 1950s-style red Naugahyde chairs and Formica-topped tables, family-style seating, and hearty, commonsense meals.

Howard Stafford liked to dress in coveralls, work boots, and a baseball cap when he visited O'Brien's in order to people-watch and absorb the cafe's pedestrian flavor. He'd never shared his get-away with anyone until now, and under normal circumstances he would never have considered Theodore Counts for a breakfast companion, but when Counts had called him the previous evening, hysterical over the fact that Oliver Lyman was dead, and lamented that a woman named Flora Jean Benson was dogging him, Stafford had decided that it was in his best interest to talk with Counts as soon as possible. Counts had capped the near meltdown by telling Stafford that a midget with spina bifida who kept Counts schooled on what was happening in Five Points had also told him that a former bail bondsman named CJ Floyd was after him.

When they'd arrived for their seven a.m. meeting, Stafford had looked back on his decision to meet with Counts as being ill advised, but he'd nonetheless ushered Counts into the restaurant, and now as they sat at a table in the far southwest corner, wrapping up breakfast, he considered himself almost home free.

"It's cold in this place." Counts ran his fork through the remnants of eggs and toast on his plate, set aside his coffee cup, and said, "And my coffee's tepid."

Ignoring the comment, Stafford took a final bite of sausage and chewed slowly before answering. "I like the food, especially their sausage."

"Then buy the sausage factory, for Christ's sake."

Stafford smiled. "That's your problem, Theodore. You think everything's about money. And it is. You just don't have the good sense to know when, where, or how to properly use it."

"Let's forget about money and food and think about our problem," said Counts.

"Your problem, Theodore. Your problem."

"Are you crazed? Lyman's dead. If that Benson woman or Floyd link him to me, they'll end up linking me to you. Count on it. To say nothing about the cops making the connection."

"Calm down, Theodore. You've done nothing wrong."

Counts looked at Stafford in disbelief. "Are you out of your mind? I stole scores of rare books from libraries. Have you forgotten about that?"

"And you've been paid. Handsomely." The expression on Stafford's face blossomed into a look of superiority. "Those books didn't belong where they were. They deserved better. Now they're in their appropriate surroundings. You offered them a better life. Much as I do when I pluck some unfortunate underdog off the street, give them a job or a position on my staff, and bless them with the gift of upward mobility. Those books are now where they belong, Theodore. And you did nothing wrong by moving them from where they were to a place of infinite more significance."

Attuned to Stafford's oddball view of the world, Counts said, "In your book maybe." He had lived through Stafford's library renovation, uncertain how he'd made it through a project that took its lead from someone so off center. During the remodel, Stafford had checked every floorboard to make certain that it was a perfect match to its neighbor. He had measured the openings for every wall-mounted fixture to ensure that each and every fixture would be an exact fit. He had made certain that the side rails on the two circulating ladders were identical, and he'd checked the satin finish on the wainscoting for flaws so many times that Counts had had to plead with him to "be done with it" so the project could be brought to a close. Looking at Stafford and wondering what on earth made a man like him tick, Counts said, "Some people just aren't as enlightened as you."

"Don't yank my chain, Theodore. I can toss you to the wolves."

Counts sat up in his chair. "And you'd be right there with me."

Stafford smiled. It was the sly smile of a nobleman flashed to a member of the proletariat. "Theodore, you're so mistaken. But let's not piss on one another for sport. There's no need. You have your worries, and I have mine. You're concerned about someone connecting you to the minor pilferage of an insignificant number of books from the shelves of a few meaningless public libraries. I, on the other hand, am concerned about having lost something priceless."

Counts looked surprised. "I thought you had that handled."

"Not completely. There are still a few loose ends."

"Like Lyman?"

Stafford took a sip of coffee without answering. When he finally did respond, his face was an unemotional blank sheet. "Make certain not to become a loose end, Theodore. I have such trouble with them. Now, where did you say you were staying until you get up enough nerve to go back home?"

"Thirty miles east of here. In Kiowa, with a friend."

"That's as good a place as any, I guess," said Stafford as their waitress appeared.

"More coffee?" asked the waitress, smiling.

"Decaf for me," said Stafford, watching the waitress fill his cup. "And my friend says his coffee's cold—can you please get him another?"

"Sure." The waitress retreated to get a pot of regular coffee.

"They're pleasant in here, don't you think, Theodore? It's like they've been commissioned to serve and enjoy it."

Counts nodded as the waitress reappeared with a steaming fresh pot of coffee. He watched the steam rise from a fresh cup as she refilled it, realizing that without considering it, he'd told Stafford where he was staying. He wished he hadn't, concerned that a man who would go to the trouble of making certain that hundreds of floorboards snuggled up in perfect harmony to one another would certainly have no trouble dispatching someone like him. He watched Stafford take a sip of coffee and glance around the room, smiling at workaday people as he caught their eye, flashing them a jovial connected look as if he were a mere commoner, just like them.

CJ was browsing a recently opened Smoker Friendly Store on a street just east of Colorado Boulevard in Denver's Belcaro neighborhood when his cell phone went off.

"Floyd here."

"You're up pretty early for someone who was out so late," Pinkie

Niedemeyer said. "Thought that after our little chat last night, I should give you a heads-up."

"I'm listening," said CJ, eyeing the star-shaped 15 percent off sign above a Christmas tree–shaped display of his favorite brand of cheroots.

"Seems as if Vannick has a hard-on for someone besides you. Got word a few minutes ago that he wants a piece of that big-breasted ex–marine corps sista you work with. Offered the some-one I talked to a reasonable sum to send her on a one-way trip."

"Damn it! I thought you said Vannick wasn't connected."

"You don't have to be to hire someone who is."

"That son of a bitch called for a hit on Flora Jean! I'll kill him!"

"Hold your horses, man. You're on a cell phone. We might as well be on a recorded line. And you're using words that I find quite frightening and offensive, do you understand?"

"Hold on a sec; I need to step away from where I am." CJ rushed out of the store, slipped into the Bel Air, and shut the door. "Okay, and for the record, I do understand. Now, will you just get to the bottom line?"

"Before you fly off the handle like some green stick right out of basic, consider the source of your aggravation, my friend."

Biting back his temper, CJ said, "I'll do that. Maybe Vannick's upset at Flora Jean because she's on to the fact he killed someone."

Niedemeyer bristled. "There you go using those awful incrim-inating words again. Let's say I give you Vannick's office address and you take the issue up directly with him."

"Fine," said CJ, seething.

"Try him at 707 West 32nd, in the Denver Highlands neigh-borhood. He drives a Porsche with vanity plates that read, *WIRED*. Got his description?"

"Flora Jean's described him for me. Thick-necked with muscle. Pockmarked face. Likes to work out."

"She's been that up close and personal?"

"They've chatted." CJ adjusted his phone to his other ear, more peeved now than angry. "One last question, Pinkie. Why so helpful?"

"Because it suits me. Why else?"

"Can the bullshit, Niedemeyer. Honesty'll work fine."

"Honesty, then. Fact is, I'm paying off a debt."

"To who?"

"A friend of your uncle's."

Knowing not to mention Mario Satoni's name, CJ said, "Funny, I've never known you to get into that kind of debt."

"You do stupid things when you're young. But the bill's almost paid. I don't expect to have to service it much longer."

"Good luck with closing out the books. And thanks for that address."

"Always enjoy helping my fellow man," said Niedemeyer. "Gotta sign off."

"Later," said CJ, pocketing his cell phone. He thought about calling Flora Jean to tell her that Vannick had called for a hit on her but decided against it, figuring there was no need to get her upset. His anger had abated and he felt clear-headed enough to go deal with Vannick. He cranked the Bel Air's engine as he tried to conjure up what Pinkie Niedemeyer could have done in his youth that would have him still paying off a debt to Mario Satoni. He didn't know the exact set of rules that wiseguys lived by, but he knew enough about their code to know that Pinkie's transgression must have been serious.

Deciding the debt he would someday pay for his lifelong affair with tobacco was going to be a whopper, CJ backed the Bel Air away from the Smoker Friendly Store and pointed the vintage Chevrolet north toward Arthur Vannick's.

The rear license plate on Arthur Vannick's Porsche gleamed in the late-morning sun, announcing to anyone with enough cryptic insight to decipher the coded message exactly what Vannick did for a living.

CJ, who'd always had the feeling that people who required vanity plates were in need of a good shrink, strolled up to Vannick's Porsche and peered inside. When he brushed one of the car's rocker panels with his leg, the alarm emitted several warning beeps.

As he stepped away from the car, a voice behind him called out, "You lookin' for somethin', buddy?"

CJ pivoted to see a thick-bodied, lantern-jawed white man approaching. The man's torso bulged from the confines of a tight-fitting muscle shirt, and his upper arms, bare and salmon pink, bore the signature bulges of a body builder. "Trying to locate Arthur Vannick."

"You've found him. You got a delivery?" CJ and Vannick now stood face to face next to the driver's-side door.

"A what?"

"A delivery for my office."

The muscles in CJ's face tightened. "Oh, a delivery. You mean the kind that delivery boys make. Afraid not, sonny."

"Then step out of the way."

CJ didn't budge.

"Move it or lose it, friend."

CJ smiled and flashed Vannick a wink. "Like Luis Del Mora and Oliver Lyman did?"

Vannick took a step back. Sizing CJ up, he said, "Who the fuck are you, asshole?"

"Somebody who's looking into why a mother lost her only son."

"Sad. Why don't you tell her to try fuckin' a little more often, make herself some more babies?"

"Don't think that would be kosher. Just like it wouldn't seem kosher for a thief to cough up everything he knows about a missing million-dollar daguerreotype or the ins and outs of the book-stealing business."

Vannick's eyes widened, his upper lip curled, and his face flushed just as a Denver Parks and Recreation truck lumbered by. As the truck's back bumper moved past, Vannick lunged at CJ, shoving him into a fifty-gallon water container that was precariously attached to the truck's bumper. The container toppled, sending a waterfall careening down onto CJ before it bounced into the middle of the street. "Next time I'll shove you in front of the damn truck." Vannick swung his car door open and slipped inside.

Standing in the middle of the street, drenched, CJ watched the Parks and Recreation truck ease back toward him. He picked up the empty container, and called out toward the truck, "Got your container," before slamming it into the Porsche's door, producing a dent the diameter of a basketball. Astonished, Vannick leaned across the front seat and popped open the glove compartment, but before he could grasp the Beretta 9-millimeter inside, CJ yanked the door open, clotheslined Vannick around the neck with his right arm, and snatched him in a near clean-and-jerk through the open door and onto the street.

He eyed the gun clearly visible in the open glove compartment, released his choke hold on Vannick, and shouted, "You better get some sense, man!"

Vannick twisted out of CJ's grasp, rose out of a half crouch, and let loose with a roundhouse left that caught CJ above the right eye.

Dazed, CJ blocked Vannick's right-hand counter with a forearm, quickly spliced both arms together with knotted fists, and took a home-run cut that connected with Vannick's left temple and dropped him like the weight at the end of a plumb line.

"Hot damn!" screamed a recreation worker who now stood in the middle of the street. Two other cars had stopped and the curious drivers had come out of their vehicles. The parks worker, a twenty-something black man with a head full of cornrows, sported a toothpick in one corner of his mouth. "I saw everything, brother. Dropped him like a sack of shit." He eyed Vannick, who was sprawled unconscious in the street.

CJ shook his head. "Don't think you did." Reaching back inside the Porsche, he grabbed Vannick's 9-millimeter.

"Shit," said the startled city worker. "The son of a bitch could've shot you."

"But he didn't."

"You wanta call the cops? I'll back you up."

Smiling at the man, CJ said, "You tell me, brother. Here I am with a rich white boy sprawled out in the street at my feet, his eighty-thousand-dollar car with my dent in it sitting next to me, and a gun in my hand. Would you?"

Copying CJ's smile, the man simply nodded as the now semiconscious Vannick let out a groan and wriggled pithed-frog-style at CJ's feet.

"Show's over," the man with the cornrows said to what was now a group of six onlookers. "Move on along."

As the onlookers moved away, some gawking over their shoulders toward CJ and the gun, CJ said to the young parks worker, "Appreciate your help," and slipped Vannick's 9-millimeter into a jacket pocket.

Eyeing CJ with admiration, the young man asked, "Where the hell'd you learn that baseball swing of yours? Sure coldcocked the shit out of Mr. Porsche."

CJ grinned. "From my uncle."

"Ever had to use it before?"

"A couple of times."

"Where?"

"In a place you never heard of."

"Try me."

"Vietnam."

The young man beamed. "Have too. It's one of them Asian places that rich folks go to for vacation."

CJ reached into his pocket, fingered the butt of the 9-millimeter, smiled, and watched Vannick, up on his knees, head to the ground, start to puke. Looking back at the young city worker, CJ said, "It's a vacation spot all right; can't argue with you there," before glancing one last time at Vannick and walking away.

It was windy and only a few degrees above freezing when Pinkie Niedemeyer checked in by cell phone for a briefing with Mario Satoni. "Weather's a pisser," said Pinkie. "One minute spring's on the rise, the next minute, fricking winter."

"What have you got for me, Pinkie?" asked Mario, accustomed to Niedemeyer's penchant for complaining.

"Got Floyd kickin' Arthur Vannick's ass over in the Highlands a little earlier. Took the thick-necked shit out with one blow. Then I got him stopping by his girlfriend's restaurant for lunch, and now I've got him back home."

"Stay glued to his rear, Pinkie."

"For how long?"

"Until I tell you not to."

"What the hell's Floyd got on you, Mario?"

"Nothing."

"Then why the white-glove treatment? You'd think he'd been made."

"You'd think," said Mario with a smile. "Just stay on his ass, Pinkie. I'll tell you when to let up."

"Okay. But I've got business I've gotta tend to, Mario, and soon. Business that's dialed in from a couple of rungs above you. Don't wanta get crossways with you on this."

"It won't come to that. Just keep me informed."

"Will do," said Pinkie. "And then maybe one day you'll tell me the whole story on Floyd."

"One day," said a stern-faced Mario, cradling the phone.

Alexie had wanted to go with Celeste, but she'd said no. She'd had enough of delegating tasks and seeing no results. She didn't need the Russian bear or his minions doing anything for her, she told herself as she crested I-25's 7,300-foot-high Palmer Divide and nosed Alexie's Range Rover toward the expanse of a broad plateau that would take her to Denver.

What she needed now was the same thing anyone needed who was engaged in a serious competition: courage, stamina, iron will, and a little luck. In life, as in sport, the end result that really mattered was winning.

She'd kill Floyd, whether today, tomorrow, or the day after that. She only had to wait for him to poke his nose out of his house, go for groceries, mail a letter, or perhaps even vacuum out his precious car. She'd stalked Floyd for months before buying into Alexie's hare-brained Moradi-Nik bombing scheme. She knew his daily regimen like she knew her own. He'd be there when she needed him to be. She just had to be a little patient. She glanced over the seat back, eyed the carrying case behind her, and smiled. She had everything she needed to deal with Floyd right there in the vehicle. The kill would be swift and, as Alexie was so fond of saying, professional.

She accelerated, nosing into a stiff twenty-mile-per-hour headwind, and briefly her thoughts turned to Bobby as she tried to imagine what their lives would have been like if he were still alive. Suddenly she was hoping and dreaming like a child, then, as quickly as the thoughts had appeared, they were gone.

Gritting her teeth, she glanced at the speedometer and realized that she was cruising at 105. She eased off the accelerator, loosened her hand-numbing grip on the steering wheel, and again glanced toward the case. "There's a time for us, a time and a place for us," she mouthed before turning her attention back to the road and the task ahead.

CHAPTER 25

CJ walked into Flora Jean's office carrying a shopping bag in his right arm. It was ten past six, and the city was busy spilling its workers back into the Denver neighborhoods and suburbs they had come from. The swelling over CJ's right eye had become a plum-sized knot. Flora Jean was about to light into him for not checking in with her all day when she noticed the lump. "Looks like you've got yourself a reason for rollin' in here late," she said, eyeing CJ sympathetically from behind her desk. "What the hell happened?"

"Had a minor disagreement with Arthur Vannick."

"Hope he's got a knot or two somewhere that matches yours."

"Didn't stick around to check. When I left him he was barely conscious. But I'm guessing he's sporting a much bigger knot than me." CJ placed the shopping bag next to him on a table and took a seat in a chair across from his old desk. Eyeing the desk with a sense of nostalgia, he slipped Vannick's 9-millimeter out of his jacket pocket and slid it across the desktop to Flora Jean. "Took this from Vannick. Any word yet on how Oliver Lyman bought it? I'm wondering if maybe I stumbled onto the gun that killed him."

Flora Jean picked up the 9-millimeter and moved it from hand to hand. "Afraid not. Vernon Lowe called from the morgue a couple of hours ago with the scoop on Lyman. Said the hole in his chest was probably from a .22 Mag. Looks like Lyman caught the same disease as Luis Del Mora."

"Still doesn't eliminate Vannick," said CJ. "It's not against the law to own more than one gun."

"Or four, or five," Flora Jean countered sarcastically. "At least we've got one of Vannick's little toys, and for now we keep him on our suspects list."

"We sure do. Along with that museum curator Sheets, Counts, and Stafford. And, although Billy wouldn't approve, Amanda Hunter."

"He sure wouldn't. I think Billy's found his Annie Oakley. Where is he, anyway?"

CJ checked his watch. "He should be back in Cheyenne by now, sticking like glue to Loretta Sheets. He drove down from Amanda Hunter's ranch first thing this morning, brought me a bag full of things he thought might be important from the scene of that break-in I told you about, and, believe it or not, handed me half-a-dozen real daguerreotypes."

"You mean I finally get to see one of those pictures that all the fuss is about?"

"Sure do," said CJ, reaching into the shopping bag and taking out several six-and-a-half-by-eight-and-three-quarter-inch daguerreotype whole-plate photographs. He smiled and handed them to Flora Jean.

"They okay to touch?" asked Flora Jean, picking up one by the edges.

"Sure are. They came out of a safe in Amanda's basement."

"They look awfully delicate," said Flora Jean, scrutinizing a photograph of the Laramie Mountains. She slid that photo aside and picked up one of a bearded man in a top hat standing beside a river. "What's the river in these two?"

"The Laramie. It runs right through Hunter's ranch. And

believe it or not, it doesn't look much different today than it did a hundred and twenty-five years ago when Jacob Covington took those photos."

"They're a little dark for my taste, but pretty enough."

"Guess that's the best you can do when you try to expose an image directly onto silver. One thing for sure, there's a puppy just like these out there somewhere that's worth over a million."

Flora Jean shook her head. "And worth killin' for. Anything else in with the goodies that Billy brought you?"

"Only this," said CJ, reaching into the bottom of the bag and taking out a small piece of tissue paper that had been folded. He laid the tissue paper on the desktop, dipped into the bag once again, and took out several 1920s-vintage Cheyenne Frontier Days postcards. He handed the postcards to Flora Jean. "Handle them gently."

"Will do," said Flora Jean, flipping through postcards that showed various rodeo events. Each card had been postmarked Frontier Days, Cheyenne, Wyoming, 1923. Beneath the postmark was a half-inch-by-half-inch imprint of the Triangle Bar cattle brand.

"Billy says Amanda's grandfather had the postcards made up to hand out as favors."

"They're mighty pristine-lookin'," said Flora Jean, setting the cards aside. "Looks like they never got distributed."

"Billy and Amanda found them scattered on the floor of the shed that was broken into. And they found this," said CJ, pulling back the corners of the tissue paper. "Don't touch," he admonished. "What does it look like to you?"

Flora Jean eyed the fragment of tortoiseshell plastic and said, "Looks like something that broke off a comb or maybe a piece of plastic off somebody's glasses frames to me."

"Two for two," said CJ. "Those are the same things Billy and Amanda and I came up with."

As if to upset the apple cart, Flora Jean said, "Or maybe a piece of plastic off a compact case."

"I didn't think of that."

Smiling, Flora Jean said, "Maybe you need to spend more time tendin' to your woman. Anyway, now that we got all these odds and ends, where do they take us?"

"I'm hoping the cards lead us to a set of fingerprints. Maybe Amanda's burglar got careless. I was hoping you'd give the cards to Alden and he'd have one of his intelligence contacts check them for fingerprints."

"It'll take some time."

"Everything does," said CJ, rewrapping the piece of plastic in tissue paper and placing the postcards back in a pile. "Now that you've seen my show-and-tell, what did you dig up at Oliver Lyman's?"

"Strange, but would you believe more collectibles? Lots of Indian pawn, you know the stuff—bolo ties, rings, squash-blossom necklaces, some old picture frames, a couple of old road maps, and a few pieces of pottery. And, now get this, a bunch of old pawn tickets with Loretta Sheets's name on a couple of 'em. What do you make of the connection?"

CJ stroked his chin thoughtfully. "Well, well, well. Collectors, collectors. Lyman, Stafford, Sheets, maybe even Hunter."

"And Vannick and Counts in their own de facto way," said Flora Jean. "Wonder what Alden'll come up with when he has those postcards dusted for prints. Wanta go through the stuff I found at Lyman's?"

"Absolutely. Who knows, we might turn up something else," CJ said, looking mildly puzzled.

"The stuff's out back on the porch. I'll go get it. What's got you lookin' baffled?"

"Just wondering, since I'm a collector myself, if we aren't missing something."

"Don't think too long, sugar, 'cause you might come up with somethin' that'll confuse the shit outta you."

CJ sifted through the things Flora Jean had brought from Lyman's without discovering anything else of interest, and Flora Jean had been gone for twenty minutes when, from his apartment, CJ called Morgan Williams to find out that Morgan and Dittier's stakeout of Alexie Borg's place in LoDo had so far produced nothing.

CJ now found himself holding on the "insurance problem hotline" of his insurance company, hoping to get a progress report on his claim. He glanced at his kitchen clock and, realizing he'd been on hold for almost fifteen minutes, slammed his open palm down on the kitchen table in frustration.

Caught between a disingenuous insurance company and Lenny McCabe's need to extract the monetary equivalent of a pound of flesh from their misfortune, CJ had the sense that things were only going to get bleaker.

He hung up the phone, pushed aside the beer he'd been nursing, muttered, "To hell with it," grabbed his jacket from a hook next to the kitchen door, and stepped outside onto the fire-escape balcony. Still calming down, he glanced past the wrought-iron stairway that spiraled up from the driveway to his apartment and toward the Bel Air parked in the driveway. Caught in the glow of a corner streetlight, the vintage machine seemed to shimmer.

A brief wind gust reminded him that it was thirty-five degrees and still very much springtime in Denver. He zipped his jacket, realized Arthur Vannick's gun was still in the left pocket, and started down the stairs, knowing that in a few minutes he'd be enjoying a meal of fried chicken, coleslaw, butter beans, and biscuits at Mavis's.

He was halfway down the steps when he remembered the swelling over his right eye. Mavis was certain to ask about the knot, and he needed an answer. A small, well-intentioned fabrication that would serve as a salve to her worries. He'd think of something, he told himself, pausing momentarily on the steps. After all, he had a full ten minutes to dredge up an explanation.

Outfitted in black and lying flat on her belly on the catwalk of an unlit billboard thirty yards from where CJ stood, Celeste Deepstream had been waiting patiently. A mechanically assisted fifty-pound compound bow and the arrow she planned to slam into the chest of the man who had killed her twin brother rested at her side. Cupping her hands to her mouth and warming them with two puffs of breath, she cocked her best winners'-podium smile.

Bobby had been the one who'd taught her to use a crossbow, how to shoot with precision and to be consistent. How to forge a stream in the heat of the hunt and not be swept away, how to use a spotting scope, even what kind of clothes to wear in order to compromise an animal's ability to catch her scent.

It had been Bobby who had taught her about quad limbs and riser locks and arm butts until she knew the mechanics of archery like the back of her hand. Most importantly for the killing business at hand, he'd taught her how to operate and shoot for accuracy when there was only the barest hint of light.

A Super Carbon Magnum arrow, machined for straightness and a smooth, quiet launch, rested just inches away.

While serving her sentence for manslaughter and looking for ways to fill the idle hours, she'd learned all she could about compound bows and arrowheads. That knowledge would now serve her well. The broad head beside her, capable of downing a 250-pound animal in the wild, could easily fell a 235-pound man. The mechanical blades were designed to lock in for flight until the instant the tip touched animal hide or human skin, producing an on-contact spiral wound that wouldn't clot. She smiled at the image, knowing that in the end Floyd's very essence would ooze from him like that of a trophy elk.

Her plan called for two shooting opportunities, an early one at twilight and a second one just before midnight. She preferred the hour at hand because the light was better, but she would take what came.

Most of what she carried with her, including her crossbow case, the compound bow, and her triple-red-dot scope, was black. Only the silver broad heads themselves, and the vanes on her arrows, had any hint of color. She'd spent two hour-long dress-rehearsal sessions on the catwalk, and she was certain she hadn't been seen either time. The toughest parts of any hunt, the stalking and the sighting, were behind her now.

She wouldn't have the luxury of checking on her kill, which meant that her first shot had to be perfect—a vital-organ shot that would silence Floyd and afford her time to escape. She had clocked how long it would take after the kill shot to vanish into the darkness and had calculated the time at just under two minutes. One minute would be spent assessing Floyd through binoculars to make certain he was dead. She'd need another half minute to pack up her things, safely clear the catwalk, and descend the billboard's ladder to the parking lot. Finally, it would take another twenty to thirty seconds to stow her gear in the Range Rover and vanish.

Her timing would have to be impeccable. There was no room for error. She ran the plan through her head one last time, rose on her knees, raised her crossbow, and sighted in on Floyd's car to get a feel for what her shot would look like. Steadying herself and mimicking a shot, she relaxed, suddenly drawn to Floyd's presence by the slam of a door and the hint of smoke rising from one of his cheroots. As she watched him move around his car from the passenger's side to the driver's side, she was struck by his slow, purposeful gait, a gait not unlike that of a big animal in the wild. He reached the front of the vehicle and stopped to check the car's antenna. As he fumbled with it, she gulped a breath of air, cocked her crossbow, and readied it. She had the perfect view of Floyd, who was now less than twenty yards away, and she could see his entire torso. His riverboat gambler's vest, his dusky-gray Stetson, the faded ever-present chambray shirt. She had no idea why he'd stopped to fidget with the antenna, but it would be his undoing. Adjusting her sight and her scope's twilight sidelight, she double-checked her arrow to make sure it was secure for what would be a steep-angled shot, steadied her finger on the lethal weapon's trigger, and squared up on her target, knowing that Floyd would briefly have to turn to face her as he opened the car door to get in.

Thinking, *Patience, Celeste,* she took a slow, deep breath. She felt her rib cage move and imagined the film of moisture that would serve as a lightning rod between the crossbow's trigger and her finger. For a split second she thought about Bobby; then, almost as if he'd been cued, she watched Floyd pivot to face her. His left hand, the one he'd used to adjust the antenna, dropped to his side as his right hand reached for the door handle. She squeezed the crossbow's trigger, a blush of wind kissed her cheek, and she heard someone shout, "Floyd!" Before she could determine where the shout had come from, her wind-aided, slightly off-course death bolt pierced the left-hand corner of the Bel Air's windshield, shattering it.

"Wind!" Only after the word exploded from her mouth did she realize she'd screamed it.

Floyd was on the ground, spread-eagled, a gun aimed menacingly in her direction. She heard the retort of a pistol and the sound of a pop just above her head; a second pop followed closely on the heels of the first.

Someone was shooting at her, and it clearly wasn't Floyd. As she raced for the catwalk's ladder, she dropped her crossbow and it plummeted toward the ground. The escape she'd planned so carefully spiraled through her head as she started down the ladder.

CJ was up on one knee, sweeping Arthur Vannick's 9-millimeter back and forth in front of him, searching for a target, when Pinkie Niedemeyer rushed from his hiding place behind CJ's garage, screaming, "The billboard! The billboard! It came from the billboard!"

Celeste jumped from the ladder's third step and onto parking-lot asphalt while both men still had their eyes locked on the unlit catwalk. She bolted for Alexie's Range Rover in an all-out sprint. She was several yards from the vehicle when CJ finally saw her. He squeezed off an erratic shot and charged after her, leaving Pinkie Niedemeyer standing beside the Bel Air.

The Range Rover roared to life as CJ charged across 13th

Avenue and raced into the nearly empty parking lot. Tires squeal-
ing, the Range Rover streaked away as CJ, steadying his arm on
a billboard support strut, squeezed off two final shots. But the
vehicle was out of range, and within seconds it had disappeared
into the night.

Floating on an adrenaline rush, CJ turned back to join Niedemeyer, nearly stumbling over the crossbow at his feet. He picked
up the crossbow, looked up toward the catwalk, and looped the
bow over his shoulder. As he crossed 13th Avenue, the wind
kicked up. The warm upslope wind kissed his cheek briefly, but it
was gone in the push of a second.

It was close to eight-thirty by the time the two cops who'd taken
CJ's statement left. He told them everything he knew about anyone who might have wanted to kill him, but most of all he told
them about Celeste Deepstream, about the bombing of his store
and Moradi-Nik and Alexie Borg and the Russian mob. What
he didn't tell them was that a hit man named Pinkie Niedemeyer,
working off a debt to a onetime Denver mobster, had probably
saved his life. He also didn't mention to them that he and the
hit man had taken five shots at his assailant.

The cops had been professional and procedural, roping off the
area beneath the billboard with crime-scene tape and going about
their job efficiently. For all CJ knew, when and if they scratched
beyond the surface of the attempt on his life, they might eventually find the two bullets that Pinkie Niedemeyer swore he'd pep-
pered into the billboard or one or all of the slugs CJ had fired.
But he suspected that it wouldn't come down to that. No one
had been killed, and there was only a damaged compound bow,

a shattered car windshield, and a broken arrow to support his story. No witnesses, no getaway car, and no woman named Celeste. They would check out his claim that a Russian mobster was somehow involved in the attempt on his life. But when all was said and done, for the Denver Police Department CJ Floyd simply wasn't front-burner material—which meant he would have to deal with his Celeste Deepstream problem himself.

CHAPTER 26

Celeste and Alexie Borg sped south on I-25 in silence on their way to Alexie's Black Forest home. Surprisingly calm, Celeste had walked into Alexie's Denver condo thirty minutes earlier and announced that she'd botched killing Floyd. Aware that Floyd, and now very likely the cops, would be dogging her, she'd offered the Russian bear the bone he'd been scratching after for nearly six months, agreeing to accompany him to Paris on a two-month-long business trip and vacation.

She wasn't certain how she'd be able to endure eight weeks of his clinging and pawing, but she'd decided that two months with Alexie beat a possible second prison stint. Besides, she knew Paris; she had contacts there and even a few friendships that stretched back to her days as an American exchange student at the Sorbonne.

Accelerating into the night, Alexie finally said, "We'll be leaving the day after tomorrow." He dropped a meaty hand onto Celeste's thigh and squeezed. "Pack as many things as you like. Everything will be first class, and very private."

Celeste forced a smile, swallowed hard, and dropped a hand onto Alexie's. She had no interest in how they got to Paris—a tramp steamer would suffice. What mattered was distancing herself from Floyd and the law. As Alexie's probing hand worked its way up her thigh, she removed her hand from his and set her mind adrift. She was no longer there, speeding down I-25 into uncertain darkness. Instead she was swimming, streaking for the bulkhead of an imaginary pool with the crowd cheering her on, hoping to be the first swimmer home.

"CJ, I've been trying to get you for over an hour. Where've you been?" Morgan growled into the mouthpiece of a pay phone outside a 7-11 a few blocks from Alexie Borg's Denver condo.

"Been talking to the cops," said CJ, who now stood in his driveway, cell phone in one hand, a flashlight in the other, checking out the damage to the Bel Air. He ran a finger around the jagged hole in the car's windshield, eyed the arrowhead puncture wound in the back of the driver's seat, and shook his head.

"'Bout what?" asked Morgan, watching a cold and shivering Dittier rock from side to side next to him.

"About somebody trying to take my head off with a bolt from a crossbow."

"Damn! Celeste?"

"Who else?" CJ slipped into the Bel Air and began picking glass off the seat. "So what have you got for me, Morgan?"

"Got Borg on the move. An hour or so ago he left his condo and walked six blocks south down Blake Street and another block north without even knowin' Dittier was on his heels. Dittier saw him get into a black Range Rover. A minute or so later I watched that same vehicle drive into the garage under Borg's building. Borg resurfaced a little while later in the Range Rover and took off like a bat outta hell up Larimer Street."

"Was anyone else in the vehicle with him?"

"Couldn't tell. The windows were all blacked out. I guess somebody could've been hidin' in the back. You thinkin' Celeste was with him?"

"More than likely. Whoever tried to take me out with that crossbow took off in a black Range Rover."

"She probably called Borg from around the corner to come get her, thinking it was safer than driving up to his building."

"No matter. I'm headed down there to have a look."

"You won't be able to get inside that buildin' of Borg's. They got it locked up like Fort Knox."

"No rush. He'll be back. Probably not tonight; things are too hot. But he'll resurface. It's his home. I want you to stay put. And Morgan, I'll be bringing you one of Julie's cell phones. You'll need it if things start moving real fast."

"Stayin' down here's okay by me," said Morgan. "But Dittier's gettin' pretty cold."

"Tell him I'll bring him a thermos of hot chocolate and my old navy peacoat."

"He'll like that. How long you gonna be?"

"Fifteen minutes at the most. Just stay put." Ending the call, CJ dusted the remaining glass off the front seat of the Bel Air and pulled the car into the garage next to his heaterless Jeep. He slipped out of the Bel Air, flipped on a light switch, and worked his way between all the inventory from Ike's Spot to a five-foot-long workbench. Kneeling, he slipped the navy footlocker he'd brought home from Vietnam from beneath the workbench, spun the combination lock, snapped the lock open, and lifted the top.

Things precious to him rested inside, most of them tucked beneath an old peacoat. He removed the coat, ignoring a box that contained his Navy Cross and a stash of porcelain license plates. He wanted two things, the peacoat for Dittier and the .45

that Ike had carried during the Korean War and he had secretly carried during Vietnam. He slipped Vannick's 9-millimeter from where he'd stashed it behind a couple of oil cans before the cops had arrived, dropped it into the footlocker, shoved the bulky, always-loaded .45 into his jacket pocket, set the peacoat aside, and relocked the footlocker. He nudged the locker back under the workbench with his foot, walked over to the Jeep, tossed the peacoat onto the front seat, and got in.

He cranked the Jeep's engine, watched a puff of exhaust rise behind him, and backed outside. When he got out of the Jeep to close the garage door, he thought about the last time he'd fired the .45. It hadn't been during Vietnam but nine months earlier when Celeste, having kidnapped, beaten, and tortured Mavis, had slipped away from him during a gunfight in the New Mexico mountains. She wouldn't slip away again, he told himself, slamming the garage door closed.

Perspiring, spent from lovemaking, and curled as tightly as her statuesque body would allow against Alden Grace, Flora Jean listened to her phone ring, finally answering it after she glanced at the flashing caller ID.

"It's CJ," she said, wiggling out of Alden's embrace. Scooping the receiver from its cradle, she said, "This better be important, CJ Floyd."

"Wouldn't have called if it wasn't," said CJ, aware from Flora Jean's tone that his call was ill timed. "Need to do a little jump start on the Del Mora case. Can you call Theresa Del Mora and have her get me Howard Stafford's daily routine? What time he leaves for work, when he comes back home, things like that."

Flora Jean sat up and leaned back against the headboard, leaving Alden Grace looking abandoned. "Are you runnin' on fumes, CJ? It's ten o'clock at night. Theresa's probably in bed; can't this wait till tomorrow?"

"Probably, but I've been gnawing on Stafford for the past half hour, trying to figure out what a rich man's angle might be in this whole daguerreotype thing."

"And?" said Flora Jean, sensing a confused urgency in CJ's tone.

"And maybe Stafford knew the Del Mora kid stole his photo and he killed him to get it back."

Flora Jean shook her head, eyed Grace, and shrugged. "There's nothin' new there, CJ." Moving the cell phone to her left ear, she said, "There's somethin' you're not tellin' me. Spit it out."

"Okay. But it doesn't have anything to do with the Del Mora case. I had a little altercation this evening, and it got me thinking."

"Altercation with who?"

"Celeste, I think. She sent me a message right outside my garage. Took the Bel Air's windshield out with an arrow from a compound bow."

"Are you okay?"

"Yeah, but that whole thing got me to thinking that maybe we've been looking in all the wrong places for Del Mora's killer, spending too much time chasing after bit players like Counts and Vannick and the Sheets woman when we should've been targeting Stafford all along."

"And Celeste sent you marchin' down this new street?"

"She sure did. She came after me herself. No middleman, no stooges, no second-string players to screw things up. Could be that Stafford did the same thing where Del Mora was concerned."

"Sounds plausible. But Stafford's not some poor run-amuck Indian princess. You're dealin' with somebody who's got influence, power, and a whole lotta money, sugar."

"I know that. But we can't dance around him forever. All I wanta know from Theresa is what time the man leaves for work."

Suspecting that for CJ, Stafford had somehow become a surrogate for Celeste, Flora Jean said, "You're bendin' the truth, CJ, playin' at being the lone ranger when what you need is help from the law. Keep it up and trust me, you're gonna end up crazy just like her. You should've given your Celeste Deepstream problem to the cops a long time ago."

"I called them tonight."

"Hope it ain't too late."

Skirting the issue, his tone insistent, CJ said, "I need to know how to get in touch with Stafford, Flora Jean."

"Okay, I'll call Theresa and see if I can get a fix on Stafford's daily routine. But remember, CJ, this is still my case. Lean on Stafford too heavy and I'm the one who comes up liable. Theresa can pull the plug on our investigation anytime she likes, and if Stafford goes screamin' to the cops, they can do even worse."

"I'll remember, and trust me, sniffing out Stafford's a move in the right direction."

"I'll call you back when I've got somethin'."

"I'll be at Mavis's."

Flora Jean smiled. "That's where you need to be a whole lot more often, sugar. Talk to you later," she said, leaving CJ listening to dead air as she cradled the phone and slipped back into Alden Grace's embrace.

Unable to sleep, CJ eyed the alarm clock on Mavis's nightstand. He hadn't told Mavis about Celeste trying to kill him, and he'd explained that the knot above his eye was the result of Morgan accidentally swinging a box of items from the store into him.

He didn't know if Mavis had bought the story; she'd had to listen to so many off-tone explanations about injuries he'd sustained over the years that he couldn't be certain. But she hadn't pressed the issue. They'd made small talk, discussed a trip to Santa Fe, and had a glass of cabernet before he'd failed miserably at lovemaking and Mavis had drifted off to sleep.

Restless and wired, he glanced at Mavis, slipped out of bed, grabbed his cell phone, and headed downstairs for the kitchen.

He didn't turn on any lights until he was in the kitchen. Opening the refrigerator, he reached inside and took out a slice of sweet-potato pie. He'd just taken the pie out of the toaster oven when his cell phone began to vibrate. He answered the phone in a whisper, "CJ."

"It's Flora Jean. I've got the information you wanted on Stafford."

"Shoot."

"He leaves his house for the office every morning around eight. Surprised somebody that rich ain't got a driver."

"What kind of car does he drive?" asked CJ, all business.

"A black Buick Le Sabre."

"Good. Tomorrow morning Mr. Stafford and I are going to have a talk."

"One thing more," said Flora Jean. "Theresa said she has a box of Luis's things that we might wanta go through. She says she forgot to tell me about it before."

"Awfully convenient."

"She was distraught, CJ. And she's a mother. No way on earth the woman would've had anything to do with her own son's murder. Now, are you sure you're up to dealin' with Stafford without gettin' the cops involved?"

"Yes."

"Okay, but remember what I said about not gettin' into a tug-of-war with Stafford. It's a war I don't think we can win."

"Unless Stafford killed someone."

"Maybe not even then," said Flora Jean, shaking her head in frustration. "I'll see you tomorrow."

"I'll talk to you early." Sensing Flora Jean's agitation, CJ flipped his cell phone closed and eyed the still steaming slice of sweet-potato pie as he tried to decide whether Theresa Del Mora's sudden recollection about her son's things was truly related to her earlier despondency. He was in the midst of enjoying the rich cinnamon-sweet flavor of his favorite dessert when his face went blank as thoughts of the Del Mora case disappeared and visions of Celeste Deepstream racing away from him with an imagined crossbow in her hand resurfaced.

CHAPTER 27

CJ had been waiting in his Jeep on the street outside the Stafford compound since seven-thirty. He'd been surprised to find that the compound didn't have on-site security personnel, just surveillance cameras, something he'd checked to make certain of when he had scaled the front wall of the compound to check things out just before daybreak.

He had no idea how Stafford would take to a black man in a battered Jeep blocking his driveway. For all he knew, Stafford had a hotline in his car to the cops, or maybe he carried a gun. It didn't matter; they were even on the second score, and CJ really didn't care about the first.

The sight of the gate opening caught CJ by surprise, the movement was so precision-quiet. CJ quickly started the Jeep, hoping Stafford wouldn't come barreling down on him, and moved the Jeep directly into the path of what he could now see was a black Buick approaching. Paul Grimes's article with a photograph of Stafford sat on the seat next to him. He had a backup plan in case Stafford wasn't behind the wheel. But no backup plan was needed. Stafford didn't come barreling down on him, and when Stafford stopped the Buick in the beam of the gate's electric eye, he was barely doing five miles an hour.

CJ stepped out of the Jeep and headed straight for Stafford. If the rich white man from Cherry Hills was afraid of a black man making a beeline for him with no one else in sight, Stafford certainly didn't show it. "Got a problem with your vehicle?" Stafford called out.

"Not really," said CJ, already standing at Stafford's door. He looked into the car and realized why Stafford had been driving so slowly. Copies of the *Wall Street Journal* and *Antique Trader Weekly* sat open on the seat next to him. Stafford had been reading and driving at the same time.

"What's the problem, then?" asked Stafford, his voice high pitched and nasal.

"Got a problem with a murder—two, in fact," CJ said boldly, deciding that swinging a ball-peen hammer was probably the best way to get Stafford's full attention.

"What?"

"Got a problem with a college kid whose mother works for you, Mr. Stafford. I can't seem to find out who killed him or his college history professor."

Unintimidated, Stafford eyed the Jeep, CJ, and then finally the gate. "I think you'd better move your Jeep," he said, backing his car out of the gate's electric-eye beam and clicking his doors locked.

CJ trotted alongside the car, his hand on the rolled-down window ledge. Stafford pushed CJ's hand off the ledge and tapped the button to close the window. The window was a third of the way up when CJ slipped a half-foot-long tree branch from where it had been holstered beneath his belt into the window. The power window ground to a halt. "I only want a moment of your time, Mr. Stafford," he said with a smile.

"I'll call the police." Stafford reached into his shirt pocket and slipped out his cell phone.

"Good. Then you and me and Sergeant Commons can have a nice long talk."

Stafford's eyes widened momentarily, but he was no less calm. Every one of his movements up to then had been made with the thoughtfulness of someone who, when faced with a difficult challenge, had the sense to systematically deal with it. That meant, as far as CJ was concerned, that Stafford had also assessed him. CJ's mention of Sergeant Commons had gotten the hint of a quiver out of Stafford, but the rich man from Cherry Hills whose parents had been early-twentieth-century Slovak immigrants seemed to have ice water in his veins.

"It's Commons or me and you," said CJ.

Stafford smiled. "Afraid it won't be either," he said, looking as if he'd suddenly come up with the solution to a monumental problem. He leaned down and reached beneath the car seat; when Stafford sat back up, CJ found himself staring at a long-barreled .357 Magnum.

Stafford lowered the window and aimed the gun barrel directly at CJ's chest.

CJ tugged the branch out of the window. Unfazed, he said, "I've got one of them real handy too."

"I'm sure you do, Mr. . . ."

"Floyd."

"Well, Mr. Floyd, here's a scenario I'd think over very thoroughly if I were you. And I don't mean this in any derogatory or racially insensitive way. Just consider it food for thought. Here I am, a prominent white man on my way to work. I'm accosted, or at least threatened, by a very large black man in my driveway. A very calculating man, I might add, who anticipated my every move. He's a man I've never seen before, and he's nosed his way onto my gated private property. We both have guns. Now, tell me, Mr. Floyd, isn't it possible that, at least for one of us, my scenario could take off in a terribly wrong direction?"

CJ eyed the gun muzzle. "It's a pretty plausible made-in-America story." CJ stepped away from the car. "We'll talk sooner or later, though," he said, taking a second step backward, upset that Stafford had sized up his potency as a threat so accurately.

"I'm betting we won't, Mr. Floyd, for two very simple reasons. I've got power and influence, and you don't. Now, if you'll take one more step away from my car, I'll give you a couple of pieces of advice." He watched CJ take a third step backward. "Good. Here's the advice. Stop trying to tie me to a murder I didn't commit—and the next time you bogart somebody like me, and I must admit you're pretty good at it, at least technically, try to look a little more menacing." Stafford smiled and, with the .357 now aimed at CJ's head, said, "Please move your vehicle out of my way."

CJ walked back to the Jeep, slipped in, moved it out of the Buick's path, and watched Stafford calmly drive away.

Flabbergasted, CJ could only shake his head. He'd come to put the squeeze on someone who wasn't very squeezable. He now had a sense of just how, as a teenager, Stafford had been able to once sit naked in a downtown Denver store window at high noon. Stafford had the arrogance and swagger born of a power broker and the iron-clad testicles of a gambler.

CJ smiled and made a U-turn in the middle of the street. He suspected that Howard Stafford was also very likely smiling. He'd remember the next time he confronted a rich white man with Stafford's chutzpah to look more menacing. As he picked up speed, he realized, however, that Stafford, hopefully without recognizing it, had also dropped a stitch. Two stitches when you really came down to it. He had blinked momentarily at the mention of Sergeant Commons, and CJ now realized that Stafford was the calculating, unflappable kind of person who would be capable of killing someone.

🦅

Howard Stafford calmly strolled into his outer office, doling out passing greetings to his executive secretary and one of his technical support staff, and stopped at the door to his office. "I'll need fifteen minutes to finish up some loose ends from yesterday," he said to his secretary. "No interruptions, please." He pushed open the door, walked across the room, and placed the battered briefcase he was carrying beside a massive battle-scarred desk that had belonged to his father. He hung his coat on the most pedestrian of coat hooks, sat down, and picked up the phone.

He'd had time to think about his encounter with Floyd, and thanks to a few connections and a series of phone calls he'd placed while driving to the office, he now had a cursory sketch of the surprisingly bold black man. He now knew that in addition to working the Del Mora case with the Benson woman, Floyd was a decorated Vietnam veteran. Acknowledging with a grin that Floyd had balls, he punched in a phone number on one of his two secure private lines.

The answer on the other end was a clipped, "Yes."

"Glad to see you can recognize an important call," said Stafford, adjusting the phone receiver to his ear.

"They're the only kind that come in on this line."

"We have a minor problem," said Stafford. "The one that you warned me could eventually erupt."

"Floyd?"

"In person. He showed up on my doorstep first thing this morning."

"Was there anyone else with him? He usually operates with backup."

"Not that I saw."

"Did he mention anything about the daguerreotype?"

"No. I didn't let him get that far."

"Inquisitive fellow, Floyd."

"Very," said Stafford, clearing his throat. "We need to talk."

"Anytime."

"Late today will work," said Stafford.

"How's seven o'clock?"

"Fine."

"Same place as usual, and don't be late."

"I won't," said Stafford, thinking that no matter the outcome of his seven o'clock meeting, he was probably going to have to teach a lesson to Mr. CJ Floyd.

CHAPTER 28

After leaving Stafford's, CJ spent most of the rest of his morning waiting for an auto-glass company to arrive and install a windshield in the Bel Air. Surprised that the credit card he'd handed the installer swallowed the $320 debit, he watched the installer drive off, suspecting that if he charged so much as a cup of coffee to the card, a *no mas* alarm would sound coast to coast.

His finances were running on fumes. He couldn't ask Rosie for another dime, and as for Flora Jean and Mavis, he wouldn't. If his insurance company came through and Lenny McCabe didn't push the issue of pooling their money, he was hoping he'd be able to float along until summer.

Flora Jean owed him for a bunch of hours, but he in turn owed Billy DeLong, who he hoped was putting pressure on Loretta Sheets, driving home the point that her onetime adviser, Oliver Lyman, had been murdered.

He and Flora Jean had cobbled together a desperate group of murder suspects that included Sheets, Vannick, Stafford, Counts, and Amanda Hunter. A strange assemblage that now had him deep in thought. Hunter seemed the least likely of the five to be a murderer, but she just might be fooling him and Billy. He'd once tracked down a horsey-set debutante out of Aspen who'd had her social registry boyfriend killed in order to get back a cache of triple-A bonds she'd given the three-timing Don Juan.

It could be that Hunter wanted the daguerreotype back as badly as the debutante had wanted those bonds.

As for Vannick and Counts, he had no question that Vannick was the kind of man that could kill straight out. He suspected that Counts, on the other hand, would only have bumbled his way into a murder.

Loretta Sheets seemed less capable of being top dog in a killing than serving as a bit player. Howard Stafford remained his odds-on favorite to have killed Luis Del Mora. If Del Mora had hijacked something precious of Stafford's from right under the eccentric rich man's nose, CJ had the sense that Stafford was just calculating enough and felt privileged enough to think that rules that applied to other people didn't apply to him—including murder.

What CJ couldn't figure out when it came to each of his suspects was how Oliver Lyman's murder fitted in. But sooner or later, he knew that connection would come. He patted the Bel Air's hood reassuringly and took the fire escape stairs up to his apartment, wondering why he hadn't seen Flora Jean all morning until he remembered that Alden Grace was in town, a sure sign that Flora Jean would be arriving late for work.

He spent the next fifteen minutes on the phone talking to Morgan and Julie Madrid, learning from Morgan that all was quiet on the Alexie Borg front and from Julie, who'd checked in that morning with Celeste Deepstream's parole office, that the laissez-faire judicial short-timer hadn't heard from Celeste in the nine months since she'd kidnapped Mavis.

CJ took the two bits of news in stride before calling to check in with Mario Satoni. An LA Dodgers fanatic, Mario was busy watching a Dodgers-Rockies spring training game when CJ interrupted.

"Damn, I'm watching the Dodgers," Mario complained.

"This won't take but a minute, Mario," CJ said apologetically.

"Hope so."

"Got any additional takes on that Russian that might help me out?"

Mario watched a Dodgers infielder muff a groundball. "Shit, the slow-ass no-fielding idiot blew a groundball!" Mario shouted at the TV screen. "Now, what was that, Calvin?"

"Borg, the Russian, middleman to my bomber. Got any more on him?"

"Nope. And by the way, the person who saved your bacon last night doesn't have anything either. Heard you got into a little scrimmage last evening with that she-devil who's out to blink out your lights."

"See somebody's real talkative," said CJ.

"I was told a story, Calvin."

"Did the person who told you the story also tell you I appreciated him being there?"

"I heard mention of it."

CJ smiled. "Wondered who in the world had him dogging me."

"Got me, but I wouldn't count on having somebody like that around all the time."

"I'll remember that. And if you hear anything else from your sources about Borg, let me know," said CJ, hearing the crack of a bat in the background.

"I'll be damned! The damn 'roid-popper parked it."

"I'll talk to you, later, Mario," said CJ, hanging up, aware that for Mario a Dodgers loss, even in the preseason Cactus League, could be a gut-wrenching disappointment.

Deciding his thoughts were far too disjointed for analytical thinking, CJ was about to make a sandwich for lunch when Billy DeLong called from Wyoming.

CJ answered with a subdued, "Hello."

"Got some news I thought you'd want in a hurry," Billy said excitedly.

"Good or bad?"

"Good, I'm thinkin'. I spent the better part of the mornin' with Loretta Sheets. Turns out she knew Oliver Lyman a whole lot better than she let on the first time we talked. When I told her he'd been murdered, she broke down like a lovesick puppy. Said she and the good professor had a thing goin' when she was a student and admitted to me when I pushed her on it that Lyman had been after that layin'-of-the-rails daguerreotype for years. Said he had a contact down in Denver who was gonna help him find it."

"Well, well. Did she mention why she was so quick to give you Lyman's name the first time you were there, knowing that it might lead us right back to her?"

"Sure did. Said she was hopin' it might lead Lyman back to her as well."

"I thought you said she was a hardcore, no-man-in-my-life feminist," said CJ.

"Guess she fell off the wagon, at least where it concerned Oliver Lyman."

"Were you able to get anything else out of her?"

"Sure did. And you're talkin' info that's killer-diller," said Billy, beaming.

"I'm listening."

"Ain't sure why she told me this. Hearin' that her onetime lover boy up and got himself murdered could've turned her real confessional. Whatever. Here's the scoop. Between bawlin' over Lyman and tellin' me how rough life had been for her without him, she told me that she and Luis Del Mora weren't the only two students that Lyman had been real partial to over the years. Turns out the good professor was usin' some of his students to run hisself a profitable little business tradin' in stolen books.

"Accordin' to Sheets, Lyman would pick out a student, spend a year or so sidlin' up to 'em real close, playin' the favorite uncle, and then get the kid to steal books, antiques, artifacts, and all kinds of other valuable stuff for him. Sheets says they stole stuff from libraries, people's houses, and even Indian reservations where Lyman spoke. They sold the stolen merchandise to secondhand stores, pawnshops, places like that."

"A real prince," said CJ.

"Yeah. And real, real calculatin'. Sheets said he'd check out a student's background before using 'em, get hisself some excuse to check out their student records, and then pounce. He preferred kids from outside the U.S., students on study visas who he could keep under his thumb. But every now and then he'd pluck a woman like Sheets right off the limb, promising 'em that if they played their cards right they just might end up becoming Mrs. Lyman, or that he'd make sure that dissertation they were workin' on sailed right on through committee. Did one hell of a job on poor old Loretta Sheets. When I left that museum of hers, she was still fightin' back tears and defendin' him."

"Sounds like Luis Del Mora fit right in. I bet Lyman thought he'd died and gone to heaven when he stumbled onto Del Mora—

lucking into somebody who not only fit his profile but also happened to be living in the midst of a rare-book and collectibles gold mine."

"Sheets said almost the same thing when I told her about Del Mora." Billy popped a fresh stick of gum into his mouth. "So now that we have the skinny on Lyman, where's it leave us?"

"A lot better than high and dry, which is where I've been thinking we were most of the morning."

"Good. Need me to do any more with Sheets?"

"Not right now. I don't think she killed Lyman, but she may have killed Del Mora. Who's to say she doesn't have another boyfriend who picked off the Del Mora kid?"

"Got any in mind?"

"Who knows? Counts, Vannick, maybe even Stafford. You never know until you've had a chance to strain the water. For the time being, why don't you stick around Cheyenne and keep tabs on the despondent Ms. Sheets. Flora Jean and I'll see if we can't come up with more on Del Mora. She's got us scheduled to meet with his mother this afternoon."

"Watch yourself. You go to steppin' around that Stafford compound and you'll be walkin' around in pretty high cotton."

CJ laughed. "I will, and I already have. Talked to the plantation master himself first thing this morning. Son of a bitch pulled a gun on me."

"I wouldn't be laughing about it, CJ. Stafford's the kind that can fricassee the likes of us and serve us up as dark meat to the hogs in a New York minute."

"I've read that book, Billy."

"Good, 'cause for a second there I got to thinkin' you somehow forgot where you were. I'll stick with Sheets and let you know if anything comes up. In the meantime, keep my warning about Stafford taped to the back of your eyelids."

"I will. Talk to you later," said CJ, hanging up and thinking that maybe he was being too blasé about Howard Stafford.

CJ and Flora Jean sat in the living room of Theresa Del Mora's utilitarian cottage, watching a sad-eyed Theresa sift through a teakwood jewelry box that contained Luis's personal effects. She set a stack of baseball cards she'd taken out of the box on the coffee table and looked up at CJ. "Luis loved baseball."

When she took a paper-clipped stack of business cards out of the box, CJ eyed them curiously. "Mind if I have a look at those?"

Theresa handed CJ the cards without responding. He shuffled through the seven cards one by one, noting that each card was for either a used-book store or a pawnshop. Recognizing the names of one of the stores and two of the pawnshops, he handed the cards to Flora Jean. "Looks like Luis was dealing with people who were into moving the merchandise."

"I don't know where he found the time," Theresa said. "He spent most of his time at the library studying."

CJ simply nodded.

"How was Luis's money situation?" Flora Jean asked, setting the business cards aside.

"We barely scraped up the money for his tuition," Theresa said, clearly incensed. "I know what you're thinking—that Luis was a common thief. But you're wrong. If he did take those books from Mr. Stafford's library, there's an explanation. He may have needed them for his studies or for some college project. Luis was no thief."

CJ suppressed the urge to tell Theresa what he knew about her son's connection to Oliver Lyman. During his bail-bonding life he'd run across many mothers in denial, even seen the mothers of three-, four-, and five-time losers, including killers, arsonists, and rapists, argue that their hardened-criminal offspring were misunderstood angels. But Theresa Del Mora's denial struck him as different, somehow proud and earnest.

"Do you have anything else you think we should take a look at besides what's in the jewelry box?" asked Flora Jean.

"No. Luis lived a quiet, humble life." She teased a yellowed newspaper clipping from where it was wedged in a corner of the box. As she unfolded the clipping and scanned it, a small tin crucifix slipped out from inside and fell to the floor. Theresa dropped to her knees and crossed herself. "Alejandro! Alejandro!" She looked up at CJ. "Luis was carrying his father's crucifix." Sensing CJ and Flora Jean's puzzlement, she rose, and sat back down. "It's my husband, Alejandro's, obituary." Holding up the crucifix, she added, "This crucifix was his. And Luis had them both among his possessions." Looking relieved, as if an excruciating burden had suddenly been lifted from her, she said, "Luis and Alejandro were estranged when Alejandro died."

Uncertain how to respond, Flora Jean asked, "How bad was their break?"

"As bad as one can be for a father and son. Alejandro was a lover of freedom. He died because of his passion. He wanted Luis to follow the path he'd chosen in life, but Luis, a mere child, didn't care to. The friction was too great for either of them to overcome."

"Can I have a look at the obituary?" Flora Jean asked, draping an arm over Theresa's shoulders.

"He was ambushed, and his car was set on fire," said Theresa, handing the obituary to Flora Jean. "I was never sure Luis understood the significance of his father's sacrifice."

"It seems that somehow he did," said CJ.

"And that makes all the difference now that I have lost them both." There was serenity on Theresa's face that hadn't been there earlier. A look that said, *Whatever comes now I can handle on my own.*

"Can I take the business cards with me?" CJ asked hesitantly.

"Yes."

CJ slipped the cards into his jacket pocket.

"Do you think the cards will lead you to Luis's murderer?"

"I'm not sure. But they represent leads we need to follow."

Flora Jean clasped Theresa's hand in hers. "We'll find Luis's killer," she said, eyeing her sympathetically.

"I know you will," said Theresa, glancing over at CJ. "Did your meeting with Mr. Stafford go well?"

"Afraid not."

"He can be crusty," said Theresa.

"I found that out."

"I can talk with him if you'd like."

"No need. We parted with an understanding."

"You don't think that he was involved in Luis's murder?"

"I'm not sure."

"There'd be no way!"

Surprised by Theresa's defense of Stafford, CJ said, "We'll see where the business cards take us."

"They'll take you away from Mr. Stafford. He's a generous, caring man." She slipped her hand out of Flora Jean's, closed the jewelry box, arose, and moved toward the door. She squeezed

Flora Jean's hand a final time as Flora Jean exited, but she made it a point to simply nod at CJ as he walked out the door.

🍃

I need a plan of my own, Theresa Del Mora kept telling herself as she sat in a turn-of-the-century Boston rocker in her living room, fingering Alejandro's crucifix, rocking back and forth in silence. A plan that would, now that she knew that Luis had made peace with his father's memory, mete out a kind of justice that she could understand.

She looked up toward the full-length mirror that hung on the wall in front of her and eyed her reflection. She looked no different than she had twenty years earlier. She remained square-faced, lantern-jawed, bug-eyed, and disfigured. She would forever be an anomalous, sharp-minded woman forced to constantly negotiate her way in a world that others traveled with ease.

She rocked back and forth, squeezing the crucifix until it cut into the fleshy part of her right hand. She wasn't certain how she could speed up her son's murder investigation, but she had a plan that would keep her more fully in tune with the progress that CJ and Flora Jean were making. A plan that would have made Alejandro proud.

CHAPTER 29

Two of the business cards Theresa Del Mora had given CJ led directly to Theodore Counts. The owners of both Bosco's Collectibles and Used Books, a store in the 8800 block of Denver's East Colfax Avenue, and Pilot's Book World and Western Artifacts in the Capitol Hill section of the city, told CJ with very little prodding after he described Luis Del Mora that Del Mora had sold them books and Western ephemera that included Santa Fe Railroad schedules, Trailways bus-line schedules, and dozens of sepia-toned photographs from the 1930s. Del Mora, both store owners calmly noted, had been sent to see them by longtime customer Theodore Counts.

CJ's attempt to pry additional information out of the two wily old traders met with a double wave of indifference. When he made the bold move of mentioning that he was investigating Luis Del Mora's murder, both men clammed up.

After leaving Bosco's, which had been his second stop, CJ headed west on Colfax in five o'clock rush-hour traffic. He was delighted that he'd pinned a donkey tail on Counts, but he wasn't certain how knowing that Counts had steered Del Mora to the two used-book and collectible dealers would actually help him.

If Counts, like Lyman, had been using Del Mora to steal valuable Western collectibles, and maybe even the book that contained the missing laying-of-the-rails daguerreotype, their relationship had to have been short-lived, especially if the only source of the stolen goods turned out to be Howard Stafford's house. That angle didn't make sense because the merchandise Del Mora had sold to both Bosco's and Pilot's had been very un-Stafford-like and pretty low-end.

Turning left onto Quebec, CJ decided to take a quick run by Counts's house. Flora Jean had told him when he'd called twenty minutes earlier to fill her in on what he'd found out, that she'd driven by Counts's place when she couldn't locate Vannick and found the front lawn littered with newspapers. He wasn't sure why he needed to go there, but he felt it was worth another try.

Peering through the Bel Air's new windshield into the glare of the fading sun, CJ flipped down his visor and continued toward Counts's upscale Hilltop neighborhood.

Theodore Counts had come home to get a credit card, enough fresh clothes to last him through the weekend, and a carton of stolen books he'd stored in his garage.

He hadn't heard any more news stories about the Lyman murder since leaving Denver, and there had been very little about the murder in either the *Rocky Mountain News* or the *Denver Post*, aside from brief pieces that each paper had run the day he'd left town. Having convinced himself that if he really were a murder suspect the police would have found him by now, he felt a strange sense of relief, but to be on the safe side, he'd decided to spend a few more days in Kiowa.

Several newspapers on his front lawn, and a nearly full mailbox told him that no one, including the police, had been around.

He picked up the newspapers, tucked them under his arm, and headed toward his garage to deal with the carton of books that could link him to Lyman.

He had pulled his car into the garage a few minutes earlier, uncertain what to expect and prepared for a full-out police assault. Convinced now that no one had been around, not even a neighbor to retrieve his newspapers, he pushed the button on his garage-door opener, watched the door rise slowly, and walked into the garage.

The incriminating carton of books sat at eye level in plain view on the third shelf of an unpainted six-foot-high storage shelf unit. He had constructed the free-standing top-heavy wooden shelves himself; they were now laden with shop tools, library-style book cartons, and cardboard boxes filled with everything from sprinkler-system parts to Christmas ornaments.

He closed the garage door and walked casually between the north-facing wall of the garage and his car toward the shelves. He had slipped the book carton he was after off the shelf, reached into his jacket pocket for his car keys, and triggered his car's trunk-lid remote when CJ, who'd entered the garage through a window just after Counts had first pulled his car inside, said, "Whattaya got there, Mr. Librarian?"

His face a snapshot of hysteria, Counts dropped the book carton and froze as CJ rose into view from behind the car's right rear fender and moved toward him. CJ had reached the car's front grill when Counts reached up, grabbed the unstable utility shelf by one of its two-by-four supports, and toppled it and its contents down onto CJ.

An old Skil saw, its blade exposed, crashed into CJ's right shoulder as he let out a loud grunt and sidestepped the shower

of unboxed hammers, wrenches, plumbing pipe, Christmas ornaments, and fencing and nails that careened down onto the hood
of the car.

Hyperventilating, Counts punched the button on his garage-
door opener and raced toward the slowly rising door. He'd almost
reached the half-raised door when CJ, his jacket and shirt ripped
and with a line of blood oozing from just above the curve of his
right shoulder, reached out with his left hand, grabbed the much
smaller Counts by his shirt collar, yanked him off his feet, and
slammed him backward into the open trunk of his car.

"You little pissant!" CJ was on top of the screaming, frightened librarian, straddling him with his hands around Counts's
throat, when he remembered that once in Vietnam he'd been
forced to kill a man with his bare hands.

Counts's screams penetrated the still, dry air until, shaking in
anger, CJ mumbled, "War's over," released his grip, and stood,
leaving the petrified librarian quivering in shock.

🍃

Counts's urine-stained khakis, a toppled storage shelf, its contents, and the six-inch-long gash along CJ's shoulder remained
the only signs that Counts's garage had ten minutes earlier been
the site of a near-death struggle.

Having explained who he was and why he was there, CJ stood
looking down on Counts. The skinny librarian, his legs still draped
over the trunk lip, continue to shiver.

CJ had dressed his shoulder wound with ointment and gauze
he'd found in a first-aid kit in the car's glove compartment. He'd
tossed Counts a shop towel to clean himself up, but Counts had
instead wrapped the towel around his neck. When CJ had pressed

Counts to explain why he'd toppled the storage shelf on him, suspecting that Counts might claim that he'd thought CJ was an intruder, Counts had chosen silence. When he'd tried to get Counts to say whether he'd been involved in Luis Del Mora's murder, Counts had remained mute.

Frustrated, CJ finally said, "Guess I'll have to call the cops."

"No. No," Counts said woefully, his voice a near whisper.

"Then tell me what I need to know about the Del Mora murder, and I'll leave."

Looking punch-drunk, Counts sat up in the trunk, eyed CJ thoughtfully, stared blankly around the garage, and in a hushed voice said, "I was brokering books."

"Brokering? Come on, Counts. You can choose a better word than that."

"Okay. I, ah, we were selling books that had an uncertain source." Counts looked frightened.

"No need to look so scared now, brother. The time for that was when you started stealing. Now, how about clueing me in on who the *we* are you just mentioned?"

"Arthur Vannick. He came up with the idea of lifting a few books out of Howard Stafford's library."

"And you just went along for the ride. Come on, Counts. I know your MO. You've been stealing books from libraries and God knows where else for years."

Sounding confessional, Counts said, "This time I got in over my head."

"Because of Vannick?"

"That and the fact that I had a chance to tap into a rare-book mother lode."

"Stafford's library."

Looking ashamed, Counts nodded. "I never should've agreed to help with the remodel job on his library."

"So you stole books from Stafford and sold them. To who?"

"Anyone who'd buy them. Rare-book dealers, private parties, museums, even other libraries."

"Did you ever sell books to secondhand stores and pawnshops?"

"Occasionally. But that was more Del Mora's territory."

"He was in this with you?"

"No. He worked his own side of the street. And he didn't work it for very long before he was murdered. I don't know how many other places Del Mora was stealing from, but I know he hit Stafford's. I also know he was careless and overeager—pretty much an amateur."

"Unschooled enough that Stafford would've figured out what he was doing?"

"Very likely."

Looking puzzled, CJ asked, "Mind telling me why Stafford wouldn't have been able to do the same thing when it came to you?"

When Counts didn't answer, CJ cupped a hand to his right ear. Grimacing in pain, he said, "I'm listening."

Counts cleared his throat and leaned back on his elbows, eyes to the ceiling. "He didn't have to. It was all part of a game we were playing."

CJ flashed Counts a bewildered look. He understood that Stafford was a crank, but he couldn't begin to fathom what kind of game he and Counts could have been playing. "Mind telling me about it?"

Counts's answer came slowly. "In case you didn't know it, Stafford's at the top of the mountain when it comes to being not only rich but eccentric. I don't think there's much that still really excites him. For some reason, that remodel job on his library seemed to get his quirky juices flowing. One day he called Vannick and me into his office for a talk, right in the middle of when we were working out the library's bookcase design and security-system grid. He had dossiers on both of us, and he knew that I had faced some . . . ah, problems and that Vannick liked to bill himself as being mob-connected. He strung us along for a while, taking us places we didn't want to go, and then out of the blue, with the two of us standing there staring at him, waiting for our pink slips, he asked if we wouldn't mind stealing for him."

Counts cleared his throat and continued. "The whole thing sounded kind of crazy, crazier still if you consider that while he was presenting his stealing proposal to us, he was grinning and licking his lips like he was somehow getting a rise out of hearing himself talk. The most bizarre part was that he wanted us not just to steal *for* him but *from* him."

CJ shook his head in disbelief. "Go on."

Looking less frightened, Counts continued, "The heart of the plan was for us to take books from his library and replace them with stolen books that were rarer and more valuable. We'd have years to play the game, he claimed. When the library was finished, Vannick and I would have the run of it. I could look through his collection, find items that needed upgrading, and then go out and search for suitable replacements. He'd get his jollies out of recognizing that a rare book was missing from one of his shelves and knowing that an even rarer book was on its way to replace it."

"The whole thing sounds ridiculous," CJ interrupted. "Where in the hell would you get the replacement books?"

"Plenty of places. You'd have to be in the book business to understand. Other libraries, museums, private collections, and occasionally antiquarian book stores and even flea markets. That was where Vannick came in. When I found a book in a place that was well protected, his job was to get us around security. Half the time I didn't need him. That's how poorly the kind of items we're talking about are secured against insiders like me."

CJ thought about Howard Stafford's well documented strangeness. His teenage department-store-window masturbating episode, his aloofness, the fact that Stafford had pulled a gun on him—suddenly the whole bizarre scheme sounded a bit more plausible. Eyeing Counts circumspectly, he asked, "And you were stupid enough to say yes to Stafford's offer?"

Counts eyed the floor sheepishly. "I'd already been stealing books for him for years. In a sense, Stafford owned me."

"And Vannick? Did he own him too?"

"No. The whole scheme simply made Vannick feel more like he was a big man."

"How far did you get with your game?"

"Not very. I only had a chance to pull half-a-dozen books off Stafford's bookshelves and find suitable replacements when Luis Del Mora's murder shut the whole thing down."

"You mean *steal* suitable replacements, don't you, Counts?" CJ could only shake his head. "The whole scam sounds like something dredged up outta *Alice in Wonderland*. What the hell was the upside for you?"

Counts hesitated before answering, as if he didn't expect CJ to believe him. "The chance to spend time going through Stafford's library collection and savor the rarity, and a chance for Vannick and me to make some money on the books we took from it and sold. The books I obtained and . . . ah, put back as replacements were, how can I best put it, free."

"And Stafford trusted the two of you enough to let you steal from him in the hope that he'd get an upgraded replacement. Sounds idiotic."

"Not if you're rich enough to take the risk, and the game you're playing gives you your jollies. Those few books I did take from Stafford's library were valuable in their own right, but their replacements were the kind of truly rare birds that would've taken him years to collect. In a sense it was just like I was shopping for a new car for him. Vannick and I got to keep the money from the trade-in, and Stafford got a brand-new car free. He really wasn't risking very much."

"So much for the money, I understand that," said CJ, still looking bewildered. "What was the big deal about having the run of Stafford's library?" When Counts didn't answer, CJ said, "You've already told me enough to guarantee yourself two to five years in prison. If you were involved in Luis Del Mora's murder, you can add another twenty. Might as well spit out the whole nine yards."

Thinking what twenty to twenty-five years in prison would be like, Counts asked, "Do you know anything about rare photographs?"

"A little."

"Do you know what a daguerreotype is?"

"I've heard of them."

"Well, for years word on the street has been that Stafford had a very valuable and historic one stashed somewhere in his house."

Deciding that it was his turn to startle Counts, CJ said, "Yeah, a missing daguerreotype of the Golden Spike ceremony. I know." He watched a look of astonishment spread across Counts's face.

"So you had your own little private gambit. You steal books both from and for Stafford, and while you're at it you search through his library for a million-dollar photograph. Sounds pretty slick."

"How'd you know about that photograph?"

CJ smiled. "The same way as you. Word on the street. The real question is, did you find it?"

"No, and I searched every nook and cranny, book, artifact, desk drawer, and cabinet in that library at least twice," said Counts, sounding frustrated.

"Maybe it wasn't in the library; ever thought of that?"

"Certainly. But since I had the run of the place, it was clearly worth looking. Even if I didn't find the daguerreotype, until Luis Del Mora got killed Vannick and I still had the book-replacement deal going for us."

CJ laughed. "Guess you and Vannick should've figured that somebody else might've also been looking to do some serious stealing from Stafford—like Luis Del Mora for instance. Maybe you shouldn't have been so quick to pass him off as an amateur." CJ shook his head. "The three of you take the cake. A rich man who steals from himself, a thieving pompous-ass brother, and a security-systems con man pretending to be a mobster. Now here's the real question: Did any one of the three of you kill Luis Del Mora?"

"I didn't!" Counts shouted.

"Well, somebody did, and it wasn't the Mad Hatter."

"What about Stafford? Maybe Del Mora stumbled across the daguerreotype before I had the chance to find it and Stafford killed him to get it back."

"Possible," said CJ, already well ahead of Counts.

"Or Vannick?"

CJ wagged an index finger at Counts. "My, my, how fast we turn on our friends."

"Vannick claims to be connected. He could've hired someone to kill Del Mora."

"And kill Oliver Lyman too?" asked CJ, watching the muscles in Counts's face suddenly go slack. "Damn, Counts, looks like you just saw a ghost. Wanta fill me in?"

Counts inched up from his uncomfortable position in the trunk. "I sold Lyman a few things over the years. In fact, he's the one who first told me about the missing daguerreotype. He had railroad-industry collectible connections."

"I see. Ever heard of a woman named Loretta Sheets? She deals in transportation collectibles."

"No."

Uncertain whether Counts was lying, CJ asked, "Sell anything to Lyman recently?"

"I sold him a couple of books I took from Stafford's library. Books that both Vannick and Stafford knew about, of course."

CJ smiled. "So now I know why you were running. You dropped out of sight hoping to separate yourself from Lyman."

"I didn't kill him!" Counts began to cry.

CJ scrutinized the pitiful little black man, scrunched into the trunk of his car, his face contorted, his body limp, and decided he'd pressed Counts to the breaking point. Rubbing his throbbing shoulder, CJ shook his head and said, "No, my friend, the only person you killed is yourself."

Amanda Hunter had come to expect that questions concerning Luis Del Mora's murder would come via Billy DeLong. She was caught off guard when, ten minutes after leaving a tearful Theodore Counts slumped in his trunk with a warning that he'd call the cops in a heartbeat if Counts didn't dance to his tune, CJ called from the Bel Air to ask her whether the person who'd called the ranch several months back asking about daguerreotype photographs could possibly have been Loretta Sheets.

Hunter dampened CJ's enthusiasm for turning his investigation Loretta Sheets's way, saying that the telephone inquiry had come not from a woman but from a nasal-sounding man. Aware that the caller could have had Sheets sitting at his side communicating instructions, CJ still refused to eliminate the feminist museum curator from his list of murder suspects.

But since Amanda's description of the nasal-sounding caller clearly fit Howard Stafford, CJ decided to give Paul Grimes a call to see if he had any muckraking insight into how Stafford might have amassed his antiquarian book and Western ephemera collection. Grimes was point-blank in his assessment: "The son of a bitch outbid or outstole the competition, the same way rich folks end up with most things."

CJ ended the call and sped through an intersection, catching the tail end of a caution light. He checked the rearview mirror to make certain the long arm of the law hadn't caught his transgression before speed-dialing Julie Madrid to see if he couldn't get a few more specifics on how Stafford might have surreptitiously assembled his rare book collection.

CHAPTER 30

"We've got action at Borg's," Morgan Williams said to CJ from his cell phone. "I've been tryin' like hell to call you for the past five minutes, and all I've been gettin's your voice mail." Morgan's eyes remained locked on the front entrance of Alexie Borg's condo.

"I've been talking to Julie about the Del Mora case," said CJ.

"Well, you best put that on the back burner for now if you're interested in hookin' up with our girl Celeste. 'Cause a big blond guy with a buzz cut and top-heavy muscle pulled up in front of the building in a black Range Rover about five minutes ago. Has to be Borg."

CJ had never seen Borg. The description he'd given Morgan was one that Mario Satoni had provided. "Does he have a woman with him?"

"Not that me or Dittier can see, and we got a direct bead on him from across the street. A valet just took three suitcases outta the back of the Range Rover. Looks like Borg's plannin' on takin' a trip."

"Wonder why he pulled up to the front of the place instead of heading straight for the underground garage."

"Thought the same thing myself. When I ran it past Dittier, he said it's because Borg's tryin' to give somebody outside the building a signal that he's ready to go."

"Could be."

CJ checked his watch to see if he had time to join Morgan and Dittier and realized he was thirty minutes late for dinner with Mavis. Shaking his head, he mumbled, "Shit!"

"What's that?"

"Nothing. Just late for something. Stay put and keep your eyes out for Celeste. I'm at 6th and Colorado Boulevard. I'll be there in ten minutes."

"You gonna fly?" asked Morgan.

"Gonna do my best." CJ floored the Bel Air's accelerator, and sped west.

CJ, Dittier, and Morgan staked out Borg's building for the next hour without sighting Borg or Celeste. The Range Rover was gone, and the chilly night air had Dittier shivering.

Morgan shook his head dejectedly. "There ain't no way in or outta that place except the garage, the front door, two emergency exits, and a trash-pickup area out back. I've checked. With all them bags he's packin', I don't think Borg's gonna use the last three."

Wrapping himself in a warming bear hug, Dittier signed to Morgan, "I'm cold."

Morgan looked at CJ and said, "I think Dittier's comin' down with somethin'. He was cold all last night."

CJ took off his jacket and draped it over the peacoat he'd given Dittier earlier. "That better? I can stay another fifteen minutes, then I've gotta head for Mavis's," he added, checking his watch.

Dittier adjusted the jacket, eyed the rip in CJ's shirt and the bloody bandage beneath it, and nudged Morgan, pointing at CJ's injury.

"How'd you get that?" asked Morgan.

"Talking to a librarian."

"Must've involved one hell of an overdue book fine."

"Give or take a million," said CJ, smiling.

Morgan whistled in amazement. "Guess from now on you'll remember to return your books when they're due."

"Sure will," said CJ, glancing up at Borg's condo, his thoughts on Celeste.

In the final fifteen minutes that CJ remained on stakeout, Lenny McCabe and Julie Madrid both checked in by cell phone, Julie to say that Jake LeBow, a friend of hers who owned an antiquarian book shop in Cherry Creek, had less than honorable things to say about Howard Stafford, claiming that in the used- and rare-book trade, Stafford not only operated without conscience but seemed to enjoy playing fast and loose with the rules.

On the heels of that call, McCabe called to say that the city engineers had given him the okay to go back into his building and retrieve his things. "And they were pretty pissed that your half of the duplex was already cleaned out," he added in a huff. "I didn't tell them that if I hadn't been scared my half of the place was gonna collapse on my ass, it would've been empty too." When McCabe asked CJ where he was, CJ glanced up at Alexie Borg's condo and said, "Out checking on our bomber."

"You got a lead on who did us in?"

"A thread of one. I've got Morgan and Dittier keeping an eye on a suspect."

Sounding relieved that the dangerous aspects of finding their bomber had fallen CJ's way, McCabe said, "Great. But I'm calling for another reason as well. I'm wondering if Morgan and Dittier can help me move some of my stuff out of the store? I'll pay them real good, and I won't need them for more than a morning."

"Not unless I get some backup here," said CJ. "Let me make a call to Wyoming and see if there's a way to free them up."

"Appreciate it. I'm here at the store. And CJ, we need to talk. Things are gonna start moving real fast once I get the okay to redo the building. I need us both on the same page, remember?"

"I hear you, Lenny."

"Just remember, you think long, you think wrong, my man."

"For now why don't you just worry about getting your stuff out of the building. Let me make that call to Wyoming. I'll call you right back."

"Call me back as soon as you hear," McCabe said.

CJ stowed his phone and walked over to Morgan, who had a pair of binoculars trained on Borg's condo. "Any movement inside?"

"Nope."

CJ shook his head and glanced over at Dittier, who was still shivering. "You and Dittier up for a warmer, higher-paying job?"

"Don't matter to me," said Morgan. "But I except it would sit real well with Dittier."

"That was Lenny McCabe on the phone. He got the okay to move his stuff out of his store, and he needs some help. You up to helping if I can get Billy to fill in here?"

"Let me check with Dittier." Morgan stepped over to Dittier and began signing. Responding to Dittier's eager nod, he turned back to CJ. "When's McCabe need us?"

"Tomorrow morning."

"When will we be done here?"

"As soon as I get an okay from Billy. Meantime, I'll stay," said

CJ, realizing he had a problem. It was an hour-and-a-half drive from Cheyenne to Denver, which meant he was going to have to cancel his dinner date with Mavis. As he slipped his cell phone out of his pocket to call Billy, he thought about which of the two calls he was about to make would cause him the most grief: asking Billy to drive down from Cheyenne at nine o'clock at night to pull stakeout duty in thirty-two-degree weather or canceling dinner with Mavis. Deep down he already knew the answer.

The temperature had dropped to thirty degrees when CJ finally passed off the Alexie Borg stakeout to a road-weary Billy DeLong and headed for Mavis's. During the drive he couldn't shake the sense, as he cruised down Welton Street and past eighty-year-old Five Points landmarks, that he was being followed.

He pulled up in front of Mavis's Curtis Street Queen Anne, took a deep breath, looked around carefully, and got out of the Bel Air. He wondered if Celeste had him so spooked that he was starting to imagine things. He was a few steps from the front stairs when Mavis opened the door. Barefoot, dressed in faded jeans, and swallowed by one of CJ's old chambray shirts, she looked relieved. "I've been worried," she said, embracing CJ as he stepped inside.

CJ kissed her on the forehead and squeezed her tightly. "Had something to take care of."

"CJ, you promised to stay in touch."

"No need. I'm close to wrapping up the Del Mora thing." CJ slipped an arm around Mavis's waist and walked her toward the kitchen. "Remember, I need the money."

Unwilling to light the flame on a midnight argument, Mavis asked, "How close?"

"A day, maybe two."

"I hope so because I can't go down that road again, CJ." Toying with her engagement ring, she said, "I'll give you back your ring first."

A knot rose in CJ's throat as he drank in the determined look on Mavis's face. "I'm just helping Flora Jean out of a bind. Two days. I guarantee it."

"I'll hold you to that."

Grasping Mavis's left hand in his and squeezing it, CJ smiled and kissed her lightly on the cheek. Uncertain how fast he and Flora Jean could really bring closure to the Luis Del Mora murder, if at all, and unwilling to mention that he and Celeste Deepstream were again engaged in their own personal war, he simply said, "Okay."

🍃

Draped in a poncho and with a black scarf wrapped over her head, Theresa watched the lights go out at Mavis's a little after twelve-thirty. She'd been watching Floyd's every move for the past six hours, locked on his tail from the time he'd left Theodore Counts's garage. She had the feeling that he might have noticed a vehicle following him when he'd left LoDo and headed down Welton Street for Mavis Sundee's, so she'd backed off briefly. Although she was tired and drained mentally, she planned to stay with Floyd until he took her to the end of the road they were both traveling, and peace.

🍃

Arthur Vannick worked out at his 24 Hour Fitness club from eleven-thirty to twelve-thirty two nights a week. He liked to boast that because his workouts crossed the midnight hour, he always maintained a lethal physical presence in two worlds. Perspiring from a heavy workout and a steaming shower, Vannick had just ambled across the first floor of the club's parking structure and up to his car when a sneaker-clad Pinkie Niedemeyer stepped from behind a concrete pillar, took two long steps forward, and jammed the nickel-plated barrel of a .44 Magnum into Vannick's left ear.

"Mr. Vannick? Arthur Vannick?" Pinkie said calmly, well aware of whom he was speaking to. "Don't move, and don't look back. I get very agitated when I'm working and people get fidgety and start to look back. Arms to your side, please."

Vannick dropped his arms and stood absolutely still.

"Real good. Excellent, in fact. I'll be brief. I understand you like to make noise about being connected. Arthur, my man, you really shouldn't do that. You're bearing false witness, and that's a mortal sin."

Vannick's right hand twitched.

"That's movement," said Pinkie, eyeing the hand. "I told you not to move."

Vannick pressed his hand to his thigh.

"Good thinking, Arthur. Now, here's the deal. I'm gonna ask you several questions, and you're gonna answer them for me. Then I'll give you a set of instructions, and I'll leave. That is, unless I don't like your answers, and I dislike wrong answers, Arthur, just as much as I detest twitching. So here we go, and please, a little honesty, Arthur. Have you been making claims you're connected, whatever in the hell that means?"

"Yes." Vannick's answer was a breath of fear.

"See, wasn't that easy? Now here are your instructions. Don't ever do that again. Are we square?"

"Yes."

"Second question. Have you been askin' around tryin' to get somebody to drop a dime on CJ Floyd or any of his friends?"

"Yes."

"Don't ever do that again. Are we square?"

"Yes."

"Final question. Do you have a gun in that phallic symbol you're driving?"

"No," said Vannick, trying his best not to tremble.

"Well, you're stupid not to." Pinkie nudged the gun barrel a little deeper. "Here's a lesson to take home with you, friend. Don't ever lie about who you know, your military record, or the size of your dick. And never, ever make the mistake of putting out feelers for a hit on somebody who's got well-connected friends. Are we square?"

"Yes."

"Good. Now step into that cock rocket of yours and move on down the line." Pinkie nudged Vannick into the front seat of his Porsche and gently closed the door. Seconds later the engine roared to life. As he sped away, Vannick stole a quick look backward to see a man wearing a Ronald Reagan Halloween mask disappear behind a concrete support.

It was two a.m. by the time Arthur Vannick finished packing his clothes and wrapping four rare books and a miniature oil painting he'd stolen from Howard Stafford's in butcher paper. Business trips were commonplace for him, so a week away wouldn't raise too many eyebrows at his office, he hoped.

He'd sent his secretary an e-mail saying he had to go back to Boston because of a family emergency and that he'd probably be gone five to seven days. He was too afraid for his life to leave a message that said much more.

Pinkie Niedemeyer slipped into bed wearing one of the half-dozen pairs of identical silk pajamas he'd had made in Hong Kong six months earlier. Now that the debt he'd owed Mario Satoni had been paid, his head was as clear as it had been in years. He and Mario were now square, and in Pinkie Niedemeyer's world, when you really came right down to it, being square was all that really mattered.

CHAPTER 31

After keeping Mavis awake half the night, and a fitful night's sleep, CJ sat alone at Flora Jean's desk sipping black coffee, deep in thought. He glanced across the desk until his gaze stopped on one of two pressed-back chairs that sat in front of the desk. Forty years earlier Ike had sawed two inches off the legs of both chairs, claiming that squat-legged chairs made for better business negotiations, giving the person behind the desk an intimidating height advantage.

He took a long sip of coffee as he considered the investigative advantages he had over Luis Del Mora's killer and Sergeant Fritz Commons. Commons almost certainly didn't know about Amanda Hunter or she would've told Billy so by now, which meant that he and Flora Jean possessed a little nugget of investigative gold. Commons assuredly had to know about Counts and Vannick, but CJ reasoned that the pesky homicide cop probably knew nothing about the convoluted game of stolen-book musical chairs that Counts, Vannick, and Stafford had been playing. More than likely only the killer or killers knew about that.

CJ thought about one very distinct additional advantage. He and Flora Jean had a distraught mother on their side, a mother who was far more suspicious of law enforcement than supportive of it; in his world well-placed distrust of cops was always a plus. Now all he had to do was outrun Commons and find Luis Del Mora's murderer.

He set his coffee aside, fished a cheroot out of his vest pocket, and hesitated, holding the cheroot in midair and eyeing it as if he'd just drawn a bad hand. He set the cheroot down on the desk and choked back a sigh, knowing that when all was said and done with the Del Mora murder, he still had Celeste Deepstream to contend with.

The entire three hours that Morgan and Dittier hauled antiques, collectibles, and just plain junk out of what was left of Lenny McCabe's store, McCabe hovered over them like a nervous drama coach. Two hours into the move, CJ had arrived. For the past half hour, he'd been standing inside Ike's Spot alone. Morgan and Dittier had loaded most of McCabe's valuable pieces into a trailer hitched to the back of a one-ton dually that McCabe had pulled up next to the garage at the rear of the store. Items meant for the trash had been tossed into a small roll-off Dumpster that sat a few feet from the front of the dually.

Walking away from the Dumpster, dusting off his hands, and glancing at Morgan, McCabe said, "Like I said, anything in that Dumpster you're more than welcome to."

Morgan forced back a frown, thinking, *Yeah, we got our choice of sticky Coke bottles, mildewed old newspapers, busted-up picture frames, and worthless coffee makers.* But since he and Dittier were each being paid $15 an hour and they were already into McCabe for almost three hours of work, Morgan decided to pass on voicing how he felt about McCabe's generosity, especially since Dittier had taken McCabe up on his Dumpster-diving offer and already had a shoebox full of discards. Morgan watched McCabe head for Ike's Spot and trotted over to check on Dittier and his shoebox of treasures.

CJ stood in Ike's Spot, glancing around the surprisingly intact empty room. He had never appreciated how narrow the store was until now. As he gazed at the walls, the empty shelves, the pockmarked wooden floors, and the slit-like windows, he realized that he'd been working in a smaller version of the same kind of New Orleans–style shotgun house as Mae's Louisiana Kitchen. He wondered if Mavis had ever noticed the similarity or if she'd noticed that the walls of his store really weren't square, or that the floors were caked with years of unstripped wax, or that the artificial interior lighting failed to mask the fact that night or day the store was always dark. He hadn't seen any of those things when he'd leased the space. He'd been too busy chasing a dream. Shaking his head, CJ stepped over a pile of broken ceiling tiles, walked to the front of the store, and raised the shade on the front door's window. He eyed the empty sidewalk, convinced that he'd made the mistake of his life eight months earlier when he'd made the decision to sell his bail-bonding business to Flora Jean.

"You look lost in space," Lenny McCabe called out from the back of the store breaking CJ's concentration. "Nothing's ever that bad." McCabe walked the length of the store, smiling, his flip-flops slapping against his heels, his ponytail looping from side to side. "I'm pretty much loaded up outside and headed for a new day." McCabe eyed CJ pensively. "You need to take the same attitude if you expect to land back on your feet, my man. I moped and meandered for a little while too until I remembered that nobody really gives a damn about old Lenny McCabe but Lenny.

You need to start traveling that same highway if you expect to survive."

"I'll work at it," CJ said softly.

"Well, you'd better start now." McCabe looked around the empty store. "Because I've got some people coming by here tomorrow to give me the scoop on how to restore this calamity. I need you on board and talking positive when they show up. Heard anything about your insurance settlement yet?"

"Yeah, and I'm afraid I can't pool my money with yours, Lenny. I've got people I owe. Construction people and folks who lost items they'd consigned to the store. Not to mention friends I'm into for loans. After I settle up, I'll barely be able to make my rent."

"Then let it all ride till you're back on your feet."

"I don't do business that way, Lenny, and I'm not interested in cutting corners and greasing a bunch of bureaucratic palms in order to resurrect a business that doesn't need resurrecting."

McCabe looked disappointed. "Don't waffle on me, CJ. I need you here in the trenches with me."

"You can always get another tenant."

McCabe looked incensed. "Hey, man, in case you've forgotten, the people who blew up *my* building weren't after me. I need you in the boat with me or we don't stand a chance of leaving shore. Besides, I've got a minor problem of my own. I more or less told my insurance company that the lease-hold improvements you made on your space were, well . . . uh . . . pretty much done on my dime."

"You what?"

"I told them that I paid for your lease-hold improvements and that I expected reimbursement."

"Are you nuts? They'll find out the truth."

"Not if you don't tell them, they won't. The whole thing's simple. You get paid by your insurance people, I get paid a little extra by mine, and everything comes out clean in the wash."

CJ shook his head. "So the real reason you need me to stay is so you can keep an insurance scam rolling."

"Partially."

"You're out of luck, Lenny. I'm not interested in doing time for insurance fraud."

McCabe shrugged. "Suit yourself, but one way or another, you're gonna have to ante up. I've got legal remedies, you know. Especially if you withheld information from me about some mad bomber being after you when I leased the premises to you in good faith."

"I'll be damned," said CJ, realizing why McCabe had, other than the day it had happened, taken the bombing of his building pretty much in stride. He'd had a plan to reinvent the place all along—a plan that would allow him to give the plain-Jane duplex a total makeover and a plan that required CJ's compliance. "Call things however you want, Lenny, but as far as your rebuilding plans are concerned, count me out."

"Don't be so hasty to run for cover," said McCabe, sensing that he'd pushed CJ into an unintended corner. "Give yourself some time to think things through."

CJ gritted his teeth and eyed McCabe from head to toe. "Thinking cuts both ways, Lenny. I'd do a little of my own if I were you."

McCabe shrugged, chagrined that he'd given CJ inside knowledge of his insurance-scamming plans. "So we think—and talk again real soon."

"We'll talk," said a stern-faced CJ, but he already knew that he and Lenny McCabe had parted company forever.

"I'll go out and settle up with Morgan and Dittier. They should be done loading everything up by now," said McCabe, recognizing from CJ's expression that it was time to leave. He pivoted and walked away without waiting for a response, leaving CJ staring out the front door.

❧

"Why you lookin' so glum?" Morgan asked CJ as he sat in the front seat of CJ's Jeep, recounting the nine $5 bills that Lenny McCabe had paid him. The Jeep, its shocks badly in need of replacement, bumped along Broadway toward downtown.

Before CJ could respond, Morgan glanced over the seat back at Dittier and signed, "You put your money away, champ?"

Dittier nodded and patted a shirt pocket full of bills before leaning forward to hand Morgan a stack of postcards.

Morgan took the postcards and turned his attention back to CJ. "Still waitin' for an answer, CJ."

"Problems," CJ said. He eased to a stop at a stoplight and glanced toward Morgan, who was casually flipping through the dog-eared stack of grease-stained postcards in his hand.

Morgan reached the next-to-last card in the stack, a Magic Marker–streaked postcard with three of its four corners missing, as the light turned green. The defaced remnant of past Cheyenne Frontier Days glory sported the Triangle Bar brand in the lower left-hand corner. CJ's gaze remained fixed on the postcard as car horns blared behind him. "Where'd that postcard come from?" he asked, his tone suddenly hushed.

"Trash pickin's from McCabe's," said Morgan.

"Mind if I have a look?" CJ pulled over to the curb as Morgan handed him the postcard.

CJ looked the postcard over, turned in his seat, and squared up to Dittier. "Where'd you find this?" he asked, holding up the card, watching Dittier read his lips.

Looking puzzled, Dittier rapidly signed an answer back to Morgan.

"Dittier says the cards were in a rusty bucket filled with broken lightbulbs, wadded-up newspapers, and a bunch of old sheet-metal screws. Worthless stuff," Morgan said defensively.

"Can I keep it for a while?" CJ asked.

Dittier flashed him a thumbs-up and a smile.

CJ slipped the postcard into his vest pocket, swung his door open, and stepped into the street.

Startled, Morgan exclaimed, "What the hell's with you, CJ? You tryin' to get yourself killed?"

"No. Just in a hurry to get someplace. You and Dittier head on down to LoDo and relieve Billy like we planned. I need to get back to Ike's Spot, now!"

"It's eight full blocks back to the store," Morgan protested.

Already on the sidewalk in an all-out sprint, CJ never heard him. Nor did he notice the vehicle two cars behind the Jeep make a U-turn or realize that the woman behind the wheel had been following him ever since they'd left Ike's Spot.

Gasping for air, CJ ended his run at the intersection of Arkansas Avenue and the alley that led to the rear of the store. Relieved to see McCabe's trailer still there, he gazed across the backyards of the two duplexes that were north of McCabe's building and spotted McCabe loading boxes into the trailer. Slipping his cell phone off his belt, he punched in Billy DeLong's number. "Billy, CJ," he panted into the phone, taking a knee behind a privet hedge that had just begun to bud.

"What's up? You sound out of breath, CJ."

"I need an answer to something real quick. Call Loretta Sheets and ask her if she ever peddled anything to an antiques dealer named Lenny McCabe back when she was stealing stuff for Oliver Lyman. Call me right back. I think I may have pieced the whole Del Mora murder puzzle together."

"Hope she's at her museum."

"Me too. If not, I'm gonna have to wing it." Watching McCabe continue to load up, CJ hung up and switched his cell phone's answer tone from ring to vibrate.

McCabe loaded two large cardboard boxes into the trailer. Leaving a lone box sitting on the ground, he walked back to his half of the bombed-out duplex and disappeared inside. CJ rose to a squat, peered over the hedges to make sure McCabe was alone, and quickly took a knee again.

Billy's return call came seconds later. "Got that poop you wanted," Billy said excitedly. "Sheets admitted that she did sell a bunch of stuff to McCabe for Oliver Lyman. She only owned up to it when I told her that you needed the information to peg Lyman's killer. She told me somethin' else interestin' too. Said that the whole time Lyman was lookin' to find that missin' daguerreotype, McCabe was lookin' for it too."

"Why the hell didn't she tell you that before?"

"I'm guessin' that after hearin' about Lyman buyin' it she was just plain scared. That and the fact that I didn't have no reason to ask her about McCabe. I only asked her if she sold stolen goods for Lyman. Never really asked her who she sold 'em to."

"Yeah," said CJ, thinking that he should've gone along on one of Billy's trips to talk to Loretta Sheets.

"Hey, Morgan and Dittier just drove up," Billy said, sounding relieved. "Need me to do anything else down here?"

"No, everything's just about worked itself to a head."

"Everything but that Deepstream woman bobbin' up to the surface. She's still out there somewhere, CJ."

"I haven't forgotten." CJ watched McCabe emerge from the duplex and return to the backyard. "Sooner or later that'll come to a head too. Gotta go, Billy," he whispered.

McCabe walked up to the fully loaded trailer, peered inside, eyed the box on the ground, and smiled approvingly. Moments later CJ stepped around the corner of McCabe's dilapidated garage, stopped a few feet from the trailer, and said, "See you're about done, Lenny."

"Sure am," said a startled McCabe. "I thought you were gone."

"Had to come back. Needed to finish up some business."

McCabe smiled. "So you've decided to take me up on my rebuilding offer?"

"Nope. Decided to see if I couldn't put a cap on how Luis Del Mora met his fate."

"What?" asked McCabe, eyeing the box at his feet.

CJ shook his head. "No, why's a better question. Like why on earth would some kid from Nicaragua end up getting killed over a couple of not-so-rare books? Even if he was a thief."

"Beats me. Maybe the person he stole the books from wanted them back, a lot more than the kid expected."

"Makes sense. Except that, as we both know, the books aren't actually missing. They're safe and sound in some police evidence locker downtown, and their owner knows that. Nope, Luis Del Mora died for other reasons."

"Like?"

"Like the fact that he fitted a profile. A profile that called for a college student who was willing to steal, sell, and barter stolen goods. Antiques and collectibles for the most part, and maybe some other things I haven't drawn a bead on yet."

"Sounds reasonable. But why run all this by me?"

"Because in a sense, Del Mora worked for you. Not in an up-front way like Dittier and Morgan did this morning. You didn't hire him; Oliver Lyman did that. You see, Del Mora was Lyman's runner, supplying you with stolen merchandise that you sold in your store."

McCabe's eyebrows arched in protest. "Have you been drinking, CJ? Or maybe you're having one of those Vietnam flashbacks they talk about. I never saw the Del Mora kid until the day he walked into your store."

"I don't think so, Lenny." CJ slipped Dittier's Cheyenne Frontier Days postcard out of his shirt pocket. "I think you knew him, did business with him, and more than likely killed him. Here's what tripped you up." He handed the postcard to McCabe.

"It's a postcard. So?"

"And an old one. From the 1930s, I'm told." CJ smiled. "I'm willing to bet that card came from a storage shed at the Triangle Bar Ranch up in Wyoming."

"Never heard of the place, and I've never seen the postcard before." McCabe shoved the postcard at CJ.

"Funny, Dittier says he got the postcard out of your trash this morning."

"Shit, the man's deaf and dumb, and he's a street bum on top of it. He's probably lying."

"I don't think so. It's not in his character. But it's sure as hell part of yours. You're lying about the postcard, about not knowing Del Mora, and about the Triangle Bar Ranch. I'd even be willing to bet you know that ranch well enough to have broken into buildings out there a couple of times."

"And why would I do that?" McCabe's ponytail looped from side to side as he shook his head in protest.

CJ eyed the swinging pendulum of hair and flashed a smile of recognition. "To look for a missing photograph. A one-of-a-kind daguerreotype of the transcontinental railroad Golden Spike ceremony taken by Jacob Covington back in 1869. You didn't find it during either one of your break-ins, but in the process you found a bunch of collectible postcards, and, pack rat that you are, Lenny, you couldn't resist bringing the postcards back." CJ eyed the trailer. "I'd sure like to see what other Triangle Bar goodies you've got stashed inside the boxes in that trailer."

When McCabe didn't respond, CJ said, "And there's one other thing that links you to those two break-ins at the Triangle Bar. A piece of plastic you left behind after your most recent visit. I spent hours trying to figure out where that little plastic fragment could've come from, and for the life of me I couldn't place the source until now, when I realized that I'd been thinking too hard about broken combs and eyeglass frames and compact cases when all along I should've been considering one of those barrettes you use to keep that ponytail of yours in place." CJ flashed McCabe his best *gotcha* smile. "Bet you if I looked hard enough, I'd find myself a toothless match around somewhere."

McCabe's lower lip quivered as he took a step back toward the trailer. "Get the fuck out of here, CJ. And don't ever set foot on my property again."

CJ didn't budge. "So where's the missing daguerreotype, Lenny? You still haven't answered that question. It wasn't in the Montana medicine book, and you didn't find it during either of your break-ins at the Triangle Bar."

There was a momentary silent standoff until Theresa Del Mora rose from where she'd been crouched in the shadow of a trailer wheel well. A .357 Magnum jutted from her right hand.

"Yes, where is it?" Theresa asked incisively. The look on her face was placid and self-assured. "Where is this priceless photograph that caused you to kill my son?" The barrel of the .357 was now aimed squarely at Lenny McCabe's chest.

McCabe's defiant look turned to fear.

"I don't think you want to go where you're headed, Theresa," CJ said, raising a hand in protest.

"Afraid I do, Mr. Floyd. And thank you for guiding me to my son's killer. Yesterday, when I decided to follow you, I knew it was a wise decision, and you've borne me out. Please don't interfere. I don't want to harm you by accident." The gun muzzle jiggled as she eyed McCabe with hatred. "In Nicaragua my husband was a freedom fighter, Mr. McCabe. He taught me to use a pistol until I became deadly accurate." She cocked the gun's hammer. "Now, please answer me. Where is the photograph?"

"Theresa, please," said CJ, gauging the distance between them.

When McCabe didn't answer, Theresa said, "I'll kill you, sir. Please believe me."

McCabe held up a hand. "I don't have the photograph."

Gripping the .357 with both hands, Theresa said, "I think you're lying."

Shaking, hysterical, and suddenly talkative, Lenny McCabe held up both hands defensively. Looking at Theresa, but talking to CJ, he said, "Luis came by the store demanding to be paid for those two lousy books he'd stolen after I had already paid him ten thousand for the daguerreotype that was in the Montana medicine book the previous evening. I told him no, reminding him that he should've already destroyed the two books since someone might have been able to trace them back to us. He said he'd taken all the risks and he wanted more money. Hell, he didn't have a clue how much that photo was truly worth. But he was stubborn and wouldn't take no for an answer. He screamed at me that I owed him two thousand more dollars. That maybe he'd even go to the cops. The next thing I know, he shows up flaunting the books right under my nose like I was a nobody, negotiating a deal for the books with you right here on my doorstep. I had to deal with him after that." Nodding to himself, McCabe stammered, "You'd seen him, CJ, and you had the books. I couldn't take the chance that you'd be able to connect the two of us if things ever started to head south. Don't shoot!"

McCabe had barely uttered the words when CJ's right arm crashed down across Theresa's wrists, sending her tumbling off balance to the ground. The gun discharged with a muffled crack into the soft, moist soil. CJ scooped up the .357 one-handed. With the other he helped Theresa to her feet.

Wiggling out of CJ's grasp, Theresa lunged at McCabe and buried her fingernails in his forehead. McCabe screamed in pain as, jamming the .357 under his belt, CJ grabbed Theresa and pulled her screaming and kicking away from McCabe. Four bloody fingernail tracks ran down McCabe's forehead.

"Where's the photograph, Lenny?" demanded CJ, feeling Theresa go limp in his arms.

"I don't have it!" McCabe shouted, watching CJ ease his hand onto the butt of the .357. "I sold it back to Stafford."

CJ nodded as if he'd half expected that answer. "For how much?"

"A hundred thousand. No questions asked."

"And Oliver Lyman—why'd you kill him?"

McCabe stared skyward without answering as rivulets of blood streamed down his face and across his tightly sealed lips.

CHAPTER 32

For almost an hour the alley behind Ike's Spot had been blocked by Fritz Commons's unmarked car and two Denver patrol units. Two uniformed officers sat behind the wheels of the patrol cars while a few yards away, a plainclothesman shooed onlookers away. Theresa Del Mora sat handcuffed and blank-faced, elbows on her thighs, on the back steps of Ike's Spot, oblivious to the surrounding commotion, while Lenny McCabe, handcuffed as well, sat in the backseat of Fritz Commons's car, head down, shivering intermittently. Commons stood in the alley talking to CJ a few feet from McCabe's run-down garage.

"McCabe's not saying anything," said Commons, glancing toward his car. "All he will admit is that the building is his, and so are the truck and trailer. He'll be even less talkative once he talks to his lawyer."

CJ shook his head. "He said he killed the Del Mora kid—that's gotta count for something."

"Under duress," Commons shot back. "He claims the kid's mother had a gun pointed at him."

"You see a gun anywhere, Sergeant?"

"Nope, but I'm guessing somebody took care of that, and I sure hope it wasn't you or one of your rodeo-cowboy friends." Commons shot CJ an authoritative stare. "I've got another set of cuffs. If it weren't for that box of things we found sitting next to the trailer and that Hunter woman calling from Wyoming, at your urging I might add, claiming that the stuff's hers, I'd have no reason to hold McCabe."

"He killed two people, Sergeant."

"You can prove that?"

"No."

"Then you'd better let the law handle this. Besides, it's awful damn funny that the Hunter woman's stolen property just happened to be sitting in a box without a top on it out in plain view screaming, *Look at me, look at me, no need for a warrant.* Of course, no one around here but a cop or maybe a bail bondsman would understand knotty little police procedural details like that. And of course you're just an antiques dealer, aren't you, Floyd?"

"I am. And it sounds like the system's getting ready to spend a pot full of taxpayers' dollars, including mine, on Lenny McCabe."

"You're right; the system may very well lose because everything you've given me up to now is pretty much circumstantial. And when McCabe's lawyers bring up the issue of him admitting to the Del Mora killing when he was in mortal fear of his life, he might even walk."

CJ eyed McCabe thoughtfully. "Do you want the right answer to work its way up out of this mess, Sergeant?"

"Of course."

"Then find the gun that McCabe used to kill Del Mora and more than likely Oliver Lyman and seal up your case." CJ nodded toward McCabe's trailer.

Commons glanced at the trailer. "You been in there digging around?"

"No. But if I was gonna do any digging, that trailer would be the first place I'd start."

"When I get a warrant," said Commons. "Now, did McCabe say anything about who might have the missing daguerreotype?"

Recalling the image of Stafford sitting smugly in his car and aiming a gun at him, CJ said, "No."

"Strange. There has to be a tie-in to someone else here somewhere."

"Keep digging, Sergeant," said CJ, having decided that he needed a very private one-on-one with Stafford. "Sooner or later you'll find the link."

Sensing that CJ wasn't telling him everything, Commons asked, "Have you told me all I need to know here, Floyd?"

"Sure have," said CJ, slipping a suddenly vibrating cell phone off his belt. "Mind if I take this?"

"Go ahead." Commons turned his attention to the trailer, hoping that a search warrant would be the key to his finding the missing daguerreotype and maybe even a murder weapon.

Cell phone to his ear, CJ said, "Floyd here."

"It's Billy. You need to get here quick, CJ. I'm glommed on to that Russian down here at his condo, and Celeste just turned up. Looks about like she did nine months ago when she was shootin' at us, except she's a good thirty pounds lighter. She's wearin' a scarf, shades, and she's dressed head to toe in black. The Russian just waltzed her outta the door to his building, and he's talkin' on his cell phone. Hey, wait a minute! One of them stretch limos just pulled up in front of the place. The Russian's motionin' for Celeste to step back under the entry canopy. Now he's talkin' to the limo driver."

"Damn! Is Morgan still there?"

"Yeah. He and Dittier are standin' right here beside me."

"Tell Morgan I need him over here at Ike's Spot in a hurry. I don't have any wheels. You stay with Borg and Celeste. I wanta know where they're headed in that limo."

"Okay. But it's gonna make me miss my meetin' with Amanda. I promised her we'd go fly fishin' later today."

"I'll make it up to you. Just get Morgan over here fast." CJ snapped his cell phone shut, turned, and found himself eye to eye with Fritz Commons.

Commons smiled. "Thought you gave up the bail-bonding business, Floyd."

"Afraid it's hard to get some things outta your blood, Sergeant. You done with me here?"

"Pretty much."

CJ glanced toward where Theresa Del Mora was standing. "What about her?"

"I've got a lot more questions for her. If I can't find that mysterious gun that McCabe keeps screaming about, she's temporarily free to go."

"She's been through a lot. Take it easy."

Commons smiled. "She'll do fine. She seems as tough as nails."

CJ walked over to the short, sad-eyed, frail-looking Nicaraguan woman, noting for the very first time how large and misshapen her head seemed to be. "I have to go, Theresa. Something urgent's come up. Sergeant Commons has a few more questions to ask you, and then you'll be free to go. I called Flora Jean. She's on her way." He took Theresa's left hand in his and squeezed it reassuringly.

Theresa could barely reciprocate. Her strength had been drained. She'd come to America searching for opportunity and

freedom, and the land of opportunity had used her up, eviscer-
ated her soul, and devoured her son. She had trusted in a place
and a culture that her husband had always mocked, and in the
end that misplaced trust had caused the death of her son.

"Theresa, are you all right?"

Theresa nodded, flashing CJ a blank, soulless stare just as Flora
Jean came rushing around the garage toward them. CJ slipped
his hand out of Theresa's and turned to leave. "I got here as fast
as I could," said Flora Jean. She stared at Theresa, said, "God,"
and shook her head.

"She's hurting pretty bad," said CJ. "Hang in there with her.
Commons has a bunch more questions for her, and it could get
rough. Try to keep him on the straight and narrow. Sorry, but
I've gotta go."

"Where?" asked Flora Jean, noting a glint of excitement in
CJ's eye.

"To settle up with Celeste."

"CJ, no!" Flora Jean's protest missed its mark as CJ rushed
across the yard, past a startled Sergeant Commons, and down
the alley toward Morgan and the open door of his Jeep.

"I'm on that limo's ass, CJ. No more than a couple of car lengths
behind," Billy DeLong said calmly into his cell phone. "Borg's in
the backseat, and so's Celeste. Now, you ain't gonna like this,
but I called the cops. Ain't seen one yet, though."

"Damn, Billy," CJ said disappointedly, adjusting himself in the
Jeep's front seat as Morgan turned onto Broadway.

"You blind to the situation, man? You ain't no bail bondsman
or bounty hunter anymore, and like it or not, you're a couple of

steps past your prime. You forgettin' that this is the same woman who had your store blown to smithereens? For all I know, she's got a bazooka or a grenade launcher in that limo. Shit, yeah, I called the cops."

Ignoring Billy's protests, CJ asked, "Did they load up any luggage?"

"Yeah, the limo driver stuffed five big ol' suitcases in the trunk."

"Stay with them, Billy. Odds on, they're headed for the airport."

Billy's cell phone crackled, "I'm locked on to 'em, and right now we're movin' pretty slow. Traffic's a mess down here. Still no helpful boys-in-blue in sight, by the way."

"Whatever you do, Billy, don't lose contact with them or with me."

"Ain't no way they'll shake me. You can count on it. And if we get cut off, I'll call you right back."

"Where are you now?"

"On the boulevard that skirts the college complex downtown."

"Auraria Parkway. They're heading for I-25!"

"Think you're right; the driver's pullin' into the left-hand turn lane. No question, he's headed for the interstate."

"All right! I'm headed north on Broadway. We're six or seven exits south of you." CJ turned to Morgan. "We need to slow down or we'll miss hooking up with that limo and Billy. Ease over to the curb for a minute."

Morgan pulled over and shot a quick glance over the seat back at Dittier. "You sure this is what we oughta be doin', CJ?"

CJ ignored the question. "Billy, we're a half block south of the Broadway entrance to southbound I-25. Tell me when you get to the Emerson Street exit and I'll have Morgan head up the on ramp. We should just about meet up with you. What's the plate ID on that limo, and how fast is he going?"

"Dream R 5, and he's cruisin' right at sixty."

"Got it." CJ checked his watch, aware that he had less than two minutes to consider anything he might have overlooked. He glanced over his shoulder and gave Dittier a wink. "We're in the thick of it now, cowboy." Nodding at Morgan, he said, "Time to hit that on ramp."

Morgan pulled away from the curb. Moments later he turned onto the I-25 on ramp from Broadway, a pothole-filled, two-lane, construction-compromised stretch of asphalt bordered on both sides by concrete barriers. A roadside bevy of cranes and heavy equipment paid homage to Denver's five-year-long I-25 lane-widening and light-rail construction project known as T-REX. Morgan slowed the Jeep as two lanes merged into one. He was just about to accelerate when, six cars ahead of him, a workman on the road shoulder flashed a handheld stop sign at the lead driver, and a front-end loader pulling a trailer loaded with concrete barriers lumbered across the on ramp and stopped.

"What the shit?" CJ sat forward in his seat as the man with the stop sign walked up to the driver of the first car and said, "Gonna be a while, buddy."

"Damn!" Totally frustrated, CJ said into his cell phone, "Got a problem here, Billy."

"Better fix it fast; I'm comin' up on that Emerson Street exit."

"Can't. We've got construction equipment blocking the fucking way."

"No way around it?"

"Not unless this Jeep of mine sprouts wings." CJ gritted his teeth and began tapping his left foot.

"Call Flora Jean, see if she can't help out."

"Might as well," said CJ, the excitement of the chase drifting past his sails. "Problem is, she's probably still with Theresa Del Mora and a cop. I'll call you right back."

"And that's what we're needin' right now, CJ, a cop," said Morgan.

Ignoring Morgan's plea, CJ eyed the trailer and the offloader that had moved up next to it, shook his head, and called Flora Jean.

"Folks up front are gettin' impatient," said Morgan as CJ ended his call to Flora Jean. "The guy first in line's outta his car."

His enthusiasm largely spent, CJ said, "Flora Jean's working on getting Sergeant Commons to have a car dispatched to DIA. I gave her the limo's vanity plate ID."

Morgan bristled. "Why the hell don't they just call the limo driver and tell him he's haulin' around a lady with a bucket full of outstanding warrants? Hell, the driver's gotta have a cell phone."

CJ smiled. "Rules, Morgan. Rules. And half-a-dozen privacy laws the cops don't wanta break. But most of all they're not calling because we don't have any clout. We're lucky that Commons even agreed to intervene."

"It's all probably for the best," said Morgan. "Us gettin' stuck like this. After all, this ain't no rice paddy, and we ain't in Vietnam."

"Nope. I'm just fighting my own private little war," said CJ, reaching for his cell phone, answering before the second ring. "Billy?"

"Yeah. And I don't think our limo's headed for Denver International. The driver cruised right on past the I-225 airport exit. He just turned onto Arapahoe Road."

"Centennial! So much for help from the Denver cops," muttered CJ.

"What?"

"Centennial. It's a private airport for commuter planes and corporate jets just off Arapahoe Road. If Flora Jean ever got us any backup from the cops, they're headed in the wrong direction."

"Yeah, yeah," Billy said excitedly. "I see the airport sign just up ahead. The limo driver's turnin' south, dead-headed for the place."

"Stick with him, Billy. I'll try to think of a way to slow them down. One thing for sure, we can't count on the airport bureaucracy helping out. There's not much airport screening security at Centennial. You pretty much drive right up to your plane, load up, and take on off." CJ adjusted the cell phone to his ear as Morgan called out, "Hey, the line's movin'. They're routin' us around that front-end loader."

"Billy, hang tight. We're rolling."

"Better make it fast. The limo just cruised onto the airport property. How far away are you?"

"Fifteen minutes, eighteen at the most," said CJ as Morgan inched the Jeep forward.

"Best aim for fifteen," said Billy. "The limo driver just pulled up to a security gate. The guy in the gatehouse is wavin' him past and out onto the tarmac. I'm across the parkin' lot from the gatehouse. There's a fifteen-foot-high chain-link fence separatin' the parkin' lot from the tarmac. I don't wanta move too close to it and chance gettin' spotted. Hold on. There're a couple of Lear-jets sittin' out on the tarmac. The limo's headed for the one that's farthest away."

"See any cops?"

"No."

"Figures."

"Won't matter one way or another in a few minutes," said Billy. "Celeste is gonna be outta here. You better haul ass."

"We're hauling," said CJ. Morgan dropped off the roadway and onto a shoulder of mud. He eased the Jeep around the loader, accelerated, kicking up a contrail of mud and gravel, and sped down the on ramp to I-25.

Sunglasses in place and with her scarf pulled tightly over her head, Celeste hurried up the steps of Alexie's Learjet. Clutching a cache of magazines and books in one hand, she stepped inside, nodded at the pilot, turned, and headed toward her seat.

The plane lacked the overhead space of a commercial jetliner, and as she took her seat, Celeste felt cramped. She placed her reading materials on the desktop in front of her seat and turned on an overhead light. The plane's interior was sterile and office-like. A computer, a printer, and a fax machine sat across from her on a desk. Four plush-looking leather chairs grouped in a quarter circle sat directly behind her. A daybed hugged the lavatory bulkhead at the rear of the plane.

Celeste adjusted herself in her seat and prepared herself mentally for the long trip to Paris. She had always disliked flying, but she'd sleep through it, she told herself.

She glanced out of the window, watched her bags disappear into the belly of the plane, and thought about how badly she'd muffed her chance to kill Floyd. She should've blown him up herself rather than count on a halfwit like Moradi-Nik, or shot him point-blank instead of hoping for a silent kill with a crossbow. But she hadn't, and it bothered her. She wondered if she was losing her edge—that physical edge that had made her a competitive athlete; the mental edge that had always fueled her curiosity and intellect; the genetic edge that had awarded her such an advantage over her twin brother, Bobby. In the end, she knew she would have her day of reckoning with Floyd. She could sense it. But as the plane's jet engines powered on and Alexie stepped inside and closed the door, she had the sudden sense that when that time came, her revenge would seem hollow.

"Ready for Paris, *mon cherie?*" Alexie called out to Celeste before nodding at the pilot and spinning his index finger winding-clock style. As the plane engines powered up to a high-pitched whine, Alexie, grinning and close to licking his lips, plopped down in the seat next to Celeste. "You'll enjoy the ride," he said. Dropping a hand onto Celeste's lap, squeezing her thigh, and eyeing the bed at the rear, he smiled, "And hopefully so will I."

"The plane's movin'!" Billy screamed into his cell phone to CJ. "Where are you?"

"Turning onto Arapahoe Road."

"They're taxiing out to the runway. Don't think you're gonna make it."

"Punch it, Morgan," CJ yelled.

Morgan floored the accelerator as the Learjet nosed its way toward the active runway. The Jeep pulled into the airport's parking lot as the plane, nose to the east, began its take-off roll.

CJ was out of the Jeep before Morgan brought the vehicle to a full stop. Stumbling and off balance, he sprinted for the fence that separated the parking lot from the tarmac as Dittier and Morgan raced after him. He was halfway up the fence when Morgan screamed, "CJ, are you crazy?" and grabbed him by the right leg. He kicked out of Morgan's grasp and watched as the jet gained runway speed. He was inches from the top of the fence when a gust of wind caught the brim of his Stetson, sending it sailing skyward. Raking his hand across the top edge of a broken chain link, CJ clenched his fist, powered his arm skyward, and screamed, "Damn!"

Celeste looked back toward the control tower and the airport's nearly empty parking lot as the jet neared take-off speed. She scanned the landscape for something familiar, a parting snapshot of the West that she could take with her to Paris. Crossing her legs, she smiled and moved out of Alexie's grasp. As the plane's nose angled upward, she noticed a Jeep hugging the tarmac's perimeter fence, and as the wheels left the ground, she could have sworn she saw a cowboy hat swirling upward in the wind. She locked the image in her mind, deciding that it would be the Western image she would take with her to Paris.

CHAPTER 33

Howard Stafford rarely entered his house by the front door, but when he saw a Jeep, which he immediately recognized as CJ Floyd's, parked in the circular driveway in front of his house, aligned perfectly with his front steps, he stopped at the driveway's edge, got out, and slowly, never taking his eyes off the Jeep or its occupant, walked toward his house. It was a half hour before sunset, and in the fading light everything appeared slightly gray to Stafford.

CJ had grudgingly come to terms with the fact that Celeste had sidestepped him, slipping away on a ribbon of air. He had left Centennial Airport hat in hand and emotionally spent, obsessively second-guessing his tactics, when Flora Jean had finally called to report that the cops had impounded Lenny McCabe's trailer and that Theresa Del Mora had disappeared.

Flora Jean's worry over not being able to find Theresa and her concern that Sergeant Commons had come by the office to voice his "official uneasiness" over not being able to further question her client forced CJ to put his war with Celeste Deepstream aside and finish what he'd promised himself he'd do after he'd left a defeated-looking Theresa Del Mora sitting on the back steps of Ike's Spot hours earlier.

He had been sitting in the Jeep waiting for Stafford for over an hour, having entered the estate without protest or fanfare by virtue of having the security code for the main gate. Luis Del Mora had jotted the code on the back of an East Colfax Avenue pawnbroker's business card.

"No need for a gun today, I hope," said CJ, stepping out of the Jeep.

"How the hell did you get in here, Floyd?"

"Through the main gate."

"Well, leave." Stafford stopped a couple of paces from the Jeep and eyed CJ's oil-stained Stetson and the bruise above his right eye. "Now. Before you end up with a knot above your other eye."

CJ smiled. "Can't. At least not until I have the answers to some questions. And just so we're on the same page, pull another gun on me and I'll make you swallow it. I'll just pretend like I didn't hear your comment."

"I'll call the police," Stafford said, a tinge of nervousness in his voice.

"Fine. I'm sure they'll want explanations, too."

"What's your game, Floyd?"

"Don't have one. But I know you sure as hell do, or did, a little shell game involving rare and not-so-rare stolen books. Found out just today that you had a couple of nincompoops *stealing* books from your library that they would then replace with rarer stolen upgrades. What I can't figure out is whether you were running your little game to scam your insurance company, to fantasize about having someone steal from you in order to get your jollies, or whether you simply wanted to come home every day and find that your library contained another Christmas present. Whatever the reason, it was one hell of a charade. Guess everyone's entitled to do what they have to to get their kicks."

"So what's your point, Floyd?"

"This. It turns out that an antiques dealer I know probably killed Luis Del Mora, and I'm pretty sure your pompous ass put him up to it. While I was waiting for you to come home, I had over an hour to do nothing but sit in my Jeep, smell the Rocky Mountain springtime, drink in the beauty of the grounds, and think about what it would be like to be rich. And you know what? At the end of that hour, I started to feel like I pretty much owned the world."

"If you're saying I hired someone to kill Luis, you're crazy."

"I didn't say that. And I'm almost certain you didn't—almost! You're at least a gnat's whisker smarter than that. Here's what I think happened, and sooner or later Lenny McCabe, that dealer I mentioned, will come clean on the whole rotten issue. His lawyers will make him. It's the only plea-bargaining chip they have to save his hide."

"It's your show, Floyd. Tell me what happened."

"Now remember, this is just a simple-minded bail bondsman's take." CJ flashed a broad, insightful smile. "What happened is this: you got yourself caught up in your book-replacement scam, with Arthur Vannick and Theodore Counts leading you by the nose, or you leading them by theirs, I'm not quite sure which, and you lost track of someone who was willing to steal from you for real—Luis Del Mora. You were so busy switching out your books for the more valuable replacements that Counts and Vannick were providing that you didn't check the henhouse for the fox. And what did those two care? They'd take your book, sell it to a pawnbroker or a used-book dealer or some unscrupulous antiques dealer like Lenny McCabe, pocket the change, provide you with a much rarer stolen replacement that was probably too hot to handle, and bingo: they've got money, they've unloaded a hot potato, and you've got a treasure locked away. When you come down to it, the whole scam was pretty much like laundering money. Oh, and by the way, Counts is the one who ratted you out." CJ took a deep, reflective breath. "And I'm guessing that everything was going along just dandy until Luis Del Mora showed up and somehow, either by having an insider's knowledge about railroads and railroad history or by watching you carefully every day and figuring out what to steal or by hooking up with a Metro State professor named Oliver Lyman who gave him guidance, or maybe just by sheer luck, he stumbled across a book in your library that contained the holy grail of transcontinental railroad lore, a photograph of the 1869 driving of the Golden Spike ceremony. And not just any old photo, mind you, but a one-of-a-kind daguerreotype. And as luck would have it, Del Mora ended up selling that stolen book, minus the photograph, of course, to me. But you already knew that, didn't you?"

Ignoring the question, Stafford said, "And this McCabe person stole the photo from Luis and killed him. End of story."

"Nope. That in fact is where the story takes, as my old riverboat captain used to say during Vietnam, a variance." CJ eyed the sudden look of confusion on Stafford's face. Smiling, he added, "Sort of like when your patrol boat starts taking on small-arms fire that couldn't possibly be coming from the shoreline and you realize you've got Vietcong shooting at you from the belly of a couple of passing sampans." CJ stroked his chin thoughtfully. "A variance. McCabe killed the Del Mora kid, all right, and he probably killed that Metro State professor, Lyman, too. But McCabe didn't steal the daguerreotype from either Del Mora or Lyman. He didn't have to." CJ smiled again. "Now, follow me on this. I've had most of the afternoon to think it through." He could see that the smile touched a raw nerve in Stafford. "Lyman had been look-ing for that daguerreotype for years, and it turns out that like all the rest of you, Lyman was an enterprising thief who had immi-grant college kids like Luis Del Mora stealing for him, and a smart capitalist who fenced his stolen goods through Lenny McCabe and others. When Luis Del Mora, fresh from plucking books out of your library, unimportant books for the most part, first turned up at McCabe's with that daguerreotype, laced of all places to the endboard of a book on the history of Montana medicine, I'm guess-ing that McCabe called Lyman, one of his stolen-book suppliers and a Western history expert, to ask for authentication. Now here's the kicker." CJ eyed Stafford sternly. "Since both McCabe and Lyman had been in the business of stealing and selling stolen books for a good long time, they realized that something as valu-able as a stolen one-of-a-kind daguerreotype of the Golden Spike ceremony would be too hot to handle, so they decided to ransom the photograph back to its owner. What they did, you see, Mr. Stafford, is sell your own photograph back to you."

"Bizarre story."

"Even more bizarre when you consider the fact that Luis Del Mora probably had no idea of the value of the photograph that he'd found in that Montana medicine book. But McCabe and Lyman clearly did. And from there things turned funky. McCabe either got greedy and tried to keep all the money you paid him to get the photograph, cutting Lyman out, or they couldn't square up on the money. Doesn't matter, really. Bottom line is, Lyman ended up with a hole in his chest, courtesy of McCabe, who'd already killed one person in his quest to get the photograph back to you." CJ flashed Stafford an incisive stare. "How much did you have to pay McCabe to get your daguerreotype back, Stafford?"

"You'll have to ask him," Stafford said smugly. "You're the one telling the story."

CJ shook his head. "I've gotta give it to you, Stafford. You're ice-water calm for a man who's pretty much responsible for the deaths of two people. Just remember, sooner or later McCabe's gonna tell his side of the story."

"And do you expect that story to carry much clout? Do you expect the tale of a murderer to possibly carry the same impact as mine?" Stafford flashed a confident grin.

"Don't know." CJ stepped back and shook his head in disgust. "But I'm sure some enterprising DA with political aspirations will be willing to slap an accessory-to-murder charge on your ass. In the end you'll answer to somebody, Stafford. The world just seems to work out its kinks that way."

Stafford laughed. "You're a naive, low-end, minor-league dreamer, Floyd. Things don't happen like that in my corner of the world. Now, if you'll excuse me, I'm late for my dinner." Stafford turned to leave. "By the time I'm inside my house, I expect you to be headed off my property. If you're not on the other side of my entry gate within three minutes, I'll call the police, or . . ."

"Or you'll pull your gun again, you privileged SOB? You triggered the deaths of two people, and you've destroyed a woman's life. I ought to kick your privileged ass."

"Don't push me, Floyd."

Checking his temper, CJ turned to leave, aware that five years earlier he would have made good on his threat. Boiling inside as he moved to get into the Jeep, he fired a parting salvo: "Try and keep your naked arrogant ass out of department store windows, freak."

Howard Stafford was already inside his house.

Stafford walked across his entryway and took the spiral stairs leading to a second-floor landing that looked back down on the entry. The landing's only window overlooked his driveway. He peered out the window and watched CJ drive away, wondering why no one from his staff had intercepted and removed the pesky bail bondsman. Loosening his tie, he took a deep, satisfying breath, deciding that answer would have to wait until later. Floyd was gone, McCabe had been pegged as a murderer, and above all he still had the daguerreotype.

He took a final glance out the window, bounded back down the steps, and headed for his library. Once there, he disarmed the keypad alarm, unlocked the doors, stepped inside, and turned on the lights. He slowly surveyed the room from left to right, eyeing every countertop, display case, bookcase, picture, and artifact in a clockwise scan. Convinced that security hadn't been breached, he walked across the room, knelt in front of a marble-topped display case, and extracted a key the size of a sewing needle from beneath the lip of the case's recessed toe-kick. He inserted the key in the titanium-lined lock, twisted it, and watched two wooden panel doors spring open.

He swung the doors all the way open and shook his head, telling himself that he should have kept the Covington daguerreotype under lock and key from the moment he'd chanced on it ten years earlier. He'd found it in the Montana medicine book at the bottom of a mildewed cardboard box that had been labeled, BOX 3, OFFICE CONTENTS, MEDICAL BOARD SECRETARY. He'd stumbled across the box on the final day of a Big Horn River fly-fishing trip outside Bozeman, Montana, a day when fishing had been lost to thunderstorms and torrential downpours. With nothing to do but read and wander, he had stumbled into an auction of water-damaged books and assorted office furnishings that had been salvaged from the old Helena, Montana, offices of the Montana Board of Medical Examiners. He'd paid $4 for the Montana medicine book and fifty cents for two others, never recognizing the significance of his find until several weeks later, when, after examining the photograph, recognizing the subject matter, quickly researching the history of the Union Pacific and Central Pacific Railroads, and devouring the Montana medicine book's section on Jacob Covington ten times over, he'd realized that he had stumbled across the find of a lifetime. Pack rat and stickler for authenticity that he was, he still had the original purchase receipt, and he'd left the photo inside the book, even saving the fishing line.

With McCabe on ice, he knew that eventually the Del Mora murder investigation would come full circle to him, but it didn't matter. Wealthy, powerful, and connected, he had always found life to be primed to go his way. Even so, he'd made mistakes, like being cavalier enough to leave the Montana medicine book with the daguerreotype inside in a place where Luis Del Mora could discover it. He suspected that prior to stealing the book, Del Mora had more than likely watched his every move for months. Del Mora had probably watched him walk the halls of his home, fondling the book, and thought that the book, not the photograph inside, was what was valuable. Stafford had no idea how Del Mora could have found the key to the cabinet, but he had, and in the end he'd found the book, the photo, and a willing buyer.

But none of that mattered any longer. It didn't matter how Luis Del Mora had found the book, or that Del Mora and some professor named Lyman were dead, or that the photo had ever been out of his possession. He had the daguerreotype back. The cost of getting it back mattered even less. His transaction with McCabe had cost him $100,000, a small price to pay for a slice of American history worth more than a million, and in the end he'd learned something valuable from the experience. There'd be no more parlor games with the likes of Counts and Vannick, no more daily making love to the daguerreotype where someone might accidentally see him. No more, as Floyd had so aptly put it, sitting in the department-store window ass-naked. It was time to close ranks. He would stop hiring Third World castoffs like Theresa Del Mora in order to soothe a guilt-ridden rich man's conscience and in the future would limit his game-playing to the things that titillated him: horse betting, making money, and sex.

He slipped the daguerreotype out of the felt-lined slipcase he'd had made for it, held it up by the outer edges, and stared at it lovingly before bringing it to his lips. He thought about what it must have been like to have been the telegraph operator who'd announced as the Golden Spike was driven, "Done!"—signaling to the world that America was now a truly united continent.

Jacob Covington's daguerreotype was indeed one of a kind, a masterpiece of alchemy and art. He stared at the photograph for several more minutes, thinking about what it must have felt like to build that which had never been built before, then he eased the photo back into its slipcase, closed the display case doors, and rose. He walked away with a smile on his face and headed for his customary predinner vodka and tonic, feeling a sense of relief. He had put the daguerreotype to bed, Floyd was a fleeting memory, and the day's turbulent events had ultimately ebbed to a manageable flow.

The fire started in Stafford's library, destroying everything inside. From there, without benefit of a sprinkler system that had been sabotaged, the fire burned its way beyond the library's massive oak doors to sweep into the adjoining hallway, engulfing millions of dollars' worth of precious art.

The smell of smoke and soot and burning timbers permeated the air as, clad only in his pajamas, Howard Stafford, hysterical, and paralyzed by fear, watched an entire wing of his house become an inferno capped by plumes of red-and-orange flames. As fire-truck sirens screamed in the distance, he watched helplessly as his most precious passions turned to ash right before his eyes.

Howard Stafford had taken something precious from her, and now, as she sped south on I-25 beyond the southern outskirts of Colorado Springs on her long trip to Nicaragua and ultimately home, Theresa Del Mora knew that without benefit of the sprinkler system, Stafford's home should be a raging inferno. She understood fire—*Only fire and water can completely cleanse*, Alejandro had once told her. Now she and Howard Stafford were even. What mattered most to him in the world had turned to ashes and a memory.

She cruised along at seventy, her conscience clear, and thought about something else Alejandro had taught her: *Freedom and family are all that really matter in the world*. Her trip to America had cost her all she had left of her family, and freedom no longer had any meaning.

She glanced toward a sign announcing the exit for the Fort

Carson Army Base, a symbol of American military might. She sped past the sign, knowing that in spite of all of Howard Stafford's wealth and power, there was no chance that he would ever see her again, much less have an opportunity for recourse. For, as Alejandro had always said about the American giant to the north, *Might in all its glory can never overpower all-out home-turf guerrilla warfare.*

EPILOGUE

CJ stood in Mario Satoni's basement, watching Mario, down on one knee, dig through one of the shoeboxes he'd gathered into a semicircle in the middle of the floor.

"It's here someplace. I just gotta find it," Mario said, sounding peeved.

"Why all the fuss, Mario? I believe you."

"Yeah. Like you believed you were gonna catch up with that Deepstream woman before she slipped through your fingers, and like you thought Lenny McCabe had your best interests at heart. Hell, Calvin, sometimes I think Mavis has it right. You do need to be nurtured."

CJ didn't answer, concerned that if he did, the inexplicable spell he had cast over Mavis might evaporate. He'd struggled for weeks to get Mavis to buy in to the story that Celeste Deepstream had been erased from his life; weeks more to convince her that he would be at the periphery, not the center, of a Lenny McCabe murder trial—a trial that was shaping up to be a slam-dunk for the prosecution.

Two weeks earlier Fritz Commons had found the .22 Magnum that Lenny McCabe had more than likely used to kill both Luis Del Mora and Oliver Lyman. The gun had been wrapped in tissue paper and stuffed in a shoebox that Commons had found beneath the bed liner of McCabe's impounded dually. CJ had let out a sigh of relief when the news media had leaked the "murder weapon found" information, knowing the find would put him a few steps further from the center of a sensational double-murder trial.

He still hadn't been able to figure out exactly where he was now headed in life, but he suspected that sooner or later a proper choice would surface. He hadn't fully abandoned the idea of continuing in the antiques business, but he knew for certain now that he couldn't completely turn his back on being a bail bondsman. He had no idea how he'd combine the two polar-opposite careers, but with Mavis's hesitant blessing, he was going to try.

"I found it!" Mario shouted. "Right here under my nose. Been a snake it would've bit me. Have a look."

CJ knelt and eyed the box's contents: a handful of gaudy costume jewelry, a couple of old Bulova watches, and a rubber-banded stack of poker chips. "Will this take long, Mario?" CJ checked his watch as Mario handed him a worn leather coin purse. "We don't wanta be late for Mavis's Easter dinner. Hope you aren't forgetting, I'm still on semiprobation."

"I'm not forgetting anything, Calvin, but you're the one who's gotta toe Mavis's mark. Just hold your horses. It's not the Last Supper. The food won't evaporate if we're a couple of minutes late."

CJ smiled, knowing Mario was right. Mavis and Rosie Weeks's wife, Etta Lee, had more than likely cooked twice as much food as they'd need to feed eleven. Earlier that morning he'd checked in and found that Flora Jean, Alden Grace, and Morgan and Dittier had already settled in at Mavis's. When CJ had called Mavis to say he'd arrived at Mario's to pick Mario up, Mavis had said that Billy DeLong and Amanda Hunter were just walking through the door. He was hoping no one would put pressure on Billy or Amanda to define their relationship, but knowing Etta Lee's inquisitiveness, he suspected she would.

"Have a look inside the coin purse, Calvin. Go ahead."

CJ unzipped the coin purse and extracted a twenty-dollar gold piece and what looked like a spent bullet. He eyed the two objects quizzically before looking at Mario, who was now standing.

Mario smiled. "The slug's from a .38. The twenty-dollar gold piece belonged to your Uncle Ike. You know that story I've been promising to tell you all these years about me and Ike? Well, you're about to hear it. But before I strike up the old band, I need to know exactly where you and me stand on a few things, Calvin."

"Stand how?"

"Stand with belonging to a two-person fraternity that requires a lifelong bond. A bond that can't be broken until one of us is dead."

Looking surprised and uncertain where Mario was headed, CJ said, "That's pretty heavy-duty, Mario."

"For most of my life I was involved in what some folks would call a heavy-duty business, in case you've forgotten."

"I know that," said CJ, stunned that Mario would even hint at his prior life as a mobster. Thirty-five years earlier, as Denver's top crime boss, Mario could have sealed anyone's fate with just a nod of his head. A mere wink would have ensured that on any given night a quarter of a million dollars passed through his hands.

"So have you got an answer for me, Calvin?"

"No offense, Mario, but you caught me off guard. Mind telling me that story first?"

Mario shrugged. "What can it hurt? You're still the one's gotta make the decision." Mario watched CJ roll the gold piece and the slug around in his right hand. "So here's the story. It was 1948, and the country was just flexing its muscle after climbing outta the Second World War. I was a twenty-three-year-old rookie in my business, working my way up. It was the second week of June here in Denver, the air was late-spring sweet, and the trees had just finished leafing out. I had a pocket full of money from a business deal I'd just closed, and Angie, God rest her soul, was expecting." Mario paused. The hurt that always filled his eyes when he talked about his deceased wife seemed magnified.

Mario cleared his throat and continued. "Duke Ellington was in town for a three-night stand, playing down on Five Points at the Rossonian. I wanted to catch him, but Angie wasn't up to it. With the strain of impending motherhood tugging at her and knowing how much I loved jazz, she shoved me out the door and told me to take in Duke on my own. Back then, when jazz was king, you could count on seeing as many white folks as black folks walking the streets of Five Points. Anyway, I sauntered into the Rossonian for the first show and took a seat at the bar. I was listening to Duke and his orchestra flow through an up-tempo rendition of 'Take the A Train' when a muscle-bound black man wearing cowboy boots, bib overalls, and a Stetson took a seat on the stool next to me." Mario eyed CJ and winked as CJ acknowledged his pinpoint-accurate description of Ike with a smile and a nod.

"We struck up a conversation that ran on the whole rest of the evening, and by the end of the second set, I knew this about your uncle. He was a World War II veteran. He'd been a member of the mainly black Red Ball Express Transportation Corps in France, and he was now a bail bondsman.

"I didn't say much about myself except to tell him that my

family was in the furniture business," Mario smiled, "which was the truth.

"I was all warm and fuzzy-headed an hour or so later when I got up to leave, but Ike, who I had found out later had been nursing iced tea all night because of his on-and-off battle with alcohol, was as sober as a mule.

"We walked out of the place together and headed up Welton Street. Ike was hoofing it back to his place on Bail Bondsman's Row, and I was headed for my car. Two blocks later, just before we were about to go our separate ways, a guy stepped out of an alley, waved a .38 at us, and demanded money. It wasn't the money in my pocket he was after, I knew that the second I saw him, but Ike didn't. What he wanted was to slide me out of certain business relationships I had developed and slide himself in.

"I reached into my pocket to give him what money I had. As I handed him the money, our eyes met; then outta nowhere, like a damn rocket, Ike clobbered the guy with the meanest clench-fisted, double-armed, baseball-bat-swinging cut I'd ever seen. The gun went off, I felt a stab of pain in my shoulder, and the next thing I knew I was bleeding from under my armpit like a stuck pig.

"When our gunman collapsed into a ball on the ground, Ike kicked him in the head like he meant to kill him. To this day I swear that kick was the very last vestige of World War II coming outta your uncle. The guy let out a grunt. Ike looked at my bloody shoulder and said, as calm as you and me are talking right now, 'We better head for Denver General.' When I told him I couldn't and pleaded with him to get me to my car, he looked at me like I was crazy. It wasn't until I said four or five times in a row that I had a special *family* doctor in North Denver who would take care of me that Ike began to recognize the kind of situation he'd stumbled into.

"When he asked me point-blank, 'You a damn mobster?' I remember laughing in pain and saying that I was a guy just like him, somebody looking for a leg up on the American dream." Mario paused and watched CJ continue to roll the twenty-dollar gold piece and the .38 slug around in his hand before continuing, "That slug you're holding could've killed me. But it didn't. I was way too stupid and ornery. Anyway, Ike slipped his arm under my shoulder, walked me to the car, helped me inside, and followed my directions to the house I was renting. By the time we got there, I'd lost so much blood I was hallucinating, thinking I was in church singing. Ike pretty much carried me up to the house, and when Angie answered the door he announced that I'd been shot. Realizing instantly what had happened, she barely gave Ike a second look. Cool as a cucumber, a lot like Mavis, I suspect, she had Ike carry me into the living room and lay me out on the couch before she ran to call her Uncle Alonzo, who was a hell of a lot more than just the family doctor. Fifteen minutes later, after Angie had helped Alonzo pump a couple of bags of fluid into me—Angie was a nurse, you know—Alonzo pulled that slug you're holding outta the fat pad just below my left armpit. Turned out the damn thing had nicked an artery.

"So much went on in the course of the next half hour that not much was said other than Angie telling Ike who she was, Ike doing the same, and Alonzo, who always saw himself as cut outta different cloth from the rest of Angie's family, exclaiming over and over that sooner or later I was gonna be the death of him.

"When Angie was convinced that I was outta the woods, and Alonzo finally shut up his complaining, she walked Ike to the door, slipped the twenty-dollar gold piece she always carried out of her pocket, and demanded that Ike take it. When Ike refused, Angie stared him down, and with Alonzo standing right there next to her, shaking his head, saying, 'No, the man's not family,' she gave the coin to Ike."

Mario let out a sigh. It was the kind of sigh that seemed to release years of pent-up pressure. "That coin you're holding has the blood of my family and Angie's coursing through it. It's been rubbed along the edge to remove the fluting, and if you look real close—you'd need a magnifying glass to see it—you'll see there's a tiny S stamped into the gold right at six o'clock. In the old days that coin carried a lot of weight, Calvin. Even today, if you happen to be the bearer, in certain circles it's worth a hell of a lot more than twenty dollars. It's yours to keep. Who knows, one day, you may need it."

"Some story," said CJ.

"There's a little more to it. Let me just finish. In the end Angie closed Ike's hand over the gold piece and ushered him out the door a few seconds before I passed out." Mario's eyes misted over. "A week later Angie miscarried. I gave Ike the slug one night at a poker party fifteen years later. Ike mailed the gold piece back to me, certified mail, two weeks before he died."

CJ watched Mario fight back tears before finally asking, his tone respectful and hushed, "How is it that after all our license-plate transactions over the years, I never knew that you and Ike knew one another until just last year?"

"Because I wanted it that way, Calvin, and so did he. There are some relationships you don't really broadcast."

CJ shook his head. "You put me in a tough spot, Mario. Prefacing that story the way you did."

"I understand," said Mario. "But think about that coin for just a moment, and consider what it represents. You no longer have Ike, and I no longer have Angie. But you do have Mavis. All I've got is a money-grubbing asshole lawyer of a nephew and his over-educated flunkies who sit around all day long hoping I take a hip-breaking tumble or lose my mind. When you come right down to it, Calvin, I really got no one I can trust but you."

CJ ran a finger along the amazingly smooth edge of the gold piece. "What do you want from me, Mario?"

"What I've always asked of you, Calvin. Your confidence and your friendship. And maybe just a little bit of protection."

"Protection from what?"

"From that nephew of mine, Rollie, and his rat pack."

CJ shook his head. "I've heard it said that there was a time when half the businesses along the Front Range ran to your pro-tection."

Mario shrugged. "Things change, Calvin. Anyway, we're not talking about that kind of protection."

"What kind are we talking, then?"

"I'll get to that in a minute, but first off I need something else from you. Something that'll keep my nephew and his asshole friends from sticking their noses where they don't belong. I want you involved in a business venture with me, one that'll explain to Rollie and his trained monkeys in business suits why you're always around. An antiques and collectibles business, sort of."

"Afraid I can't help you there, Mario. I'm tapped out financially."

"Then I'll get you retapped. Money's not an issue. I need you in this venture with me, Calvin. We won't have to run a fancy business out of a store like you were doing at Ike's Spot. We can have a different sort of operation. A virtual kinda store. We can sell things, yours, mine, even consigned stuff, by appointment or on eBay right out of this basement. That way you can have your cake and eat it too. You get to spend part of your time with Flora Jean doing what you've always done and the rest over here with me offering up antiques and collectibles for sale—and a little protection."

"Mario, do you realize you're talking about me getting crossways with people who are your blood kin? A special kind of kin involved in a special kind of business that's never taken real well to outsiders."

Mario paused, looking as if it hurt him deeply to say what came next. "So was the guy who Ike cold-cocked and stomped in the head that night in Five Points. He was kin too. How else do you think I realized right off what that sham holdup was really all about? He was family, Calvin, and he was gonna kill me if Ike hadn't stepped in. My nephew and his wolf pack are nothing more than a twenty-first-century refinement."

"I'm an outsider, Mario," CJ protested.

"So was Ike. Don't worry so much. If you take me up on my offer and the shit really does end up hitting the fan, we've got ourselves an inside ringer."

"Who?"

"Pinkie Niedemeyer." Mario smiled. "You never heard any more from that Vannick character after Pinkie talked to him, did you? One little visit from Pinkie, and Vannick and his friend Mr. Counts were singing about Stafford and Lyman and even McCabe to the cops. Guess they weighed the lesser of two evils and punted. Pinkie may think he's out of my debt, but you know what, the man still owes me."

"Damn, Mario. This is starting to sound deep woods serious."

"Life and death, Calvin. It's not just my money that Rollie's after. There are things I know about him. Things that tend to make my Stanford-educated nephew uncomfortable, sometimes even sweat. When you come right down to it, he's a lot like that Howard Stafford guy you brought down: haughty, rich, and above it all. Except Rollie's a hundred times more ruthless."

"That's a hell of a comparison, Mario, but not such a good one for getting me to agree to your request. Stafford's still walking the streets. The DA hasn't been able to get anything close to an accessory-to-murder charge to stick, and Stafford's lawyers and PR people have him looking for all the world like a victim in every media outlet from here to Albuquerque. Stafford's probably sitting at home laughing his head off."

"Trust me, Calvin. They'll peg Stafford with something in the end." Mario flashed the hint of a grin. "They got Capone in the end, didn't they? And he had just as much money and a lot more muscle than Howard Stafford. Besides, I thought you told me that the dead kid's mother already settled the score."

"In her own personal way, she did."

"And we can do the same thing with Rollie," said Mario.

"What! Burn his house down and disappear?"

"No. Send him a message."

"And you and me going into the antiques business will send him that message?"

"It'll tell him that I've got people on my side. He already knows about Pinkie, and the two of us working together will send him the message that I'm not into half-stepping anymore. Besides, he already knows who you are."

"What?"

"Listen, Calvin, I need folks around me who ain't afraid of

shit." Mario paused to let his message gather steam. "Bottom line is, you and Pinkie fit that bill. I need you in on this, Calvin. At least consider it?"

CJ took in the look of concern in Mario's eyes. "Am I missing something here, Mario?" he asked, moving the coin and slug from his right hand to his left.

"Nope," said the insightful onetime Denver crime boss, sensing that for the time being he'd pressed CJ as far as he dared. "Just think about it. That's all I'm asking. Right now, let's say we head for that Easter dinner you've been promising me all week."

"And the gold piece and the slug?"

"Like I said, they're yours to keep." Mario handed CJ the coin purse. "Slip 'em back in here."

CJ slipped the gold piece and the slug back into the coin purse, zipped it shut, and followed Mario toward the basement steps.

When Mario reached the top of the stairs, he turned back to CJ. "Hope you got your sunglasses. It's awful bright outside." He swung his back door open and stepped out into the noonday sun. "We takin' my car or the Bel Air?"

"Let's take the Roadmaster," said CJ, slipping the coin purse into his vest pocket.

"Good choice," said Mario, walking across the backyard toward his garage.

"Why's that?" asked CJ, surprised by Mario's comment, knowing it was a rare Sunday that Mario took the 1953 showroom-spotless Roadmaster out for a spin.

"Because it's the choice Angie would've made," said Mario, lifting the garage door. "Always drive your top rollin' stock on special occasions or when you're off to visit kin, is what she would've said."

CJ nodded. As he slipped into the vintage machine, he decided to take out the twenty-dollar gold piece and the .38 slug for one last look. As he did, there was a momentary unsettled look on his face that caused Mario to ask, "Something the matter, Calvin?" as he cranked the big Roadmaster's engine and eased the car back out into the warmth of the sun.

"No," said CJ, fingering the two objects in his hand as if he were somehow in his mind's eye weighing good against evil. "Just considering your proposal."

"Well, take your time," said Mario, nosing the Buick east toward Mavis's. "Rome wasn't built in a day."

"I know," said CJ, squinting pensively into the sun as he moved his fingers back and forth between the gold piece and the slug.